Hilary Norman and The Murder Room

>>> This title is part of The Murder Room, our series dedicated to making available out-of-print or hard-to-find titles by classic crime writers.

Crime fiction has always held up a mirror to society. The Victorians were fascinated by sensational murder and the emerging science of detection; now we are obsessed with the forensic detail of violent death. And no other genre has so captivated and enthralled readers.

Vast troves of classic crime writing have for a long time been unavailable to all but the most dedicated frequenters of second-hand bookshops. The advent of digital publishing means that we are now able to bring you the backlists of a huge range of titles by classic and contemporary crime writers, some of which have been out of print for decades.

From the genteel amateur private eyes of the Golden Age and the femmes fatales of pulp fiction, to the morally ambiguous hard-boiled detectives of mid twentieth-century America and their descendants who walk our twenty-first century streets, The Murder Room has it all. >>>

The Murder Room
Where Criminal Minds Meet

themurderroom.com

T0352011

Hilary Norman

Hilary Norman was born and educated in London. After working as an actress she had careers in the fashion and broadcasting industries. She travelled extensively throughout Europe and lived for a time in the United States before writing her first international bestseller, *In Love and Friendship*, which has been translated into a dozen languages. Her subsequent novels have been equally successful. She lives in North London, where she has spent most of her life, with her husband and their beloved RSPCA rescue dog.

By Hilary Norman
(titles that appear in bold are published by The Murder Room)

If I Should Die

Hilary Norman

This edition published by
The Orion Publishing Group Ltd
Orion House
5 Upper St Martin's Lane
London WC2H 9EA

An Hachette UK company
A CIP catalogue record for this book is available from the British Library

ISBN 978 1 4719 0762 3

www.orionbooks.co.uk

For Walter Neumann,
whom I never had a chance to know

Acknowledgments

My special thanks are due to Graham Rust, for his vast knowledge of pacing, and his generosity in sharing it with me; to Dr. Romeo J. Vecht, who also gave me so much valuable time; and to Sgt. Marjorie O'Dea of the Detective Division, Chicago Police Department, for her good humour, patience and expertise.

Grateful thanks also to Dr. Herman Ash, David W. Balfour, Howard Barmad, Carolyn Caughey, Sara Fisher, John Hawkins, Herta Norman, Dave Risley of London Zoo, the excellent and helpful staff of the Ritz-Carlton Hotel, Chicago, Helen and Neal Rose, Dr. Jonathan Tarlow and Sharon Tarlow, Michael Thomas, and Rae White.

Now I lay me down to sleep;
I pray the Lord my soul to keep.
If I should die before I wake,
I pray the Lord my soul to take.

Anonymous. First printed in a late edition of the *New England Primer*, 1781

Monsters are chaos beasts, lurking at the interstices of order . . . The dragon, for example – perhaps the most widespread monster in myth and folklore – is born through a mixture of species . . . by the joint generation of a man or worm and a metal.

Encyclopaedia Britannica

May you not hurt your enemy, when he struck first?
Aeschylus, *The Libation Bearers*

Prologue

Sunday, January 3rd

It was one of those special January mornings in Boston when winter felt like a real childhood treat. Fresh snow had fallen the previous day, but the main streets were pretty much clear and the busiest sidewalks safely gritted, and the Public Garden looked like an old-fashioned Christmas card. Not a Swan Boat in sight, but the sky was perfect azure, the sun shone brightly, every branch of every tree was blanketed, every twig of every shrub ethereally frosted, and large expanses of sparkling icing sugar landscape were satisfyingly untrodden.

To Jack Long, this morning was just another bonus to add to his new-found sense of well-being. In his early forties, sandy-haired, lean and more than passably attractive, Jack was aware that he hadn't felt this good in years, and that every moment of this unplanned, enforced time-out was making him feel even better, fitter, stronger and more optimistic.

He had cleared the snow off a bench with his gloved hands, and now he sat facing the water, watching an old lady with a cane feeding small scraps of bread to the ducks. The sun felt so warm that he had taken off his anorak, and he was snug in his thick white turtle-necked sweater. So long as his hands and feet were warm, Jack had never minded the cold. He was comfortable now, his breathing calm and even, forming feathery ribbons of steam.

He looked around, took it all in, then closed his eyes, and gave himself up to the sunshine and the clean air and the sounds of birds and muted traffic.

He was almost asleep when it happened. He felt nothing, for it happened too fast for sensation. One minute, Jack Long was alive, a still-youngish man with everything to live for. The next, he was gone.

Rose O'Connell, seventy-eight years old and mad as hell with the arthritis that had, in recent months, slowed her former briskness, saw it happen, just as she was turning away from the water's edge, her bag of bread scraps empty now. A sudden jolt, thrusting the young man's upper body forward convulsively for an instant, the way electroshock therapy had jerked the patients around in the hospital Rose had worked in in the bad old days.

She stood for a moment, resting on her cane, watching the man, her eyes intent and puzzled. He was perfectly still again now, slumped back against the bench, and she supposed he might be sleeping, but his hands were so limp in his lap and his sandy head lolled in such a way that Rose, with a chill passing through her that had nothing to do with the weather, knew better.

She began to limp closer, moving slowly, cautiously, until she was just a few feet away. She looked down, and the fingers of her right hand clenched the handle of her cane. She had been a nurse, had seen plenty of spilled blood in her time, much of it created by violence, and she knew she would not faint.

The man's blood spread slowly and steadily, oozing over his white sweater like a blooming, ever-expanding red rose, and dripping down through the slats in the wooden bench onto the white snow.

It was not the blood that made Rose cry out. It was something else entirely, something she had never seen in all her years of nursing, either in the operating theatres or in the emergency rooms.

It was rising from the hole in his chest, in a swirl of black. Smoke.

xii

1

Monday, January 4th

He was a cop, and she was a ballet teacher. Joseph Duval was thirty-eight years old, living in Chicago, Illinois, with his wife Jess and her nine-year-old daughter Sal from a previous marriage. Hélène Duval, his sister, known to everyone as Lally, was twenty-three, living in West Stockbridge, Massachusetts, with Hugo Barzinsky – her lodger, best friend and business partner in Hugo's, their café – and her cat. Joe had known from the age of ten that he would, in time, move away from home. Lally had never doubted that she would live in New England until they buried her. Those were the most significant differences between Joe and Lally Duval. In most other ways, especially in the ways that counted most – in their hearts and minds – they were about as similar and as close-knit as any brother and sister could be.

When Joe telephoned Lally at a little before quarter to five that Monday afternoon, he was at his desk in the station in the Logan Square district of Chicago, and Lally was in her bedroom some nine hundred miles away, brushing her dark brown, almost waist-length hair up into the sleek ponytail that would, with a little deft pinning, become the neat bun that was obligatory in the ballet world.

"Whatcha doing, sis?"

Lally smiled at the welcome sound of her brother's deep, warm voice. "The usual – I just delivered a fresh batch of croissants to the café, and now I'm getting ready for class." Nijinsky, her three-year-old Siamese, near the door, watched her swinging hair through friendly slit eyes. "Are you at the office?"

1

"It's a paperwork afternoon." Joe paused. "How are you, kid?"

"I'm wonderful," Lally said. "We got a fresh load of snow last night, but today's been gorgeous. How about you guys?"

On average, Joe and Lally made a point of speaking to each other at least once a month. So far as Lally was concerned, she'd have been happy to talk to her brother once a day, but being a lieutenant in the Chicago Police Department's Violent Crime Unit meant that Joe's life was wild and full, and Lally knew that his occasional long silences didn't mean he thought about her any less.

"We're all pretty good this end," Joe said, "knock on wood." He rapped smartly on his desk.

"How's Jess feeling?" Her sister-in-law was recently pregnant, and Lally knew that she and Joe and sweet Sal were all on tenterhooks because Jess's last two pregnancies had both ended in miscarriage.

"So far so good." Joe was a man of deep emotion but few words.

"Is she taking it easier this time?" Lally felt his anxiety over the line.

"A little. You know how independent Jess is, but I think she'll do just about anything to keep this baby, even if it does mean letting Sal and me carry the shopping and take care of the gardening."

"It must be hard for her."

"You bet it is."

Lally checked her alarm clock and finished pinning her hair. Her brother's beloved features, his long, sharp nose and soft grey eyes, so like her own, were as clear in her mind as if he were seated opposite her.

"How's work?" she asked, grabbing her black leotard and pulling it snugly up her body. She knew it was a pointless question, that in spite of the honesty between them in most things, the confidences of the Chicago Police Department couldn't be safer if they were locked in a high-security vault.

"Like always," Joe said, easily. "You know."

She didn't know, but she thought she was probably glad of that. She worried about Joe all the time as it was, and maybe her imagination was worse than the real thing, but somehow she doubted that. She had seen reality – brutal, bloody reality – the day their parents had been killed in a car crash over four years ago, a few days after her nineteenth birthday. With Joe so far away, it had been left to Lally to make the identification at the morgue in Pittsfield. She had been aware, even in those most terrible moments of her life, that there was a kind of mercy in their going together, for they had been the closest married couple she had ever known,

2

more like twins than husband and wife, and it was almost impossible to conceive of either one being left behind to mourn the other. But that hadn't helped Lally, not that day, nor in those that followed, to come to terms with the violence of their end. She'd worried about Joe ever since he'd joined the police force – she guessed she always would.

"Are you okay, sis?" Joe asked. "You sound breathless."

"Just getting changed – class is in ten minutes."

"You wanna call me back later?"

"You're never there – will you be there?" She tucked the receiver under her chin, stepped into her blush pink rehearsal skirt, then tugged on leg warmers.

"Probably not."

Lally smiled again. "Okay, let's do a round up. I'm well and happy, Hugo had a cold but now he's okay, the roof needs clearing, the path needs sweeping and gritting again, but otherwise the house is fine – " The Siamese came and rubbed around her ankles. "Nijinsky sends his love – he's great." She picked up her pointe shoes. "One of the children I teach isn't so great, and I'm worried about her, but everything else is just wonderful, and I love you and I miss you, and I wish you'd all come and live back here."

Joe, too, grinned. "I miss you, too, sweetheart, and everyone this end's great, too – and Sal was talking about you this morning, said that if you don't get over here soon, you'll wake up one day and find her on your doorstep."

"Tell her any time."

"I love you, sis."

"Joe?"

"What?"

"Be careful."

"You, too."

Nature, Lally always felt, had struck an almost perfect balance in the Berkshires. No mountain or valley or lake was too massive or too daunting. There was a wonderful blend, an almost perfectly harmonious mix of natural landscape and the human factors of villages, small towns and country roads, of farms, large and small, of handsome churches and old colonial graveyards. There were the seasons, so clearly defined: youthful springs and richly blooming summers, memorable, glowing autumns, splendid, uncompromising winters. Visitors came from far and wide to the region, drawn by its beauty and its cultural appeal, for the Berkshires were famed for their summer festivals of dance, theatre

3

and music. But for Lally Duval, so deeply rooted in western Massachusetts, there was an earthy solidity, a sense of permanence and belonging that had little to do with those things.

Her mother, Ellen Carpenter Duval, had been born and raised in Lee, just a few miles away, in a family who had lived in the area for five generations, and even Jean-Pierre Duval, of French-Canadian extraction, was a second-generation resident of West Stockbridge. There must have been at least one other Duval over the decades with travel lust, but Joe was the only one who'd ever up and gone anywhere for keeps.

"Are you sure you want to stay in town?" he'd asked Lally when she'd found her new house a few months after their parents' death. It was a white clapboard Cape-style home with blue shutters, a porch and a sun room with a bay window and a view of the distant Berkshire hills, and it stood on Lenox Road, not much more than a mile from their old family house on Main Street.

"Of course I am," Lally had reassured him. "It's home and I love it – not just because of the past, but because of the present and future. I can't really imagine wanting to live anywhere else."

She had felt no desire to alter anything much about her life; that wasn't why she'd agreed to sell their parents' home. She had always been independent, even as a young child, and both Jean-Pierre and Ellen had respected their daughter's individuality and need for space. A house, with land – even a small scrap of land – was something Lally felt she could stamp herself on, something she could grow within, in which she could expand and extend herself. Besides, a dancer needed both space and the confidence that the thumping of her entrechats and the echoing of her beloved music would not disturb neighbours, especially if – as happened quite often – the urge to dance woke her up out of sleep in the middle of the night.

Lally had known since she was fourteen that she would never be a great ballerina. In the first place, she had grown too tall, and in the second, dance was not everything to her. It was what she looked forward to doing every day of her life, and it was something she could not conceive of giving up, but Lally loved life in general a little too much to dedicate herself utterly to ballet. She had never been a slave to ritual, and if the weather was especially gorgeous or the air particularly invigorating, she would always much rather have gone outdoors than go to ballet practice, and if a friend needed a helping hand or a shoulder to cry on, Lally never thought twice about her priorities, for people naturally came before dance. And so early on, she had sought her own compromise, and had found it in teaching.

Classes at the Lally Duval School of Dance were held in an old converted barn next to Lally's house. She taught children from the ages of five to twelve, and this afternoon's class was made up mainly of ten-year-olds, including Katy Webber, the student she'd referred to on the phone to Joe.

Katy was one of the most promising children Lally had ever taught, a pretty, slender, fair-haired girl with the look of a fragile fawn and the underlying constitution and determination of a prizefighter. Katy never missed class, had every ounce of passion, ambition and courage necessary for a dancer, and yet Lally had always been glad to note that she combined those gifts with a normal capacity for fun, and it was plain as the nose on her face that the healthy balance in the child was nurtured by her parents, Chris and Andrea Webber, who both encouraged and patently adored their daughter.

Lally had noticed the stiffness first – a slight loss of flexibility in Katy's back – during class a couple of months ago. On questioning the child, Lally had sensed an unusual evasiveness in her, and had refrained from pressing the issue, and two days later, Katy had seemed back to normal. When, the following week, Lally saw her wince during an arabesque, she had ordered her to stop and to see her at the end of class, but by the time the rest of the children had made their customary final curtseys and bows, Katy had gone.

Andrea Webber had telephoned that evening.

"Katy wanted me to apologize for leaving without speaking to you."

"That's okay," Lally said easily. "It was just that she seemed to be having a little difficulty today, and I wanted to be sure she was all right."

"That's why Chris and I didn't let her wait when we picked her up. Chris had an idea Katy might be coming down with something, and so we got her home and tucked her up right away."

Katy had missed her next class, and Lally had assumed that the flu, or whatever, must have caught up with her, but three weeks later, when Lally came into the girls' changing room to check on a leaking radiator, she caught a glimpse, just before Katy had time to cover herself with a towel, of a large black bruise on the child's right buttock. It was the look in the ten-year-old's eyes that had stopped Lally in her tracks, freezing the question in her throat. Lally knew suddenly, without being told, that the bruise was not the result of an innocent accident. She knew it from the split

5

second's fear and embarrassment in Katy's blue eyes.

"What should I do?" Lally had asked Hugo next morning in the café.

"There's nothing you can do, or at least nothing you should do."

"How can you say that if there's a child at risk?"

"Kids are always getting bruised." Hugo shrugged, and his pony tail bounced. "It may not mean anything."

Since Hugo Barzinsky had come to live in Lally's house two and a half years before, he'd become her closest friend. Hugo was thirty-four, tall and skinny, with a hawkish nose, a gentle smile and straight, light brown hair, receding a little for which he compensated by wearing it long, usually in a pony tail. Until his twenty-sixth year he had danced with the Joffrey Ballet in New York, but then a violent mugging in Greenwich Village had left him with a back injury that had ended his career and brought him back home. Their community being a small one, Lally had known all about Hugo's rise and fall, yet they had hardly exchanged more than a courteous greeting until two summers before, when they had both chosen, on an especially lovely day, to eat their respective lunches on a bench in the Berkshire Botanical Garden off Route 102. They'd chatted about the weather for a moment or two, exchanged sandwiches and a little local gossip, and had swiftly discovered not only that they had dance in common, but also that they loved good food, baked their own bread, hated Wagner and liked crime novels. Their friendship had blossomed; in a matter of months, Hugo had come to live in Lally's house as a paying lodger; within the year, *Hugo's* had opened its doors on Main Street, and with their combined talents, there was seldom a free table to be had in the café.

Many people in the community thought that Hugo was gay, which he was not, but Hugo didn't give a damn what anyone else thought about his sexuality. The only person he really cared about at all these days was Lally, and since that day when they'd shared their sandwiches in the Botanical Garden, he'd never looked at another woman. So far as Lally was concerned, their relationship was one hundred per cent platonic, but though Hugo knew he would never risk telling her how he felt, he still fantasized, sometimes, like a teenager with a crush, that Lally – who had no special man in her life – might wake up to her own feelings for him, but she never had and he doubted that she ever would.

"What if Katy's bruises do mean something?" Lally asked Hugo now.

"You mean what if someone's hurting her?"

"Of course that's what I mean." The thought made Lally feel physically sick. "I can't stand by and do nothing."

"That's exactly what you should do," Hugo said, gently. "You have no real evidence, Lally – you said yourself it was more of a gut feeling, and I respect your instincts, but they're not proof, are they?"

"I guess not."

"That doesn't mean you can't keep an eye on her."

"You bet I'll keep an eye on her."

Lally clapped her hands.

"Into the centre, girls."

The children assembled neatly in the middle of the studio. There were nine girls and three boys, some more graceful and natural than others, but all pink-cheeked, sparky eyed and eager to please.

"Okay, we'll start with grand plié in second position, ending with the right arm in third position and the left in second."

She walked towards them. Katy Webber was in the front row. Lally saw it right away, could hardly understand that she'd missed it until then. She felt a kick of horror in the pit of her stomach.

"Madame?"

Lally blinked. Thomas Walton, one of the boys, was looking expectantly at her. All the children were waiting.

She tore her eyes away from Katy and took a deep, steadying breath.

"Turn your bodies to the right," she directed, "and step on the right leg in second arabesque . . ."

The class went on.

She called Hugo at the café directly the children had gone.

"It's on the inside of her left arm," she said. "It looks like a bite."

"Did you ask her about it?"

"She said that one of her mother's German Shepherds bit her – a nursing bitch, upset because Katy picked up one of her pups."

"Sounds reasonable enough." Andrea Webber ran a dog-breeding business from their house in Stockbridge.

"Does it?" Lally was in the kitchen, Nijinsky twining himself around her ankles. "Katy's been living around her mother's breeding kennels ever since she could walk. She knows better than to pick up a brand-new pup."

"What are you saying, Lally?"

"That I don't think it was a dog bite." Her voice showed her distress. "Hugo, it was her face, her expression. Katy's such a transparently honest child, and I'm sure she was hiding something."

7

"Or someone."

"I think so."

"So what now?"

"I'm not sure."

"You could go to her school, talk to her teachers, see if they've noticed anything."

"I could, or I could pay the Webbers a visit."

"Lally, you can't do that – you can't just walk into someone's home and start talking about something as sensitive as this."

"I know I can't," she said wretchedly.

"So what? You'll try the school?"

"Maybe." Lally heard voices at Hugo's end. "Customers?"

"It's pretty busy in here."

"Go on then."

"Promise you won't do anything on impulse?"

"Don't worry about me."

"*Promise* me."

"Okay, okay, I promise."

The dizziness hit her about five seconds after she put down the phone, catching her unawares. Lally grabbed the edge of the pine table to stop herself falling, then stood very still, hunched over at the waist, for a moment or two after it had passed, and then, slowly, she straightened up again.

"What was that about?" she said to the cat.

Nijinsky made one of his small low chirruping sounds, and went on rubbing.

"You're right," Lally said. "It was nothing."

She wasn't especially concerned. Probably she'd eaten too little for lunch – in winter, she needed extra fuel, particularly when she was teaching – or maybe she was getting her period a little early, which sometimes affected her strangely.

She put it out of her mind, and returned her thoughts to Katy Webber. She might not have any idea who was hurting the girl, but she was certain now that someone was. She didn't know yet exactly what she was going to do about it, or even how best to begin to tackle the problem without running the risk of making life worse for Katy instead of better.

She only knew that she had to do something.

2

Tuesday, January 5th

The man leaned back in his chair, and wondered if it had begun. Outside, the sky was as dark as it ever became over the city. Snow flurries blew past the plate-glass windows, beyond the sealed room. Inside, the filtered air was warm, maintained at just the right humidity, not too dry, not too moist, the lighting an even pre-dusk, electronically sustained.

The man led a full, vigorous life outside the room, yet there was no other place in the world where he felt so comfortable, so at ease. He encountered dozens of people every day, yet the only friends he trusted were here, within these walls. He confided in them, he cared for their every need, he sustained their life processes. He controlled their very existence, which was why he felt able to trust them. He had always found power intensely satisfying, and he knew now that the absolute power he had created extended beyond the room, further, perhaps, than even he could hazard, but no one else knew that yet. Though they would know soon enough.

"Mother would be so proud," he told his friends.

He often spoke to them about his mother. He had lost her a long time ago, and he had waited interminable, patient decades to punish those he blamed for that loss.

"She taught me many things," he told them, softly. "But there were three rules of life more important than the rest. Mother's Rules of Life. Identity – knowing and never losing sight of who I was and where I sprang from. Self-control . . ."

9

It was his litany, repeated daily, sometimes aloud, often silently, in his mind. Self-control meant denial and suffering, sometimes even humiliation, but without it you were lost.

"And the third rule." He regarded his friends with benign tolerance. "Never to forget the existence of dragons."

They'd heard it all before, many times, but they never seemed to grow bored and, after all, they couldn't have complained if they were. The man often talked to them about dragons, sometimes for hours on end. They were out there, he said. Outside the room, in the city, in the country, all over the world.

"Mother told me once that she lost self-control for a while – early in her life – and the dragons were out there, waiting to pounce. They take many forms, but they're always out there, always waiting.'

His music was playing, his beloved Wagner. *Götterdämmerung* – 'Twilight of the Gods'. His mother's favourite. All about heroes and dragons, about Siegfried, the dragon slayer.

"She called me her little hero." He lay back on the reclining leather chair and closed his eyes, remembering. He'd squashed a dragonfly when he was six, and that was when she'd begun calling him her little Siegfried. Dragonflies were known as the devil's darning needle, she'd told him, because they could sew up the eyes and ears and mouth of a sleeping child. Mother had admired heroism more than anything.

He opened his eyes and looked at his friends in their glass enclosures. His own little captive dragons. Nine of them. Five *gekkonidae*. Two *iguanidae*. And the most dangerous, his favourites, *helodermae suspectum*, the two Gila monsters. Each family lived in its own vivarium, required its own special environment, set up so that each home had areas of light and shade. The man had provided no large rocks or tunnels for them to hide in, for they were there for his pleasure, for him to observe, to master.

He had felt intense fear when he'd first brought them to the room. The first time he'd touched one of them, he had experienced such revulsion and terror that he had vomited. But once he had placed them safely into their vivaria, a new excitement had begun to replace the revulsion. Touching them now, sometimes, brought him to erection. He suspected that the greatest elation of all might come from killing them, but for now, at least, he chose to dominate them instead, and to practise self-control.

He tried not to think too much about the terrible days, such a long time ago yet still so clear in his mind. The night he had lost her, when they had robbed him of her, when he had become aware that her breathing had ceased and that she had left him. And then those other days, worse even than the loss itself, when they had humiliated her, when they had laughed.

If he thought about it now, the pain was still intolerable, and he would have to punish himself to expunge the agony from his mind. Sometimes, he would use his fingernails to gouge into his flesh – always on his lower abdomen or on his buttocks, so that no one would see what he had done – and sometimes he used lighted cigarettes to burn himself. He never smoked, but he still bought the same brand of cigarettes that she had liked, partly because he needed the aroma to help himself, partly because she had used them to correct him. Very seldom, of course, for Mother had nearly always been kind to him, almost an angel really, and if she had found it necessary to administer a little discipline, then he knew that it was just as necessary for him to continue.

Their punishment had been a long time in coming, but now the time had come. Those who had killed her, those who had humiliated her, those who had laughed, at her, at him, would all pay now. And innocents, too, would suffer, but that was unavoidable. Sad, but inevitable.

The man stared out of the window, into the dark, snowy night. He wondered if it had begun.

3

Wednesday, January 6th

On icy winter mornings like this one, Sean and Marie Ferguson liked nothing better than having their breakfast in bed. Not that they needed to stay under the covers to keep warm, since their townhouse on North Lincoln Square in Chicago's near north side was as lavishly heated as it was furnished and decorated; but with Marie fully occupied with her patients for between ten and fifteen hours a day, Sean liked keeping his wife as physically close as possible every moment he could, and besides, the sunny Renoir painting that hung over the fireplace directly opposite their bed made them both feel spiritually summery every morning of their lives.

"How're you feeling?" Sean looked across at his wife, just pouring her second cup of lemon tea.

"Great."

"Really?"

Marie smiled at him. "Really."

"No symptoms?"

"Not a single one." She spread honey on a slice of rye toast. "You have to stop worrying about me, Sean. We've all told you and told you, there's really no need."

"It's only been three weeks."

"And I'm trying to forget about it."

"I know you are. I'm sorry." Sean looked penitent.

"No need to apologize for loving me. It's just that I wish you'd believe that I'm feeling one hundred per cent okay."

12

"Honestly?"
"Cross my heart and hope to die."
"Don't *say* things like that."

Marie was the only child of William B. Howe, a multimillionaire industrialist and fine art collector whose wife had died in childbirth. Marie's father had expected his fair-haired, green-eyed daughter either to take over his business empire or to marry suitably, preferably a man of sufficient means to complement and expand the Howe fortune. Marie, however, had confounded her father by insisting on studying medicine and then specializing in obstetrics. Upon his death, she had inherited the house on North Lincoln Square which she loved for its beauty and its happy childhood memories, but she had sold two other major properties, one in San Francisco and the other in Newport, Rhode Island, in order to fund the creation of the Howe Clinic in the Rogers Park district. Her partner, John Morrissey, a cardiologist, shared Marie's ideals. The clinic was luxurious and scrupulously well run, its fees on average no lower than most similar establishments, but it was not unusual for more than one room at a time to be occupied by impecunious patients, and Marie had been known to look after women from first pre-natal to final post-natal checks without charging a single cent.

Her marriage to Sean Ferguson five years earlier had raised the collective eyebrows of the extended Howe family to even greater heights. Her husband was a writer – part journalist, part poet, part novelist of modest success – a passionate, dark-eyed man who adored and admired his wife unreservedly. He knew that the father-in-law he had never met would have disapproved of him intensely, but Sean never held that against William Howe's memory, for he knew that Marie had loved her father deeply. He was also aware that most of Howe's contemporaries, and many of Marie's, suspected him of having married for money, but both he and his wife knew those suspicions were wholly unfounded, and Sean didn't give a damn what anyone else thought. He would gladly have lived with Marie in a tent, but he had enough common sense to realise that the old Howe home was infinitely more comfortable and aesthetically pleasing, and Sean did not believe in depriving his wife for some idiotic, senseless male pride.

Until that day just over three weeks ago, Sean had never seen Marie sick. She'd had the occasional light cold, of course, but nothing more significant, not even the flu two years back when he and most of Chicago had crashed with it. When she'd developed the sudden

13

irregular tachycardiac heartbeat that John Morrissey had explained might become lethal unless they fitted her with a pacemaker, Sean had been terrified despite Marie's calm. She understood the wonders of modern pacing, knew that she could go on to lead a perfectly normal life even to the point of delivering twins at four in the morning, but Sean was so panicked by the description of what needed to be done, so anguished at the very idea of a thoracic surgeon being called in, that Marie and Morrissey had both banished him from the room while the procedure was carried out. Ten days later, after the surgeon, technicians, nurses and John Morrissey himself had all sworn that Marie was no longer at any risk, that everything was fine, perfectly fine, and that they could both go home and forget all about it, Sean had begun to allow himself to be persuaded. But while Marie regularly pleaded with him to allow her to forget all about it, her husband could not imagine that he would ever be able to obliterate it from his own mind.

"Are you ever going to make love to me again?" Marie had asked him last night, just after he'd turned the light out.
"Of course I am."
"How about now?"
"I'm a little tired right now, sweetheart."
"I don't think you're a bit tired."
"Sure I am."
"I think you're still scared."
"Of what?"
"Of giving me a heart attack."
"That's crazy, Marie."
"I know that, but do you?"
Sean had not answered.
"You still don't believe what John told us about getting back to normal, do you?" In the dark, Marie's voice sounded even, but her upset showed through. "He said I could do anything and everything I used to do – exercise, work, sex – everything."
"I know what he said."
"But you don't believe it."
"Of course I do – I know John wouldn't lie, not about you – not about anything, but especially not about you – "
"But?"
"But you're right. I am scared." Sean stared into the dark, holding her hand tightly. "I'm so afraid I might hurt you, and I'm sorry for that, and I love making love to you more than almost anything, but I'd sooner go without for the rest of my life than risk your health."

"Well, I wouldn't," Marie said firmly. "Even if there was a risk, which there isn't."

"How would you feel if it was me with the problem?"

"That's just it, Sean, I don't have a problem any more." Marie sat up and turned on her bedside lamp. "But if you'd had the pacemaker fitted instead of me, and if I'd heard everything John told you, I'd be just as horny right now as I already am."

Sean grinned. "Are you?"

"Of course I am. Aren't you?"

"No."

Marie craned her head to look at his face. "I think you're lying. You're always horny when I am."

"Not tonight," Sean said, still smiling. "I'm too tired."

The problem was that she was dead right, that he did want her just as much as she wanted him, as much as he'd always done – that not touching her, hardly even kissing her in case things got out of hand, was driving him half crazy. He'd gone to sleep the night before longing for her, and he'd woken up this morning with an erection, and he knew that Marie had been caressing him while he slept, and he only got out of trouble again by insisting that he, instead of Hilda, their housekeeper, was going to make breakfast for her, because she liked his scrambled eggs better than Hilda's.

"Are you writing today?" Marie asked him, after she'd eaten the last of her rye toast. Her appetite had always been good, and though it had dipped a little a few weeks back, even Sean had to admit that her enjoyment seemed back to normal.

"Not till this afternoon," he said, leaning back against his pillows. "I'm going to drive you to the clinic this morning and then go look at the lake for a while." He often strolled or just stood for hours, staring into Lake Michigan's vastness, seeking inspiration for a story or a poem.

"So you're in no particular hurry?"

"No hurry at all," he said, lazily. "Why? Something you need?"

"If it's no trouble," Marie said, politely.

"You know better than that." And it was true, for Sean never tired of doing things for his wife, didn't even mind going shopping with her, loved waiting around for her when she bought dresses or shoes, though shopping with Marie couldn't have been less trouble, since she was almost always in a rush to get back to the clinic, or to visit a patient at home.

"Then there is something I need," Marie said, still carefully polite.

"Sure." Sean looked at her. She looked especially beautiful this morning, even in the harsh January light. She was wearing one of her pale green silk nightdresses, cut low in the front in a V-shape, the lines softened by lace and by the warm swell of her breasts. He realized suddenly that she had not been wearing that nightdress before he'd gone down to the kitchen to make their eggs.

"Don't you want to know what I need?" Marie asked.

His mouth was dry. He knew perfectly well now what she needed, and the damnedest part of it was that he was rock hard again, and she just looked so pretty, her curly fair hair falling so sweetly around her face, she just looked so completely *well* – and maybe it was time to believe her and John, and maybe they could get back to normal, and if she could, then who was he to risk ruining their happiness, the ongoing wonder of their marriage?

"I know," he said, and his voice was husky.

"Please, Sean."

"Are you sure?" His arms ached to hold her, his mouth yearned to kiss her breasts.

"You know I am."

"And you're certain it's safe?" He knew she'd won, knew he was seconds away from slipping his hand inside that soft silk nightdress.

She didn't answer this time, just moved closer to him, close enough to brush her hair against his cheek, knowing how much he loved that. And Sean closed his eyes and breathed her in, smelled her fragrance, and then his arms were around her, gently, then more fiercely, and then they were kissing, and it was as though all the fears were being extinguished by their kisses. Marie took his right hand and guided it to her left breast, and he felt its roundness, its warmth and softness, and its hard, wondrous nipple, and the last of the fears disappeared, and she helped him pull the nightdress up over her head, tousling her hair, and she tugged at the cord of his pyjama trousers, and they began making love, and it was like coming home after a war or something, and she felt and smelled and tasted like sweet heaven on earth . . .

He had just entered her for the first time in almost a month, when it happened. His eyes were open, watching her face, for he loved seeing her expression at that moment, and she never hid anything from him, and he could see the joy in her eyes, and the excitement, and the pleasure.

It happened so quickly, so without warning, that he thought, for just a moment, that Marie was climaxing, that she had wanted him so much that she had already reached her orgasm. She gave a cry, her back arched violently, and her face contorted, and he began to let go, too, but it was only for that one, remaining instant, before the fear came back, and then that, too, was not enough, because it was so much more than fear that Sean felt, it was terror, unspeakable terror and more.

He pulled out of her, but she was already limp in his arms. He was trembling violently, he heard loud, wild breathing, hardly realizing it was his own. Gently, very gently, he laid her back against the pillows. And then he saw.

The blood. The hole.

And the smoke.

Sean Ferguson started to scream.

4

Thursday, January 7th

In the fading light of the New England afternoon, Lally parked
her ancient Mustang outside Chris and Andrea Webber's house
on Route 102, and sat staring out of the window, contemplating her
last chance to back out. Hugo had counselled her repeatedly against
the risks of interfering in something she was ill-equipped to handle,
but the bruises and that bite mark on Katy Webber had haunted
her every waking moment since Monday.

While Lally lived in West Stockbridge, the much more exclusive
town of Stockbridge itself, a few miles down the road, was an
infinitely greater magnet for tourism and money, old and new. It
was, in many ways, the archetypal New England town, with a
charming main street – immortalized by its famous late resident,
Norman Rockwell – a thriving colonial inn, bustling stores and
galleries, and a cluster of large and handsome houses.

The Webbers' home, three storeys, white and solid, less than a
mile from Stockbridge's Main Street, was set back from the road,
surrounded by a white picket fence and partially shielded by two
fir trees. Chris Webber's Jeep Cherokee stood in the driveway, his
wife's Dodge pickup behind it, a good two inches of fresh snow
piled on their roofs and layering their ski racks. The house looked
friendly enough, the porch lights already switched on. Lally knew,
from Katy's glowing descriptions, that it had previously been a bed
and breakfast inn and had more rooms than they needed. Webber
was an artist and author of teach-yourself painting guides, and Katy
had told Lally that her father had knocked three top floor rooms

18

into a large, airy studio, using one end for painting and the other for writing his teach-yourself guides, while her mother – who apparently spent most of her time caring for her dogs in specially-built kennels in their back yard – used one room on the second floor as her study, and Katy had two rooms of her own, one for sleeping in, the other large enough for homework and ballet practice.

It was certainly not a home, Lally reflected, as she sat in the comforting security of her Mustang, where lack of personal space might cause friction.

Do I cut and run? she asked herself one last time, tension rising and tightening in her chest. *Or do I go ahead and stick my nose into their business?*

The decision made, she reached for the door handle, took hold of her big canvas shoulder bag, and got out of the car. A moment later, she was standing on the snow-cleared porch, her finger on the bell. For a long time, no one answered. She began to turn away, tension giving way to relief–

The door opened. "Miss Duval, what a nice surprise."

Chris Webber looked fraught. Not exactly dishevelled, but for a man she'd always thought of as calm-looking and solid, he looked decidedly frayed around the edges. He wore denim jeans, sneakers and a big blue handknitted sweater, all paint-stained and what Lally would have expected of an artist, but his short curly fair hair was rumpled, his dark blue eyes were guarded and there were two long scratches on his face, one on his strong straight nose, the other beside the cleft on his chin.

"Have I picked a bad time?" Lally asked.

"For what?"

She took a breath and plunged into her pretext for calling.

"I've come about Katy's pointe shoes." It sounded lame, even to her own ears. "It's quite a small problem, but it's really important."

"Katy's only just back from school," Webber said. "She's changing her clothes, and then she has a history assignment."

It was evident to Lally that this man, who had always seemed friendly and outgoing when he'd picked Katy up after classes, did not want her coming inside. Lally reconsidered backing out and going home, but then she remembered Katy's bruises and stood her ground.

"It's a safety point," she persisted. "I really need to talk to Katy before her next class."

Chris Webber saw she wasn't going to go away.

"Of course," he said. "Come in." He stepped back and she went

19

inside. The entrance hall smelled of paint and coffee. A carved wood coat rack overflowed with hats and scarves, and three pairs of snow boots lined up against the wall beneath it.

"I'm sorry to seem so inhospitable, Miss Duval." He showed her into the sitting room, a large, cosily decorated room filled with big old furniture, a blazing wood fire burning in the hearth. "It's just a difficult time of day, you know?"

"It's my fault for not calling first." She paused. "And please, it's Lally."

"And I'm Chris," he said.

They stood awkwardly for a moment. Lally was tall, but Webber was at least six-two and broad-shouldered. She had seen him jogging from time to time around Stockbridge, and once or twice in the summer she'd seen him cycling with Katy along Route 102. He looked very fit. He also looked embarrased as hell at having her there in his sitting room.

"Have a seat," he said. "Make yourself at home – I'll go find Katy."

Alone, Lally sat down in a pretty chintz covered armchair. A young German Shepherd bitch, entirely black except for beige wisps over her eyes and on her paws, got up from the rug in front of the fireplace and came over to sniff at her boots.

"That's cat you're sniffing," Lally said, softly, glad of the company. Her heart was beating fast and her palms, normally dry and cool, felt moist. The dog picked up a red rubber ball from behind the armchair and tossed it into her lap. "Well, thank you," she said.

The minutes ticked by on the grandfather clock in the far corner. Lally glanced around the room, taking in the photographs on the big oak dresser and the paintings – two landscapes and a portrait over the mantelpiece of Andrea Webber, painted, Lally guessed, a few years back. Her eyes went on roaming around the room, over the bookcase – one shelf filled with Chris Webber's own works, another crammed with ballet books, a blue leather dog's lead lying on the middle shelf beside a couple of silver trophies for some achievement or another. It all looked solid, snug, secure, the perfect American family home, yet somehow, Lally thought, it didn't feel safe.

Imagination, she told herself. *I'm building this feeling up.*

From out back, she heard fretful barking, and from somewhere upstairs she heard voices, and no one was actually yelling, but Lally could tell that a quarrel was in progress.

The dog was staring at her.

"Want your ball back?"

The tail thumped. Slowly, carefully, Lally rolled the ball off her lap onto the carpet. The dog pounced, chewed at it for a moment or two, then threw it back again.

She heard footsteps on the stairs.

"I'm sorry." Katy ran into the room. She wore denims and a white sweatshirt and she was clutching her new pointe shoes. Her face was flushed and her eyes were pink, and Lally thought she'd probably been crying. "There was some work I had to finish."

"That's okay," Lally said, easily.

Katy managed a grin. "That's Jade. Isn't she gorgeous?"

"She's wonderful." Lally had never noticed before how like her father Katy was; she had her mother's turned-up nose and her fair hair was straighter than Chris Webber's, but their dark blue eyes were almost identical and she had the same little determined cleft in her chin.

"Daddy said you want to talk to me about my shoes." Katy was anxious. "Did I do something wrong?"

"Nothing big," Lally reassured her. "Just a small technical point – but an important one." She took a breath – her chest still felt tight with nerves. "It's about your ribbons." She bent and opened her shoulder bag, and took out a sample pair of shoes. "Bring yours over here and I'll show you the problem."

The argument upstairs began again. Lally saw Katy's flush deepen, saw her eyes grow more distressed, and she knew now that if she'd been looking for the source of Katy's injuries, she'd come to the right place. She wished she hadn't. She wished she was home or at *Hugo's*.

Katy focused hard on her shoes. "Did I sew the ribbons on wrong?"

"The stitching's perfect," Lally praised her. "And you used just the right heavy-duty cotton, but you sewed them on a little too far forward. See?" She showed her. "I know it seems like a tiny detail, but these ribbons are very important for support."

They heard footsteps on the stairs, and an instant later Chris Webber reappeared, clearly more agitated than before. A swift look of mutual dismay passed between father and daughter, and Lally knew, without a doubt, that whatever trouble did exist in this household, it was not between these two. She felt more like an intruder than ever.

"How's it going?" Webber asked.

"I sewed my ribbons on in the wrong place, Daddy."

"Did you, honey?" He looked at Lally, gave a small smile, and sat down on the couch. Jade padded over to him and rested her

21

head on his left knee. Webber put out one hand and began, absently, to stroke her. "Please," he said, "don't let me interrupt."

Lally went on talking automatically. She was repeating the standard pointe shoe lecture she'd given Katy's class only days before, but Katy listened politely and attentively as if she'd never heard it before, and Lally sensed that perhaps it was a welcome respite for the girl.

"So tell me again the things you need before putting on your shoes."

"Surgical tape to wrap around each toe," Katy recited, her voice soft but eager. "Lamb's wool – pure alcohol to pour into shoes when they're new – "

"Really?" Chris Webber raised an eyebrow.

"It's to help break them in," Katy explained. "Lally says it helps mould the shoes to your feet."

Webber's tension was hitting Lally like a stone wall. It was time to end the charade. "Katy," she said slowly, "could I please have a drink of water?"

Katy stood up. "Would you like juice? We have orange and apple."

"Water's fine, thank you."

Katy left the room. The dog got up from her place beside Webber, wandered over to the fireplace and flopped down again, resting her head on her front paws.

"Am I right in guessing," Webber said, very quietly, looking at Lally intently, "that your coming here today has nothing at all to do with ballet shoes?"

Lally flushed hotly. "Am I so transparent?"

"Probably not to Katy."

She nodded. "I'm here because of Katy. I'm worried about her."

The door banged open. Andrea Webber stalked into the room.

"You bastard," she said.

The dogs in the back yard began barking again, louder than before.

"You lousy *bastard*, walking out on me like that."

Lally was frozen in her seat. Andrea hadn't even glanced at her. Her feet were bare and muddy, and Lally thought she might have been in the back yard, though it was freezing cold and almost dark outside. She wore old, torn denims and a long, baggy red sweater, and her hair, always so immaculate when she came to pick up Katy from class, was unkempt. She wore no make-up except for smudged mascara, and her dark eyes, red from crying as Katy's had been, were filled with anger.

Lally wanted to be invisible or gone. She could smell the drink

22

from across the room. Whisky and beer. Andrea Webber was drunk. Not just a little, but absolutely, stinking drunk.

"Andrea," Chris said, calmly. "We have a visitor." He had risen from the couch, and his face was very pale. "Miss Duval's come to talk to Katy about her shoes."

"Bully for Katy," his wife said, slurring her words.

"I think I should go," Lally said, quietly.

"Not on my account," Andrea said, still not looking at her.

"Why don't you sit down?" Chris asked.

"Why don't you go to hell?"

"Andrea, please." Chris moved towards his wife. He put out his right hand as if to touch her arm, and she lashed out hard, hitting him on the chest.

"Son of a *bitch*," she snarled.

"Andrea, for God's sake – "

"And the worst of it is you're such a *sanctimonious* son of a bitch." She turned away, staggered a little and bumped against the wooden dresser, rattling ornaments and framed photographs. "You used to at least take a drink with me, not spend all your time criticizing me."

"No one's criticizing you," Chris said quietly. "Why don't you just calm down, so that Lally – "

"So it's Lally now." Andrea turned back. "I call her Miss Perfect." For the first time, she looked at Lally. "Did you know that?"

"Andrea, stop it," Chris said, more sharply.

"I guess you know my daughter thinks the sun shines out of your neat little backside, Miss Duval?"

Lally didn't know what to say or do. Why, in God's name, hadn't she listened to Hugo? Why had she exposed herself to this, why had she been so *egocentric* as to imagine she could do anything to help?

"Maybe you should leave," Chris said to Lally. "I'm so sorry."

"It's all right," she said, getting up and stuffing her shoes back into her bag. "I shouldn't have barged in this way."

"No, you shouldn't," Andrea said, nastily.

"That's enough, Andrea," Chris said.

"Is it? Am I embarrassing you, Mr High and Mighty? You think you're so much better than me, don't you?"

"No, I don't?"

"Sure you do, you all do." She was out of control, close to tears.

"Why don't you go upstairs?" Chris said, trying to stay gentle.

"I don't want to go upstairs." Andrea's voice grew louder with booze and anger. "I'm not some inconvenience to be kept out of the way – I'm your wife, remember? I'm your *wife!*"

Chris tried to take her arm again, but she shoved him away harder than the first time. Appalled, Lally took a step forward, then stopped.

"Mommy, don't."

They all turned. Katy stood in the doorway.

"Please, Mommy."

"Go away, Katy," Andrea said.

Katy looked at Lally, then back at her mother. Her eyes were pleading. "Stop it, Mommy, please."

"Go to your *room*, Katy," Andrea snapped.

Lally saw the child steel herself, knew how much easier it would have been to do as she was told, to run upstairs and shut herself away, but Katy didn't budge, just stood there bravely.

"I want to help you, Mommy," she said.

"I'll tell you when I need your help."

"Katy, honey," Chris said, gently. "Why don't you go on up?"

The girl hesitated and then, while Lally held her breath, she walked right up close to her mother. "Mommy, why don't you come up with me?" She held out her hand.

"Why don't you leave me *alone?*" Andrea kicked out her right foot, and hit Katy's shin.

"You *stop* that!" Whirling around, Chris pushed Andrea against the wall, shocking her fleetingly. Katy burst into anguished tears. Over by the fireplace, Jade sat up and growled softly.

"Come on, Katy." Lally stepped forward again, more decisively. "I'll take you up."

"Oh no, you don't!" Andrea pulled away from Chris and seized Katy's left arm. "I won't have you taking over my daughter – "

"I wouldn't dream of taking over," Lally said incredulously.

"Oh, no?"

"Of course not!"

"That's why she talks about you night and day – you should hear her, you'd love it." Andrea let Katy go, turning on Lally, and the child rushed weeping from the room and up the stairs. "I suppose Chris has been telling you all about me." She came very close, and Lally could feel her warm, liquor breath. "About what a lousy mother I am."

"He hasn't said anything, not a word."

"Andrea, for pity's sake, will you stop this right now?" Chris's anguish was written all over his face. "I won't have you subjecting Miss Duval to this kind of abuse."

"So it's Lally to you, and Miss Duval to me." Andrea's cheeks

24

were scarlet now, and she was panting with rage. "That just about says it all, doesn't it?"

Lally picked up her bag, her hands shaking. "I'm going," she said to Chris, not looking at his wife. "Please don't worry about me. As far as I'm concerned, this never happened."

She started for the door, but Andrea grabbed her wrist.

"Let me go," Lally said, coldly.

"How dare you give me orders." Her fingers gripped like a painful vice. "This is my house, not yours."

"Let her go, Andrea." Chris stepped between them, and even Andrea saw from the expression on his face that she'd gone too far. "Let her go right *now!*"

Andrea released Lally and with a great sobbing moan she ran out of the room. An instant later, they heard the back door slam. Chris sank back down onto the couch and put his head in his hands, and Jade went to him, sat close, leaning against his legs.

"Will she be okay?" Lally asked, weakly. She felt sick and shaky.

Chris nodded, his head still down. "She'll probably stay with the dogs for a while." His voice was muffled by his hands. "When she gets like this, they're the only beings she can stand to be with for long."

"Do you want me to leave?"

"If you want to."

"Can I do anything to help?"

He didn't answer. Lally looked down at him helplessly for a moment, then sat down again, on the edge of an armchair. She felt riddled with guilt, as if her coming to the house had created the ugly scene, though she knew full well that there must have been any number of incidents worse than this one, and that they were the reason she had come in the first place. She thought about poor Katy, all alone upstairs, and how frightened she must be, how humiliated by the public exposure of her mother's frailty.

Chris raised his head at last. He looked up at Lally, and there was such a frank sadness in his eyes, and Lally realized then that she was the first outsider to have witnessed this family at its lowest ebb, and it felt a little like being an eye witness to a crime. She couldn't even try to slip silently away because Andrea Webber had reached out her hand and drawn her right into the messy heart of it. She was involved now, whether she wanted to be or not. She felt it, and she knew Chris Webber felt it too. She had lost her right to walk away. And looking at the man right now, at all that hopeless-ness laid bare, and then thinking of Katy upstairs in her bedroom, Lally found that she wasn't sure if she really wanted to walk away.

For several minutes they sat in silence. From time to time, the dogs in the back yard barked and Jade cocked her head to one side, listening, but staying where she was. Inside the sitting room, the grandfather clock ticked on. Outside, in the street, a neighbour shovelled snow, and the traffic on Route 102 continued its steady flow.

"I'm so sorry," Chris said, at last.

"Not your fault," Lally said. "I came uninvited. I interfered."

"You were a guest." Chris's eyes were still pained. "I hope she didn't hurt you when she grabbed you."

"No," Lally said, though her wrist was still throbbing. "You were right. I didn't come to talk about shoes or ribbons. I came because of Katy's bruises. I shouldn't have come."

"I'm glad you did."

"Why? I haven't exactly helped, have I?"

"I think you've helped me reach a decision." Chris's jaw was very taut. For a moment, he hesitated, weighing something up. "And now I think I need to ask you for your help, and I have absolutely no right to ask."

"More right than I had to come here." Lally paused. "I'd like to help any way I can."

"Do you think you could take Katy home with you – just for an hour or two? Get her out of the house, occupy her while I start trying to unscramble this mess – I know it's asking too much, but – "

"Do you think she'll want to come with me? I'll be more than happy to have her, but is it the right thing to do?"

"I think it is," Chris said slowly. "It's time for me to take some action, to work out what I'm going to do about our problems. I think it may be easier if I don't have to worry about Katy, for just a little while."

"All right," Lally said. "If she agrees."

"I've kept hoping that I could keep things together, superficially at least." He shook his head. "But I know it's gone too far now. I know it's time. To take care of things."

"Of Andrea."

He nodded. "She needs help."

Lally bit her lip. "I think Katy's going to need some help, too."

"I know she is."

"I'm sorry," Lally said.

"Me, too."

5

Thursday, January 7th

J ust over one hour after the autopsy into the death of Jack Long – delayed for over three days by an eleven-vehicle pile-up on the Massachusetts Turnpike and a rash of fatal shootings – had been completed at People's Hospital in Boston, the autopsy on the body of Marie Ferguson began at Chicago's Memorial Hospital.

The autopsy room, next to the pathology laboratory, was in the basement, an artificially bright, subterranean world apart from the rest of the hospital. About thirty feet square, it was a cold, cheerless place made out of stone, stainless steel and marble. If a stranger were to enter at a time when the room was in use, he might, for an instant, believe he had entered a regular operating theatre, but though some of the sights and sounds were similar – the gowned and masked men and women, the clatter of instruments, the occasional grating of a bone saw or the buzzing of a drill – he would quickly observe the absence of anaesthetist and nursing staff, the less urgently focused concentration than that of a surgical situation, and the fact that there were four tables instead of one. For the patients who lay on the marble slabs in this room were beyond hope and beyond the help of surgeons.

It was a quarter after six Thursday evening when the young associate medical examiner completed his external examination, made his first incision and stared intently down into Marie Ferguson's body.

"Most of the chest wall has been destroyed." He spoke, as he

27

worked, into a microphone suspended over the table. "Pieces of skin and subcutaneous tissue are hanging around the left side of the chest wall."

All four tables were occupied, and the autopsy room was buzzing with activity, but the pathologist was already wholly engrossed. He wore a mask, gloves, apron and shoe covers over green scrub clothes, and three of his senses, touch, sight and smell, were on full alert.

"Part of the skin has a blackish colour. Part of the right side of the chest wall has also been destroyed, but there is some normal tissue left in the axilla of the right side. Remnants of a pacemaker are visible. Remnants of pacemaker wires are present." Picking up a scalpel, the medical examiner bent lower over the patient, sniffing. "There is a smoky odour apparent in all tissues of the chest."

The paramedics who had responded to the 911 call at the magnificent house on North Lincoln Square the previous morning had believed, at first glance – as had the first police officers on the scene – that Marie Ferguson had died of a gunshot wound. As the early investigation had begun to unfold, however, and as the victim's traumatized husband had continued, until medicated into sleep by the attending physician, to protest his innocence, it had become clear that nothing about the case was as it had first appeared.

The medical examiner's autopsy protocol confirmed Sean Ferguson's bewildered, hysterical statement. His wife had not been shot, yet her heart had blown open, her left lung had collapsed and there was blood in the pleural cavity.

"*Cause of death: destruction of the pericardium and the heart muscle*," Commander Isaiah M. Jackson read to Lieutenant Joseph Duval just before eleven that night, from the protocol that had been rushed to his office.

"And they think it was the pacemaker that caused it?" Joe Duval asked. His grey eyes were keen and puzzled.

"They seem pretty sure of it." Jackson played with a gold Cross pen on his desk. He had long, delicate fingers, a tall, athletic body, a strong, seldom humorous face and a gleaming black, entirely bald scalp.

"Has it ever happened before?" Bending down, Joe peered at the gory evidence packed into two glass jars on the commander's desk. The containers were tightly sealed, but the office already reeked of formaldehyde.

"Not so far as they know." Jackson grimaced. "What a way to go."

28

"So it's accidental death, and we ship this off to the manufacturers?"

"Who just happen to be Hagen Pacing in Logan Square." Jackson shook his head. "I knew Mrs Ferguson's father, William Howe. Hell of a man."

"And a powerful family," Joe commented.

"You got it. So let's take care of this fast, Duval." The commander wrinkled up his nose. "This stuff smells like skunk's pee."

Joe was already at the door.

"We need the Hagen people to guarantee that this was a one-off," Jackson stopped him. "Some kind of freak accident."

"You think there might be more, Commander?" Joe said.

"God forbid."

Isaiah Jackson waited until Duval had closed his door, and then he sat back in his chair and stared at the jars on his desk. They were making him feel sick to his stomach, and it had nothing much to do with the stink. His own pacemaker had been fitted three years ago, and he had, thank God, never felt better, but still, freak or not, Marie Ferguson's death made him uneasier than anything else had since a spate of senior police shootings five years before by a demented retired officer.

Gently, cautiously, he rubbed his chest.

"Talk about heartburn," he said.

6

Thursday, January 7th

Lally had taken Katy home. The ten-year-old had protested weakly at first, but both Chris and Lally had observed that she was relieved, more than anything, that someone else knew their secret, and that maybe now her mother might let her father give her the help he said she needed.

They sat for a while at the kitchen table, drinking home-made lemonade and playing with Nijinsky, and then, even though it was dark, they built a snowman in the back yard, before heading into the barn-studio for a little barre practice; and Lally switched on all the lights and put on a Prokofiev tape and they began to improvise, and before long they were both throwing discipline to the wind and releasing all the accumulated tensions in their minds and bodies the best way they knew how.

Her sudden attack of breathlessness took Lally by surprise.

"I have to stop," she gasped, laughing a little and leaning up against one of the wall mirrors. "You've run me ragged, Katy Webber – I think I must be getting old."

Katy stopped whirling and came to her, concerned. "Are you okay?"

"I'm fine," Lally said, though she felt oddly exhausted. "But I think maybe I've had enough for the moment."

She switched off the power and they put on their snow boots and coats and went back to the house, and there was a message on the answer machine from Hugo at the café, wanting her to call, but Lally didn't feel up to explaining things to Hugo just yet. What they needed, she told Katy, was hot chocolate with marshmallows, and the child, needing to keep busy, helped make the drinks and fussed around her teacher and petted the cat. Neither of them broached the subject of Andrea. Lally knew it would be wrong to question Katy without her father present; her only rights in the whole miserable affair were to see her pupil out of danger. She watched Katy fondling Nikinsky's ears, listened to her softly humming the Prokofiev, and wondered what was happening at that other house a few miles down the road.

Chris arrived just after nine that evening. Lally had made supper early, after Hugo had telephoned to say he would be out all night at a friend's, and then, seeing that Katy was exhausted, Lally had persuaded her to take a nap on her bed, promising to let her know when her father came or called.

"Come in," she said, softly.

He looked haggard and sad, and Lally saw, with new horror, that there were fresh scratches on his right cheek and left hand, but she restrained herself from mentioning them, just invited him to come and sit down by the fire.

"Katy's having a sleep," she told him. "I said I'd wake her when you came."

"Would you mind if we left her a while longer?"

"Of course not. She needs the rest."

The sitting room was very hushed.

"Can I fix you something to eat?"

"I'm not really hungry."

"It's all ready – just needs heating up. It's no trouble, and you look as if you could use something."

Chris nodded wearily. "Maybe you're right."

They sat at the big pine table in the kitchen, and Lally set down a dish of chicken casserole and mashed potatoes, and in spite of his misery, Chris found that he was pretty hungry, and Lally, having eaten very little with Katy, joined him and, after just a moment's hesitation, she opened a bottle of red wine and poured two glasses.

It was a strange meal. Two virtual strangers, knowing just the bare essentials about each other, the way people did in a small community, their only real common link asleep upstairs. Chris was a married man, the father of a pupil, and there was no real reason for Lally to feel the slightest intimacy with him, and yet she was aware that she did feel that, and that it wasn't just because of what had happened that afternoon. If it hadn't been for Andrea's bizarre attack on her, Chris would probably never have felt able to enlist

31

her help, but sitting there now, watching him eat, feeling his pain, Lally realized, with a pang of guilt, that there was something disturbingly attractive about Chris Webber, and that it bothered her more than a little.

"Would you mind," he asked, after a while, "if I talk to you about things?"

"Not a bit," she replied. "So long as you don't feel obligated."

"I'd like to talk," Chris said. "I think I've needed to open up – to unload, I guess – for a long time." He paused. "But I have no right to burden you."

"No burden," Lally said.

He spoke slowly but candidly, letting it out a little at a time. He was from Philadelphia, but had come north-east on a long painting vacation thirteen years ago and had fallen in love with the Berkshires and with Andrea. They had married within six months and settled in Williamstown, and it had seemed in the early days to be a good, loving marriage of equal minds, until Andrea had started to experience some irrational anxieties about what she regarded as her own inadequacies. No matter how often Chris had tried to reassure her, Andrea felt that she was too inhibited, that she was unpopular, that she was a poor wife. She had never drunk liquor of any kind before, having grown up in a teetotal household, but about a year after marrying Chris, she had taken her first glass of wine at a party, and had become, out of the blue, the life and soul of the evening. Chris had enjoyed watching Andrea's self-confidence bloom that night, and if she'd stopped there, it might have been okay, but one glass had become two and then three, and then she'd begun experimenting with spirits, and that was when her new-found abandon had turned to aggression.

"The drink changed her so much – literally changed her," Chris told Lally. "From being irrationally self-critical and a little obsessive, she became resentful and belligerent."

"But only when she drank?"

"Absolutely." Chris picked up his own wine glass, then set it back down on the table. "It wasn't as bad then as it is now, and after she became pregnant, things got a lot better because she stopped drinking."

"And after Katy was born?"

"She started again."

With their child to consider, and aware to a degree of the bad effect liquor had on her, Andrea seldom took a drink outside the home. She wanted to be as good a mother as possible, and up to a point, she had always been great, but ever since they had moved to Stockbridge things had become worse.

"My brilliant plan," he said wryly. "My great hope for the future. Andrea had always been crazy about dogs, so I figured that going into the breeding business might be just what she needed to keep her happy. I guess I hoped that all that space and independence might help her to quit again."

It hadn't helped. From lashing out verbally, Andrea had begun to react physically, and so long as she hadn't taken out her rages on Katy, Chris had managed to control his own anger, but since the first time she'd struck their daughter, he'd been living in a nightmare.

He paused for a moment. Lally's kitchen was warm and snug, the only sounds the low hum of the refrigerator and Nijinsky's loud purring from his comfortable spot on Lally's lap.

"You don't have to go on," Lally said.

"It feels strange, opening up this way," Chris admitted. "I've always been a pretty private man. And in spite of everything, I still feel disloyal talking about Andrea this way to – " He stopped again.

"To an outsider?" Lally smiled. "But isn't that just why you feel you can talk to me? Because I'm not involved, other than with Katy."

"To be candid," Chris said, "you don't exactly feel like an outsider."

"Because of this afternoon," Lally said quickly. "Because I was there."

"I guess so."

Lally took a sip of wine, then went on stroking the cat.

"I've pushed Andrea as hard as I can to quit," Chris said. "I've offered her every kind of help I could think of, but she's rejected them all. She claims that she could give it up if she chose to, but that she doesn't choose to. She says it's what she needs to make life with me bearable."

Ever since he had found the first bruises on Katy a couple of weeks before, Chris had known that the writing was on the wall. If it hadn't been for their daughter, he would have done Andrea a favour and left years earlier, but he hadn't wanted to break up the family.

"And now?" Lally asked, gently.

"I know the situation can't be allowed to continue."

"No."

"I tried talking to her before I came here tonight, but she was way too far gone for anything to get through."

"I saw the scratches," Lally said. "They look sore. Would you like something to put on them?"

Chris shook his head. "They're nothing."

"How about some coffee then?"

"Good idea."

Lally set Nijinsky on the floor, and cleared the table. Chris started to help, but she motioned to him to stay where he was. The silence was there again, but there was nothing too uncomfortable about it, it felt easy, almost intimate. Lally made a pot of coffee and poured them both a cup.

"I've made up my mind about three things," Chris said. "Number one, I have to protect Katy from this moment on. Number two, I have to get Andrea into a clinic, with or without her agreement." He stopped.

"And number three?"

"I have to accept that my marriage is over."

"Are you sure?"

"Andrea wasn't a drunk before she married me. She wasn't unhappy before she married me, and she started drinking because she was miserable." He shook his head. "I'm not taking all the blame, believe me, and I want to help her – I'm *going* to help her. But it was marrying me that changed Andrea. And it's high time we ended it."

Chris asked Lally if Katy could stay with her the rest of the night. He knew it was a great imposition, but it seemed cruel to wake her now and take her back home. And besides, with Katy safely out of the house, Chris would be able to tackle Andrea more easily when she woke, talk to her about his feelings before she had a chance to start the day's drinking.

Lally showed Chris to her bedroom, watched him stoop and gently kiss his daughter's hair, but she was sleeping soundly.

"I should write her a note," he whispered. "So she'll know I haven't just abandoned her."

"She wouldn't think that."

Chris looked at the bed. "Where will you sleep?"

"I have a spare room," Lally whispered.

"Are you sure you don't mind?" He looked anxious again.

"I can sleep anywhere." Lally looked down at the sleeping child. "And to be honest, I think I'll be happier knowing she's here tomorrow morning, rather than – " She stopped.

"I know," Chris said. "You're right."

The dizziness hit Lally again at the front door. It was a worse attack than the one a few days earlier, and she thought for a moment she was going to fall down in a real faint, but Chris was beside her, holding her up, and in another minute it was gone.

"What in hell was that?"

"I don't know. I just got a little dizzy."

He helped her back into the sitting room, and made her sit down on the sofa. "Are you sick?" he asked, anxiously. "You seemed okay before – you had a good appetite."

"I'm fine," Lally assured him. "I've been a little off colour lately, that's all."

He was appalled. "And you took the time and trouble to come to our house, and all you got was a pile of abuse. And now I've sat here all evening telling you my troubles – " He started for the door.

"Where are you going?"

"To wake Katy."

"Don't you dare wake her." Lally got up, then quickly sat back down.

"Are you dizzy again?" He returned to her side.

"No, I'm all right. But you mustn't wake Katy – I'm fine, truly."

"You almost passed out."

"It was just a little dizzy spell, no big deal."

"Easy for you to say – you didn't see how white your face was."

"All the more reason to let Katy stay. Hugo's out for the night – it'll be nice to know there's someone else in the house. Not that I'm going to need anyone," she added, quickly.

"You're sure?"

"Absolutely."

"Can I get you something before I go?" He hesitated. "Should I stay?"

"No," Lally said firmly. "You're needed at home." She managed a smile. "Anyway, I really am okay now. See?" She stood up, and it was true enough, the dizziness was gone.

"You're quite sure?"

"It's time you left, Chris."

"I don't know about this."

"Do you want me to turn pirouettes to prove I'm okay?"

"No! Definitely not."

"Then go home, please."

It was another ten minutes before he drove away, finally satisfied that she wasn't about to pass out and injure herself. Though Lally did have to admit to herself that she felt pretty sick, as if she'd run a marathon without water. If she didn't perk up in a day or two, she guessed she'd have to see Charlie Sheldon, though it was years since she'd last visited the doctor.

Maybe I'm just more upset about Katy than I realized, she thought. She walked upstairs slowly, holding onto the banister rail just in case. She went into her bedroom very quietly, took the things that she needed for the night, looked down at the sleeping child for a moment or two, and then, leaving the door ajar and the light on in the corridor, Lally went to bed in the spare room.

7

Friday, January 8th

The five factories that made up Hagen Industries occupied a site of nine acres of land behind Western Avenue in the Logan Square district of Chicago. Most of Hagen's employees reported for duty between seven and nine in the morning and went home between four and six o'clock in the evening. During their eight or so hours of work, they had no real call to leave the complex; Hagen Industries was a paternalistic employer, and everything its people needed was on tap. There was a restaurant and a coffee shop, a branch of North Community Bank and a post office, a grocery and drugstore, and a doctor's office.

Most of the men and women who worked for Hagen Industries had the satisfaction of knowing that they were producing articles that benefited mankind, none more so than those who worked for Hagen Pacing. Their factory was the smallest of the five in the complex, and it was accepted by the parent company that this was one area where financial growth was considered a lower priority than continued quality, for Albrecht Hagen, the president, was known to care more passionately about the further development of these brilliant pieces of gadgetry than anything else in his business empire.

The modern pacemaker was the most reliable electronic device ever made by man. It needed to be, for it was called upon to correct, without discomfort or even awareness, natural imperfections of the human heart, and each device was expected to provide more than three hundred and fifty million pulses in its own lifetime. At least three hundred and fifty thousand pacemaker implants were performed worldwide each year, and since its beginnings in the mid-seventies, Hagen Pacing had steadily and meticulously built itself a substantial slice of the manufacturing cake.

The pacemaker factory was divided into two main areas, Research and Development, headed by Olivia Ashcroft, PhD, and Production, headed by Howard Leary, a scientist whose first ten working years had been spent designing weapons systems, but who had told Al Hagen, after joining his corporation, that he felt he'd come home. Ashcroft and Leary were both devoted to the company and its products, but at forty-five and fifty-two respectively, both were aware that they were now virtually over the hill. The peak of an electronic engineer's career these days came much earlier than that of almost any other profession. There was so much new development to absorb, and so much growth, that within three years of an engineer starting out, he would have forgotten half of what he had learned, and would only be able to keep up with half of what was going on in his own area. There was nothing that Ashcroft and Leary did not know about pacing, but when it came down to the most crucial area of all – quality – the number one in the factory was Fred Schwartz, the Quality Assurance Manager. Schwartz lived and breathed for his work. Everyone who reported to him had been trained to check, check and check again that whatever they handled was one hundred per cent perfect, but no one had a sharper eye and a more acutely developed instinct for the most minute flaw that Schwartz himself.

They had never needed him more than now.

They assembled in the president's office at 6 a.m. The factory was still silent, and Al Hagen's office, too, had a strained, hushed atmosphere. It was a cool, rectangular room decorated and furnished in stark black and white; monochrome photographs, mostly of uncompromising landscapes, hung on the walls, and a built-in Bang & Olufsen hi-fi system with four speakers was a focal point.

Hagen had called Ashcroft, Leary and Schwartz at their homes within moments of being alerted by Security to the two faxes from the Boston and Chicago Police Departments. Ashcroft and Leary had crawled, dazed and ragged, from their beds, but Schwartz, who prided himself on being able to get by on less sleep than most people, had already been dressed for work. The shock of the news imparted to them by Hagen guaranteed that none of them would rest easily for the foreseeable future.

"Is it really true?" Schwartz asked Hagen.

"I'm afraid so."

Neither Ashcroft nor Leary spoke.

"One death in Boston, last Sunday. The second on Wednesday morning, right here in Chicago." Hagen's light blue eyes pierced them all from behind his round wire-framed glasses. He was generally thought of by his workforce as a benevolent leader. Fifty-one years old, six feet tall and stoop-shouldered with grey, fuzzy, close-cropped hair, he tended to dress like an ageing college boy, with bow ties and white socks and long, colourful woollen scarves in winter. He looked anything but benevolent today. He looked stunned, and he looked accusing.

"Do we have details?" Olivia Ashcroft recovered first. She was usually crisply elegant and poised, wore matte, understated makeup and tailored suits every day of the working week. This morning she wore blue denims, a sweater and anorak, and her hair was rumpled. She looked almost, though not quite, vulnerable.

Hagen passed across the faxes. "See for yourself."

In the rush, Ashcroft had forgotten her glasses. She held the paper a little away from her face, and both Howard Leary and Fred Schwartz craned their heads to read at the same time.

"Jeesus." Leary, smartly dressed for business despite the frantic call, was a red-haired, green-eyed man with a quick temper, poor digestion and a sallow complexion. Reading the Chicago fax, he grew paler than usual.

Ashcroft glanced at him. "What?"

"Don't you recognize the name?"

She peered back at the fax. "Marie Ferguson?"

"That's Marie Howe Ferguson," Hagen said. His voice, usually gentle, had a harsh note. "Head of the Howe Clinic in Rogers Park, daughter of William B. Howe. Major money, major citizen."

"Oh, God."

Schwartz remained silent, still staring at the faxes, too shocked to speak.

"Nothing to say, Fred?" Hagen asked, quietly.

"What can I say?"

"You'd better think of something," Leary said.

Schwartz was a quiet, modest man, with hazel eyes, mousy hair and a small nose and mouth. "I'll be trying to track both shipments – " He sounded unsteady. "But since the faxes say that the explosions eradicated every trace of all serial numbers . . ." His voice trailed away.

39

"You're going to need as much information as possible," Hagen said.

"Their physicians will have our delivery notes on file," Ashcroft said.

"The pacemakers could have been hospital or doctors' stock," Schwartz pointed out. "I don't have to tell anyone here that the delivery notes will only guide us to the relevant shipments. Many shipments are made up of devices from different production batches – if either Mr Long's or Mrs Ferguson's pacemaker was one of our biggest sellers – " He came to a halt, his mind already hard at work sifting through possibilities.

"Depending on when these two devices were manufactured," Hagen continued the line of thought, increasingly appalled as the immensity of their predicament became clearer to him – "most of the others in their batches will probably have been implanted too. If not all."

"We'll still have the master copies," Schwartz said.

"Jesus," Leary said again, more softly.

The focus turned relentlessly on Schwartz. In the ten years this man had worked for the corporation, no one had ever seen him at a loss. Schwartz might be the quiet type, but he exuded a brand of confidence that others found reassuring. He was a gifted engineer with a fine scientific understanding; there was nothing flamboyant about him, neither in the drab clothes he wore nor in his unremarkable face. Only his clear, 20/20 vision, hazel eyes and his hands, long-fingered and nimble, betrayed his high intelligence and skill. So long as Schwartz was around, Hagen and the others knew things would be ticking along nicely. Or at least they had, till now. Now, just when it mattered most, he had nothing to offer.

"This is a catastrophe," Howard Leary said flatly.

"How, Fred?" Ashcroft was gentler. "How can this have happened?"

"In theory, it can't," Schwartz replied.

"According to the police departments of Boston and Chicago, it has." Al Hagen's narrow face was filled with tension. "According to the medical examiners in two cities, it has."

Since Schwartz had taken over quality control, not even the tiniest, most benign flaw had slipped through his net, but he had, nevertheless, laid down simple, straightforward procedures in case of unlikely hitches. To begin with, every component that went into a Hagen pacemaker had its own serial number, and all components were bought or produced in batches of one hundred, of which thirty-three were used in the current production cycle, another thirty-three were set aside to be used in three months, and a further thirty-three in a year. The remaining component in each batch was kept right out of production, and in that way, if something did go wrong, not only was the relevant component readily available for inspection, but the potential for trouble had been divided by three.

Because the faxes made it clear that the explosions had obliterated every part of both pacemakers, including the serial numbers on the electrodes at the generator box end of the pacing leads, Schwartz had no alternative but to await full details of the shipments that had contained the devices; without that information, even if the Hagen Pacing computer could tell them how many pacemakers had been shipped to Massachusetts and Illinois locations in the past two months or so, there was no guarantee that one or both devices had not been awaiting use in Boston and Chicago for a year or more, since they would still have been well within their use-by dates.

"How long till we get whatever's left of the devices?" Schwartz asked now, in the early morning hush.

"We'll have Mrs Ferguson's later this morning," Hagen replied. "They'll be flying the Boston remains to us as fast as they can." The president shook his grey head. "God knows what the press will make of this if it gets out."

"We have to stop it getting out," Leary said.

"What is the situation on that score?" Ashcroft asked Hagen. "How much have the families been told?"

"That's another problem," Hagen said. "Sean Ferguson, the husband, is a journalist." A hint of despair touched his voice.

"Shit," Leary said.

"According to the police, they were together when it happened – and I mean together." Hagen folded his hands and laid them on his desk, visibly shaken but still fighting to stay calm. "That poor man saw it happen. Whether he's read the autopsy report yet or not, he saw his wife die before his eyes because of one of our pacemakers."

"We *have* to stop this getting out." Leary was very grim. "There'll be chaos, pandemonium – patients clamouring to have their pacers removed."

"Stop it, Howard," Ashcroft said.

"Jesus Christ, Olivia, about twelve thousand people a year entrust their lives to us!"

"And losing our tempers won't help any of them."

"What do you suggest?" Leary glowered at her.

41

Schwartz stood up. "I have only one practical suggestion to make at this point." His voice grew a little stronger. "That in the absence of any more information, I start getting some kind of investigation under way."

"How long, Fred?" Hagen asked.

"I can't answer that."

"Couldn't you at least hazard a guess?" Leary was sarcastic.

"How can he?" Ashcroft reasoned. "He needs facts – some place to start."

"I'll see that you get everything you need," Hagen told Schwartz.

"It's going to be tough today." Schwartz spoke directly to Hagen, ignoring Leary. "We obviously can't involve anyone else, so I'll have to keep production moving, and work alone after hours."

"Thank God for the weekend," Leary said.

"Looking on the black side," Ashcroft came in again, tentatively, "if we have no answer by Monday, shouldn't we consider halting production?"

"Once the FDA get hold of this" – Hagen was dismal – "I doubt we'll have much choice, but for now – " A new thought struck him. "This could be pretty dangerous for you, Fred. Once you start checking master copies or whatever's left of the batches – I mean, we can't be sure they're not lethal too."

"They're not," Schwartz said, decisively. "I'd stake my reputation on it."

"We're talking about staking your life," Ashcroft pointed out. "And no matter how confident you may feel, we have to consider protecting the rest of the workforce."

"Olivia has a point," Hagen said.

"A point that could mean halting production." Leary was very blunt. "A point that would mean withdrawing lifesaving treatment from hundreds of patients, at least – not to mention telling our employees and everyone they know that we're too dangerous to work for. Why not just buy a full page in the *Tribune*? You'll destroy Hagen Pacing, and you'll panic every pacemaker patient in the country."

Schwartz sat down again. "I hate to say this," he said, 'but in some ways having two deaths may make things a little easier – "

"Easier!" Hagen was appalled.

"Only in that soon we should at least have two sets of clues to feed into the computer, maybe narrow the problem – if it *is* our problem – down to a single production batch."

"Jesus, Fred," Leary said, sarcastically, "maybe you'd like a whole string of explosions."

"Take it easy, Howard." Hagen focused back on Schwartz. "Do you really think there's the remotest chance this might not be a production problem?"

"I *know* it can't be," Schwartz replied steadfastly. "There is simply nothing in the devices that could possibly cause anything like this to happen."

"The batteries are combustible," Leary said.

"And hermetically sealed – we've never had any trouble with them. Which is one of the reasons I'm not all that concerned about the danger of examining the master copies – to myself or to anyone else on the premises."

"You'll still have to take precautions," Hagen told him. "Protective clothing, goggles, gloves – "

"Of course."

For a moment or two, no one spoke.

"Okay," Hagen said. "First things first. Aside from getting every ounce of available information, I'm going to do everything I can to persuade the people who already know about this not to break this story wide open." He paused. "I don't have to tell any of you how crucial it is that no one else in the complex or outside gets to hear even a whisper."

"Of course not," Ashcroft said.

"No one'll hear it from me," Leary confirmed. "You'll have to be more careful than any of us," he told Schwartz. "You're the one at the sharp end down there on the floor."

Schwartz's resentment was plain. "Don't you think that I, of all people, can't see the catastrophic consequences of a leak?"

"Come on, folks," Hagen soothed. "Let's all try to keep calm."

"I'm calm," Schwartz said.

"I'm so calm I scare myself," Leary said, wryly.

Olivia Ashcroft rose. "I'm going home to change – unless there's anything I can do for you right this minute, Fred. We all know you work better alone – "

"I have to work alone, while we're trying to maintain normality."

"But if another head or pair of eyes would make a difference, behind the scenes – ?"

"I'll let you know." Schwartz smiled at her. "Thank you."

Leary looked at Hagen. "Al, I need a quick word." He glanced at the other two. "On a separate issue."

"Sure," Hagen said. "See you later, Olivia." He nodded at Schwartz. "Good luck, Fred."

Ashcroft and Schwartz left the room and Hagen sat down again.

"What's up, Howard?"

Leary kept his voice low. "Are you sure he's up to this?"

"You mean Schwartz? More than anyone else I know."

Leary looked sceptical. "I know we've always thought he was a whiz, and nothing major has gone wrong since he's been with us. But let's face it, Al, most of our systems were in place before Schwartz joined us. He's never faced a real test before."

Every muscle in Hagen's face was tautly drawn. "Right this minute, Howard, I'd be lying if I told you I was sure of anything." He paused. "But I do think I've come to know Schwartz pretty well over the years, and there is just one thing I am certain of, and that's that Hagen Pacing means everything to him."

"I think that applies to all of us." Leary shrugged. "Maybe I'm just frustrated at having to leave the detective work to him. Just a few years ago, I'd have been the one working twenty-four hours a day with my eyes glued to a microscope. It isn't easy leaving it to someone else."

"Schwartz may not have your flair, Howard, or your qualifications," Hagen said, gently, "but even you have to admit he's the most conscientious and meticulous man you could hope to find."

"So you don't think we should consider bringing in outside help?"

"Not until we have to," Hagen said fervently. "Lord knows there are too many people involved already." He glanced at his watch. "I have to get moving on some calls. Over the next couple of hours, I'm going to have to persuade the Chicago and Boston Police Departments and the Ferguson and Long families that we're moving heaven and earth to nail this down."

"You have to keep them quiet, Al."

"We'd better all hope and pray that I can." Hagen's eyes were very grim. "Because if I can't, and if they do insist on making this public, all hell is going to break loose."

"Tell me something I don't know," Leary said.

8

Saturday, January 9th

Though ribbing, gentle or otherwise, was as much a part of life in the Chicago Police Department as drinking with the guys at the end of a shift, ever since Lieutenant Joseph Duval had almost single-handedly doused the flames of the multiple arsonist-killer known as *The Inhuman Torch*, few of his colleagues mocked his hunches. They teased the sharp-nosed, sharp-jawed detective because he stayed thin no matter how much he ate, and they scoffed at him because he could get drunk on one bottle of beer, but they respected his well-known tenacity and they seldom kidded around when Duval had one of his gut feelings.

Within fifteen minutes of entering the president's office at Hagen Pacing early on Friday afternoon, Joe's sixth sense – which always began in the form of a weird prickling along his spinal cord – had warned him that not only was this going to turn into a case, but that, sure as shit, it was going to be a big one.

"I hate scientists," he confided to Commander Jackson on Saturday morning at the station. "They're on another planet. We have two bodies, a man and a woman nine hundred miles apart, their chests blown to chopped liver by their pacemakers, both made by these guys, and all they can say is that it couldn't happen."

"According to Al Hagen, it couldn't," Jackson said.

"But it *has* happened." Joe shook his dark head. "Apples don't explode either, but if forensics sent me a report proving that two Red Delicious had blasted into atoms, that would be good enough

45

for me. But not for these people, with their formulae and their lists of components."

"All of which supposedly prove there's nothing in these things that could explode."

"Which means either they're wrong, and there's been some kind of chemical reaction they never envisaged – "

"Impossible, according to Hagen."

" – or," Joe continued, "those two devices contained a little something extra."

"You're talking about sabotage, Duval."

"I'm talking about homicide."

"You're talking about bombs."

"I guess."

"There's no real evidence."

"Not yet."

"I want you to be wrong on this one, Duval," Jackson said.

"I want me to be wrong, too."

"But you don't think you are?"

"No."

"Jesus." The word was softly spoken, almost a murmur.

"All they seem to know so far is that both pacemakers were produced months ago," Joe said. "The Quality Assurance Manager – a guy called Schwartz – swears the factory is clean."

"Hagen says they need time," Jackson said.

"How much time can we give them, Commander? It's been almost a week since Long died."

The two men fell silent. Within the dark wood-lined walls of the commander's office, with its framed certificates and photographs of its occupant shaking hands with distinguished men and women from the mayor to the Superintendent of Police, it was generally possible to seize a fragment of calm, while outside in the big open-plan office filled with chipped desks, dented filing cabinets, a bunch of detectives and secretaries, there was usually an atmosphere of noisy chaos. Isaiah Jackson, always trim, always well dressed, hated noise, disliked people who tried to yell at him to get a point across, and despite his deep, resonant voice, was known for his ability to bawl people out in a whisper.

"Do you trust Hagen?" Joe asked.

"I've never met him." The commander paused. "But I told you I knew Marie Ferguson's father, William Howe." He leaned back in his chair and pointed at one of the black and white photographs on the wall to his left. "That's him – the tall guy in the hat. If he were alive today, Al Hagen might have been boiled in oil by now."

"The folks at Hagen are nervous of Sean Ferguson. You know he's a freelance journalist?"

"Can't say I blame them."

"Maybe not, not if they're scared he might write a piece that's going to give thousands of patients heart attacks." Joe was grim. "But I had the distinct feeling when I met Howard Leary – that's the Head of Production – that he, for one, was more interested in covering his backside."

"I take it you didn't care for Leary."

"I thought he was an arrogant asshole, but I think he's probably right about keeping it away from the press for as long as possible."

"If you're right about this," Jackson said, "Leary's a prime suspect."

"Along with everybody else at Hagen Pacing." Joe paused. "So what's the plan, Commander? Do we bring in Bomb and Arson and close the place down?"

"Hagen agrees with Schwartz – says they need time."

Joe shrugged. "I guess we don't have much choice if we want to keep things under wraps. And they are the experts." He thought. "How about we give them the rest of the weekend, but start moving in, discreetly? Give them all the help we can and do some checking of our own."

"What do you need?" the commander asked.

"I'd like to wander around the factory the rest of today and tomorrow. Then from Monday, I think two of us should go in – just two – keep it tight. Go in undercover, make out we're doing some kind of time-and-motion study." Joe pondered. "Lipman would make a pretty good scientist-type, if she's free."

Jackson nodded. "I'll consult with Chief Hankin, then call Hagen and set it up."

"On a strictly need-to-know basis," Joe added. "Only those who already know what's going on." He glanced down at his notes. "Leary, Olivia Ashcroft and Schwartz." He paused again. "I liked Schwartz. He was too busy to talk to me, but he looked haunted, like this thing was killing him."

"What about Ashcroft?"

"I didn't meet her, she was home with her family."

"What did you make of Hagen?"

"He reminded me of one of my college professors." Joe considered. "First impression, I thought he cared – not necessarily just because of the business."

The commander looked intently at the lieutenant. "This could just be a terrible accident, you know, Duval."

47

"I hope it is."
"But you've got one of your damned hunches, haven't you?"
Joe grinned as he got to his feet.
"Thank God I'm not infallible," he said.

9

Sunday, January 10th

After Chris Webber had come to take Katy to school on Friday morning, Lally had found her house uncommonly quiet. He had arrived early to have time for a word with his daughter before they left, and Lally had found their conversation almost unbearably poignant.

"Mommy's fine this morning, sweetheart," Chris had begun. "But we both know that doesn't mean she isn't sick any more. And I think the time has come for us to make sure that she gets the treatment she needs to make her better."

"But Mommy isn't really sick, Daddy, is she?" Katy said. "It only happens when she's had too much to drink."

"But that's just it, Katy, that *is* the illness." Chris's eyes were distressed. "We've talked about it before, remember? The different ways too much liquor affects people?"

"I remember," Katy said. "Some people fall down, and some get sick to their stomachs, and some people get real dumb or real sad."

"Usually," her father went on, "they're just a big pain in the neck, but with a few people, alcohol really changes them. Even if they're usually kind and normal and gentle, a few drinks makes them mad."

"Like Mommy," Katy said.

"Exactly like Mommy."

"So how will they make her better, Daddy? Will the doctor give her medicine, or what?"

Chris took his daughter's hand. "This isn't like having the flu or tonsillitis, Katy. It's possible that Mommy may have to go to a hospital for a little while."

"How long?"

"I'm not sure yet."

"Two days?"

"More than that," Chris said.

"A whole week?"

"Maybe a little longer than that." Seeing Katy's expression, Chris squeezed her hand more tightly. "But you'll be able to see her, sweetheart, and it'll be worth it, don't you think, if the doctors can make Mommy feel better again?"

"I guess." Katy sounded doubtful.

Alone again, Lally had tried to busy herself with baking for the café, but she had felt strangely lonely. Hugo often stayed out at night with friends, and Lally was happy enough by herself as a rule, but having Katy stay over, and then having Chris to dinner – all those confidences, all that unburdening and sharing – had given her a sense of rare intimacy. In practical terms, of course, Lally hardly knew the Webbers at all, yet there could be no denying that as of now, she was involved with them, like it or not.

But do I like it? she asked herself, folding eggs into her dough mixture.

There was no simple answer to the question. She hated the fact that a ten-year-old girl was being exposed to fear and hurt and too much adult misery. She'd loathed seeing Andrea Webber transformed by drink, and she certainly hadn't liked seeing the pain and dismay in her husband's eyes. But she had to admit that she had liked the hours she and Chris had spent together and, if she was entirely honest with herself, she'd liked hearing him say that his marriage had been over for years. Though of course he'd said nothing of the kind to Katy that morning.

Speared abruptly by guilt, Lally shook herself. There was nothing between her and Chris Webber, and even if she had been attracted to him, there had been not the slightest indication that the feeling had been mutual. The man had a hundred things on his mind, and she was certainly not one of them. Besides, so far as the Webbers' marriage was concerned, nothing was over until it was over. And wouldn't it be far better for Katy if her family life could still be salvaged?

Certainly that's what Katy feels, Lally thought, *and that's what matters.*

They did not come back after school that afternoon, and Lally, who'd given just one class that morning and then gone directly to *Hugo's,* had to admit to herself that she felt a sharp sense of disappointment that Chris had not called to let her know what was going on. Probably, she told herself, he was embarrassed about having talked too much to an outsider – for that was, of course, what she still was to him: his daughter's ballet teacher who'd poked her nose into their private business and gotten more than she'd bargained for.

Chris did call Friday evening, just after nine, while Lally and Hugo were watching an old movie on TV.

"Sorry it's so late," he said. "I've only just got Katy to bed." He sounded awkward.

"You didn't have to call at all," Lally said, carefully and politely. "It was a pleasure having Katy stay over." She was aware of Hugo, sitting four feet away, listening to every word she said, could feel his disapproval without looking at him.

"I wanted to call," Chris said. "I wanted to let you know what happened."

"Don't feel you have to," Lally said swiftly. "I mean if I can do anything more, I'll be glad to, but otherwise – "

"Do you mind hearing about it?"

"No, of course not."

"Because to be candid, talking to you feels like the first sane, halfway normal thing I've done all day."

Chris told Lally that he had persuaded Andrea to admit herself to a clinic near Springfield that afternoon. He didn't say much about what it had taken to talk her around and to get her there, but Lally read between the lines and guessed that it had been a nightmare for them both. She thanked him for telling her, and Chris asked her if she was feeling better, and the conversation ended warmly enough, but it seemed to Lally more than ever that she had misread the atmosphere the night before. There was nothing going on between them, nor could there be.

"Careful, Lally," Hugo said after she put down the phone.

"Of what?"

"You know what."

"Do I?"

"I think so."

That was all Hugo said, but Lally knew that he could almost always read her mind, and she knew, too, aggravatingly enough, that Hugo's warnings were usually valid. She often accused him of being overly cautious, especially in human relationships, but Hugo was her best friend, more constant than anyone she knew except her brother Joe, and she generally paid more attention to his advice than she would have him believe.

51

Chris Webber, when all was said and done, was a nice man, desperate to share his problems with another adult. Lally couldn't even kid herself that he had chosen her to confide in, because she'd been the one who'd stumbled in on their disaster. She had achieved what she had set out to: a possible end, ultimately, to Katy's nightmare. Andrea was going to get help now and, with luck, before too long, she'd be home again and the Webber marriage would be back on track.

Now, however, on this grey and snowy Sunday morning, Lally had to admit that Chris and Katy Webber were not paramount in her thoughts. She had her first dizzy spell of the day right after rising, and then another one, less than twenty minutes later, at the foot of the staircase. Hugo, just coming out of the kitchen, almost dropped his coffee cup, and insisted on picking her up and carrying her to the sofa in the sitting room.

"I'm not moving an inch from here until you tell me exactly how long this has been going on," he said, standing over her.

"It's nothing," she said, too weakly to be credible.

"Bull."

"That's not very nice, especially on a Sunday."

Hugo was wearing a robe, and his long hair was loose, and with his hawkish nose and tall, lean body, Lally thought he looked almost biblical.

"I don't feel very nice," he said. "My favourite person just passed out – "

"*Almost* passed out, and I'm feeling better already."

" – just almost passed out, and she's already let slip that it's happened before, and I want to know why in hell you never said anything."

"Because I knew you'd make a fuss." She started to get up.

"Don't you dare move. Damn right I'll make a fuss – and if you don't tell me everything right this minute, I'll call Doc Sheldon."

"Okay, okay, I'll tell you – and there's no need to look so worried. It was just a little dizziness – it's probably just some kind of virus."

"Have you ever passed right out?" Hugo demanded.

"No."

"Sure?"

"*No.*"

"How many times has it happened?"

"Hugo, will you please shut up and let me tell you."

Five minutes later, he was on the phone to Charlie Sheldon anyway, insisting that Lally needed to be seen right away, and though Hugo was acting calm now, what worried him more than anything else was that Lally wasn't really arguing.

The nightmare began about fifteen minutes after Charlie Sheldon had started his examination. He was about sixty-three, perhaps older, wore ancient tweed suits, cut his own wispy white hair and smelled of pipe tobacco, and he was always a quiet thoughtful man, not prone to making snap decisions or diagnoses. But it seemed to Lally this morning in his old, companionable surgery, its walls lined with Rockwell prints, that Charlie was even more ruminative than usual, offering scarcely more than a grunt or two as he took her blood pressure, looked into her eyes and ears, listened to her heart and lungs, checked her reflexes, weighed her, took a little blood and then sent her to the bathroom to produce some urine to accompany the other sample to the laboratory.

The doctor was on the telephone when Lally came back into his office, and it was a moment before she realized that the appointment for tests he was setting up in less than an hour's time was for her.

"Charlie, what's going on?" she asked as he put down the receiver.

"Just fixing up a few tests." He took off his glasses, old as his suit and roughly mended with adhesive tape, and rubbed the bridge of his nose.

"I heard." She looked right into his face. "Where's the fire, Charlie? What are these tests?"

He looked right back at her. "I'm concerned, Lally. With another patient I might fool around with the notion that the dizzy spells were stress related, but I've known you too many years for that."

"They could be."

"You believe that?"

She said nothing.

"Okay, let me be straight. I don't much like the sound of your heart."

She felt a sharp jab of fear. "What's wrong with it?"

"I'm not sure, which is why I ordered the tests. Okay?"

"Not really."

"But you'll have them."

She gave a small, helpless shrug. "You're the doctor, Charlie."

Hugo, still in the waiting room, blanched visibly when Lally told him, trying to sound calm, that she was going directly to the Taylor-Dunne Hospital in Holyoke for a few tests.

"Right now?" Hugo looked at Charlie Sheldon standing in the

doorway behind her. The doctor nodded.

"I think Charlie gets bored on Sundays," Lally tried to joke.

"All that's happening," Sheldon told Hugo, "is me trying to do my job, just trying to rule a few things out."

"What kind of things?" Hugo asked.

"He won't tell you," Lally said, and took his arm. "He's a doctor, they study for years just for moments like this, so they can pretend they know stuff when they don't really know anything at all."

"Doc?" Hugo looked back at Charlie again.

"Just get her over to Holyoke. Folks over there are busy enough without patients being late for their appointments."

Walking out to the car, Lally recognized the barely concealed fear in Hugo's eyes, and she remembered that he'd been a little phobic about hospitals ever since his own back injury. "Why don't I just get a cab?"

"Oh, sure."

She pulled him to a stop. "Hugo, I'm sure there's nothing to be worried about, and I think you'd be better off opening the café – I mean, what use is a business partner if he doesn't take care of business when you're sick?"

"Nice try, Lally." He started walking again.

"Maybe I'd rather be alone."

"No, you wouldn't."

She leaned against his shoulder. "No," she said, "I wouldn't."

She was examined more thoroughly than she'd ever been in her life, and asked about a hundred questions, before she gave more blood, underwent a brain scan and an EKG, in which electrodes were applied to her chest, wrists and ankles. They took spinal and chest X-rays, and performed a calorific test in which the outer canals of her ears were briefly flooded with water and her eyes then checked for normal reflex flickering to rule out labyrinthitis. The doctors, nurses and orderlies were all gentle, reassuring and efficient, but Lally had never felt so terrified and alone. She'd made Hugo stay in a waiting room, but she thought now that she might have liked a familiar hand to hold, and when the sudden memory of Chris Webber's face flashed into her mind, she let herself grasp at it for just an instant, remembering the dark blue eyes and curly fair hair and strong straight nose. And then she let the image go again. She was on her own, and that was okay. She was good on her own.

Her brain was just fine, so were her ears, and so was all the rest of her, except for her heartbeat, which was pretty much what Charlie Sheldon had thought. Against her will, Lally was ordered into a wheelchair and pushed to the office of one Dr Lucas Ash, a cardiologist, where she waited for almost three-quarters of an hour, in pristine, pearl-grey leather and chrome silence, while he completed his hospital rounds.

"I'm sorry," he said, as he swept into the room.

"That's okay." Lally looked at him with fascination. He was about forty-five, blond and almost too handsome, with a Roman nose, violet-blue eyes and the kind of perfect skin that looked as if it were scrubbed clean and moisturized on the hour.

"Excuse me while I flip through your notes?" He smiled at her disarmingly, then bent his head over the file. Every now and then, he picked up a pair of tiny fold-up spectacles from his desk and put them on, almost, Lally felt, as if he needed to prove that he really was a doctor and not an actor in a medical soap.

He didn't make her wait too much longer for his diagnosis. He listened to her heart for a while, took her pulse and blood pressure, double-checked her family history, and asked, loud and clear, if she was perfectly sure she hadn't taken any drugs whatsoever in the last week or so.

"Not even an aspirin," Lally said.

"Okay."

She waited, focusing on the window behind the doctor's chair. It was snowing again outside, and the hospital gardens, the whole world, seemed closed off behind the veil of white.

"You have a condition called bradycardia. In lay language, that really just means an abnormally low rate of heartbeat. That's what's been causing your blood pressure to drop, hence the loss of energy, weakness and dizzy spells." Ash paused. "Have you heard of heart block?"

Lally shook her head. Her hands were very cold.

"In simple terms, it's an interruption, or a blocking of the passage of impulses through the heart's conducting system. The contractions of the upper and lower parts of the heart are not properly synchronized, and though in some cases the problem can be partial, in your case, it's what we call complete heart block." He paused again, watching her face. "Now that's nowhere near so alarming as it might sound."

"How serious is it?" Lally's voice was very soft.

"Very serious, but only if left untreated. It could lead to a seizure, even a cardiac arrest."

"You mean it could kill me?"

"Only if we did nothing about it."

A sense of unreality and disbelief was making Lally feel as if she were floating somewhere above the room, looking down at herself sitting in the chair, facing the doctor.

"I don't really see how this can be true," she said, very slowly and still quietly. "I'm a dancer. I exercise all the time – I mean not just dance, I work out every morning. I've always had more energy than I know what to do with. I'm a strong person."

"Not quite so strong lately, though," Lucas Ash suggested.

"No, that's true, but couldn't this just be one of those weird viruses you hear about?" Lally began to hear the suppressed terror in her voice. "Neither of my parents ever had any kind of heart problem – no one in my family has, so far as I know."

"Your mother and father died young, in an accident." The doctor was kind, but matter-of-fact. "And I doubt if heart disease was exactly a regular topic of conversation in your home. It never is, till something goes wrong."

"And now it has." A fist of dread was twisting itself around in Lally's stomach. Suddenly she wanted to cry like a child, wanted someone to take her in their arms and tell her that everything was going to be all right.

"There's nothing for you to be afraid of, Lally," Dr Ash said. "I told you that this would only be a problem if it was left untreated."

Lally looked at him guardedly. "How can you treat it?"

"By fitting you with an artificial pacemaker."

"A pacemaker?" The small relief at being told she could survive was instantly wiped away by images of artificial hearts, pictures of her lying on a bed with tubes and wires. She saw herself being wheeled by Hugo to her dance studio, pale and fragile, heard herself tell her students that she couldn't teach them any more, but that they weren't to be afraid for her –

"How much do you know about pacemakers?" The doctor's question brought Lally back to earth.

"Very little, I guess." She flushed pink. "I've heard about them, of course, but I've never knowingly met anyone who had one."

"How big do you think they are?"

Lally shrugged, and held up her hands vaguely in the shape and size of an orange. "About so big? I don't know."

Dr Ash smiled and opened a drawer in his desk.

"This is a modern pacemaker." He saw the surprise in her eyes. "Not much bigger than a matchbook, is it? Take it." He offered it to her. "Light, too, isn't it?"

"It's amazing." The fear came back. "This would be attached to my heart? I know it's small, but how could I move around with something like this inside me?"

"Easily, believe me." The cardiologist fished in his deep desk drawer for something else, then stood up and turned around to remove a book from one of his shelves. "Lally, come and sit down over here." He gestured to a grey settee and waited for her to settle. "In the old days, the early days of pacing, this was the kind of device patients had to put up with." He held out a large metal object. "Take it."

Lally held it in her right hand. It was about seven times bigger than the first one he had shown her. "It's so heavy," she said, startled.

"Nevertheless, the first recipient of the first pacemaker in the late fifties is still alive today."

"Really?" The first spark of genuine relief lifted her.

"And when you go on to learn how extraordinarily sophisticated pacemakers have become over the last thirty or so years, that information alone ought to be enough to wipe out most of your fears."

"I guess so." Her lack of conviction showed in her voice.

Lucas Ash looked at her with genuine sympathy. "I'm not dismissing your anxieties, Lally. The symptoms you've been suffering would scare anyone, and in just the last few hours you've had all kinds of tests, and then I come in – a complete stranger – and tell you that you have a serious heart condition."

"But one that's not going to kill me, right?"

"Absolutely right." The doctor took the old pacemaker away from her. "But you're still scared, aren't you?"

Lally nodded.

"Then the best way to deal with that is to explain to you exactly what we're going to do, and then to do it."

"When?"

"Right away."

"You mean today?"

"Absolutely today." Lucas Ash smiled. "It's a comparatively simple procedure, Lally, not really surgery at all. No general anaesthetic, just a few days in the hospital to rest up, and then home and back to normal."

"What do you mean by normal?" Lally asked.

"I mean just that, normal."

"By whose standards?"

"Anyone's."

"What about a dancer's?"

Dr Ash leaned forward. "Lally, listen to me. I'm not in the business of lying to my patients, okay?"

"Okay," she said, tensely.

"For the first two or three days after the procedure you'll feel a little sore from the small superficial wound on your chest, just above your left breast – you are right-handed, aren't you?" She nodded. "Then, for another week, you'll be advised to take things gently, though with each passing day you'll probably feel more and more like doing pirouettes, or whatever it is that ballet dancers like doing." He saw her manage a weak smile. "And after that, if things go well, you'll be able to do exactly what you've always done."

"What might not go well?" Lally asked quickly.

"Nothing disastrous. Sometimes, adjustments have to be made at the post-implant stage, but all that means is that a piece of gadgetry gets waved over you, and everything gets put one hundred per cent right without the slightest discomfort or risk."

"Sounds like a piece of cake," she said.

"It is."

"But does it really have to be done today? I mean, I have responsibilities – my dance classes, the café. Hugo and I – Hugo's the friend who brought me here – we run a café in West Stockbridge together, and he needs me to do the baking, and – "

"I'm sure Hugo will get by."

"Maybe, but – "

"But nothing."

Lally stopped talking.

"We need to do this right away, Lally," Lucas Ash said again, patiently. "Most probably, if we didn't, you'd be okay, get away with it. But you'd be running an unnecessary risk."

"You mean I might have a seizure or something."

"I mean, in theory, that you could die. Which would be an awful waste, don't you think, considering that a pacemaker would take care of the problem completely."

Lally was silent for another moment.

"Okay," she said.

"You're sure? You understand what I've told you?"

"I think so."

"If you wanted a second opinion, I'd have no objection, provided there was no delay."

"I don't need a second opinion," Lally said. "I trust you."

"You trust him?" Hugo, in the waiting room, had gone from pale to ashen.

"Yes, I do." Lally sat down beside him on a navy blue couch. "And so does Charlie Sheldon, which is more important."

58

"But shouldn't you have a second opinion?"

"No, not really." The unreality had come back, filling her with a delusive and definitely temporary calm. "In a way, Dr Ash *is* the second opinion – it was obvious Charlie knew what was going on the minute he listened to my heart."

"But why do they have to do it right now?"

"Because it would be pretty dumb to risk me dropping dead for the sake of one more day."

"Don't say things like that," Hugo said furiously.

"Only if you promise to stop looking so scared." Lally managed a smile. "Nothing's going to happen to me, Hugo, I promise."

Hugo's brown eyes were tender and terrified. "Aren't you scared?"

"What do you think?"

"I'd better call Joe."

"No," Lally said quickly.

"You have to tell him."

She shook her head vehemently. "No, I don't. Joe's worried enough about Jess and the baby. It might be different if this thing were a week away and he could maybe fly out."

"He's your brother, Lally," Hugo said. "He has a right to know."

"And I have a right not to scare him." Lally was immovable. "You're not to call him, Hugo. A preoccupied cop is a vulnerable cop – Joe's told me that himself, and I don't want to have to start worrying about him." She laid a hand on his arm. "Promise you won't call him."

"If that's what you want. I still don't agree."

"Promise me, Hugo."

"Okay, I promise." Hugo was silent and wretched for a moment. "Do you want me to be with you when they do it? I could hold your hand."

"And have you pass out in the middle of things?" Lally said lightly. "I don't want Lucas Ash having to concentrate on anyone except me."

"I wouldn't pass out."

"Maybe not, but you'd hate every second of it, and I've got better things to do than feel sorry for you."

"You make me sound like such a wimp."

Lally put her arms around him. "You're anything but a wimp, Hugo Barzinsky. You're a strong, sensitive, wonderful man, and I don't know where I'd be without you."

Hugo blushed.

The procedure began at four o'clock. Lally was wheeled into the catheter laboratory in the Department of Cardiology, fully conscious and as appraised as possible of what was going to happen to her. Charlie Sheldon had come over to Holyoke to see her, and that had helped a little. Charlie was not a liar. If he said that having a pacemaker implanted was nowhere near as nice as a day on the beach, but nowhere near as nasty as having a tooth pulled, she was inclined to believe him. And she did trust Lucas Ash, even if he was too handsome to be real.

There were two other people in the laboratory.

"Hi, Lally, I'm Joanna King." A statuesque black woman of about thirty came over to shake her hand warmly. "I'm a radiographer, and I'm going to be monitoring the implantation on our X-ray equipment."

"Thank you." Lally didn't know what else to say, though even in her white coat, the woman looked more like a Paris model than a radiographer, and she was beginning to wonder what it was about this place that made everyone look so good.

"And this is Bobby Goldstein." Lucas Ash indicated the young, kindly-faced, bespectacled technician on the other side of the room. Goldstein, busy doing something, raised a hand to wave to her. "Bobby's going to be in charge of operating your box of tricks, okay?"

"Okay." Her voice sounded hoarse.

Sitting there, waiting for them to start, Lally was part relieved, part alarmed that they were clearly not in an operating theatre. The laboratory was scrupulously clean, and there was an instrument trolley, but Mozart was playing from a speaker in one corner, and there was no daunting operating table and not too much dazzling steel or harsh lighting, and there was no awful, sickly smell – but then again, if something went wrong, she couldn't help wondering, where was the resuscitation equipment?

The pacemaker consisted of a little generator box like the one Dr Ash had shown her in his office, two insulated wires that would be attached to the box and that would carry the electrical pulses from the generator to her heart, and at the end of those wires, two tiny electrodes that would ultimately be planted in the right atrium, the upper chamber, and the right ventricle, the lower chamber. Aside from the prick of the local anaesthetic that would deaden the entry point on her chest, Lucas Ash had assured Lally that there would be no actual pain, just some unusual sensations, not even any significant discomfort. The puncture would be made on her chest a little way under her left shoulder, and the wires would be

60

introduced into the sub-clavian vein and advanced, slowly and carefully, under Joanna King's X-ray supervision, towards their destination.

"Once the electrodes are firmly in place in your heart," Bobby Goldstein told Lally before they began, "I get to take over for a while, testing to see that they're perfectly positioned, and taking all kinds of measurements."

"And when Mr Goldstein's finished," Lucas Ash went on, "I'll link the generator box to the two wires, and then I'll make a small pocket under the skin above your left breast, tuck the box into the pocket and suture you up – and then the whole device will be programmed precisely to your body's needs – "

"Taking my dancing into account," Lally said, tensely.

"Absolutely, just as I explained earlier." The cardiologist was patient and gentle. "Your pacemaker knows everything it needs to about the effects and demands of extreme exercise – do you remember, Lally, or would you like me to go over the details again?"

"No, I remember."

"You're sure? I don't mind. There's no rush."

"I'm sure." She made a small grimace. "About that, anyway."

"What aren't you sure about?"

"I'm not sure I should have bothered getting up this morning."

Lally had never believed in the word 'discomfort'. If a doctor or dentist said that something was going to cause a little discomfort, then to her mind that usually meant it was going to hurt. Likewise, if they said that something was going to hurt a little, more than likely it was going to hurt one hell of a lot.

She sat very still when Dr Ash began, trying desperately to relax and give herself up to the Mozart, but she was rigid as steel, and though Lally seldom perspired outside the dance studio, she could feel beads of sweat trickling down her back under her hospital gown. Joanna King was concentrating too hard all through the procedure to watch Lally's face, but Bobby Goldstein saw her terror, and until he was needed to do his stuff, he pulled up a stool and sat quite close beside her, and at one point, when Lally felt a strange sensation and winced involuntarily, the technician took her hand in his and squeezed it, and for the second time that day, Chris Webber's face sprang unexpectedly into her mind, and for just a few precious moments, Lally stopped thinking about the wires prodding into her heart.

It was all over in less than an hour.

"That's it," Lucas Ash told her.

"Is it working?"

"Perfectly."

"Why are you holding your breath?" Bobby Goldstein asked.

Lally flushed and took a tentative breath.

"See? Nothing awful happened, did it?" Dr Ash smiled, and patted her right hand. "Nor will it, Lally, not now."

"And that's really it?" She could hardly believe it.

"You can relax," Goldstein told her. "Your heart's working perfectly."

"And it's going to go on that way for another ten years or so," Lucas Ash added. "And even then, the only thing that should need replacing is the little box, which is really no big deal."

Lally felt her body relax, had not entirely realized until that instant how rigid she had remained throughout the operation. Suddenly she wanted to cry with relief and, to her shame, the tears did begin to well up in her eyes, and she scrubbed at them hastily.

"Here." Joanna King handed her a box of Kleenex. "Go right ahead."

"I'm sorry," Lally wept.

"A lot of patients weep when it's over," Bobby Goldstein assured her.

"Hell," Joanna King said, with just the merest touch of scorn, "I've seen the biggest, toughest, most composed men cry all the way from start to finish."

"But it didn't even *hurt*," Lally sobbed, in wonder.

"Didn't I tell you it wouldn't?" Lucas Ash asked, mildly.

"Yes, but I didn't believe you – " Lally blew her nose. "I mean how could wires being poked through my veins right into my heart *not* hurt?"

"Well, that small wound will start hurting a little when the local wears off," Ash pointed out, "but we'll give you something for the pain, and in a day or two even that will be reduced to a minimal soreness." He paused. "The big thing is that it's all over, all taken care of, and you can relax."

"I'll be seeing you a few times during your stay," Goldstein told her, "to do some more measuring and to make any tiny corrections to your programming that may be necessary."

"The idea," Lucas Ash went on, "is that you get to go home without fear and without symptoms."

Lally blew her nose again.

"Have any of you ever known a pacemaker to go wrong?"

"Not for many years," Dr Ash replied steadily and honestly. "In the old days – and then only very seldom – generators displayed a few minor faults, and occasionally wires fracture, but those problems are so rare as to be discountable – you really are more likely to be knocked down by a bus." He paused. "Infection, of course, is still a potential hazard, as with any surgical procedure, but I applied a local antibiotic before I sutured you up, so that's not likely to be a problem, either."

"All you have to do now," Joanna King said, "is to let yourself get tucked up in bed and looked after for a few days."

"And then a little more rest, a little monitoring," the cardiologist added, "and if everything looks as good as it does now – and there's no reason why it shouldn't – then you'll be able to forget all about it."

"Back to normal," Lally said, and smiled for the first time.

"Absolutely."

10

Monday, January 11th

Joe Duval and Linda Lipman arrived for duty at Hagen Industries at eight-thirty Monday morning. Lipman was everything Joe had hoped she would be: pin-striped suit about nine years out of date, the new frosting she'd had put into her fair hair dyed right out, sensible shoes, colourless nail varnish, the picture of the effective statistician in the field, not a hair out of place but far too busy to concern herself with up-to-the-minute fashion.

"I love your horn-rims," she said, grinning at Joe's glasses as he parked their car. "Can you see anything through them?"

"They're clear glass."

"Don't leave them lying around."

"Got your stopwatch?" Joe switched off the ignition.

"Got your clipboard?"

"Check."

"Let's go."

"We were hoping, as you know," Al Hagen told them in his office ten minutes later, "that Schwartz might be able to link both devices to a single production batch, to give us a better chance of tracking down every potentially dangerous unit."

"But that hasn't proven possible?" Joe asked.

"Regrettably, no. In the first place, whereas Mr Long had what we call a single chamber demand pacemaker, Mrs Ferguson had a dual chamber pacemaker, which means that if it was some kind of production problem, we're looking for at least two suspect batches."

"But you haven't traced them," Lipman said.

"We're getting there, but slowly," Hagen replied. "Our paperwork logs details of each production batch included in every shipment, so although we had no serial numbers to go on immediately, we were able to narrow the problem down to three possible suspect batches in the Boston case, and just two batches in the Chicago case."

"That's good news, isn't it?" Joe presumed.

"I wish I could say it was." Hagen was grim-faced. "We produce pacemakers in batches of one hundred, which for safety's sake are divided down into three segments of thirty-three each, to be delivered at three-monthly intervals, with one master copy held back for security. Two out of the five batches in question were produced last September, one in October and another two in December." He paused. "Looking only at the September batches, chances are every one of the devices in the first segment, and a number of the second segment, will have been implanted in patients by now."

"Surely you can trace the patients," Lipman said.

"Until we can narrow this down further, Detective, we're talking about a minimum of over two hundred devices, many of them inside human beings all over the United States, some perhaps even further afield."

"But you still have the final segment of thirty-three from each batch to examine, plus the master copies," Joe said.

"Yes, we do. And logically, whatever problem caused these two tragedies ought to have been evident in those control copies."

"But they haven't been?" Joe asked.

"Not a trace – everything just as it should be." Hagen shook his grey head. "And it's going to be a long, slow job checking each and every one of the other devices – we don't want to take any risks." He slipped his right index finger up under his glasses and rubbed the bridge of his nose. "On one hand, the fact that the master copies were perfectly normal makes me more hopeful that the other pacemakers are all sound too. On the other hand, it makes me even more nervous, because we still have no hard proof."

"Surely you can recall the devices that haven't been implanted?" Lipman said.

"You make it sound so simple, Detective."

"That part of it does seem simple to me." Lipman was terse. "Aside from anything else, the FDA are bound to force a recall."

"Detective Lipman, the Food and Drug Administration will know that it's too soon to quantify the real risk. Those two hundred or so suspect devices could, God forbid, be just the beginning." Hagen's colour was heightening. "If we wanted to play it one hundred per cent safe, we'd be talking about recalling and checking *thousands* of pacemakers." He turned to Joe. "Do you begin to understand what might happen, Lieutenant?"

"I think I can imagine," Joe said.

"I suppose you imagine a warning going out to hospitals and physicians and cardiologists – maybe you go further, and picture the panic and chaos if the press and TV networks get hold of the story."

"Naturally we do," Lipman said.

Hagen turned his attention to her. "Suppose you had a pacemaker fitted, Detective, and you got wind of the news. What would you do?"

"I'd run like hell straight back to my doctor."

"And what would you want him to do?"

"Tell me that my pacemaker was safe."

"And if he couldn't be sure?" Hagen paused. "You'd ask him to take it out and put in one guaranteed not to blow up."

"I guess so," Lipman agreed.

"Can you imagine what removing a potentially explosive device from a living, breathing human being would entail?" Hagen was white-faced again now. "If you were a surgeon, would you care for the risk? If you were on the board of governors of a hospital, would you give permission for your operating theatres to be used?"

Lipman did not answer. She, too, had grown paler.

"I could go on."

"We get the picture," Joe said.

"This isn't like the Anacin scare, Lieutenant Duval. You can't just tell people not to swallow their pills. That's why we've been praying that Fred Schwartz would at least be able to focus in more tightly. If we could pinpoint two batches that we *knew* for certain to be faulty – and I have to tell you that still seems almost an impossibility to all of us in the company – then at least the nightmare scenario of operating theatres on red alert could be kept to a minimum."

They all sat in silence for a long moment.

"What's Mr Schwartz doing now?" Joe asked finally.

"Obviously, he's begun testing the undelivered devices from the batches we've discussed, and then he's going to start examining and testing every single master copy set aside from every batch produced in the last six months." Hagen paused. "I have to tell you that Schwartz still believes there's no way this can have happened in this facility."

"What do you believe, Mr Hagen?" Lipman asked.

"I don't know what to believe right now." Hagen paused again. "Since you and Lieutenant Duval are from the Violent Crimes Division, it's pretty clear you're looking for a more sinister cause than an accident."

"Since Mr Leary and Mr Schwartz have both made it plain that nothing normally in your pacemakers could explode on its own," Joe said steadily, "criminal intent does have to be a consideration."

Hagen flushed again. "Have you any idea how unthinkable that seems to me?"

"I think we have, sir," Lipman gave Hagen one of her deceptively tender smiles. When she was being herself, Linda liked wearing vivid pink, sometimes even scarlet lipsticks, but today she was all face powder and muted colours.

"We're not just here to investigate, sir," Joe said, gently. "We want to help you any way we can."

"For which I'm grateful," Hagen said. "As I told your commander."

Joe stood up, and Lipman followed suit. "I guess we should get to work." Joe took the horn-rimmed glasses from his top pocket. "We're going to be watching and listening and taking notes – have your people been told there's a T & M study starting today?"

"Of course. The only people here who know the truth are Leary, Olivia Ashcroft, and Schwartz." Hagen hesitated. "And I think it would be helpful to confide in my personal assistant, Cynthia Alesso – she's been with me from the beginning. I'd trust her with my life."

Joe put on the glasses. "I'd be happier if you kept what you told her to the barest minimum."

"I agree."

Hagen came with them into his outer office and introduced them to his assistant. Cynthia Alesso was around fifty, with keen nut brown eyes and dark curls strewn with silver. She reminded Joe of a blackbird, her movements sharp and swift, her voice high and musical. Hagen went back into his office and closed the door, and a moment later, they heard the sound of classical music, loud and vibrant, piercing the walls.

"Wagner." Cynthia Alesso smiled ruefully. "I've always hated Wagner, but the boss is crazy about it, says it relaxes him when he has problems to work out. The bigger the problem, the louder the music."

* * *

Joe Duval knew that his desire for a career in law enforcement stemmed, in good part, from the time after his best pal Tom Harris had been shot to death in a raid on a drugstore while his mother was buying aspirin and shampoo. Joe and Tom had been the closest of confidants in the third grade, and after the tragedy Joe had been left bereft and confused, emotions the local police force had seemed to fully comprehend and share as they had dealt with the nightmare rapidly, compassionately and effectively, nailing the two drug-crazed gunmen within two weeks. The police officers had become heroes to most of the kids at school, but to none more than Joe Duval.

Apart from the terrible months after Tom's death, Joe's childhood had been pretty much a joy, yet from an early age he'd known he was not destined to stay in the Berkshires. He and Lally shared the same colouring, the same dark brown hair and grey eyes, and they loved each other beyond words, but in some ways they were immeasurably different. Lally's roots meant everything to her, whereas the day Joe had left West Stockbridge to go to John Jay College in New York City, to study criminal justice and psychology, had been one of the most exciting of his life. And it had all gone so beautifully, so exactly as he'd planned: first college, then the Police Academy, and his first years on the force with the NYPD. And then he'd fallen in love with Jess and with sweet Sal, her daughter, and he'd relocated to Chicago so that they could be married. And nothing too much had really gone wrong with his adult life until his parents' premature death, and then Jess's miscarriage last year – and those sorrows had felled him, though looking back on them from a distance, in a bizarre kind of way he was almost grateful to them for forcing him to fully understand the fragility and preciousness of love and family and the stuff that really mattered. Ambition, hard work and achievement had their places right enough, but they weren't what really mattered, not by a long chalk.

It was tough, sometimes almost impossible, being a good husband and father when you were a cop, but Joe was luckier than most, because though he knew Jess was as afraid as any policeman's wife, she never gave him a hard time about the dangerous situations he got involved in, seldom nagged him about the long hours he worked.

"I knew when I married you," she said simply.

"But don't you hate it?"

"How can I, when it's so much a part of you?"

He was a lucky man in so many ways. Soon after his promotion to sergeant, he'd been accepted by the FBI for a ten-month training programme with the Behavioral Science Unit within the NCAVC – the National Center for the Analysis of Violent Crime – and hard on the heels of Joe's new-won experience in criminal personality profiling had come his first major case. The arsonist who had terrorized Chicago for almost four months – self-styled *The Inhuman Torch* in letters sent, at first, to the *Chicago Tribune*, and as the investigation got under way, to Joe Duval himself – had liked burning people more than property, and had liked knowing they had burnt alive and conscious; and the fact that he never knew his victims seemed only to increase, not lessen his satisfaction. Effective teamwork, routine detection, BSU profiling techniques and good luck had led to the *Torch*'s arrest, but not before the killer had set a fire that he boasted would burn at least a hundred victims. Joe had interrogated him every way he knew, not all of them orthodox, and the fire, in a children's hospital, had been stopped just in time. He had been promoted to lieutenant within three months.

Everything changed less than one hour after Joe and Lipman's arrival at Hagen Pacing, when Cynthia Alesso asked Joe to return to Hagen's office to take a call from the commander.

Jackson was curt and to the point. "Someone in the ME's office found traces of plastique explosive in Mrs Ferguson's remains."

"I thought that had been ruled out," Joe said, picking his words carefully with Hagen there in the room at his desk.

"Yeah, I thought so too," the commander said. "Is Hagen still there?"

"Yes."

"He knows."

Joe looked at Hagen. He seemed dazed.

"Do you want us to come back, Commander?"

"No point wasting time." Jackson's voice was grim. "I've talked to Boston, and Chief Hankin's informed the FBI and FDA. Under the circumstances, given our jurisdiction, they're letting us put together our own task force, including Bomb and Arson, and the FBI will give us access to computers, transport, whatever we need."

"Who's going to head the task force?" Joe asked.

"You are."

Joe said nothing. A swift stab of excitement gripped him, followed by a wave of guilt. It was often that way for him, getting caught up in a homicide investigation. All the right motivations, sure, but then that nasty little worm of conscience reminding him that a job done well could further his career, the way all those poor burned people had brought him his promotion.

"You got *The Inhuman Torch*" – Jackson was a mind reader – "and more to the point, you trained in their Behavioral Science programme, so the FBI's behind us on this, for the moment at least. It's all yours, Duval."

"Thank you, sir." Joe pushed the guilt aside and started focusing hard on the case.

"It'll be around the clock," Jackson went on, "and you can't talk about this one to anyone, not even your wife."

"I realize that, sir." Joe hated keeping stuff from Jess – they were the kind of couple who liked to share.

Hagen got up from his desk and went out of the room, closing the door quietly behind him.

"Hagen just left," Joe said. "He looks pretty shell-shocked."

"Tell the others – Leary, Ashcroft and Schwartz – see how they react – and make damn sure they know it's for their ears only."

"It could be any one of them," Joe said.

"It could be anyone in the whole goddamned place." Jackson paused. "Hagen says Schwartz is going to test samples from the last six months' output. Think he's up to it, or do we bring someone in?"

"I think it might be a mistake replacing him at this stage," Joe said. "He knows better than anyone exactly what goes into these things." He remembered the man's haunted expression, remembered that he'd liked him on first impression, then put the thought away. "He'll have to be supervised every working moment."

"And he has to work in a secure testing area, away from the rest of the work-force," Jackson said. "Who do you want on the task force?"

"Lipman, for sure. And Tony Valdez from Bomb and Arson," Joe said without hesitation. "He's the man to stick with Schwartz and the production line." He paused. "And Cohen."

"Cohen has a pacemaker." Involuntarily, the commander laid his right hand on his own chest. Aside from Chief Hankin, he thought no one in the department knew about his trouble.

"He's had it for ten years," Joe said. "It'll make him extra sensitive."

Jackson winced. "He may not think it's such a hot idea."

"I think he'll want to help," Joe said. He and Sol Cohen went back a long way.

"I'll talk to them both, and get back to you."

"Thank you, sir."

"Just find out how the hell this happened, Duval, and get the bastard who did it." Jackson's voice grew more resonant. "And for

70

the love of God, find out if those two were the only ones."

"We'll do our best, Commander."

"Not good enough, Lieutenant."

Joe looked at the dead receiver, and put it slowly back on the hook. The commander wanted results, Chief Hankin demanded results, and if Joe didn't give them what they needed – and soon – if this horror was allowed to get out of hand, the whole country would be after his blood.

Joe knew he had the case of a lifetime. He had never wanted one less.

11

Tuesday, January 12th

Hugo came to collect Lally from the hospital at three in the afternoon.

"Are you sure you're ready to leave?" he asked her.

"I've been ready to leave since yesterday morning."

"But Dr Ash wanted you to stay till tomorrow."

"And then he changed his mind."

"Because you drove him nuts."

"He wouldn't be letting me out if he thought I wasn't ready."

"Depends how nuts you drove him."

"You make me sound terrible."

"You are."

"Hugo."

"What?"

"Take me home."

She knew he was still frightened for her, and in a way she was grateful for that fear because it strengthened her, gave her someone else other than herself to think about. That had probably been the worst part of the last few days, the sudden awareness of her own body, the constant battle with her mind not to count every heartbeat. Hugo had said, in one of his braver moments, that she looked fine, a little on the pale and interesting side, but nothing that a few home-cooked meals and a lot more sleep wouldn't set right. Lally still felt pretty sore, though that did seem to be getting better with almost every passing hour, but apart from that, she found it hard to describe exactly what she felt.

"I feel emotionally weird," she told Hugo on the drive home.

"How weird?"

Lally tried to find words. "Some of me still feels shocked, I guess – by the drama, by the speed of it all." She paused. "Some of me feels vulnerable and anxious, because maybe not all of me believes that such a simple procedure could really put right something so dangerous."

Hugo glanced across at her. "But it has put it right, Lally. I've done a lot of checking around since Ash put in the pacemaker. They're wonderful things, completely reliable."

"I know they are." She smiled at him. "I'm just trying to be honest about what I'm feeling." She ran her fingers through her long, dark hair. "I can't wait to get in the shower and wash my hair properly."

"I'll do it for you."

"Maybe I'll let you help dry it."

"You're too kind."

Lally stared out of the window, relishing the snowy landscape, the beauty of the hills in the distance. "I know it's foolish," she said, quietly, "but another part of me feels heroic and euphoric, as if I've been smoking dope and drinking champagne. I get these moments when I feel I've stared death in the eye and told it to take a running jump."

"That doesn't sound foolish to me," Hugo said.

"But the weirdest thing of all is that I keep alternately forgetting and then remembering with a jolt that I have this *thing* embedded in my body, this alien thing powering my heart – "

"It isn't powering it, it's just making sure it steers a safe course."

"I know. Still."

There were two bouquets waiting for Lally at the house, pink roses from Hugo with a card telling her how much he loved her, and a bunch of sweet peas from Katy Webber, saying that she wished Lally would get better real soon and would she mind if she came to visit?

"Don't look at me like that." Hugo saw Lally's accusing stare. "I had to tell some people – you're not going to be taking classes for a few weeks yet."

"Maybe."

"Definitely." He raised a hand defensively. "Don't worry, I didn't tell Joe – though I still think he ought to know."

"He will know, when I'm better," Lally said, definitely. "And not before."

"I guess it's up to you," Hugo said.

"It is." Lally looked at the flowers again. "I'd better put those in water."

"I'll do it. You go upstairs and get into bed."

"I've just got out of bed."

"Dr Ash said you could only come home if you rested, and he meant staying in bed."

"I could lie on the sofa," Lally said.

"With a pillow and a blanket," Hugo compromised.

"Deal."

"Then go put on something comfy and I'll cut you a slice of your welcome-home cake."

Lally's eyes brightened. "Chocolate?"

"What else?"

She was settled on the sofa before Hugo brought her the cake and a cup of camomile tea. "This came for you this morning." He handed her a brown paper wrapped parcel.

She looked at it curiously. There was no address, written or printed. It had clearly been hand-delivered. "Who's it from?"

"I was asked to say nothing," Hugo said. "I guess it's some kind of gift."

Lally held the parcel for a few moments, examining it for signs. It was rectangular in shape, about eighteen inches by twelve, and about two inches thick. She gave up trying to guess, and tore off the paper to find a brown cardboard box. Her hands grew more impatient.

"Careful," Hugo said. "It might be fragile."

"It's a painting." Lally's eyes widened. Gently, she lifted it out of the box, and saw that it was a portrait of herself, on canvas and framed in pale polished wood. She was barefoot and dressed in the leotard and cotton rehearsal skirt she often wore for classes, her hair was fastened in a bun, and she was holding a pair of pointe shoes. Her eyes filled with tears.

"There's something written on the back." Hugo's voice was tight.

She turned it over. *Thank you*, it said. *Be well, and safe. Chris.*

"He's called a few times," Hugo said. "I didn't know how much you wanted him to know, so I didn't tell him where you were, but once the surgery was over, I told him you were fine and when I expected you home." He paused. "He sounded pretty upset when he heard you were sick, and then he kept on calling, leaving messages."

"Why didn't you tell me?"

"I'm not really sure," Hugo said, slowly. "I wasn't too clear how you felt about the Webbers."

"Don't you mean how you felt?" Lally asked, gently.

"Maybe." Hugo sat down on the end of the sofa, and she moved her feet to make space for him. "You know I was uneasy about your getting involved with them. It was upsetting you, and the man's married, with problems – "

"I understand," Lally said.

"But then, this morning, he got here with the parcel before I was even out of bed, wanting to know exactly what time I was going to fetch you." Hugo gave a wry smile. "He's probably sitting at home right now, chewing his nails, wanting to talk to you."

"I should call him."

"I suppose you should. I'll bring you the phone."

Chris answered on the second ring.

"It's me," Lally said, and watched Hugo leave the room.

"You're home." His voice was full of relief.

"I'm calling to thank you for my gift," she said, trying to be careful, though she knew her heart was in her voice. "It's the most wonderful present I've ever been given."

"I've been so worried," Chris said.

"I'm fine now."

"When Hugo told me what had happened, I couldn't believe it."

"I had a little trouble believing it myself."

"I kept remembering that you almost passed out when I was with you the other night, and that I just went home and left you."

"Because I insisted. You weren't to know."

"I should have stayed. I should have called a doctor."

"Chris, I'm fine now. It's all over."

"Hugo wouldn't let me visit you – he wouldn't even tell me where you were. I would have at least sent flowers."

"I was only there two days, and they didn't encourage visitors."

"At least you're home now."

They were both silent for a moment.

"How are things with you?" Lally asked, tentatively. "How's Katy doing? Is she home right now? I'd like to thank her for her sweet flowers."

"Katy's doing pretty well," Chris replied, "but she's at a friend's house – doing homework together, or so the story goes."

Lally hesitated only briefly. "And Andrea?"

"Not so good," Chris said. "She's still fighting them and me, still refusing to admit how bad her problems are."

"I'm sorry."

"She seems to understand, though, that if she doesn't stay in the clinic, I'll take Katy away from her. Andrea may not care about our marriage, but she loves our daughter far too much to risk losing her."

Hugo came back into the room, clucking like a mother hen to let Lally know that he thought she'd talked for long enough.

"I have to go now," Lally said. "My nurse wants me to take a nap."

"You should," Chris said quickly. "You need all the rest you can get."

"Thank you again for the painting, so much. It'll be a lovely reminder to me to do as I'm told so that I can get back to teaching as fast as I can."

"Katy'll be glad of that," Chris said.

Lally put down the phone and looked back at the painting. She hadn't liked to suggest that he come to visit her, and Chris had clearly felt awkward about butting in where he might not be wanted, but the portrait stopped her from feeling deflated. She saw the fineness of the brush strokes and saw, too, that if it was true that the beauty of a subject was in the eye of the beholder, then this particular artist definitely thought she was beautiful. Right now, wise or not, that notion made Lally very glad.

Hugo waited till later that evening, after he had served Lally a bowl of goulash soup with fresh baked bread, to bring up the subject again of the Webber family and Lally's involvement with them.

"May I be honest?" He sat down in one of the armchairs.

"You always have been."

The sitting room felt like a haven. Hugo had switched off the overhead light and turned on the two lovely red and yellow glass lamps that Toni Petrillo had had commissioned for Lally by one of their local craftsmen two birthdays ago, and the only other illumination came from the fireplace and the world beyond the windows. Lally had asked Hugo not to draw the drapes, because it was snowing again, and she loved sitting snug inside watching the flakes tumble past the street lamps outside.

"You've fallen for him, haven't you?"

Lally remained silent.

"You don't have to answer. I know you have. And it's just as clear to me now that Webber feels the same way about you – and so he should, but – "

"Don't go on," Lally said, softly. "There's no need – I know everything you might want to say to me. Chris is a married man

76

with a sick wife and a load of problems, and Katy's a pupil of mine, and it's a lousy situation to rush headlong into."

"But sometimes," Hugo said, "emotions take over from common sense, don't they?"

"They sure do." Lally looked up at Chris's painting propped on the mantelpiece. It was like having him in the room with her. She thought maybe she ought to find that a disturbing notion, but she didn't.

"And right now," Hugo went on, "you're extra vulnerable. Maybe too much so to be capable of making sensible decisions. You're usually a pretty sensible woman, Lally."

She smiled at him. "Right now, Hugo, I have to admit that being sensible is not my first priority." She wriggled her toes comfortably under her blanket. "Tonight, at any rate, I'm too busy being glad to be alive and home again, and with you."

"I reckon the only person in the world almost as glad as you is me."

"I know," she said, gently.

"Will you at least try to be a little careful?"

"I might not want to be exactly sensible," Lally said, slowly, "but for the time being, I don't feel like taking too many risks either. Not with my life, not even with Chris Webber."

12

Wednesday, January 13th

Sam McKinley had been back on the job for a week, but today was his first day on active duty. The medical officer had read and approved all his hospital reports, and, having checked him over personally, had agreed that Sam was good as new.

The San Francisco Fire Department looked after its own, and Sam had wanted for nothing during his brief illness, an illness that had scared the hell out of him for a few days, but which had proven, after all, to be nothing that couldn't be put right with a simple operation and some tender loving aftercare.

The other thing that had worried Sam almost as much as his initial fear of premature death, had been the possibility that they might not let him come back to work. Sam McKinley was not capable of doing a desk job; he had juices running through him that responded to action, to excitement, to the unique comradeship of his particular line of work and, when all the chips were down, to danger. If Sam had to die young, he always told his brother Andy – not his wife, of course, no one ever, *ever* talked to Susan about death – it sure as shit wasn't going to be in bed.

Not that Sam had any kind of death wish. If he'd ever, for a second, believed he might have had, all those thoughts had been wiped clean away the day his trouble started. Those juices that he knew made him function had all but stopped then, and when Sam had stared at himself in the mirror, he'd seen a face that had seemed, structurally at least, to have been his own, and yet it had not been *him*, for the essence had gone from the friendly old brown eyes that had winked back at him every morning of his life when he shaved and got ready to go to work.

Still, all the worry was behind him now, and he was back in the Department amongst his colleagues, and waiting for the first call of the shift. J.D. had said to him a half-hour ago that he hoped, for Sam's sake, that their first morning would bring nothing more serious than stranded cats and elevators, but Sam had a notion that something else was coming.

It came all right.

It was at a warehouse not too far from Fisherman's Wharf, and no one seemed to know how or why it had erupted the way it had, suddenly, out of nowhere, but there were two blocked exits and there were men trapped inside with Christ knew what kind of noxious fumes, and time running out.

Sam fought it with the others from the outside for more than an hour, and the heat was indescribable, the way it always was – once in a while, Susan asked him how it felt, but he always shrugged it off because he knew she couldn't take knowing – but then he heard that J.D. had gone inside and that he was in trouble, and that was the old red rag to the bull within Sam McKinley, because J.D. had saved his life three years back in a big blaze on Fulton Street, and they'd been best buddies way before that, and if J.D. was in trouble, Sam was going to get him out.

He saw him right away, saw that he was okay except for a big wooden crate on his leg, pinning him down, and it was hard for them to talk, with the respirator masks over their faces, and impossible to hear, what with the roar of the fire and the hoses, and anyway, there was no need for words, for the relief in J.D.'s eyes when he saw Sam coming for him was more than enough, and Sam had too much work to do to bother with talk.

He got the crate off J.D.'s leg, and he snapped off a long stick of wood for a cane, and they started out together, Sam keeping J.D. ahead of him so that he could be sure he got out okay – and that was when it hit him, like ten sledgehammers, like all the fireworks on all the Fourth of Julys rolled into one.

And all the juices that were Sam McKinley rocked and rolled for a split second, and then were quiet and laid to rest. And J.D. was outside before he realized that Sam wasn't with him, and there was no one else left inside the warehouse to see the spurt of blood.

And anyway, there was too much smoke.

13

Thursday, January 14th

The man still made time to come back to the room for a while every night. It felt good to be there, as it always did. Better than home, better than work, better than anywhere. And they needed him to come, his little dragons, to change their water and clean their enclosures and make sure they were feeding properly.

He liked watching them eat. The geckos ate live insects – crickets, wax moths, locusts, anything the little creatures could easily overpower. The two green iguanas, with their big spines and dewlaps, could stay healthy on a diet of chopped cabbage or dog food, but once in a while the man brought them mice or birds' eggs. And then there were his favourites, his Gila monsters, almost pretty with their black and pink bands, and smaller and gentler than the iguanas, but the most respected, the most feared, for the grooved teeth that conducted the venom from the glands in their lower jaws.

"They have very poor eyesight," the reptile house keeper at the Chicago Zoo had told him. "And they're real slow moving, they can't go for the big, fast animals, so they go for baby rats and fledglings, voles, eggs – anything small enough to swallow whole. They're nocturnal, too, and real shy, so we don't know as much about them as we'd like to, but we think their venom is mostly a defensive mechanism, because unlike snakes, they kill their prey almost instantly by crushing with their jaws."

"So the venom's a secondary thing?" the man asked.

"It's the trauma of the bite that kills, the venom follows

involuntarily. These creatures have tremendous jowls and muscle – if they bite you, it's real hard to get them off because they hang on, and those grooved teeth are very sharp."

The man had stared at the single stocky lizard in its glass enclosure.

"Could they kill a man?" he had asked.

"They've killed a few, so I'm told, but usually a bite is just damned painful and makes you real sick for a while."

The man was meticulously careful with his Gila monsters. But then, he was always careful about everything. And patient, too. He'd endured decades of patience. And now it was over. It had begun.

The finished design for his revenge, complete with scale drawings, mathematical calculations and blueprint for operation, had taken him less than forty-eight hours to conceive. He had taken one summer weekend, had shut himself up in the room with everything he needed for inspiration; had stocked up from Kuhn's Delicatessen, bought champagne from House of Glunz, slotted in his new compact disc version of *Siegfried*, and settled down, opposite the vivaria, to begin.

There had been countless possibilities, many diverse ways of achieving his aim. He understood perfectly every single component that went into a pacemaker, every millimetre of circuitry; he could read and comprehend it all in the way ordinary people read newspapers or comic strips or stared at their TVs. And that summer weekend, for once allowing his brain full, brilliant, free rein, he had sifted through the endless permutations, suggesting and dismissing, seeking perfection, purity and flawlessness.

And he had found it.

It was laughably simple, when you came right down to it.

The second stage, the active planning, had proved almost as rapid. He had begun in late August to assemble what he would need, and by mid-September everything had been in place on his workbench in the room. Everything except the plastique. He didn't want that stuff anywhere near him until he was ready to begin.

Hagen Pacing was, at that time, producing eight hundred pacemakers each month, at a rate of two hundred per week. Manufacture was, as always, divided into batches of one hundred, each batch in turn divided down into a further three divisions of thirty-three pacemakers, with one master copy set aside for security. The first hundred were manufactured between Monday morning and Wednesday noon, the second between then and Friday evening.

He had considered plans of far greater complexity, had been tempted almost beyond endurance by the prospect of producing whole generator boxes, was confident of his ability to make perfect replicas of the genuine articles. But he knew, nonetheless, that simplicity was best, and so he had controlled his impulses.

On Tuesday and Thursday nights each week, a number of partially assembled boxes were left on the production line, their batteries soldered onto their circuits one stage before being slipped into their titanium cases and welded shut. His plan was to remove a given number of the partly-assembled devices and bring them to his room, where he would detach the batteries and replace them with his own, specially created for his purposes. No one would ever challenge him, for his presence during the evenings and sometimes late at night was taken for granted by the security guards.

He had to admit that his own tiny batteries were ingenious, real beauties. Several times during the planning and execution, he had experienced a wave of irrational desire to show Ashcroft what he was doing. Best brain at Hagen Pacing, and she knew it, how she knew it, in spite of her refined, quiet manner. He'd have liked to have seen her face, to see the naked admiration in her eyes. But Mother's voice still sounded a warning rebuke in his head. Self-control above everything.

The lithium batteries used in all the Hagen pacemakers were manufactured by an independent supplier. They were tiny and powerful – they had to be since they were expected to provide life for the pulse generators for ten to twelve years. His plan was to duplicate the stainless-steel casing of these batteries and to insert four components into each of these hollow cases. A smaller battery, identical in chemistry to the original. A piece of micro-circuitry. Half an ounce of plastique explosive. And a detonator.

Being smaller, his active battery would not operate the pacemaker for anywhere near as long as the larger battery would, but under the circumstances that hardly mattered. A major consideration during planning had been that though under normal circumstances most pacemakers would be implanted well within one year of production, all Hagen devices were released from the factory with a use-by date of two years from their date of manufacture. He had elected, therefore, to incorporate within his battery a timing circuit to ensure that the countdown to detonation would only begin after implantation.

82

There, he had encountered some problems. Hagen Pacing ran rigorous checking and testing procedures, including post-assembly tests designed to mimic the effects of implantation in the human body, to ensure that each pacemaker would work effectively when needed. His circuitry, therefore, would have to distinguish those tests from the real thing, and so he had incorporated a simple counter to register the current being drained from the battery at all times. While a pacemaker was in storage, the drain was tiny. Once implanted, it went up in a great leap. The change from quiescent to operational was easy enough to detect, but the same leap would, of course, occur during the checks after final welding. Those checks took fifteen minutes, and so his circuitry had not only to detect that the battery was running in its pacing mode, but also to count a given number of pulses in that working mode.

All patients receiving a pacemaker implant remained in hospital for at least twenty-four hours, and a week to ten days after the procedure they returned for a check-up and further testing of their device. It was vital, therefore, that detonation did not take place until after the final discharge of the patient. Once again, the solution had been devastatingly simple. Set to count at a rate of sixty pulses per minute, all that the circuitry within his battery needed to do was to count to one million pulses in the pacing mode, and then, automatically, to arm its own secondary timing circuit and to count down from there to the point of detonation.

Only one more problem had remained. Once it began – once people had begun to die – it was just a matter of time until they started X-raying patients to check out their pacemakers. On regular hospital X-rays, the steel-cased battery in a pacemaker showed up a small, opaque mass, but when they increased the kilo voltage for a higher penetration beam – and they would, once they knew what they were looking for – they would be able to see his added circuitry – not the plastique explosive, of course, but they would see his timing device, and that would just make it too easy for them. They could set up mass screenings and for all but the few, the very select few, the panic would be over. It wasn't that he planned to get away with it in the long-term – that wasn't the point of this at all, not for him. It was his game. It was their pain, their nightmare, their punishment. And he planned to draw it out for as long as possible. He'd waited too long for anything less.

Screwing up the X-rays for them turned out to be simple too. Easy as falling off a log. He'd make three times as many, that was all. Two-thirds with added circuitry only, one-third with circuitry and plastique. Just to throw them off, to increase the confusion, the fear, the hysteria.

From the last week of September until the penultimate week of November, he had removed six partially assembled pacemakers every Tuesday and Thursday evening, replacing them in the early hours of the next morning with his own batteries soldered to the Hagen circuitry, two of them the real thing, the other four dummies. He was perfectly confident that all his Midnight Specials, as he called them, would pass every inspection. The cases were impeccable in every way, right down to their serial numbers.

By the time his work was complete, ninety-six customized pacemakers had sat snugly in their titanium, laser-welded, hermetically sealed cases, awaiting delivery to hospitals and cardiologists' offices all over the country. Thirty-two of them were miniaturized time bombs. The man could easily have made twice or three times as many, but this was more than adequate. This would kill, this would baffle, bewilder and terrify. This would master and slay dragons.

He had dismantled his workbench and equipment, burned what he could and driven everything that could not be burned to a dump site halfway between Chicago and Gary, Indiana. He had kept precisely detailed records of what he had done, and then, for his very last trick, he had created five more sets of records, all of them equally intricate but false, so that if and when they finally tracked it down to him, he'd be able to take the torture a step further, set phoney trails, drive them crazier. Make them beg. Make them pay.

Just two weeks into the New Year, and innocent people were dying.

But then, they always did.

14

Friday, January 15th

The new case was proving the real bitch Joe had guessed it would be. Hagen's quality control man, Fred Schwartz, was as able and thorough as Hagen had claimed, but his steadily increasing dismay, frustration and weariness were obvious, his small mouth still set with determination but the hazel eyes ever more red-rimmed and darkly shadowed. Each nighttime since Monday had seen the factory taken systematically apart in an effort to find evidence, but not a shred had been found, and so Hagen Pacing remained, for the moment, in business. Meantime, in a secure area well away from the workforce, Schwartz was dismantling and checking every master copy and all the remaining suspect stock, assisted and overseen every inch of the way by the eagle-eyed Tony Valdez from Bomb and Arson, but their progress remained painfully slow. Checks on the backgrounds of every member, past and present, of the Hagen workforce and the freight company they used had, thus far, yielded not a single criminal record nor apparent motive. Commander Jackson, with the chief on his back, was gnawing at his well-kept fingernails, and Joe, guilt-ridden about his inability to take care of his pregnant and vulnerable wife, had suggested to Jess that she take Sal to her parents for the visit she'd been planning for months.

"This would be a real good time for you to go, Jess."

"Why?" Her soft brown eyes were suspicious.

"Because I'm going to be working around the clock on this new case – and I mean around the clock – and because I'm going to be

85

bringing the paperwork home with me, and because I'm not allowed to tell you anything about it, and you know me, I hate it when I can't share important stuff with you, and it's going to drive me nuts."

"So this has nothing to do with any kind of danger?"

Joe knew she was afraid. "No danger, Jess, I swear it. Just a heap of work, and I'm not going to be nice to know until it's over."

"So it's another big one."

"The biggest."

"And you're going to get crabby, and you think I need looking after because of the baby, and so if I'm around, you'll just feel guilty and that'll make you even crabbier."

"You got it."

"And you swear you're not in any danger?" Jess raised her chin in a challenge, bouncing her chestnut curls a little.

"Cross my heart and hope to die," Joe said, and winced inwardly.

"I'll call Mom in the morning."

"I love you, Jess."

"I know."

Joe hated sending her away. But then he hated just about everything about this case. There was such a nasty element of remoteness about it all. Not seeing the victims, thank God. Not being privy to the immediate, overwhelming horror that normally fuelled the rage that was a part – a necessary part – of any homicide investigation. Whenever Joe saw a murder victim, saw men, women, sometimes children – most of all, the children – slashed or cut up, or shot or beaten, or burned or Christ alone knew what, he suffered the same kind of agonies that most of his colleagues did in the struggle to detach from them. And then, too, in most murder cases, there was the need to learn about the victims, to discover every last detail about them, anything that might help them get the killer. But it had quickly become plain that all of that wouldn't get them anywhere in the pacemaker case. The victims in Boston and Chicago were not connected in any way; they were random victims, their only link here, at the point of their pacemakers' origin. There was no reason for Joe to discover anything more about Jack Long or Marie Ferguson than he already knew. They were simply victims, and it all felt so *cold*, so passionless, and though Joe had learned, over the years, the importance of professional detachment, he was aware that passion, to him, was still a necessary evil in any investigation.

He had been working on the profile of the killer every night that week, seldom catching more than two hours' sleep and vainly trying to limit his caffeine intake, knowing he had to keep an even keel.

Since the birth of the National Center for the Analysis of Violent Crime in 1984, the FBI had assembled on their computers a massive data bank on violent criminals. The scientists and special agents who worked full time on criminal profiling at Quantico were not detectives but behavioural scientists, their role not to psychologically analyse the criminal mind in order to understand why they committed crimes, but to analyse the crime in such a way as to help lead them back to the perpetrator. They regarded crimes as symptoms, backtracking from the acts themselves in an attempt to try to work out the type of individual who might display such symptoms.

"In the most simplistic terms," one of Joe's tutors had told him, "it's like a pathologist being presented with a severed foot with only a big blister on its sole for ID. The kind of blister points to a particular brand of sports shoe, which points to an athlete of some kind. The fact that the blister has formed over old scar tissue indicates that the runner may be the obsessive kind, the kind who won't give it up even if it hurts, and so on. We're looking for clues – usually a lot more subtle than that blister – that may give us insight into the mind of the criminal."

Mass murderers or serial killers seldom knew their victims, frequently gloried, sometimes suffered, during the killings, but the behavioural scientists had also studied, with the help of interviews with convicted serial killers, the way they behaved after each kill. In this case, with the two deaths taking place hundreds of miles apart, and in the absence of media coverage to date, there was little or no chance that the pacemaker killer had been able to return to the scene of the death either to gloat or to observe, though there was every likelihood, of course, that he or she was returning to – or had never left – the scene of the crime itself: the place where the lifesaving devices had been transformed into death traps.

"Let's go over it one more time," Joe said to Lipman and Cohen during a snatched meeting in their office at the factory on Friday morning. They had been allocated a medium-sized, utilitarian room on Al Hagen's floor, with two desks, a computer terminal, four telephones, a fax machine and a coffee maker. "Hagen, Leary, Ashcroft and Schwartz all give the same reasons for claiming it's virtually impossible for the crime to have been committed here."

"Though since any one of them could be our bad guy," Sol Cohen said, "what they tell us may not be worth bubkes." Detective Cohen was seventeen years older than Joe, chubby and balding, and he and the lieutenant were as fond of each other as if they were uncle and nephew.

"It's gotta be one of the A Team," Lipman said. "Someone with access to the place at a time when no one else is around to watch, and according to security, no one beside the top guys ever stays late at night. And it's mostly the men," she added, "though apparently Leary hangs around less than Schwartz, or Hagen himself. Ashcroft told me she likes to get home to be with her family, and her assistant confirmed that."

"Valdez agrees with Schwartz that you can't break into a pacemaker after it's been finally sealed," Cohen said. "So there's no way it could have happened past the final checks without being noticed."

Joe nodded. "Yet Schwartz claims that none of his workers, however dextrous – and even if they had the capability, which he doubts – would have had the time to tamper on the production line without being caught."

"But Schwartz may just be covering his ass," Lipman reminded them.

Valdez came into the office in a rush, sending papers on one of the desks flying. When he was dealing with explosives, Valdez moved as sweetly and smoothly as a cat, but off the job he enjoyed moving fast, being careless, even clumsy.

"Al Hagen just went home with the flu, and he's the third this morning."

The entire Hagen Industries complex had been stricken with influenza since mid-week, men and women dropping like flies.

"Get someone on his apartment building," Joe told Cohen. "Keep it discreet."

"Sure thing." Cohen was already on the phone.

"Schwartz looks like hell too," Valdez said.

"How close are you guys to getting through the checking?" Joe asked.

"He's slowing down. He's tired and he's sick." Valdez paused. "I guess I was hoping he might incriminate himself and save everyone a pile of trouble."

"I still don't believe it's Schwartz." Lipman shook her head. "We've all watched him for hours on end. He never lets up – I've never seen anyone so focused, so dedicated, so meticulous."

"Maybe." Joe picked a sheet of paper out of his briefcase, and read. "*. . . perfectly proper, a regular man . . . no jewellery, no flashy ties or clothes . . . quiet, polite, methodical, prompt.*"

"Your profile?" Lipman asked.

Joe shook his head. "James Brussel's profile of *The Mad Bomber*."

"Frank Kulak?" Lipman wrinkled her brow.

"Another one – guy called Metesky in New York in the early fifties. Blew up Radio City Music Hall and a few other theatres."

"And a couple of train stations," Valdez added. "You used his profile in the arson case."

Joe nodded. "Like our friend here, Metesky used precise, scientific methods to target random victims and kill through preparation, not hands on."

"Leary wears a Rolex and two rings," Lipman said, thinking of the profile.

"And Hagen's too flamboyant," Cohen, off the phone, joined in.

"Schwartz is certainly as capable as Leary and Hagen of pulling it off," Lipman mused. "Though I'd rather it was Leary."

"You, too?" Joe had disliked Leary from first meeting.

"He's such a smart-ass. And he spent ten years designing weapons systems."

"I think Schwartz is okay," Cohen reconsidered.

"Me, too," Lipman agreed.

"Can't hang a guy because he doesn't wear flashy clothes," Valdez said.

"I hope it's Leary," Lipman said again.

"Can't hang a guy because we don't like him either," Valdez pointed out.

"What next?" Cohen asked.

"We stick to the A Team like glue," Joe said. "I'll take over Schwartz for a while, until he drops. Lipman, you take Leary – flirt with him if you have to."

"Thanks a bunch."

"Cohen can take Ashcroft – I don't think she's the flirtatious type – and Valdez, just go on sniffing around. All of you use your clipboards, look and listen hard, tape a zillion notes, get everyone as much on edge as you can." Joe went to the door, grabbed the handle and turned around again. "Maybe we've made them too cosy, too complacent. I want us to really breathe down their necks for a while, get under their skins a little."

"You want us to make them crazy?" Lipman asked.

"The crazier the better."

The news about the death in San Francisco came in just after five that afternoon, and the collective blood pressure of Joe's task force and the Hagen A Team shot volcanically higher as the decision was made that Hagen Pacing would be shut down by morning. Within an hour, Fred Schwartz, by now running a high fever, went home to bed, and the only members of the A Team still on the premises were Ashcroft and Leary. As the crisis had deepened, with Hagen and Schwartz becoming sicker and Ashcroft growing more worn and harassed, Howard Leary seemed, increasingly, a model of composure.

"What happens now?" Ashcroft asked Joe in Leary's tastefully decorated office a little after seven o'clock.

"We stop pretending to be statisticians and start an open investigation," Joe replied. "We'll be joined as soon as possible by two more detectives from our Violent Crime Unit, two more from Bomb and Arson and two FBI scientists – and before morning, this building will be sealed off from the rest of the complex and the only employees beside yourselves will be the key personnel you asked for."

"What's the cover going to be?" Leary looked comfortable and smooth in a flawlessly tailored dark suit, his pale grey tie knotted in a manner that Joe knew he could never achieve if he stood in front of a mirror for three hours straight.

"Building cracks," Joe replied.

"Cracks?" Leary raised an eyebrow.

"Subsidence," Joe explained. "We'll tell them it's probably a foundation problem. Discovered late today. No danger with a skeleton staff, but normal weight loads hazardous. Those locked out will be told they'll remain on full pay, and given a special number to call daily for updates, so that we can keep tabs on them if necessary."

"That poor fireman," Ashcroft said. She looked pale and tired. "I can't help wondering if he might be alive if we'd gone public."

"That's illogical, Olivia," Leary argued. "The only difference is he might have died standing in line at his doctor's office instead of in a fire, and he would have died in terror instead of at work." He paused. "How long do we think we can keep this whole mess quiet, Lieutenant?"

"Not too much longer," Joe answered. "Not without a lot of cooperation. Too many people know – family, medical examiners, physicians – one journalist that we know about."

"I still believe secrecy's vital," Leary said.

"Even though there may be men and women – perhaps even children – walking around with time bombs in their chests?" Ashcroft asked him. "I'm not so sure they shouldn't at least have the right to try to save themselves."

"As of tonight," Joe said, "the FDA still agree with Mr Leary that there's more to lose by going public. I gather there's going to be some kind of high-level meeting tomorrow morning to see how secrecy can best be maintained."

"Are you getting anywhere with the investigation, Lieutenant?" Ashcroft asked.

"We're still ruling out a lot of possibilities."

"In other words, you're getting nowhere," Leary said.

"We don't have a resolution yet."

"At least you're half honest."

"No sense not being."

"Do you still suspect me?" Leary asked.

"What makes you imagine I might?"

Leary shrugged. "I'm not a likeable man."

Olivia Ashcroft sat very still, and Joe regarded Leary's ironically raised red brows, narrow green eyes and sallow face. "That doesn't automatically make you our number one suspect."

"What about Hagen?" Leary asked.

"What about him?"

"Do you consider him a suspect?"

"Howard!"

"Don't look so shocked, Olivia," Leary said. "You know perfectly well it could be any one of us."

"It's much more likely to be some brilliant insane person masquerading as a cleaner or working in the despatch department," Ashcroft insisted.

Joe focused on Leary. "Why should we suspect Hagen?"

"Because of his mother."

"What about her."

"You don't know?" Leary was gently mocking.

"Apparently not."

"His mother died of a heart condition."

"Millions of people do," Ashcroft said.

"Not when they might have been saved by a simple intervention."

"A pacemaker." Joe's spine prickled briefly, but he kept his voice flat.

"That's right."

"When did she die?"

"In the mid-fifties. Hagen was fourteen."

"Pre-pacemakers," Joe said.

"Only just. He heard about them soon after she died."

"I didn't know," Olivia said.

"He told me years ago."

"What else did he tell you?" Joe asked.

Leary smiled. "You mean did he tell me he resented pacemakers because they came too late to save his mother?"

"Did he?"

"On the contrary," Leary said, "he told me it was a prime motivating force behind his takeover of the pacemaker company."

"Makes sense," Joe said.

"It would seem to," Leary agreed.

"Of course it does," Ashcroft said warmly.

"You have another opinion?" Joe asked.

"Not really. Just thought I'd throw it in, if your people hadn't already picked it up." Leary paused. "I imagine you feel I might have told you sooner."

"It comes to mind." Joe contained his irritation well. He, Lipman and Cohen had all interviewed Leary on several occasions, and the possibility of any known grudges had been raised each time. He flicked mentally back over the folder of information they'd accumulated on the boss of Hagen Industries. *Albrecht Hagen, born 1941, Chicago. Father, Helmut, born 1916, Cologne, W. Germany. Electrical engineer. Died 1950 (lung cancer). Mother, Annaliese, born 1921, Chicago. Housewife. Died 1955 (myocardial infarction). Marital status: single. Children: none.* So far as he remembered, sixteen other personnel files had revealed familial deaths from heart-related diseases.

"Anything else you'd care to mention?" he asked Leary.

"About Hagen?"

"Or anyone else."

"Would you like me to leave?" Ashcroft asked with a touch of acid.

"Not necessary." Leary smiled again. "Did you know Al dropped out of college?"

"Yes, I did," Ashcroft said, still coldly. "Is it relevant?"

Leary's shrug was slight. "Probably not."

"It certainly didn't hold him back," Joe commented.

"No, it didn't," Ashcroft agreed. "Al built up Hagen Industries on his own, he didn't inherit it. He's a very gifted man."

"Who pays us for our qualifications," Leary said. "We're the brains, he's the boss."

"I think that's a gross overstatement," Ashcroft said. "And Hagen Pacing's the apple of Al's eye. What you're suggesting makes no sense."

"No sense at all," Leary agreed amicably.

"Are you suggesting he may resent his lack of qualifications?" Joe persisted quietly.

Leary shrugged again. "He knows we know we're brighter than him." He glanced across at Ashcroft. "Especially Olivia – however vehemently she protests – who's the most brilliant of us all." His green eyes were amused. "You could certainly have done it, though I don't know of anything in your background or past to motivate you to do such a thing."

"Thank you, Howard," Ashcroft said scathingly.

"You're welcome."

"What about Schwartz?" Joe asked. His inner eye reviewed the start of that personnel file. *Frederick Schwartz, born 1951, Chicago. Father, Siegmund, born 1920, Düsseldorf, W. Germany. Artist. Died Chicago 1950 (road accident). Mother, Eva, born 1924, Chicago. Housewife. Died 1962 (cerebral thrombosis). Marital status: single. Children: none.* Schwartz had not known his father and had lost his mother young, as Hagen had lost both parents, but Joe recalled nothing else of special significance.

"A lesser man," Leary said. "Al doesn't agree with me, though I think you do, don't you, Olivia?" She made no comment. "Schwartz's dedication has always seemed genuine enough to me. He's of German descent, same as the boss, big on the work ethic – lives alone, too, so far as I know, but other than that I know very little about him." He paused. "He could have done it, too. As I said before, any one of us could have."

There was a tap on the door, and Lipman came in.

"The guys from Bomb and Arson are here, Lieutenant."

Joe checked his watch. Almost eight o'clock. Before too much longer the newly magnified task force would be starting to take the Hagen Pacing building apart in earnest, section by section, rooting through every file, every stockroom, every sheet of paper, every air-conditioning duct, every foot of pipework, if necessary, for the evidence that might help them move on to a conclusion. Not a moment too soon, so far as he was concerned.

"You'll excuse me?" He stood up.

"Of course," Ashcroft said.

"Good luck." Leary paused. "You probably know this already, but both my parents are still alive. So are my wife and three children. There's no history of heart disease in my family, and I have no grudge against the company, other than the fact that it's probably about to go down the tube."

"Putting you out of work," Ashcroft said, mildly.

"And every other member of the workforce," Leary said.

"Obviously." Joe went to the door, where Lipman waited.
Leary smiled one more time.
"Except Al Hagen," he said.

15

Saturday, January 16th

At half past eleven on Saturday morning, while Hugo was at the café and just as Toni Petrillo was leaving the house after a visit, Chris and Katy Webber arrived to see Lally. The hour that they stayed was, at least for Lally, one of the most miserable and frustrating she could remember.

She had realized, ever since seeing the painting, that her attraction to Chris was almost certainly mutual, that he, too, had perhaps been guiltily counting the moments till they might meet again, and this morning, when he'd walked through her front door, she had looked up into his face and had seen her own emotions, raw and confused, mirrored in his eyes.

But the child was there between them, preventing them from speaking their minds, from reaching out and touching even so much as a hand or a cheek. And Andrea Webber – for all that she was shut up miles away in a clinic, or perhaps all the more because of it – stood between them too. Or perhaps, Lally thought, it was simply their twin consciences, silencing their voices, stamping on their feelings, on their right even to *consider* their own feelings.

"When are you going to start classes again?" Katy wanted to know.

"Not for a little while yet," Lally told her.

"But you are going to be okay?"

The girl's anxious dark blue eyes were so like her father's. Lally knew she would never be able to look at her again without thinking of him.

"Lally's going to be perfect, Katy," Chris said.

"Yes." Lally smiled at him. "Of course I am."

They talked about ballet, about the conditions on the ski slopes at Bousquet, about an icicle that had dropped like a spear from the lintel over a grocery store on Elm Street two days earlier, narrowly missing Katy's head. They talked about Jade and the other dogs at the big house down the road, and how Katy had promised her Mommy that she would help look after them while she was away. They talked about the imminent publication of Chris's new teach-yourself painting guide. They talked about everything they could think of, except Andrea Webber's alcoholism, or Katy's bruises, or the fact that Chris and Lally were guilty of having fallen in love with each other, and that they both knew there was no future in it, no hope.

When they had gone, Lally went into the kitchen and tried to make a soufflé, but it sank like a stone in the oven and then she put on a tape of *Swan Lake*, but she felt afraid to dance even a few steps. And it was snowing again, and suddenly she hated all the whiteness and the muffled sounds and the grey skies, and she felt trapped and claustrophobic and more depressed and alone than she could remember feeling in years.

Hugo came home a little after four that afternoon, and found Lally curled up on her bed under a patchwork quilt, Nijinsky asleep beside her. Lally's eyes were closed, and Hugo wasn't quite certain if she was really sleeping, but there were tear stains on her cheeks, and a fresh bunch of sweet peas in a little vase beside Webber's portrait on her dresser, and he knew who had been in the house and who had caused those tears.

And Hugo, who seldom drank spirits – never drank any liquor that early in the day – went quietly downstairs and poured himself a glass of whisky, and stood at the sitting room window sipping and staring out through the veil of white steadily blanketing Lenox Road and West Stockbridge and most of the Berkshires. The whisky tasted sour, but little more so than his own jealousy.

Chris Webber had made Lally cry, and Hugo hated him for that, but at the same time he despised his own hypocrisy, for the hatred implied that if Webber were able to make Lally happy, Hugo might like him better.

Nothing, of course, could be further from the truth.

16

Sunday, January 17th

On Sunday morning, the sun shone on Chicago for the first time in almost a week. It was bitterly cold, the wind blew off the lake and the snow lay, caked to lethal icing, on the sidewalks and piled up on the kerbs, but the sky was pure azure and the sunlight bestowed such a brilliance on the city that Joe felt better than he had in a while. His moods had always been influenced, if not controlled, by weather changes; he functioned better on days such as this, which was just as well today, considering the two appointments that lay ahead of him.

Heading south on Lakeshore Drive, Joe found himself thinking about Lally. His sister flitted into his thoughts most days – brief feelings of fondness, mostly, when he drank his first cup of coffee each morning facing two of his favourite photographs of her on the opposite wall – but during the course of the last few days, in spite of the craziness of the pacemaker case, he'd found his thoughts switching to her at less likely moments. If Jess had known that his sixth sense, as she called it, was tweaking him, if she hadn't gone to her parents with Sal, she would have made sure he made time to call his sister, but Jess wasn't there, and it was less than two weeks since he and Lally had last talked, and Joe hadn't felt exactly troubled about her, but all the same, as he parked the car and turned off the ignition, he made up his mind to call her again real soon.

With Hagen Pacing still being turned inside out – still fruitlessly – and with the FBI's computers linking with Hagen Industries' to prepare as complete a list as possible of pacemaker recipients at potential risk, in case a decision had to be made to try to organize mass explantation, Joe was concentrating on going after two of the three men who still remained his chief suspects and whose illness now gave him an excuse to enter their homes. The plan this morning had been for Lipman to accompany Joe when he visited Hagen and Schwartz, but she, too, had gone down with the flu last night, and Joe wanted Valdez and Cohen to stay at the factory in case some scrap of evidence – hell, he was ready to settle for crumbs, they all were – finally showed itself. So he was on his own, getting out of the car opposite Lake Michigan, sparkling today like a great frosted ocean, and climbing the curved reddish stone steps up to the entrance of The Carlyle.

It was one of the most expensive looking buildings in perhaps the choicest residential street in Chicago; a handsomely designed sandy-coloured stone building of around forty storeys, erected in the mid-sixties, identified only by a discreet sign, too small to be seen from the street. The entrance was locked. Joe waited a moment before ringing the bell, turning around to look back at the lake. It was part frozen, though not thickly enough for ice fishing. Some years, if it froze hard enough, the fishermen took chairs out onto the ice, made holes, sat down and fished through. Joe saw no chairs this morning.

Upstairs, on the thirty-third floor, Hagen opened his own front door. From within, Joe heard music, opera, probably Wagner again, remembering what Cynthia Alesso had told them.

"Good morning, Lieutenant." He wore a black silk dressing gown with matching pyjamas and wine-red slippers, and a white silk scarf was wrapped around his throat. His voice sounded hoarse and though he'd taken the trouble to shave, Joe thought he looked like hell, and there was certainly no question that he had gone down with the same flu bug that had now felled Linda Lipman.

"How are you, sir?"

"Pretty lousy. Come in, if you dare."

Hagen closed the door, and an aura of wealth enfolded Joe. He noted bronze sculptures and paintings, recognized a Dali and guessed it was an original. Not that they hadn't known it anyway, but Leary had been right in one respect. If Hagen Pacing went down the tubes, this man would not, at least financially, suffer unduly.

"It was kind of you to agree to see me here," Joe said. "I hope you're up to it."

"No problem. In fact, it's something of a relief." Hagen led the

98

way through the magnificent marble entrance hall into a huge, bright sitting room, all ice blue furnishings and creamy rugs and crystal chandeliers, a world away from his black and white office. "I can't begin to tell you how guilty I've felt walking out on you the way I did, Lieutenant, but I spent most of yesterday barely able to get out of bed."

"Perhaps you should sit down, sir."

Hagen nodded weakly, and settled himself on a high-backed settee, indicating to Joe that he should sit wherever he wished. A silver tray with matching coffee service stood waiting on a table beside the settee, and Hagen poured for them with hands that trembled a little.

"So," Hagen said, "how can I help you, Lieutenant? Or has there been some progress you want to tell me about? I've spoken to Chief Hankin several times, of course, and Howard and Olivia have been keeping me informed."

"I wish I could say there's been a breakthrough."

"But still nothing." Hagen looked wretched. In spite of the incongruously boyish scarf around his neck, the youthful quality that had been apparent on the previous occasions he and Joe had met was not in evidence this morning. Today, the close-cropped fuzzy grey hair was not so much a style decision, just grey, the skin on his throat showed every one of its fifty-one years, and the eyes behind the round wire glasses were dismayed.

"Tell me about Mr Leary," Joe said, suddenly.

"What would you like to know?" Hagen paused. "I'd have thought, by now, that you'd know most things about us all."

"I thought that, too."

"But something changed your mind?"

"Just reminded me how fallible our checking systems can be." Joe smiled. "Most citizens still have surprisingly few details on file, in spite of our national paranoia about lack of privacy."

"I'd have thought the FBI would have a reasonably detailed file on Howard," Hagen said, "in view of his years of work on military projects."

The music, well-modulated, crescendoed softly and ended.

"May I speak frankly, sir?"

"Of course."

"Has Mr Leary any particular reason to dislike you?"

Hagen's eyes flickered only a little. "This isn't actually about Leary, is it, Lieutenant?" he asked shrewdly. "It's about me."

"It's about both of you," Joe said, carefully. "About everyone in the company."

"But Leary's told you something about me."

"He's talked about you."

"Something that's made you suspicious of me?" Hagen's voice was very calm. "Or perhaps I should say, more suspicious, since we must all be prime suspects."

"He told me about your mother."

"My mother?" Hagen looked puzzled. "What about her?"

"He referred to her death."

"My mother died many years ago."

"Yes, sir."

Joe saw the anger move across Hagen's face. It was no flash of heat, merely a change of mood, though a little more than irritation.

"Mr Leary mentioned the fact that your mother's life might have been saved by a pacemaker."

"That's true, had they been available," Hagen agreed. "They had, of course, been invented, but no living human patient had yet received one."

"You were very young when she died."

"Fourteen years old. I was younger when my father died."

"But it influenced you enough to start manufacturing pacemakers more than fifteen years later."

Hagen nodded. "I'm sure it was a motivating force."

Joe picked up his coffee cup. It was fine porcelain, and he was glad he'd never been a clumsy man. He felt, for the thousandth time that week, that he was getting nowhere. Hagen undoubtedly resented this new line of questioning, but he still remained scrupulously courteous, the picture of a man who understood that since he must be a suspect, he must, therefore, tolerate some invasion of privacy. Joe wanted, more than anything, to look around, to see the rest of the apartment, but he knew there would be no opportunity, at least not on this occasion.

"I have no deep-seated hatred of pacemakers, Lieutenant, if that's what you, or perhaps Leary, were thinking," Hagen said. "If I stop to think about it, I do still feel a certain sadness at knowing that my mother might have lived many years longer than she did – but I might just as well loathe all the surgeon generals who didn't ban cigarettes, because my father died of lung cancer."

Hagen picked up a cup and saucer, his hands still trembling – though almost certainly more from the effects of the flu, Joe thought, than from emotion or guilt – and then he set them down again on the table before him.

"I've been prouder, Lieutenant Duval, of my role in producing

100

pacemakers than of anything else I've ever done in my life."

Joe nodded. "I can imagine that, sir."

"As to Howard Leary, did he say anything else of consequence?"

Hagen gave a wan smile. "This is a rare opportunity to learn a little more of what my colleagues think of me."

Joe noted the use of the word colleagues instead of employees. He had no sense that it had been used for effect.

"He referred to your college career."

"To my lack of qualifications."

"To your dropping out."

Hagen smiled again, less bleakly this time. "Howard's never dared say it to my face, but he's always enjoyed feeling superior. Olivia's the only one of us he respects, because he has no choice – she's easily our best brain."

"How does he feel about Fred Schwartz?" Joe asked.

"He trusted him well enough, until this happened, but even then, I felt it was his effectiveness he mistrusted, not his innocence."

"Mr Schwartz has been the most obviously distraught since this began," Joe said.

"I've always been fond of Fred." Hagen shrugged. "That doesn't mean I haven't thought of him as a potential suspect too."

"But you've rejected the idea?"

"I think so." Hagen leaned back heavily. "I'd much rather think we've had an enemy working for us somewhere on the line, someone from a rival firm, perhaps."

"That's still a possibility, of course, sir, though it seems increasingly unlikely," Joe told him.

Hagen looked very tired. "We really are getting nowhere, Lieutenant, aren't we? Hagen Pacing has been shut down, and you've found neither the perpetrator nor the method – we still don't even know how many devices have been tampered with."

"We may not know that until we find the person, or people, responsible."

"And in the meantime, they're presumably laughing at us."

"Presumably."

"I'm not laughing," Hagen said darkly.

"No, sir. I know you're not."

"Do you?" Hagen shook his head. "I don't think you know much more than you did when you came in here, Lieutenant."

Joe didn't answer.

"How much longer," Hagen asked, "before we're forced to go public?"

"I don't know, sir."

"Leary's right about that much, you know. It would be a nightmare."

"There may be no alternative."

Hagen made an effort, and stood up. "Do something for me, Lieutenant."

"If I can."

"Put an end to it." Behind the glasses, Hagen's eyes glinted with what Joe thought might almost be tears. "Stop pussyfooting around us all, stop being so damnably *polite*, and get a result."

Fred Schwartz's apartment building was not too much further north on Lakeshore Drive than Al Hagen's, yet in social and economic terms Joe knew it might as well have been a continent away. It looked okay, brownstone and solid enough, but Joe guessed that the residents probably fought a running battle against the things most ordinary solid citizens had to. In a place like The Carlyle, if something went wrong with the electricity or air-cooling system or elevators, or if someone found a nest of bugs in a supply room, Al Hagen would doubtless never have to know about it. Schwartz's building would probably have had a string of residents' action committees, aborted one at a time through a mixture of apathy and a case of too many chiefs. Hagen lived on the thirty-third floor of The Carlyle. Schwartz lived on the twenty-second of his building. Hagen's terrace overlooked Lake Michigan, with the Magnificent Mile a few hundred yards over to the right. Schwartz's side-facing apartment had no balcony, but if he leaned right out of his sitting room window, he could probably see the lake, too. The interiors might be vastly different, Joe mused later on, and he didn't know if Schwartz had ever been inside his boss's home, yet there was no question in his mind that Schwartz had gotten as close to Hagen's lifestyle as possible, though whether it was a case of flattery or of envy, he could not tell. It was, at least, interesting. It was, at least, *something*.

"It's kind of you to have agreed to see me, sir," Joe said at the front door.

"I'm happy to see you, Lieutenant. I've seen no one except my doctor since I left the factory on Friday."

If Hagen had looked like hell, Schwartz looked worse. He, too, wore a silk dressing gown, though his had a paisley pattern and looked old, if scrupulously clean and pressed. His wispy, mousy hair was carefully combed, the unremarkable, small-featured face looked pasty, the whites of his bleary hazel eyes were pink, and his forehead and upper lip were beaded with perspiration. He wore burgundy pyjamas beneath the robe, and he smelled of menthol, as if he'd been rubbing his chest.

"Shouldn't you be in bed?" Joe asked, genuinely concerned.

"I felt worse in bed," Schwartz said, and stepped back. "You should keep your distance, Lieutenant. You don't want to catch it."

"If I haven't caught it yet, I'm hoping I may be immune."

For such a quiet, modest man, Schwartz had a startlingly opulent apartment. Joe stepped over Persian rugs as the other man led the way into his sitting room. There were bookshelves – books had been surprisingly absent at Hagen's, but maybe Carlyle apartments had their own libraries – and heavy drapes, and a central, glittering chandelier. Music played softly from two speakers in a thirties-style mahogany wall unit. Opera. Joe smiled inwardly. Another shared love. Or another imitation.

"You have quite a place, Mr Schwartz."

"Thank you, Lieutenant. Won't you sit down?" Schwartz gestured to a brocade-covered armchair. "Can I get you something to drink?"

"No thank you, sir." Joe, sat and looked up at an ornately framed portrait hanging above the sofa. "That's a beautiful woman."

"My mother. Painted by my father."

"It's lovely."

"Thank you." Schwartz, too, sat down, grimacing a little, as if his joints pained him. He took a white linen handkerchief from his dressing gown pocket and mopped his forehead. "This is damnable," he said. "I haven't been sick in years."

"Detective Lipman went down with it last night."

"Poor lady, I'm sorry," Schwartz said.

Joe hesitated. "Shall I come straight to the point, sir?"

"I'd be grateful."

"I've come to the conclusion that you really do know more about the current range of Hagen pacemakers than anyone else, including Mr Hagen."

"That's probably true." Schwartz was matter-of-fact.

"I know you still believe that this can't have happened in your factory."

"You mean I don't want to believe it," Schwartz said.

"Perhaps. Though I want you to know we're looking elsewhere, too."

"I've never doubted that you'd have to." Schwartz wiped his face again, then coughed and cleared his throat before continuing. "I know the factory as well as I know this apartment, Lieutenant, and I've found not a shred of evidence of anything untoward – and your Detective Valdez is a very thorough man, too."

"And you all – including Valdez – insist that the devices are impregnable, once sealed."

"That's correct."

"Yet the cardiologists and thoracic surgeons involved in the three cases so far," Joe went on, "all maintain that they would have known if the pacemakers had been tampered with."

"I'm afraid I don't believe that," Schwartz said.

"They say that pacemakers are always visually examined and handled prior to every implantation."

Schwartz shrugged. "What else would you expect them to say?"

Joe smiled. "Maybe you're right." He paused. "I'd like to ask you a favour, sir, if you're up to it."

"Anything that will help, Lieutenant."

"If you're too sick, or too exhausted, just tell me."

"Of course."

Joe sat forward. "If it were you, Mr Schwartz – if you had done this thing – how would you have done it? If you wanted to turn one of your pacemakers into a bomb, knowing all that you do, how would you go about it?"

Schwartz showed no sign of being offended. "I take it this is on the assumption that I would do it before the devices were sealed?" He watched Joe nod. "And also assuming I had full access to the production area." He paused only briefly. "I'd use the battery. It's the most combustible component in the generator box – the part of the pacemaker implanted in the chest wall."

"Go on."

"It was the first thing Leary and I talked about at the beginning, since lithium batteries are potentially explosive under certain circumstances. I shared the knowledge with Detective Valdez, of course."

"Certain circumstances being extreme heat or flames, for example."

Schwartz nodded. "Which might feasibly have caused the fireman's death, but which does not, of course, explain the other fatalities."

"Could enough explosive be inserted into the batteries to cause the deaths?" Joe asked.

"In theory, I imagine so. I'm not an explosives expert." Schwartz began to cough again, a longer attack than before. His face reddened, the veins on his neck and temples stood out.

"Can I get you some water?" Joe stood up.

"Please." Schwartz pointed to the door, trying but failing to control the coughing. "Kitchen's to the right."

Joe went back out over the Persian rugs. There were two closed doors. He opened one, hoping not to get the kitchen first time. Schwartz's bedroom was warm and stuffy, the bed tidied but uncovered. A large box of Kleenex, a bottle of red capsules and a tumbler of water stood on the bedside table, and that same menthol smell filled the air. He heard Schwartz coughing, closed the door and found the kitchen, fastidiously clean and neat. The cupboards were glass-fronted, everything clearly visible and in its place. Joe opened the big old refrigerator. There was nothing of interest, no sealed containers that might have held sinister substances, a few cans of sardines, two cartons of skimmed milk, a bottle of German beer, half a Saran-wrapped roast chicken, a supermarket pack of ham, some Diet Fleischmans margarine and three eggs. Not exactly the dream refrigerator of a master bomber.

Joe ran the cold water faucet, filled a glass and took it back into the sitting room. Schwartz was mopping his face again with his handkerchief, and his breathing seemed more laboured than before. Joe gave him the glass.

"I couldn't find any bottled water."

"I never bother with it." Schwartz sipped a little. His hands trembled. "Thank you, Lieutenant. I'm sorry to be so much trouble."

"I'm the one who should be apologizing. You're sick, and I should be letting you rest, not picking your brains."

"I'm not unflattered. Or should I be wary?"

Joe sat down again and smiled. "Not unless you did it." He paused. "You were about to try to tell me how the plastique explosive could be inserted into the pacemaker batteries."

"In itself, in theory again, I guess that would present no great problem." Schwartz paused. "Aside from the obvious hazard of being seen to do it. But it would mean opening the sealed outer case and welding it closed again afterward, which would be noticeable on checking." He shrugged, weakly. "If it was the batteries, it's more likely that they would have been tampered with during their production."

Joe nodded. "We've been checking that out. To date, it doesn't look likely."

"Okay. But even that would only give us a part of the picture – I'm sure our bomber would have found many more complex problems than inserting the explosives."

"Such as?"

Schwartz shrugged again. "The possibilities are endless." He shook his head. "I'm sorry, Lieutenant. You're asking more of my brain than it's fit to give you today. Surely your explosives

105

technicians must have come up with something by now?"

"Not much more than you and Valdez. Traces of plastique, the possibility that the batteries were tampered with, and minute traces of electronic circuitry that mean timers were probably used."

Schwartz nodded. "Time bombs," he said, softly, dully.

"None of them went off before they were in the patients."

"And I suppose no one's been able to make a connection between the three victims."

"Nothing except for their Hagen pacemakers."

Schwartz shook his head again, slowly and painfully, and the dampness of his pasty cheeks glistened. "It goes from bad to worse, doesn't it, Lieutenant?"

"We'll get there," Joe said.

"But how many more people may die before you do?"

"Let's pray none."

"How much longer will the factory be shut?"

"I can't answer that, Mr Schwartz."

"It's dreadful for Al Hagen."

"And for many others," Joe said.

"But Al's always cared so deeply about Hagen Pacing. More than any of his other companies."

"You care, too, Mr Schwartz."

Schwartz nodded. "It's been my life for the past ten years."

Joe rose from his chair again.

"You and Mr Hagen have a lot in common."

Schwartz's smile was wan.

"I guess we do."

17

Monday, January 18th

O n Monday morning Hugo drove Lally to the hospital in
Holyoke for her eight-day check-up. Persuaded that there
would be no invasive procedure on this occasion, he came into the
laboratory with her and held her hand while Lucas Ash, Joanna
King and Bobby Goldstein checked her over, ran a final X-ray and
used their magical electronic gadgetry while Lally alternately sat,
jogged on a treadmill, lay down and walked, to ascertain that her
pacemaker was properly programmed for the individual needs of
her heart.

"One hundred per cent," Dr Ash pronounced when it was over.

"Really?" Lally, nerve-racked, icy limbed yet clammy, looked
suspicious.

"I've told you before, Lally, I don't lie to my patients."

"I'm sorry." She flushed.

"No need to be sorry, so long as you believe me."

"I'm trying to."

Hugo, his own palm damp, gave her hand one last squeeze and
let go.

"Well, I feel better," he said.

"I'm sure that's a relief to us all," Joanna King said, drily but not
unkindly.

Hugo took no notice. "This means Lally's really going to be
okay?"

Lucas Ash shook his head. "Okay implies survival, or something
merely adequate. Lally's going to be better than okay – she's going

to go on being Lally, leading the lifestyle she chooses – dancing, baking, whatever."

"It's so hard to believe," Lally said, though a fresh and wonderful feeling of warmth and relief was stealing through her entire body and mind. "I mean, I am starting to believe it, truly, but it was all so sudden, so *serious*, and now – " She shook her head, impatient with herself. "I'm sorry, I'm being a real pain."

"No, you're not," Bobby Goldstein said.

"No more than anyone is at this stage," Joanna King added. "I know I'd be no different if it happened to me."

"But you can go home now," Dr Ash said, with finality.

"And then what?" Lally asked.

"Forget it."

"Honestly?" This time it was Hugo who sounded disbelieving.

"I'd like you to start slowly, dance-wise," the doctor addressed Lally, "but you can, and you should, make a start. Gentle warm-up exercises, barre work, nothing too exerting for a week or two – not because it's going to kill you," he added swiftly, "or even harm you. But I don't want you overdoing things and scaring yourself. I want you to take it easily, and come to terms with the fact that the thing in your chest is your friend, a part of you now."

"Think of it as a new lover," Joanna King suggested, "who's going to turn into the perfect husband. At first you don't quite believe how good things are, you can't quite trust him, but gradually you settle down and realize that things are better than they've ever been."

"And then you take him for granted." Bobby Goldstein grinned.

"In this case, a good thing," Lucas Ash said.

"What about check-ups?" Hugo asked.

"One month from today," Dr Ash replied. "Then six months, and after that, it'll be annual."

"And the batteries?" Lally asked.

"Should last ten to twelve years."

Lally sat back in her chair and relaxed. No more questions came into her mind. She looked around the laboratory and then at the people surrounding her. The sun had poked through the grey outside, and its sudden yellowish winter glow illuminated the doctor's golden head, giving him a cartoon aura that made her smile.

"How about a vacation?" Hugo asked.

"Good idea," Dr Ash said.

"A vacation?" The word sounded good. Lally hadn't been anywhere – other than to Chicago to visit Joe – in a long time. "What kind of vacation?"

"Any kind you like." Ash paused. "I'd prefer you didn't actually climb a mountain just yet, but walking or riding or swimming – like most things in life, everything within reason."

"Skiing?" Lally asked.

"Sure, why not?"

"I don't really feel like skiing," she said. "I think I'd like to get away from all this snow."

"You love snow," Hugo said.

"Not the last few days. I've hated it."

"We could go to Florida," Hugo suggested, then looked awkward. "Unless you want to be by yourself."

"I don't."

"Or with someone else."

Lally looked at him steadily. She knew he was thinking of Chris Webber. "There's no one else I'd rather go with, Hugo."

"That seems to be settled then," Joanna King said.

"Florida?" Bobby Goldstein queried. "You don't look like Miami Beach people to me, if you don't mind my saying."

"I don't think we are," Lally smiled at him.

"I might be," Hugo said. "I've never been."

"Me neither," Lally said. "But I've always wanted to see the Everglades."

"Go to the Keys," Goldstein told her. "Great for creative types – get the best of all worlds. Swamps – if you like alligators – "

"And deer," Lally said. "And otters and thousands of birds."

"Do you know that at least six Pulitzer prizewinners live on Key West alone?" Goldstein had a misty look in his eyes. "It's where I'll be heading when I write my bestseller."

"Don't anyone hold their breath," Joanna King said.

"So that's settled." Lucas Ash's brisk voice broke the spell. "Lally and Mr Barzinsky are going to Florida."

"When?" Lally asked him.

"Whenever you like."

"You mean I could go now – right away?"

Dr Ash shrugged. "Maybe go home and pack a few things first."

The sunlight had already vanished, but the warmth continued to fill Lally. She felt good.

"I hate alligators." Suddenly, Hugo looked apprehensive.

Lally smiled at him.

"I'll protect you," she said.

That evening Lally decided it was time to call Joe. She listened for a few minutes, then put down the receiver.

"What's up?" Hugo asked.

"No one home."

"What about the answering machine?"

"I didn't know what to say."

"Tell them what's happened, but that you're okay."

Lally shook her head. "I don't want to do that. Joe'll worry unless he speaks to me direct."

"Tell him you're so okay that we're taking a vacation."

"He might not believe me."

"Lally, you have to tell him." Hugo sounded severe.

"No, I don't." Her face was stubborn. "I know my brother a lot better than you do." She dialled again, listened to the machine picking up and raised a finger to her lips to hush Hugo before leaving her message. "Hi, everyone, it's Lally, just calling to say hello. I'm fine – Hugo's fine – Nijinsky's fine – we're all fine, and everything's good, and Hugo and I are going on vacation for a few days, so don't worry if you can't reach us. Love you."

"Lally – " Hugo said.

She put down the phone.

"Hugo."

"What?" He glared at her.

"Stop being such a bully."

18

Tuesday, January 19th

H e was dozing on the couch in the room when the gecko woke him. He felt it on his chest, hardly any weight at all, just enough to bring him out of sleep, raise every hair on his body, and open his eyes.

Fear swamped him, sickened him, but the man controlled it, remained very still, watching it. It was so small, so deceptively attractive, with its leopard spotted skin and clever golden eyes. He remembered he'd held one of these little creatures one morning soon after he'd brought them home; he had held it up in his thickly gloved hand against the sunshine from the window, and the light had seemed to shine right through its head, and he had quivered with excitement and fear at the gleaming display of its powers.

He had never felt it on his naked flesh before, till now. It must have climbed out of the vivarium while he had changed its water. Slowly, it began to move down towards his belly. He felt a wave of nausea as the terror increased, and then, as he watched the spotted, pointed tail, he felt his own excitement begin to rise, saw his penis grow engorged and powerful and swordlike and, as if in a dream – for he could not have done it otherwise – he reached down and plucked it off his belly with his bare hand. It wriggled against his palm, panicking, writhing, particles of freshly shed skin flying into the air, and the creature's fear strengthened the man and, carefully holding its tiny jaws closed, he sat up a little and began to rub it over his own body, over his nipples, back down over his belly and against his testicles and penis. He felt the fire in him, felt the surging and the agony and the heat and then the shuddering, groaning release, felt the milkiness of his semen against his skin. And the movement in his hand had ceased, and when he looked down, he saw that he had squeezed the life out of the little creature, and it was the first time he had killed a dragon in physical combat, and the release and relief and vindication were overwhelming, and the man knew that it was a sign.

A little later, having disposed of it, he lay down again and closed his eyes and allowed himself to drift back. Past his mother's death, past the anguish and humiliation, back to the days and nights of pleasure and sweet pain, at her hands and in her arms, in her big bed at home, and in her own special place.

Waiting for the deaths to begin had been hard, but oh, it had been so thrilling. Like all the childhood treats Mother had made him wait for. Like the times when she'd baked his favourite spiced cookies into letter shapes, but her rule had been that he had to spell out two names from *The Ring of the Nibelung* with the cookies before he was allowed to put the first one in his mouth, and it had always been worthwhile for the deliciousness, but oh, the waiting had been so tantalizing.

Mother had made him wait for other delights, too. Like letting him stay up late at night till she got home from her special place, or allowing him to brush her hair – so soft and silky and golden – or sharing her bed with him. And once she had allowed him in, then she had made him wait an eternity before she had begun to caress his back and rub his shoulders, and stroke his chest and stomach, and then – the thing he loved most of all – to tell him stories about Father, his favourite heroic stories about the old days.

She hadn't always been gentle with him. Her work had wearied her, and often, when she'd come home bone-tired, her temper had flared, and she'd had to punish him with her cigarettes or with her hands, but that harshness had only made the tender moments more precious to him. He had never been able to resist asking her about her work, and often his questions had elicited a slapping or worse, but sometimes, lying in bed with him, she'd given in and told him about it, and shown him, too, and then the room in which they'd lain had seemed almost to disappear as brand new, fascinating mysteries unfolded and became exquisitely clear to him.

Mother had taken him, once, to her special place, and he'd been awed by its magnificence. By the crystal chandeliers and red velvet drapes, tied in flounces with thick, braided ropes, by the bedrooms with their canopies and ceiling mirrors, and by the strange, haunting paintings and tapestries that had depicted the ancient German myths and legends that Mother had made so much a part of their lives. One painting in particular, called *Siegfried, the Dragon Slayer,* had been his favourite, and after his mother had died and her special place had closed its doors for ever, he had gone there before the auction and had arranged for one of the chandeliers and that painting to be set aside for him.

Now that he had time on his hands, the man permitted himself to dwell in the past for more hours each day than he had allowed himself in years. There was too much time, in a way. It made the waiting harder, made the need for self-control even greater. He found that he had revelled in his acting ability, in the factory and at the apartment. The lieutenant had left on Sunday morning without a shred of doubt that he was a sick man. It hadn't been too hard feigning the flu, not nearly so taxing as the role he'd been playing for so many years, and if he was honest with himself, this past two weeks had been the most fun he'd ever had. Watching them all squirm and thrash around, the way the little gecko had before it had died. It was almost a pity to be out of the centre of things, away from the focus of the investigation. Safer of course, but less absorbing.

He came to the room twice daily now and stayed for longer than he had in the past, sometimes watching his little captive dragons, sometimes reading his logs, the records of his work, other times just resting or thinking or remembering. The cops weren't likely to return too quickly, not without calling first, and he kept his answering machine switched on most of the time, the way a sick man might, and even if the good lieutenant did grow suspicious, as he surely must, given enough time, he was ready for him.

This was a new phase of waiting, perhaps the hardest and the most tantalizing yet. Waiting to be caught. To play a different kind of game with them. Face to face.

19

Wednesday, January 20th

L ally and Hugo had spent Tuesday night on Key Largo, the first and largest of the islands strung together by Route 1, the great Overseas Highway. Any ideas that Lally might have had about camping, canoeing or hiking in any of the Everglades wilderness areas, had been firmly stamped on by Hugo before and during their flight to Miami.

"We'll go camping, we'll hire a boat, we can swim or snorkel or walk or fish, or do whatever you damn well please," he'd told her on the plane, "but wading around in a swamp with a bunch of mosquitoes and alligators is just plain unhealthy."

"It's winter," Lally said. "You don't get many mosquitoes."

"You always get mosquitoes in that kind of climate."

"You get jelly fish in the ocean too," she taunted him.

"Then you'll swim and snorkel alone."

"You'd leave a sick woman to snorkel alone?"

"You're healthy as a horse, you told me so."

"I'm still a little fragile."

"Then you can lie under a parasol and sip exotic drinks."

"For one day," Lally consented.

"How about five?" Hugo had never been an outdoorsman.

"One. Then we go snorkelling."

"Anything to please a sick woman."

"And camping?"

"Whatever." Hugo settled back in his seat and shut his eyes.

"Hugo?"

"What?"
"How do you feel about bats?"
He didn't open his eyes. "I hear they only go for women's hair."

The Keys were a subtropical necklace of islands off the southernmost tip of Florida, marking a narrow dividing point between the Atlantic Ocean to the south and east and the Gulf of Mexico to the west. Their history was full of tales of piracy and shipwrecks, but even today, in spite of modern communication and the inevitable fast-food and motel chains along Route 1, the Keys still smacked of freedom and romance, and Key Largo was its gateway. Parking the rental car they'd picked up at Miami airport and heading for the stores in town, Lally and Hugo had found everything they'd forgotten to pack in their haste to leave the New England snow – insect repellent, sunblock, film and sandals – and then they'd checked into a modern hotel overlooking the bay, partly because Hugo wanted to be sure of at least one night with a comfortable bed and bathroom, and partly because it was the only hotel they could find with two vacant rooms.

They'd eaten well that night at a place called Sundowner's, dining on yellowtail stuffed with crabmeat and drinking Chardonnay, and then they'd wandered through town again, more leisurely now, people-watching and listening to the gaggle of the tourists' languages, before returning to their hotel and lazing about for a while on the terrace with a nightcap, enjoying the peaceful, evocative sounds and smells of the ocean.

"This is heaven," Lally said, quietly.
"I can't believe we're really here," Hugo agreed.
"It's so warm, and so – " Lally fumbled gently for the word.
"Soft," Hugo finished.
"Yeah," Lally murmured. "Soft is right."
"Lally?"
"Mm?"
"Are you sure you want to go camping?"
She smiled. "I want to do everything. I want to lie under the stars and swim with dolphins and watch otters and turtles – and I don't care if I don't get to see alligators, but I do want to see eagles, and I want to fish for those crabs you can throw back in the water – you know, the ones who grow back their claws?"
"Stone crabs," Hugo said.
"So clever of them."
It was a balmy night, with a sweetly cooling breeze coming off Florida Bay. Lally stretched out her long legs in their white cotton

jeans, and rested her drink on her lap, and closed her eyes for a few minutes and Hugo, studying her, thought, as he almost always did, how incredibly beautiful she was, and how little she realized it, and how much he loved her, and how much it still hurt to know that her love for him was such a lesser creature than his own.

They slept soundly and started out easy on Wednesday morning, with breakfast in the hotel garden and then a ride in a glass-bottomed boat over at the John Pennekamp Coral Reef State Park. A little later, Lally persuaded Hugo to try his hand at snorkelling, floating on the surface in the shallow, spectacularly brilliant areas, and after a while it was hard to persuade him out of the water, and the famous laid-back atmosphere of the Keys that they'd heard about was already having its effect, and time had begun to lose its meaning. And by three o'clock, back on the highway heading south past Tavernier towards Islamorada after their first tastes of conch chowder and Key lime pie, they were both singing old Dylan songs and gazing to left and right at the stunning greens and blues of the ocean and Gulf with wide eyes and mostly wordless pleasure.

They would camp that night near the Atlantic, shaded by tall Australian pine trees, and Lally would see gumbo-limbos, and Jamaican dogwoods, and mangrove swamps, and she would lie beneath the stars and be more grateful than she had ever been for her life. And already memories of sickness and doctors and hospitals, and thoughts about troubled families and alcoholic mothers and unhappy little girls, and men with dark blue eyes, seemed light years away in another, alien world.

20

Thursday, January 21st

J oe's day had begun badly, and grown steadily worse.

He'd been relieved to hear Lally's message in the early hours of Tuesday morning, but by the time he'd gotten around to calling her back later that day, her own machine had been switched on, and he supposed she and Hugo had left for their vacation. For a while, he'd put her firmly out of his mind, but then that odd, gnawing sense of discomfort about her had returned, and the knowledge that there was no sound reason for it and nothing he could do about it, hadn't helped at all.

Today had begun with a face-to-face confrontation with Marie Howe Ferguson's grieving husband, Sean, and Dr John Morrissey, her close friend, cardiologist and partner. Given the commander's blessing to do and say anything within reason that would hold the two men in check at least a while longer, Joe had met with them shortly after eight in the drawing room of the Fergusons' town house on North Lincoln Square. It was a room that had made even Al Hagen's apartment look almost cheap. Fine art, antiques, Georgian silver, a glistening piano topped with a mass of framed photographs, a handsome fireplace with logs blazing, every last detail exquisitely understated. It was old money, and none of it anything much to do with Sean Ferguson, who looked as if he might have been more at ease in a converted loft but who also, it was plain to see, had adored his wife passionately, and was ready to go into battle with everyone from Lieutenant Joseph Duval through the President of Hagen Industries up to the Director of the FBI, if necessary.

"My wife is still in the morgue, Lieutenant," Ferguson had told Joe, his dark wounded eyes full of fiery anguish. "I want to bury her, but they put me off and off. I know what I saw, and I know what killed her, and now I want to know how and why and *who* – "

"Mr Ferguson – "

"And we've both had a bellyful of reassuring noises, Lieutenant," Ferguson rode over Joe's words, "and the reason you're here is because we want to know everything, and we want to know it right now."

"And we'd be sitting with the Superintendent himself," John Morrissey, a distinguished, silver-haired man had said, very quietly, "if Chief Hankin hadn't sworn that you know more about the investigation than anyone else in the country."

"And if we don't get chapter and verse now, this morning," Ferguson had added, "we're going to go public, whatever the consequences."

Joe had watched them, and listened carefully, and looked at the photographs of the late Marie Ferguson, a pretty lady with honey-coloured hair and green eyes and an expression that reminded him of Jess, and he'd gone with his instincts and told them every single thing he could. And although it was a still-miserable tale of fruitless searching and sniffing around, Morrissey and Ferguson had seemed to accept his honesty and integrity, and that though things had started too damned slowly, all that could be done was now being done; and the practical physician in Morrissey couldn't help but agree with the consensus that mass explanation, without more information, was still a nightmare scenario.

At eleven o'clock, Joe had attended his second and infinitely more gruelling meeting of the day, held in the far less congenial surroundings of a conference room at City Hall. Also present had been Chief Hankin, Commander Jackson, and the Regional Director of the FBI along with two special agents, the Director of News Affairs for the Chicago Police Department, the Commissioners of Public Safety from Chicago, Boston and San Francisco, the press secretaries from the mayors' offices of each of those cities, and an emissary from the Surgeon General of the United States Government. The agenda was a pooling of information and an analysis of the current situation; the formulation of a joint decision with regard to the level of confidentiality that could reasonably be demanded from chiefs of surgery around the country once contingency plans and lists of patients at risk were shared with them; and finally, their approach to the media.

Jackson had presented his report on the investigation to date, and no criticism of Joe's heading of the pacemaker task force had been voiced during the meeting, though Joe felt that the coolness of the eyes surveying him had spoken volumes. Time, it was generally accepted, was running out. With so many people in three states in possession of a dangerously minimal amount of information – if all hell was not to break loose some time during the next few days – it was agreed that meetings would have to be held with all the news agencies and broadcasting companies without further delay to try to agree a temporary news blackout.

It was after two in the afternoon when Joe returned to Hagen Pacing and found Cohen waiting for him in the lobby, his face wrinkled with anxiety.

"It's okay," Joe reassured him. "They didn't fire me yet."

"I need a minute, Joe."

"Sure." Relief at having escaped the heavy artillery had buoyed him up a little. "What's up?"

"In private."

Joe glanced at him quizzically. "What's happened?"

"There's something you have to see."

"What is it?"

"In the office."

Since the expansion of the task force, another desk and two more filing cabinets had been squeezed into their allotted office. A heap of computer printouts lay on the desk closest to the window. No one else was in the room.

"I was looking over the patients' names," Cohen said. He sounded nervous. "Maybe it's because of my own pacemaker, but I really feel for all those people – I mean, thank God they don't know yet, but – " He stopped.

"And?" Joe was being patient. "Sol, what's wrong with you?"

"One of the names."

"Someone you know?" Concern began to rise. "Who is it?"

"I think you should take a look."

Joe picked up the concertina of computer sheets.

"And I think you should sit down."

Joe remained standing. He saw the pencil mark Cohen had made to the left of the name, and the blood drained out of his face.

Hélène Duval, Lenox Road, W. Stockbridge, Mass.

He sat down, trembling.

"It can't be. It's a mistake."

"I don't think so." Cohen's face was wreathed in sympathy. "Joe, I'm sorry. I kept looking, and I couldn't seem to take it in."

Joe still stared at the computer sheets. "I don't understand. Why didn't she tell me?"

"Didn't you even know she was sick?"

Joe shook his head, too dazed to speak.

"You told me you talked to her the other day," Cohen said, gently. "You said she was taking a vacation."

"We didn't speak. She left a message." Joe's voice was hardly more than a whisper. "I've been thinking about her so much, worrying – I didn't know why, it made no sense – but things were so crazy here, and then when I heard her voice, she sounded so normal." He shook his head again. "So *well*."

Cohen pulled up one of the other chairs, a typist's upright, on rollers. He sat astride it, facing the back. "We have to find her, Joe. Where did she go?"

"I don't know." The daze began to dissipate. Panic swelled in its place. "Sol, I don't know, she didn't tell me."

"So we'll call her friend Hugo."

"They went together."

"Who else would know?" Joe didn't answer. "Who else, Joe?"

"Toni Petrillo, her neighbour."

"Good. You have his number?"

"Her number. No, I don't."

"No problem." Cohen picked up the phone. "I'll get it."

Joe stared at the computer printout. He remembered wondering, when he'd heard Lally's voice on Tuesday, where they'd gone. Skiing, he'd guessed. An image had flashed across his mind then, of Lally the last time he'd seen her on the slopes at Bousquet, wearing a crimson one-piece suit, long dark hair flying, waving a ski pole at him and laughing. The image had made him smile. Lally almost always did.

But she couldn't have gone skiing, Joe knew that now, because she'd been sick, real sick, and the vacation must have been arranged as convalescence. Something had been wrong with Lally's heart – with his own sister's *heart* – and he hadn't even known. It was typical of her, not wanting to worry him, knowing he had Jess's pregnancy to concern him, but goddamnit, he had a right to worry about his own sister, didn't he? And now she was out there, somewhere, and she had this thing in her chest –

"Joe."

Joe blinked. Cohen had put down the phone.

"No answer from Toni Petrillo, but I just realized we're going about this the wrong way. There's no reason to assume Lally's pacemaker was even made by Hagen – this is just a list of everyone in the country who's had an implant in the last six months. We need to talk to her doctor."

"Charlie Sheldon." The first surge of panic had receded, and Joe felt numb. "He's been our doctor for ever."

"Number." Cohen nudged him gently. "Joe, give me his number."

"He's the only Dr Sheldon in Stockbridge."

Charlie Sheldon was out, too. An hour passed, and Toni Petrillo continued not to answer her phone, and the doctor's answering service thought that maybe his beeper wasn't working or was out of range, because he usually called in right away when they tried him. Joe knew they'd reach him before much longer, and failing that, he knew that the local police would go get him. And somehow, just a little later on, they'd find out where Lally and Hugo had gone, too, and by then they'd probably have learned that Lally's pacemaker wasn't a Hagen at all, and none of it would matter any more.

But in the meantime, somewhere, in the snow or in the sun, by the ocean or deep in the heart of the countryside – maybe even in a major city – maybe even thirty or forty thousand feet up in the sky – Lally was sitting, or walking, or swimming, or eating, or maybe dancing, without the slightest suspicion that the alien thing in her chest – the tiny object plugged into her heart that was meant to be keeping her alive – might instead be a killer.

21

Friday, January 22nd

The commander had been understanding. For the commander.
"Take the next few hours, Duval."
"I might need a little longer than that, sir."
"You want me to take you off the case?"
"No."
"Then take the next few hours."
Joe was almost out of his skin. The numbness had long since evaporated, and all his nerve ends seemed to be on fire. He had managed to avoid yelling at too many people in his efforts to track Lally down, aware that offended New Englanders could become frigidly uncooperative. When he'd finally gotten hold of Doc Sheldon early Thursday evening, he'd been so shocked by what Joe had told him that for a moment Joe had been afraid he might have a heart attack himself, but then the doctor had dragged himself into action, promising to get hold of Lucas Ash, the cardiologist, right away.

It had been ten o'clock before Joe had heard from him again.

"I'm sorry, Joe," Sheldon said.

Joe's stomach took a dive. "It's a Hagen."

"No, not that – I meant I'm sorry I have no news for you. Dr Ash is out of state, and can't be reached."

"Why in hell not?"

"Because he's en route between one convention in Los Angeles and another in Honolulu."

"What about his office?"

"The office closed at six today for an early weekend, and his

IF I SHOULD DIE

answering service is referring emergencies to another physician."

"He must have staff – a secretary. Someone must have access to his files so we can find out what he put in Lally. Where is Ash's office, for Christ's sake?"

"In Pittsfield, but no one's going to be there till Monday morning."

"What about the hospital where Ash did it?"

"Place called the Taylor-Dunne in Holyoke. I already tried them." Sheldon sounded exhausted. "They said Ash always uses his own stock of pacemakers. I'm sorry, Joe, but until he arrives in Honolulu and checks into his hotel, there's nothing more I can suggest."

Still failing to reach Toni Petrillo by phone, Joe made the decision to stretch the commander's few hours by taking the earliest available flight out of O'Hare on Friday morning to Albany, New York, and catching Route 90 south-east to Stockbridge. It was lunchtime when he arrived at Lally's house, letting himself in with his spare key. There, in the sitting room, watering his sister's plants without a care in the world, was Toni Petrillo.

"Where have you *been*?"

"And hello to you, too, Duval." Toni, five feet two inches tall with springy golden hair, innocent blue eyes and chubby cheeks, always took an insouciant attitude with Lally's big brother in order to hide the outsize crush she'd had on him since childhood.

"I've been calling you for almost twenty-four hours."

"Really?" Toni was surprised. "I've been home – at least when I wasn't at Hugo's or here."

"Then why didn't you answer the phone?" Joe asked belligerently, and swept right on. "Where are they?"

"I presume you mean Lally and Hugo." Toni set down the copper watering can on the sideboard, Nijinsky wound around her ankles, rubbing.

"Don't be cute, Toni. Where are they?"

"On vacation."

" I know that, but where?"

"Why? What's up?" For the first time, Toni looked concerned. "What are you doing here, Joe? Did Lally know you were coming?"

Joe took off his anorak and tossed it onto the settee. "Toni, for the last time, tell me where they are."

"They're in Florida."

"Florida?" It was one of the last places he'd thought of. He pictured matrons sunning themselves on Miami Beach and new alarm filled him. For Lally to have submitted to Miami, she must have been really sick. Not that that was nearly as important as it

123

ought to have been, given the circumstances. He refocused on Toni. "Where in Florida?"

"I don't know."

"You must know." Joe glared at her.

"I don't." Toni's mood notched up a gear from concern to anxiety. "Joe, I don't know because Lally didn't know herself. She and Hugo decided at the last minute, and all she told me was that they were flying to Miami, and that they were probably heading for the Everglades, or maybe the Keys."

"Jesus." Joe remembered reading somewhere that the Everglades National Park alone covered well over a million acres.

"Joe?" Seeing his expression, Toni's anxiety shot all the way up the scale to fear. "Tell me what's wrong."

"I need to find Lally." His voice was very strained. "And fast."

"Can't you tell me why?"

"No." He grew gentler. "Toni, think back and think hard. Did she say anything – *anything* at all that might narrow it down a little. We're talking about thousands of square miles."

Toni shook her head, then brightened a fraction. "I did hear Hugo complaining in the background – something about hating alligators. Lally laughed at him, but you know how soft she is, she'd never make him do anything he really hated." She paused. "Joe, does this have to do with her being sick? She's fine now, she's going to be okay – "

"So you think they might have gone straight to the Keys."

Toni stared at him. "I don't know."

Joe sank down in an armchair. The light flashing on Lally's answering machine caught his eye, and he stood up again. Six messages. Only one was his. He rewound the tape and listened. Two of the messages were from mothers of pupils, wanting to know when Lally would be starting classes again. Three were from a man called Chris, wanting to know where Lally was. His voice was warm, but growing increasingly urgent by the final message.

"Who's Chris?" Joe asked Toni.

"Chris Webber. His daughter's one of Lally's star pupils."

"He didn't sound like he was calling as a father."

Toni hesitated only briefly. "I think he's interested in Lally."

"Is she interested in him?"

"Yes, and no."

"What does that mean?"

"It doesn't mean anything."

Joe was in no mood for evasion. "Are they seeing each other?"

"No." Toni hated talking about Lally behind her back. "Nothing's happened between them."

"But he's married, right?" A brief flicker of anger passed through Joe, but he doused it. Concerns like that belonged to normality, to a life in which his sister wasn't walking around with a time bomb inside her.

"Is Lally in some kind of danger, Joe?" Toni was growing more afraid. "You have to tell me at least that much. I don't understand what's going on."

Joe's mind was working. "Where can I find Webber?"

"He lives just outside Stockbridge, on 102."

"Where does he work?"

"He's an artist, he works at home. Joe, it isn't like that – there's nothing to get heavy about. Chris's wife is – "

"I'm not concerned with their relationship, Toni," Joe interrupted. "Lally might have said something about the vacation to him."

"But you heard him – he doesn't even know they've gone."

"She still might have dropped something." Joe was back on his feet, picking up his anorak. "Do you have his address?"

Toni was up, too, the local directory in her hands. She tore a corner off the *Berkshire Eagle*, wrote down the address and phone number and gave it to Joe. He zipped up his jacket and walked out to the front door.

"This isn't fair." Toni was near frantic. "You can't just leave me like this. At least give me something I can do."

Joe relented a little. "Poke around, see if you can find anything to help – maps, or maybe they marked some guide books, or wrote something down, whatever. And keep thinking back – maybe she said something you didn't think was important, something you've forgotten." He stooped and planted a kiss on her head. "I'm sorry, Toni, I wish I could share this with you, but I can't." He opened the door, then turned around. "If Lally or Hugo were going to call you, they'd try you at home, wouldn't they?"

"Or at the café. But I don't expect them to call." She thought. "But what if my phone's broken? You couldn't get through."

"When you've finished looking around here, go home and have the operator test it – tell them it's an emergency – give them my name if it helps. And tell whoever's working at the café to make sure that if Lally or Hugo call, they take a contact number and tell them to stay put. Stay *put* – you got that?"

"I've got it."

Joe had expected to dislike Webber on sight, but he didn't. The man was home alone, apparently painting, judging by the smell of varnish and the fresh smears of colour on his blue fisherman's sweater. Two friendly German Shepherd dogs stood behind him, wagging their tails at the sight of a visitor. Joe watched Webber's face as he introduced himself. At the mention of Lally's name, the other man seemed almost to light up. There was no wariness, no shadowing of guilt. Joe knew right off that Chris Webber was in love with his sister, and that he had no problem with Joe knowing about it.

Chris knew nothing whatever about the vacation.

"I didn't even know they were going."

"But you knew she'd been sick."

"Yes." Chris saw Lally's grey eyes duplicated in her brother's sharp face. "You didn't?"

"No."

"I saw her last Saturday." Chris tried to be reassuring. "She was in really good shape. These pacemakers are wonderful things. The doctors say she can do anything now that she could before."

They were still standing in the hall. The atmosphere between them was thick enough to cut.

"Can I get you a cup of coffee?" Chris asked.

"You can."

The kitchen was big and airy. The draining board was crowded with pots and pans washed but not put away. A loaf of bread stood on a board on the oak table, surrounded by crumbs, a mug of stale, cold coffee beside it. Joe wondered about Webber's wife, and another touch of anger bristled down his spine, but he put it firmly away.

"I need to find Lally urgently," he said. "You're absolutely sure she said nothing about a vacation when you last saw her? Has she ever said anything about wanting to travel to Florida?"

Chris shook his head. "I haven't known Lally well for long. And no, she never talked about travelling anywhere. I kept leaving messages because I was getting anxious about her not being there – in fact, I was going to go to the café later on today if I didn't hear from her."

He poured fresh coffee into two cups and set them down on the table. With his right hand he brushed the crumbs into his left, and tossed them into the waste disposal. The two dogs hung around for a moment, then lay down together in the far corner.

"Can I get you something to eat?"

"No, thank you." Joe noticed the clock on the wall. It was almost two o'clock. "Can I use your phone? It's long-distance, but I'll get time and charges."

126

"No need." Chris moved a white telephone with a long cord from one of the work tops and set it down next to Joe. "I'll be in the next room."

Joe called Hagen Pacing and asked for Cohen.

"Joe, where are you?"

Joe told him.

"And Lally's in Florida?" Cohen was dismayed.

"Probably in the Everglades or the Keys, but no one knows where." Joe swallowed some coffee. "Did you check to see if Dr Ash is a Hagen customer?"

"Yes, and he is – but apparently he buys from other companies too, so it doesn't necessarily mean anything."

"But we can't rule it out. Has Dr Sheldon been trying to reach me?"

"No, but Jackson wants you. Ferguson's been on Chief Hankin's back."

"I'll go see Sheldon again, try to talk the local force into letting us into Ash's office in Pittsfield."

"When are you coming back?"

"As soon as I've located Ash or Lally."

"You're not thinking of going to Florida?"

"If I have to."

"You have to be here, Joe. You've a task force to run."

"We're talking about my sister's life," Joe said tightly.

"They can find her without you." Cohen knew how stubborn Joe could be, and he was talking fast. "You don't even know Florida – and even if you do find her, and even if her pacemaker was manufactured by Hagen, that's even more reason to find the son of a bitch who did it, so the medics can decide how to get it out of her safely."

"I have to get off the phone now, Sol."

"You have to call the commander."

"I will."

"Ferguson wants to talk to you."

"Tell him I've nothing new to say."

"You can't just let everyone down, Joe, you know that."

"I know that my sister's life is in danger." Joe kept his voice down. "I know there's an outside chance that any moment now she could die, just like Marie Ferguson or Jack Long or the fireman."

"Joe, let me help with this." Cohen became more urgent. "Go see the doc, try getting into Ash's office or whatever, and meantime, we can contact the Florida State Police about searching for Lally." He, too, lowered his voice. "If you get suspended, it's not going to

127

help her or any of the others. You've got to stay inside the investigation, you have to."

"I'm going now, Sol."

"Call the commander."

"I will."

"Now."

"Soon."

"And mind you stay in touch." All Cohen's affection and concern were in his voice. "Good luck, Joe."

"Thanks." Joe put down the receiver.

"What's going on?"

Joe looked around, startled. Webber stood in the doorway, his face pale, his expression shocked.

"I heard what you said. What's going on?"

"I can't tell you."

"Sure you can."

Joe shook his head. "It's a police matter."

Chris came and sat down at the table. His hand were clenched into fists. "You said Lally's life is in danger."

"I didn't know you were listening."

"I was on my way in to get a rag." Chris's voice was cold. "If you didn't want me to hear, you shouldn't have made the call in my kitchen."

Joe didn't answer.

"What happened to those other people?" Chris persisted. "Marie Ferguson and Jack Long and the fireman. Who are they? What happened to them?"

"I can't tell you," Joe said again.

"If Lally's in some kind of danger, I want to know."

"Do you consider you have some kind of special right over my sister?"

"No right at all, except that I'm in love with her."

Joe looked at the ring on Chris's left hand. "Does your wife know?"

"No."

"Are you living together?"

"My wife's in a clinic," Chris answered steadily, "being treated for alcoholism. And before you ask, nothing at all has happened between Lally and me. She doesn't even know how I feel about her – or at least I haven't told her." He paused. "You said on the phone that she could die at any moment. So I take it we have to find her." His jaw was set tightly. "I want to help."

"You can't." Joe stood up. "I have to go."

Chris got up, too. "You can't."

"Are you going to stop me?"

"Are you carrying a weapon?"

"No."

"Then I'll certainly try to stop you if I have to."

Joe looked the other man in the eye for one more moment. He was a married man with one daughter that he knew about, and he'd fallen in love with Lally while his wife was sick, and he knew he ought to have despised him on sight, and at another time he'd probably have punched him in the mouth. Yet right now, with all that was happening, he found himself trusting Webber, and it made no sense to do that, but it was another one of those gut reactions, and he knew he was going to go with it.

"Okay," he said, and sat down again.

"Thank God."

Chris poured fresh coffee for them both and came back to the table.

"If there's some kind of official secrecy involved," he said, "I'll sign a paper, or whatever you need. Just tell me what's going on."

Joe told him. The expression of rage in Webber's eyes when he finished, confirmed that he'd been right to confide in him. He looked the way Joe felt.

"What do you need?" Chris's voice was shaky but strong.

"Wait till I've gone, then call this number." Joe took a pen and notebook from his inside pocket and tore off a sheet. "Detective Cohen's the man I was just talking to. He's okay, but I don't want to get him fired. If he can't talk to me direct, they can't expect him to get me back to Chicago."

"What do you want me to tell him?"

"That I've confided in you – God help us all – and that I want him to keep you informed of all developments from his end, as and when."

"And meantime?"

"I'm going to find Charlie Sheldon and I'm going to consider breaking into Ash's office." Joe stood up again. "Find out how fast I can get to Miami." He glanced down at the telephone and made a note of the number. "I'll be in touch."

Chris waited until he heard the front door close, and then he went out into the back yard and walked past the kennels. The dogs barked, but he took no notice. The snow was piled over a foot deep even on the path, and he wore only sneakers, but he didn't notice the cold or wet. He thought about Lally. About her beauty, her kindness, her courage. He thought about the magic that had flared up between them so fiercely, and about the way they'd both backed off because of Andrea and Katy. He thought about Lucas Ash, and about the little pacemaker that was supposed to have saved her life, and he thought about those other people – all with normal lives and hopes and dreams – blown to kingdom come by a maniac.

He felt a wet nose on his left hand, and looked down. Jade, the bitch Lally had met when she'd come to the house two weeks ago, was nuzzling him gently, and Chris only realized then that there were tears rolling down his cheeks and that the dog was trying to comfort him.

"I'm okay, girl."

He took a look around. The sun was already starting to dip, but it was still there and the heavily laden branches of the fir trees were glowing pink. In south Florida it would be warm, and somewhere Lally might be getting ready for a blazing sunset and thinking contentedly towards her future. A future that might never come to pass, unless they found her.

He turned and went back into the house to call Cohen.

Joe telephoned Chris at six o'clock.

"What do you have?"

"Cohen wants you to call him."

"So what's new?"

"Any luck with Ash?"

"His office is in a high security building, so no chance. We're going to have to wait for him to get in touch from Hawaii. Have you found a flight for me?"

"For us."

"No way."

"You can't stop me."

Joe took a second. "Do you have a decent car to get us to Albany fast?"

"A Jeep Cherokee – want me to pick you up?"

"What about your daughter?"

"I've already sent Katy to stay with a friend. She's ecstatic."

"You sure about this?"

"Where are you?"

"Lally's house."

"I'm on my way."

Joe called Cohen from the airport.

"Thank God."

"What's happened?"

"Jess is going nuts."

"What's wrong?" Fresh terror gripped Joe. "Is it the baby?"

"I'm not sure – she's not sure – "

"Tell me what happened, for Christ's sake."

"Jess called, sounding really upset. She's been having some kind of pains, and she wanted to talk to you, and then her mother got on the phone and said if you were any kind of husband you'd be here when she needed you." Cohen sounded distraught. "Joe, you have to come back. I know how hard it must be, but you've got no choice."

Joe felt as if he was tearing in two. He saw Webber looking at his watch and pacing, and he thought of Lally, somewhere, blissfully ignorant, and then he thought about Jess, his sweet Jess, and he knew Cohen was right.

"Have you called Florida?"

"They have all they need. I went to your house and got one of Lally's photos to fax through to them, and they'll have the real thing tomorrow." Cohen paused. "What do I tell Jess?"

"Tell her I'm coming."

"It's not your fault, Joe. Don't beat yourself up."

Joe put down the phone. Webber was at his side instantly.

"Something's happened," Chris said tersely.

"I have to go back to Chicago."

"You can't."

"I have to." Joe wanted to scream, but his voice was very quiet. "My wife may be losing our baby, and she needs me."

Chris stood still for a moment.

"I'm going to Florida," he said.

"The state police have already started looking for Lally." Joe looked at Webber. "Are you sure about this?"

"You know I am."

Joe nodded. "I'll tell them you're on your way, and that they have to let you help. But you have to do it their way – they're experts, okay?"

"Okay."

The flight was being called. Chris picked up his bag.

"Find her," Joe said.

"I will."

"And try not to scare her too much."

Chris managed a half-smile. "I'm scared enough for both of us."

"She'll need you to be strong for her."

"Trust me."

"I do." Joe picked up his own bag. "God help me, I do."

22

Friday, January 22nd

They had camped for two nights, and tonight they had taken time off – "for good behaviour," Hugo said, for Hugo would never adapt too well to life in a sleeping bag or under canvas – on Conch Key, staying in a tiny wooden cottage with its own screened porch close to the beach. They were sharing the bedroom, and Hugo felt heroic and unmanned at the same time, felt his love for Lally spilling over and over, certain that she must, at last, notice, hoping that she would not, praying that she would.

"Bahia Honda tomorrow," Lally said, dreamily, before they went to sleep. "White sand beaches, silver palms and turtles."

"You sound like you swallowed the guide book," Hugo commented into the dark.

Lally smiled. "And evening bats."

She had begun thinking about Chris again. She hadn't intended to, had almost believed herself free of him, of the sheer impracticability of falling in love with such an encumbered man, but he had slipped neatly back into her mind with the beauty of the settings they had seen over the last few days and the knowledge that such scenes could not be captured with their Pentax, that only a great photographer or an artist could begin to seize the magic of it. The real truth was, Lally confessed to herself under cover of darkness while Hugo gently snored in the next bed, the unvarnished and shameful truth was that, joyful as it was having her dearest friend to share this vacation with her, she wished that Chris could be here, too, so that she could watch him, his reactions, his responses, could spend time with him away from his troubles, could learn something about the man himself, the individual. And if she had allowed herself, Lally knew she was a whisker away from turning wishing into fantasy, and she was behaving like a schoolgirl, and she knew it had to stop.

You don't know him, she told herself for the hundredth time. *And he isn't here, and he can't be here or anywhere else with you, and there's no point wishing for things that can't be.*

And yet she did.

23

Saturday, January 23rd

In Orlando, Florida, Alice Benton Douglas was at the hairdresser, having her first permanent in twenty years. The last time, the day before her thirtieth wedding anniversary, she'd treated herself, hoping that a little change might put some extra spice into their celebrations, but it had been a disaster, all frizz and split ends, and Martin had refused flatly to be seen out in public with her, telling her she looked like an over-used scouring pad.

This time was very different. In the first place, Martin had been dead for three years, and though Alice often missed him and wished she had a little company in the evenings, at least there would be no man to mock if it all went wrong again. In the second place, *Melvyn's* was a class act and terribly expensive, and Alice had yet to see a single scouring pad walking out of this salon. Everyone and everything was sleek and elegant, and Alice, too, felt transformed already, even after her first shampoo.

Everything was different these days, of course, what with Walt Disney and Epcot and all. And then there was the building work – so many new buildings, all those beautiful houses, all those strangers flooding into the area. Most of her friends, her contemporaries, complained that the landscape was being destroyed, cluttered, but Alice loved it. The new homes were wonderful, she thought, like movie sets and so luxurious, and they had brought life, youth and prosperity with them. And shopping malls and neat little strip malls, so easy to park close to, with places like *Melvyn's*, places that had been out of reach in the old days.

Everything about Alice was transformed now, of course. Had been ever since her surgery. Surgery. A big word for such a small 'procedure', which was what they'd all called it in the hospital, only Alice hadn't believed them for a moment, for how could anything that involved cutting a hole in her chest be dismissed as a simple procedure? And yet they'd been right, she'd admitted that almost immediately – once the terror had subsided and she'd realized not only that she was still there, still alive, but that she felt a thousand per cent better already.

Transformed, she thought, resting back comfortably while her head was wrapped in a snowy white turban. *The new Alice Douglas.* The hair would only be a small part of the process, scarcely significant, as would be the new dress she intended buying herself later that afternoon or, if she was too tired, tomorrow morning. *But I won't be tired,* she thought contentedly. *That's the whole point. I'm never going to feel dog-tired again, not without a damned good reason.*

The boy who had shampooed Alice's hair, tilted her chair upright again and helped her onto her feet, and Alice thought, for an instant, of rejecting his help, but she had been brought up in a time of comparative chivalry, and she knew that it was discourteous to spurn kindness of any sort.

She was looking into the mirror when it happened. Sitting in the chair – a funny, quite unpleasant kind of chair, really, that got pumped up by a pedal till you were the right height, a little too much like the dentist's chair – and listening to the young woman who was going to give her the permanent explain to her that nowadays there was absolutely no reason for frizz or even curl when all that was needed was a little extra body.

"A little extra body," were the last words Alice Douglas ever heard, for everything else was drowned out by the sound of a hair-dryer being switched on nearby, and by the strange, small boom inside her chest, and by the shrieking of the stylist just rolling the first strands of hair into the first roller as Alice's wet head jerked forward and then slumped back again, flopping and dead.

For the first few moments, everyone kept their distance, backed away. And then, in a small, shocked rush, they all moved forward again, closing in on poor dead Alice Douglas, staring in wide-eyed horror at the blood that had sprayed the mirror and the white plastic hairspray and gel bottles and the folded towels that stood on the counter ahead of her.

And at the hole, bloody and ragged, in her pale green gown.
And at the smoke.

24

Saturday, January 23rd

The man knew he was very sick. He might have been shamming when the good lieutenant called on him last Sunday, but looking into his bathroom mirror now, seeing the stark contrast between the hectic flush on his cheeks and the whiteness of the rest of his face, seeing the pain in his eyes and the dark ringed shadows beneath them, he knew that he ought to be in the hospital.

One of the Gila monsters had done this to him. His favourite dragons. And his own impulse decision to play one more game with the enemy, when they came to find him. He had decided to bury his six sets of records – one the precise log of the work he had done, the other five his intricate false trails – in the vivaria. He'd toyed with the notion of burying two in each enclosure, but the big iguanas still unnerved him and so he'd decided, in the end, to bury the whole package, fastened together with elastic bands, with the monsters.

They had not been visible when he'd unlocked the glass door of their enclosure and gone inside; they were shy creatures, often burrowing deep into the sand. The day before, the man had played a tracking game with the dim-sighted creatures, placing two newly dead baby rats first in one part of the enclosure, then moving them, again and again, and observing how, slowly but doggedly, the lizards turned towards the scent each time until finally the man had rewarded them with dinner, which they had, as always, swallowed whole. They had eaten well, and often, after a good meal, they burrowed and slept for days. He had not anticipated their waking.

Nor that he might accidentally tread where one of them slept.

Nor that it might bite him.

He knew about the creature's bite, about the grooved sharp teeth that could be almost impossible to dislodge, but nothing could ever have prepared him for the pain of the bite, nor, a mere thirty seconds later, for the sheer agony of the venom as it was released through the teeth into the punctured flesh on his left heel.

He had screamed with the pain, had fallen to the floor and kicked at it with his other foot, had grasped at its fat body and pulled, but the monster's teeth had only held tighter. He had crawled madly out of the vivarium, scattering sand and grit and faeces all over the room, seeking a tool of some kind, or a knife, but he had cleared everything out of the room after his work had been completed at the end of last year, and still the monster had hung on, and still the venom had poured into his foot. And then he remembered reading a case where hot water had dislodged a Gila monster from a victim's hand. He had forced himself to the kitchen sink, filled the kettle and boiled it, crying softly all the while with the pain, and then he had poured the water onto his foot and the creature, and finally it had released him, and he had begun to vomit with agony and then he had passed out. And when he had come round again, the dragon had still lain beside him, dead from the scalding water, and in spite of the exquisiteness of his own pain, the man knew he had triumphed again.

He had cleaned up the mess as well as he could, locked the vivarium, slid the lizard's corpse, wrapped in newspaper, down the chute to the communal trash area, and stumbled back to his apartment. He had disinfected the wounds and put antiseptic cream on the blisters, and bandaged his foot, but he was growing weaker and was unable to eat. He supposed he had a fever, but had no energy to use a thermometer. He knew what he might expect from the venom. Local pain and swelling, general weakness, nausea, ringing in his ears, perhaps respiratory distress. Even, in the worst cases, cardiac failure. But he knew that would not happen to him. He would not die.

In time, they would come to visit him again, and when they saw how badly his condition had worsened, he guessed they would send a doctor, perhaps even take him to hospital. He would not tell them about the bite, would wear socks and slippers, however painful, and even when they found it, he would be silent, would not give the other dragons the satisfaction of knowing what one of their kind had done to him. There was no antivenin for the bite of the

Gila monster. All they could do was care for him, while he toyed with them.

Mother used to care for him when he was sick.

25

Saturday, January 23rd

J oe was functioning on automatic. He was numb again, with fear, with guilt, with being torn to pieces. Jess was in the hospital, and all the tests so far indicated that the baby was okay, and they were praying that things would settle down and that Jess could go home. But right now the doctors wanted her to rest up, and it was such a struggle for Joe to keep from telling her about Lally, and the trouble was that his feelings always showed in his face – Jess always said he'd make a lousy poker player – but this time he was hell bent on keeping the nightmare from her, and so far he'd managed it.

There had been a storm in Hawaii, and Joe's temper had blown when Cohen had told him that Lucas Ash had still not been in touch because there was a problem with the phone lines, but at least the Florida State Police had gotten the prints of Lally's photographs, and they were already out there, looking and asking questions. Apparently they thought it a real possibility that Lally and Hugo might be in Everglades City because the big seafood festival was on, and Joe saw some sense in their reasoning that no one who liked food as much as they did was likely to resist it.

The searching and sifting at both Hagen Pacing and the battery plant had been completed, and nothing, not a sliver or fragment of evidence, had been found to prove that the sabotaging of pacemakers had happened at either site. Hagen and Schwartz were still home sick – Hagen, he had reported to Cynthia Alesso by phone, with a secondary chest infection that looked like turning into pneumonia – but Linda Lipman, younger, fitter and made of strong stuff, was back on duty and had gone to visit Ashcroft and Leary at their homes. Olivia Ashcroft had pretty much fulfilled her expectations, but Lipman had been startled to find Howard Leary markedly different than at the office, a surprisingly convincing family man with a pretty schoolteacher wife, a long-serving and contented Spanish housekeeper, and three normal, boisterous children at different stages of orthodontia.

Joe badly wanted to search Hagen and Schwartz's apartments, but he didn't even bother making out a complaint for a search warrant, for he knew that without specific proof no judge would agree to sign it. The more Joe thought about it, the more he felt the two men's illnesses were too damned convenient, but since about a quarter of Chicago had the flu, that was no evidence either. Because of Jess, and his genuine concern over Lally, the commander had said comparatively little to Joe about his trip to Massachusetts, but Jackson was less than appreciative about Chris Webber having been told what was being kept from the rest of the country.

"Just what do you know about this man, Duval?" he asked on Saturday night.

"Very little," Joe admitted.

"Yet you've foisted him on the Florida police." Jackson's tone was as soft as usual, but held an unmistakable note of menace.

"I think he can help."

"And what if he opens his mouth to the wrong person?"

"Webber's only interest is in finding my sister, Commander," Joe said. "He could care less about selling his story or worrying about other patients in the same position. He may remember to care about those things after they've found Lally – I don't know enough about him to be sure – but right this minute, I'd stake my life on his doing anything to help."

The commander took a long look at Joe.

"When did you last sleep?"

"I caught a nap on the plane."

"Go home now. You look like hell."

"I can't."

"It wasn't a request, Duval."

"I won't be able to sleep, Commander."

"Wanna bet?"

Joe went home. The house was lonely without Jess or Sal, and it

141

seemed suddenly to be crammed with reminders of Lally. The photographs, books she'd given him, the watercolour of the Berkshires she'd bought to keep home fresh in his mind, the silver candlesticks she'd given him and Jess for their fifth wedding anniversary. He flicked the TV remote until he found a rerun of *The Odd Couple,* found a frozen pizza and heated it in the microwave, and drank a beer, and normally that was all it took to knock him out, but tonight, if he was hoping to get any rest, he knew he'd need more, so he followed it up with a shot of Jack Daniels. And the comedy show ended and *The Red Shoes* began, and Joe knew it was one of Lally's favourite movies, and suddenly he was drunk, and sadder than he could ever remember feeling in his life, and with no one there to see, he began to choke up a little, sat there looking at the screen and sniffing like a teenage girl.

He woke up as the closing credits were rolling, and it was after two, and his head ached. He dragged himself out of the armchair and filled a glass with cold water and drank it down, and then he called the hospital to check on Jess, and called Florida to check on Lally, but no one anywhere had any news for him, and so, very slowly and rather painfully, he went upstairs and pulled off his clothes and went to bed, and slept like a dead man.

26

Sunday, January 24th

Chris had never felt so useless in his life. He had thought over the last few years that he had cornered the market in helplessness as he'd watched Andrea drink herself over and over from Jekyll into Hyde, but running around south Florida like a headless chicken for the past twenty-four hours, scanning tourists and staring into cars, getting more and more frustrated and weary, knowing that he was about as likely to run into Lally Duval as he was to see a snowflake, he had become increasingly filled with a sense of self-mockery and despair.

Chief Hankin having asked his Miami counterpart for assistance in the search, had enabled Joe Duval to ask the local police to meet Chris at Miami airport on Friday night, and they already knew that Hugo and Lally had rented a red Pontiac Sunbird, and every available officer from Miami to Key West had a copy of the car description and Lally's photograph. It would have been useful if someone had thought to give them a snapshot of Barzinsky, too, but never mind, because now that they had their licence place number they were one hundred per cent better off than they had been before, and no one put up a fight when Chris told them he'd decided to go it alone rather than stick with any one group of officers.

"You do have people on all the islands?" he'd asked one young officer with a golden crew cut and snub nose.

"Pretty much."

"What do you mean pretty much?"

"Word's gone out, sir. To all the camp sites and tourist offices."

"And hotels?"

"There are hundreds of hotels and motels, Mr Webber. We can't get details to all of them, but they'll all get checked out in time." The officer had looked and sounded patronizing.

"How much time?" Chris had asked.

"As long as it takes, sir."

"You know how important it is that we find Miss Duval, don't you?" Chris was a non-violent man, but he'd experienced a sudden intense desire to shove this young asshole up against a wall and show him his fist.

"Yes, sir, we know, and we'll be doing our best."

"Then it won't matter to you if I look for them on my own."

"So long as you don't go getting yourself into trouble, sir. You wouldn't want to use up any more valuable manpower, would you?"

Chris gritted his teeth. "I'll keep in touch, in case you have news for me."

"You do that, sir."

Assuming that even if they had spent time in the Everglades they'd have long since moved on south by now, away from the wetlands to the Keys, Chris had stayed at a hotel in Florida City on Friday night. Saturday morning had proven hotter than he'd anticipated, and he hadn't stopped to pack properly, and his denims and sneakers felt too heavy, but he had no intention of wasting time shopping for shorts or sandals, and gradually he'd grown acclimatized. As the day went on, everywhere he'd looked there'd been young women with long, straight dark hair, but whenever he ran up to them, or honked the horn of his own rented Mercedes, or touched them on the shoulder, they turned around, looking startled or amused or angry, and none of them had those soft grey eyes or that magical slenderness, or that wonderful dancer's neck, and he knew it was hopeless, worse than hunting for a needle in a haystack, because there was no way of knowing if she was *in* this particular haystack or in another, twenty or forty or even a hundred miles away.

He had tried, from the start, to envisage the trip through Lally's eyes. She was an energetic young woman, and a creature of impulse, he knew that much, but she had been sick, so there must be some limitations, and he guessed that even if Lally didn't want to accept that, Hugo Barzinsky would take care of her. Chris had seen the way Hugo looked at her, the way his eyes changed when he talked about her, and he recognized that look, for he'd seen it in his own eyes in the shaving mirror over the last two weeks.

There were two ways Hugo and Lally might have tackled the Keys, either driving all the way through to the last island, Key West, and then backtracking leisurely, or dipping in to some or even all the Keys on their way down to the tip. He wasn't sure about Barzinsky, but he didn't see Lally as a methodical traveller, so Chris had taken a chance on the second alternative, and he'd bypassed Key Largo on the assumption that, as with the Everglades, they'd have been and gone by now, and headed straight for the Islamorada group of islands.

"Have you seen this woman?"

He'd asked the question over and over again, feeling like a cheap private eye in a bad movie, except that most people he asked were happy to look at Lally's picture, or too polite to refuse to. But no one had seen her, and it *was* hopeless, and he understood the young cop's attitude a little better already, for according to the leaflets he'd picked up at the tourist centre there were at least a dozen sites that might have attracted them, and any number of hotels, motels and mom-and-pop establishments they might have stayed at, or restaurants, diners and cafés they might have eaten at.

He'd hit pay dirt on Saturday evening.

"Have you seen this woman?" he'd asked the man at the cash desk at the entrance to one of the camp sites on Long Key.

"Yes."

Chris stared at him. "You have?"

"Sure." He was Hispanic and had an easy, swinging accent. "Like I told the cops, she and her friend camped here Wednesday and Thursday night. What did she do?"

"What do you mean?"

"Why are you all looking for her?"

"She didn't do anything."

Chris couldn't believe it. There were sixty camp sites on Long Key, and he'd struck the right one first time.

"So they left yesterday morning?" His spirits soared, his feet stopped aching, the throbbing in his head went magically away.

"I guess so."

"Do you know where they went from here?"

"How should I know?"

The headache came back. "Is there anyone else they might have talked to about their plans?"

The man shrugged. "Maybe a turtle, maybe a bird."

Another wise-ass. Chris had thanked him and gone to a payphone to check in with the police. They had been there before him, and the discovery hadn't gotten them much further along, but they said that it was good to have confirmation of their presence in the Keys, and it was only a matter of time before they were found.

It wasn't that Chris didn't believe that. The trouble was, he couldn't be be sure they had the time.

Sunday morning he felt no better. He'd spent the night in a motel on Route 1 and now he was back on the road, heading south, and he felt like a washed-up gambler, sticking pins in the map to decide where to try next.

He was filled with self-disgust. He was an amateur, and arrogant, and a damned fool. He also had a wife in a clinic in New England, and a ten-year-old daughter he should have been looking after, and if anyone was going to find Lally, it was almost certainly not going to be him. But he'd promised Joe Duval that he would do his best. And besides, he was in love. He was thirty-five years old, and he was head-over-heels in love with a woman who was not his wife. A beautiful, talented, impulsive, decent young woman whose life was in unthinkable, unbearable danger.

There was a red Sunbird three cars further along. Chris's pulse-rate quickened. He put his foot down, swung out to get a better look, but it wasn't a Sunbird at all, it was a Japanese import, and the driver and his passenger were both black.

He bit down hard on the disappointment, and drove on.

27

Sunday, January 24th

J oe heard the phone ringing while he was in the shower. He grabbed a towel and ran, making wet footprints on the bedroom rug, a thing Jess abhorred.

"Yes?"

"Lieutenant Duval?"

"That's right."

"This is Lucas Ash. I treated your sister last – "

"I know what you did." Joe was curt. The sabotage might not be the cardiologist's fault, but so far as Joe was concerned, the communications breakdown had been unforgivable.

"I want to apologize for the delay in getting back to you – "

"Thank you." Joe cut him off again. "Do you have the information, sir?" He knew that his tone was too brusque, but he couldn't help it.

"I do, Lieutenant."

Joe heard the grim note in the other man's voice, and knew.

"It was made by Hagen Pacing?"

"I'm afraid so."

"Are you sure?" Joe clutched at straws. "Have you confirmed it with your office?"

"I have, and in any case I remember every detail about your sister's case, Lieutenant. I'm afraid there's no doubt."

Joe's mind raced, going nowhere.

"Lieutenant?"

"Yes."

"I'm arranging to return right away. I'd like to be on hand in case I'm needed." Ash paused again. "I understand from Detective Cohen you're having some difficulty locating your sister. I told him I knew she and Mr Barzinsky were probably going to Florida, but I'm afraid I had nothing more to offer."

Joe went silent again.

"I'm sure you'll find her soon."

"I hope so." Joe's voice was stiff.

"I'm so very sorry, Lieutenant." There was no mistaking Ash's sincerity. "You sister's one of the loveliest young people it's been my privilege to meet."

"Yes," Joe said. "She is."

He put down the receiver. There was a pool of water around his feet, but he didn't notice. The phone rang again, and mechanically he snatched it up.

"Did you hear from the doc yet?" It was Cohen.

"Just now. It's bad news."

"Oh, my God."

"Anything else, Sol?"

"Nothing from Florida yet, but it's still early." Cohen hesitated, "I had a visit from Ferguson."

"What's up?"

"I told him about Lally."

"You did what?"

"I know, I know, but the man was really on shpilkes, and then when he heard you were in the Berkshires, he got it in his head you were taking a break, and I got mad and told him. Joe, I'm sorry."

Joe heard his wretchedness. "Right now, Sol, Ferguson knowing or not knowing is the least of my worries."

"Anyway, it really shut him up. He was very shocked, wanted to know if there was anything he could do for you, and I told him no, thank you, but at least now he'll stay off your back." Cohen took a breath, and changed the subject. "Any news on Jess?"

"No change."

"Thank God for that."

"Yeah."

"They'll find Lally today, Joe."

"Yeah."

"You okay?"

"What do you think?"

28

Sunday, January 24th

The names were heavenly. Big Pine, No Name, Big Torch, Little Torch, and Sugarloaf. The Lower Keys began below the Seven Mile Bridge, and their character was different again from the islands that had come before. If Lally and Hugo had felt well-being and relaxation washing over them as far back as at Key Largo, these less commercialized islands, with their easy access to Atlantic coral reefs, their wildlife refuges and tropical hardwood forests, and their quieter, calmer attitude to life in general, all but stopped them in their tracks.

On Big Pine Key on Saturday afternoon they had seen their first alligators close to, lying tranquilly near the shore of a big freshwater pond, and on Sunday, in the early morning mist in one of the wilderness sections of the refuge, they spied two of the elusive, tiny white-tailed Key deer, the smallest in the world. For the first time since she'd become sick, Lally felt like dancing for joy, but she controlled the impulse and stood very still, and Hugo, too, scarcely dared to breathe, and the two exquisite, fragile creatures seemed almost to be posing for them, and though neither Lally nor Hugo risked touching their camera for fear of disturbing the animals, it was a moment they both knew they would retain for ever.

Chris Webber noticed no alligators, no deer, nor herons nor pelicans. He was an artist faced with deep and gentle colours, with lush vegetation and rare creatures and an atmosphere so peaceful that at another time he would have put up his easel and not moved for hours or even days. But his eyes were still seeking the red Sunbird, and the dark-haired, grey-eyed girl, and nothing else counted, nothing mattered, not the hungry growl in his stomach when he forgot to eat, nor the nagging ache in his head from the sun and ceaseless looking, and when, just after noon he checked in with the police on Sugarloaf Key, he didn't know that he was less than two hours behind Lally and Hugo, though for all the good that was, they might just as well have been a thousand miles apart. But he forced down some local fish, and drank another cup of coffee, and though he tasted neither, they renewed his strength and his determination, and he got back in his car, back onto Route 1, and drove on again.

Key West took Hugo's and Lally's breath away. It shimmered in the sun, was fragrant and lush with frangipani and hibiscus and mango trees and oleanders and coconut palms, and lively and colourful with fishing boats and yachts and attractive houses and contented humanity.

"Spanish explorers named it *Cayo Hueso* or island of bones," Lally told Hugo when they arrived just after two o'clock. "They found all these human remains scattered on the shore, and no one ever discovered why they were there or who they'd belonged to, but the name stuck."

"Not exactly descriptive," Hugo said, his voice softened with wonder. "I don't think I've ever seen anything more perfect. I may never go home. Maybe we could open *Hugo II* here."

"And we could both write novels." Lally joined in the fantasy. "You remember what Bobby Goldstein said about all those Pulitzer prizewinners."

"You could teach ballet here."

"I'm not sure Nijinsky would like the heat."

"It's not all that hot."

"That's because it's only January."

"Oh well," Hugo sighed. "If the cat doesn't like it, we can't come."

Chris Webber hit Key West at ten minutes past four. He parked the Mercedes in a lot in the Old Town and found, as he had in every town, the police station.

"They're here," an officer at the desk told him. "Their car was spotted an hour ago."

"And?" Chris's pulse-rate rose again.

"And that's it for now."

"But you said someone saw their car."

"Sure."

"So?"

"So nothing else yet." The police officer observed Chris's growing flush of frustration and anger. "Mr Webber, this is a busy town with a lot of traffic, but assuming they haven't been here too long, most people stay a while because they like it."

"So you do have people out looking?" Chris didn't trouble hiding his irony.

"Naturally we do, sir."

"Thank Christ for that."

The officer was amiable. "This is the end of the line for the Keys, sir. They can't go any further, unless they rent a boat, and we'd hear about that, so the only thing we have to worry about is getting a hold of them before they get back on the highway and head back the way they came."

Chris went to the payphone and called Joe Duval collect.

"I'm in Key West, and they're here, too."

"Thank God."

"But we don't have them yet," Chris said quickly. "Duval, how much do the local police know about what's going on?"

"The cops on the street know they need to find Lally fast."

"But they don't know she's in danger."

"Not exactly."

"Can I tell them?"

Joe took a breath before answering. "No."

"I think it might help if they knew."

"It might help Lally, but it wouldn't help anyone else." Joe's voice was tight with the strain.

"She's your sister, Duval," Chris protested.

"You think you have to point that out to me?"

"No. I'm sorry."

"Don't waste time being sorry," Joe said. "We have a clinic on red-alert here in Chicago, waiting for Lally." John Morrissey, Marie Ferguson's partner, had called Joe direct to place the Howe Clinic at Lally's disposal for the explantation of her pacemaker. "Just get back on the street, Webber, buy yourself a street map, and start walking. Go to every café, every hotel, every restaurant, every tourist attraction. Show people the photograph, keep your eyes open – "

"Believe me, my eyes are open."

"Find her, Webber. Time's running out."

Chris's stomach dipped. "You've heard from the doctor."

"It was made by Hagen. They're still crosschecking to see if it belongs to any of the other batches we know for sure were tampered with."

"But it's a possibility."

"I wouldn't still be telling you to find her if it weren't."

Chris followed the tourist trail blindly, playing a half-crazed game of hide and seek, with no cries of 'hot' or 'cold' to aid him. He went to the aquarium, scanning the backs of the heads of people watching sharks being fed; he visited a house that had originally been owned by a US marshal who'd saved a neighbour from Key West's fire of 1886 by dynamiting their street; he went to the Hemingway House and saw the six-toed cats rumoured to be descended from the writer's own animals; guessing that Lally might feel like a break from commercialism, he drove to a wildlife refuge outside town, and then he drove back again to visit a bizarre cemetery where stone caskets rested above the ground and many of the epitaphs were more humorous than poignant. *"At Least I Know Where He's Sleeping Tonight"* seemed one of the favourites, but Chris hardly read any of them as he half walked, half ran from grave to grave, looking at faces and backs and tuning into voices, trying but failing to find the one he sought.

"They haven't checked in to a hotel or guesthouse yet – though of course most of them are full – but we'll be doing the rounds again in an hour or two."

Chris was back in the police station. It was five minutes before six o'clock, and the sun was going down.

"Have you been showing the photograph?" he asked the officer on duty.

"Yes, sir, we have."

Chris raked his hair with one hand and suppressed an urge to hoist the other man by his collar. "This is crazy. I mean, you told me they were here, and you've supposedly been searching for them since three o'clock – what are you people *doing*, for Christ's sake?"

"Everything we can, sir." The officer was as cordial and maddening as his predecessor had been almost two hours before. "And we'll have a couple of men at the Mallory Docks in about ten minutes."

"What happens there?"

"Sunset, sir." The officer smiled. "If your friend's in Key West, it's a fair bet that's where she and most every other tourist'll be."

"How do I find it?" Chris was already halfway to the door.

"North-west end of Duval Street." The other man grinned again. "Even named the street after her."

The place was jammed with life and noise. Men, women and children from everywhere, some there to entertain or to sell their wares, most there to be entertained and to spend money. Chris's eyes were dry and sore with staring, and he'd never especially enjoyed large crowds, but now he loathed them, had a wish to wipe them out, wanted them all to lie down and shut the hell *up* so that he could yell out her name and have her hear him.

He saw jugglers and acrobats, mime artists and fire-eaters. He saw clowns and street vendors, and dogs wearing bonnets and two men with tattoos over every visible inch of their bodies. Twice, he saw young women with long dark brown hair, and he sprinted towards them only to brake sharply when he saw they weren't Lally, and once he thought – he *swore* – he saw Hugo eating ice cream and laughing, but then he was gone, vanished off the street like one of Kirk's crew beamed up to the *Enterprise*. And Chris wanted to scream, wanted to tear his hair out and scream like a madman, and if he'd thought it might have helped, might have drawn Lally from the mass, he'd have done it without hesitation, but there was so much going on, so much fun, so much pleasure and music and laughter and squealing, he doubted she'd even have noticed.

"It's going!" someone yelled.

The sun gave a final dip, and hit the horizon, and the crowd cheered as if all their home teams had simultaneously scored the greatest winning touchdown of all time.

And Chris heard a bang.

Everyone around him heard it, too, craned their heads to see what had caused it, then lost interest, shrugging and smiling and gazing back at the ever-darkening horizon.

But Chris was terrified that he knew what it was, and he saw two police officers less than a hundred yards away, and they were looking, too, trying to fathom where it had come from, and he felt the blood roaring through his arteries into his head, thought that if he was right, he might die too, and he couldn't bear it if he was right, he just couldn't *stand* it –

He saw the cops start walking, fast, away from the square, and he started running like a demented thing, crashing into people, knocking over a postcard rack and a bicycle, almost sending a small girl flying, stopping just for a second to check that she was unhurt and to pacify her enraged mother. The cops were moving up Duval Street, turning into Caroline, and Chris was almost on top of them when there was another bang, and they all ground to a halt, and it was just a kid, a teenaged boy, letting off firecrackers, and the two cops laughed – he heard them *laugh*, and okay, he felt relieved, too, more than he could easily express, but still he wanted to bang their heads together for laughing, and he couldn't understand what was happening to him, because he was such a peaceable man as a rule, but then again he'd never experienced such frustration, never felt such fear for anyone, not even Katy, as he felt for Lally Duval, for this woman he hardly knew.

"What a circus," Hugo said.
"Fun, though," Lally said. They linked arms as they strolled, leisurely, out of Mallory Square. "Where to now?"
"Food?"
"Sounds good."
"And we still need somewhere to sleep," Hugo pointed out.
They'd stopped in at a few places, but the prices were insane, and most of them were fully booked anyway, though some people had suggested they return later on in case of no-shows.
"We can always leave town and camp again," Lally said.
"I think I'd rather sleep on the beach."
"I think we might be arrested."
Hugo shrugged easily, and they strolled on.
"If I were any more relaxed," Lally said, softly, "I'd be comatose."
Hugo looked down at her fondly. "You feel good, don't you?"
She smiled up at him. "I feel wonderful."
"God bless Lucas Ash," Hugo said.
"Amen."

The red Sunbird had been found parked in a lot not too far from Mallory Square, but the Key West Police Force still insisted that neither Lally nor Hugo had checked into any known hotel, motel, resort, guesthouse or bed-and-breakfast establishment on the island.
"At least we'll make contact when they return to the car," a sergeant told Chris. "Until then, there's not too much more we can do except keep our eyes open." The officer looked at his exhausted face. "If I were you, sir, I'd try to grab a little shuteye."
Chris ignored the advice and went back outside. He located the parking lot, found the car, saw the note from the police and added one of his own, wrote it in bold marker pen and taped it right over the driver's side of the windshield, where they couldn't miss it. He began walking again. By the time all this was over, he reckoned,

he'd probably have tramped every foot of Key West several times over, and yet he doubted if he'd have noted anything of the slightest consequence about the place itself. He thought of calling Joe Duval again, could have used a conversation with someone who knew what he was feeling, but it wasn't fair to bother Duval when he had nothing to tell him.

He went into a bar, had a Coke, then hit the streets again. There were fewer folk out now, since most people were eating dinner. Chris had a restaurant guide in his pocket, and a blister on his right big toe. He walked into five places in and around Duval Street, scanning the diners and walking out again. In the sixth, he saw another pair of cops showing Lally's picture around, and he felt a sudden rush of warmth for them, felt just a little bit less alone, but still, they hadn't found her, and by now he was beginning to wonder if they ever would, if Lally and Hugo hadn't perhaps just dropped off the edge of the world, never to be seen again.

He didn't know what took him back to that particular section of that particular harbour. He'd visited it three times since he'd arrived that afternoon, and now it was almost midnight, and aside from a few perfectly laid-back glamorous types sipping nightcaps on the decks of their yachts, there were hardly any other people around.

There was a fishing boat up ahead, a beautiful old vessel, its sails neatly furled. It was pale in the moonlight, graceful and peaceful. An old grey cat sat on a ledge near the stern, washing itself in silent concentration. *All cats are grey in the dark.* Chris stood very still, watching it. It was the first time in days that he'd consciously taken time out to look at anything, really *at* it, and he realized that for tonight, at least, he'd about given up. He supposed he was too tired to look any more. He supposed there was nothing more he could do, except maybe catch some sleep somewhere, even if it was only back in his car.

The cat stopped washing. It looked at him.

"Hi," Chris said.

It stiffened a little, not actually rising, but still looking.

"Don't mind me," Chris said.

And then he realized that it wasn't looking at him, but past him, to a spot somewhere behind him.

"Chris? Is that you?"

He didn't move. He thought he was hallucinating.

"Chris?"

He turned. She was there. No more than ten feet behind him. She wore a flowing skirt and a dark, halter-necked top. Her arms

155

were bare and her long slender legs showed through the diaphanous fabric of the skirt. Her long straight hair blew in the gentle breeze off the Gulf of Mexico, and the moon, behind her, surrounded her with an aura of silver. She was the most incredibly lovely sight he had ever seen.

"It is you," Lally said, softly, unable to believe her eyes.

"I thought – " He stopped, his throat so dry that the words were almost too husky to hear. He swallowed. "I thought you were a ghost."

She stepped closer. "No ghost."

"Thank God," he said.

"What are you doing here?" Her voice was so sweetly puzzled, so calm. "I couldn't believe it was you. Are you on vacation, too? Is Katy with you?"

Chris licked his lips. "Where's Hugo?"

"Having a nightcap with some people we met." She turned her head, nodded in the direction of one of the smaller yachts moored some way back. "I felt like strolling a little, and – " She stopped, seeing his expression. "Chris, what's wrong?"

He managed to smile, though his heart was pumping, and every last fragment of weariness had vanished. He'd been dreaming of this moment for the last two days, had fantasized about finding Lally, about sweeping her into his arms and keeping her safe and never letting her go again. Yet now, seeing her standing there just a few feet away, they were like polite half-strangers bumping into one another on vacation, and she looked so happy, so well, so *normal*, and he knew he had to rip it all apart, to bring terror, not safety, into her life, and he didn't know how to do it, and he wished to God that Joe Duval were there instead of him, and he experienced a sudden and intense urge to run.

Instead, he stood absolutely still.

"Lally," he said, "I've come here to find you."

29

Monday, January 25th

C hris refused to tell her anything until they'd fetched Hugo,
and were all sitting down, away from other people, on a pier
wall. The stone felt cool and solid beneath her, and the sky was
still clear and beautiful, littered with brilliant stars and that
magnificent moon.

"There's a problem," he said, at last, "with your pacemaker."

"What kind of problem?" Hugo sounded half afraid, half
aggressive, as if a part of him suspected that Chris Webber had
come haring down to Florida just to break up his vacation with
Lally.

"Of course, it may be nothing at all – "

"What *kind* of problem?" Lally asked.

Even in the darkness, Chris's face was white. "They're recalling
all the recipients of pacemakers manufactured by the company who
made yours. There's probably no problem with it at all, but your
brother felt – "

"Joe?" Lally was bewildered. "What does Joe have to do with it?
I didn't even tell him I was sick."

"I know." Chris had repeatedly rehearsed the way he would break
the news to Lally, the way he would try not to frighten her too
much, but he knew now that that was an impossibility. "The
manufacturers asked the police to help track down all the patients.
Your brother saw your name on a computer printout."

"How did you get involved?" Hugo asked.

"Lieutenant Duval came to Stockbridge on Friday, looking for

157

Lally." He mustered a smile. "And we've both been trying to find you ever since."

"Is he here, too?" Lally asked, suddenly icy. The prospect of Joe taking time off work, and leaving Jess and Sal, seemed more alarming than anything else Chris had said.

Chris shook his head. "He wanted to be, but he had to go back to Chicago. He's waiting to hear from you."

"You still haven't told us what kind of problem this is," Hugo said.

"That's because I don't really know the facts. All I know is that it's urgent that we get you to Chicago."

"Why Chicago?" Hugo asked. "Why not home?"

"If it's so urgent," Lally said, very softly, "wouldn't it be safer to deal with it in Florida, quickly?"

Chris's insides wrenched with pity and fear. "According to your brother, there's some special equipment in Chicago they wouldn't have here."

"Nor in New England?" Hugo was openly suspicious.

"That's right." Chris willed Hugo to shut up. "Okay with you, Lally?"

"No. Not unless you tell me the truth." She saw the dismay on Chris's face, and grew gentler. "I can cope with trouble better when I know what I'm up against."

Chris didn't speak.

"Tell me, Chris." Her voice was surprisingly calm. "You didn't leave Katy and Andrea to come chasing us all over Florida because of some possible problem with my pacemaker. It's worse than that, isn't it?"

Still Chris didn't trust himself to speak.

"It's my heart, Chris. I have a right to know."

"Tell her." Hugo was shivering in spite of the night's warmth.

Chris focused on Lally's grey eyes. Even in the darkness, they were every bit as beautiful as he'd remembered.

"Okay," he said. "But I swear to you, the odds are heavily against your pacemaker being affected. I swear that by all that's holy."

All Lally's calm went away. "Go on," she said.

He told her everything he knew.

They drove through the night to Miami, abandoning the red Sunbird in favour of Chris's larger, faster, smoother Mercedes. Hugo wanted Lally to lie down and rest on the rear seat, but she was a million miles from sleep, felt wired enough to power the whole state of Florida single-handedly.

"Are you okay?"

"I'm fine."

They kept asking her that, trying, but failing, to mask their fear, and she kept responding, though she no longer really knew how she did feel. It was simply too insane to take in, too terrifying to cope with. The anxiety, when she had first been taken ill, that her heart might stop beating, had been awful enough. The knowledge that there was a possibility – no matter how remote – that it might actually be on the point of being blown to kingdom come, was, when all was said and done, too much to contemplate.

Hearing Joe's voice on the phone, when they'd called him from Key West, had lent her only a grain of comfort.

"Don't think," he'd told her. "Thinking'll make you crazy. Just get to Miami and get on that plane and come to me, and we'll take care of it."

"Why can't I go to a hospital here?" she'd asked, her voice thin and unfamiliar to her own ears. "Why can't they just take it out here?"

"They're not equipped there, sweetheart. You have to come to Chicago. Everything's all set for you here."

"I'm scared, Joe."

"I know you are."

"Aren't you?"

"Not any more." He sounded very decisive. "Not now we've found you. You're going to be fine."

"What about Miami?" she'd asked, clutching at straws. "There are major hospitals there – couldn't they take it out?"

"No, sweetheart, they couldn't They need special equipment, and we have that here." Joe had paused, and she'd realized that he was fighting to control his own emotions, and suddenly Lally had felt a great rush of anxiety for him.

"I love you, Joe," she'd said.

"I love you, too, Lally."

It was the same now, with these other two frightened, loving men, both striving so hard to seem normal as they drove, taking turns, for safety's sake, for they were both dog tired. While Hugo drove, Chris sat in the back beside her, holding her hand, saying little but communicating a lot through his touch, and when he took over the wheel, it was much the same with Hugo, though Lally had the sense that he was closer to cracking than either Chris or herself. When Hugo looked at her now, the love in his eyes was more naked that it had ever been, and she'd always known how he felt about

159

her, though neither of them had ever talked about it, and maybe now they never would.

She watched the nape of Chris's neck while he was driving, saw him glancing at her every few moments in the rearview mirror. There was no more room for doubt about his feelings for her now. This man, whom she hardly knew, had dropped everything, had left his wife in a clinic, had even left his own daughter, to chase her through half of south Florida because she was in danger. If she hadn't been so terrified, she thought that might almost have made her happy. But it was hard to daydream about happiness when she was so painfully aware that both these men who loved her were speaking in soft, cautious voices, as if they feared that a loud sound might detonate the thing inside her.

The thing. That was the way she'd thought of it when she'd first been released from the hospital, but then it had seemed a strange, yet benevolent alien, a lifesaving thing. Not a killer.

They reached Miami airport before sunrise. At the United check-in desk, Chris found a message to call Duval in Chicago without delay.

"What's up?"

"Can Lally hear us?" Joe asked.

"No."

"You can't fly."

"What?"

"They won't let Lally fly."

"They have to."

"No chance." Joe's tone was terser than ever. "There's been another death, in Orlando. There was a small piece in a local paper, though the full story's been kept away from the media. But the FBI notified the FAA, and the guys down there know you want to bring Lally back to Chicago, and they're treating her like a walking bomb."

Chris was silent, his mind working overtime.

"I'm getting something underway from this end," Joe said, "but it's going to take time."

"We don't *have* time."

"Tell me about it."

"I'll get her there," Chris said.

"How?" Joe was sceptical.

"I'll charter a plane."

"You'll never find a pilot willing to do it."

"I'll find one, for the right money."

"It'll cost a fortune." Joe was close to tearing his hair out. "There's no way I could even begin to – "

"I can afford it," Chris said. "And I won't want paying back."

"I can't let you – "

"Goddamn it, Duval, do you want your sister back in Chicago in time to save her life or not?"

"Go get a plane," Joe said.

30

Monday, January 25th

The man lay in his hospital bed in the early hours, neither asleep nor awake, his mind spiked by the fever. They had brought him there last evening. He had not told them yet about the bite on his heel. They would find it soon enough.

He closed his eyes. His foot hurt, and his head. His brain swam. *I saw a dragon once. In Mother's special place.*

In a strange room in a long corridor with a padded door. A red, glowing light spilling out through the crack, and strange, unfamiliar sounds that scared him, but not enough to make him run, until he crept up to the door and peeped inside, and the terror swelled him like a huge balloon expanding in his chest and choking him.

The dragon was great and scaly with a hideous head and a huge tail and human arms and legs, all hairy and ugly, and it lay on top of the woman, pinning her to the bed.

He wanted to scream, but he knew it might turn on him, and he wanted to run then, but he found that he couldn't look away, and he felt a funny feeling watching them, a hot, strange sensation deep down, like the feeling he got when Mother stroked him in her bed. There was a mirror on the ceiling, and he stared up and saw the woman's face, and her eyes were closed and her mouth was open, and she was moaning and writhing –

And he knew that the dragon was killing her – and he must have made a noise then – gasped a little, and maybe he cried out, because the dragon turned around to look at him, and its eyes were so red and fiery, and then everything went dark until Mother woke him with her cool fingers on his forehead, and they were back in her office and he was lying on the couch, and the dragon was gone.

"*I saw a dragon,*" *he whispered.*

"*I told you,*" *she answered, still stroking him.* "*I warned you.*"

"*It was killing a lady,*" *he said.*

"*That's what they do.*" *Mother's touch was so gentle.* "*They kill people.*"

"*I thought it was going to kill me.*"

"It's all right," the voice said. "You're okay now."

"It was going to kill me," the man said. "The dragon was going to *kill* me. I saw it, and it saw me, and – "

"There are no dragons here," the voice told him.

He opened his eyes. And saw the nurse. And though his head still hurt, and his chest was tight, and his foot burned like fire, he smiled at her.

"Oh, yes," he said. "There are."

31

Monday, January 25th

At seven-fifteen, Cohen called Joe at home to tell him that both Hagen and Schwartz had been admitted to Chicago Memorial Hospital.

"Complications from the flu," Cohen said.

"Easier to keep tabs on them," Joe said, without sympathy.

Fifty minutes later, just after Joe had arrived at the station, John Morrissey telephoned.

"Sean Ferguson needs to see you urgently, Lieutenant."

"What's up?" Joe was grateful as hell to Morrissey for his offer of the clinic for Lally, but he needed another encounter with Marie Ferguson's grieving husband like a hole in the head.

"He said to tell you it might be a breakthrough in the investigation."

"What kind of a breakthrough?" Joe asked wearily.

"He wouldn't tell me, but Ferguson's not a time-waster, Lieutenant. If he says he has something, I think you should listen."

"Is he at home?" Joe felt the first tingle of interest.

"No, he's here at the clinic, in Marie's office."

Ferguson was pacing, his boots making indentations in the soft, pale green rug. His late wife's office had been cleared of surface paperwork, but otherwise Joe guessed it was pretty much as Marie Ferguson had left it. It was a workmanlike but unmistakably feminine room, and Joe realized now that the whole clinic was stamped with her personal style.

"Lieutenant, thank God." Ferguson wore denims, a black turtle neck sweater and leather jacket. His dark hair was tousled, he looked a little wild, but there was a touch of triumph in his almost black eyes.

"What do you have?" Joe got straight to the point.

"A motive."

Joe felt the old, familiar prickling in his spine. "Go on."

Ferguson bent down and pulled a folded piece of paper out of a battered pigskin attaché case. "Research is what I do best, Lieutenant. Journalists get used to digging, and fiction writers are even better at it when they're determined to find exactly what they need to make a story fit." He laid the paper on Marie's desk.

"You want me to read?" Joe was impatient.

"In a moment." Ferguson gave a small wry grin. "Forgive the theatricality, Lieutenant. I've felt so helpless since I lost Marie, and knowing that you guys weren't getting anywhere hasn't helped. This thing I've found may not pan out, but I have a hunch – I get hunches, you know – and this one says it's the real McCoy."

"I know all about hunches," Joe said.

"Okay." Ferguson sat down behind the desk and motioned Joe to sit down facing him. "I found an old newspaper cutting. Four columns, with a picture. There was never a follow-up story, but I did a little more digging of my own."

Joe waited.

"Seems a crematorium on North Lincoln Avenue got blown up – that is, the chamber and furnace exploded – at the end of a service." Ferguson paused. "Seems it happened because the body being burned had a pacemaker with an old-style battery made of mercury zinc cells. Seems that happened a few times in different places, which is why there's a law now decreeing that pacemakers must be explanted prior to cremation."

Joe sat on the edge of his chair. He watched the other man's dark, excited eyes, and thought that he might have been more suited to life as an actor than a writer.

"Does the deceased have a name?" he asked, softly.

"Yes, it does."

"Do you think you could tell me the name?"

Ferguson glanced sideways at a photograph on Marie's desk of his wife and himself, arms around each other. Slowly, and with satisfaction, he picked up the paper off the desk, unfolded it and passed it across to Joe.

"Mean anything to you, Lieutenant?"

Joe was already on his feet.

"Oh, yes," he said.
"And there's more," Ferguson told him.

"It's not enough for a search warrant," Jackson said when Joe called him at the station.
"Sure it is, Commander."
"We have no more hard evidence than we had before."
"His whole personnel file is full of lies."
"Could just be full of errors."
"You don't believe that, sir."
"Maybe not, but we need a lot more and you know it."
"His mother was a madam. His file says she was a housewife."
"I can't see a judge blaming him for lying about that."
"His file says his father died in Chicago in 1950, but there's no record to say he ever really existed."
"So he lied about being illegitimate – or maybe he didn't even know."
Joe fought to hold down his rising anger. "His childhood was probably warped as hell, Commander. His mother – his only parent – wasn't just some small time hooker, she ran her own whorehouse. Lord knows what the boy might have gone through, and that was *before* his mother got blown sky high in the middle of her cremation when he was just a boy."
"It's all hypothesis, Duval, not hard proof."
"It's *motive*. He fits the killer's profile almost perfectly now. He's been harbouring this obsession for decades – we're talking revenge, for God's sake."
Jackson was immovable. "You're probably one hundred per cent right, and Christ knows I'm just as anxious to get a result on this as you are – "
"I seriously doubt that," Joe snapped into the phone. "Your sister's not going half crazy wondering if her heart's going to explode any second."
Jackson's tone grew crisper. "With respect, Lieutenant, there may be hundreds of people out there in the same condition, only they don't have a crack team of surgeons and bomb squad officers and half a private clinic on stand-by."
Joe tried to hold on to his self-control, knowing that losing it wasn't going to help Lally. "I have to get into that apartment, Commander. He's in the hospital – it's the perfect opportunity."
"You can't. Not yet. Get me more."
Joe opened his mouth, then shut it again.
"Go talk to him first chance you get, Duval. You have to wait till

the doctors okay it – if he's real sick the hospital won't let you near him yet. Take Cohen with you – better yet, take Lipman – get her to offer to bring him stuff from home. Talk to him about his mom, make nicey-nice, goad him a little if you have to. Take it as far as you can, but for Christ's sake be careful."

"We're running out of time, Commander."

"Do us all a favour, Duval. Go have some breakfast, then occupy yourself – catch up on all that paperwork sitting on your desk."

The phone in Joe's hand went dead.

32

Monday, January 25th

Lally, Chris and Hugo took off from Miami at eleven minutes past nine. Lally panicked a little as they climbed on board the Cessna, terrified suddenly that her pacemaker might explode in mid-air, killing them all and God-alone-knew who else on the ground, and Hugo, too, had wavered, but Chris had taken over, and the pilot, a near-silent, square-jawed, grey-haired man in his late fifties seemed laid-back and unconcerned, and so Lally just let it happen.

The skies were clear over Florida and for much of the flight, but over Georgia they hit a little turbulence, and later, starting their descent towards O'Hare, the little plane bucked and rocked repeatedly as their pilot battled his way through snow and high winds, and by the time touchdown came, Hugo was pea green, and Lally's face was white as her knuckles, and only Chris seemed cool and unshaken.

"Everyone okay?" the pilot asked, emerging from the cockpit.

"Fine," Chris said.

"Ma'am?"

"Yes, thank you," Lally said, a little shakily.

"I'm sorry it got a little rough for a while," the pilot said.

"It wasn't so bad," Lally said.

The pilot attended to opening the door.

"All right?" Chris asked Lally, very gently.

She swallowed. "In one piece." She managed a smile. "Thanks to you."

"It did get a little hairy up there."

"At least it was real," Lally said.

"Real?"

She tried to explain. "The turbulence, all that buffeting. I felt I was part of it – I could feel it happening to me." She shook her head. "All the rest of this has felt so *unreal* – do you understand?"

Chris looked down at her. "I think so."

Hugo stood up, hating the closeness between the other two, despising himself for hating it. "If you don't mind, I think I'll take a scheduled flight when it's time to go home." His long legs were shaky. "But thanks for getting us here."

"My pleasure," Chris said.

Joe, pale with tension, was waiting for them with another man, silver-haired and in great shape for his sixty or so years. Joe and Lally hugged each other tightly for several seconds, both holding back their tears, and then Joe pumped Chris's hand vigorously and shook his head at Hugo.

"Do me a favour, Barzinsky. Next time you take my sister island-hopping, remember to stay in touch with someone."

Lally saw Hugo's flush, and came to his defence. "Don't you dare blame Hugo for any of this – if it had been up to him, we'd have been sitting in the shade at some hotel in Miami Beach."

The silver-haired stranger spoke. "Perhaps we should get out of here?"

"Lally," Joe said, "this is Dr John Morrissey, head of the Howe Clinic, which is where we're taking you right now."

The clenched, sick feeling in Lally's stomach that had vanished for a few minutes at the sight of her brother, came back. She looked at the man. He had a trim grey beard and a kind face.

"How are you doing, Miss Duval?" he asked her.

"I'm doing okay, thank you."

"You must be very confused."

"Yes, I am."

They all started walking. Joe had his left arm around her, and Chris strode along on her other side, with Hugo beside the doctor. Lally had little sense of where they were. All that seemed important now was to get to wherever they were going as quickly as possible. She'd had plenty of time to think on the flight, before the bad weather had started shaking them up. When Joe had told her on the telephone that they couldn't take out her pacemaker in Florida because they needed special equipment, she'd felt anger and bitterness as well as fear, but once she'd begun really thinking about it, she'd understood. They were talking about some kind of bomb. That meant a risk factor for everyone who came near her. A surgeon most of all.

They emerged from the terminal building into the icy air. Joe's old green Saab waited at the kerb. Joe opened the back door.

Lally looked at the doctor again.

"Are you sure about this, Dr Morrissey?"

"About what?"

"About having me in your clinic."

"Absolutely."

"I don't want to endanger anyone."

His smile was warm. "We'll take every precaution, Miss Duval. Though you do realize there's only a very small chance that your pacemaker is one of the affected ones."

"Why doesn't that comfort me as much as it should?"

"Get in the car, Lally," Joe said.

She stayed where she was.

"What's up?" Chris asked.

"I think I should travel alone."

"Why?" Hugo asked.

"Why do you think? In case."

"Lally, get in the car," Joe repeated.

"I think the others should get a cab," she said, stubbornly.

"It didn't worry you in the plane," Hugo said.

"Of course it did, but I didn't have much choice."

"Lally, for the last time – "

"May I say something?" Morrissey intervened.

"I wish you would," Joe said.

The doctor took Lally to one side. To left and right, people surged from the airport building carrying bags, wheeling carts, searching for cabs, tipping Red Caps, some of them taking their first breaths of freezing Chicago air, others coming home.

"Will you trust me?" Morrissey asked Lally quietly.

"I think so."

"My partner and dearest friend, Marie Ferguson, died nineteen days ago."

Lally stared at him. "Because she had one of these pacemakers?"

"Yes, but that's not the whole point." Morrissey looked right into her eyes. "The point is, her husband was in bed with her when it happened. They were about as close to each other as they could get. And nothing happened to him. Not a scratch."

"I'm so sorry," Lally said.

"Me too." Morrissey managed a smile. "So will you get in the car now, Lally? You don't mind if I call you Lally, do you?"

"I wish you would." Lally paused. "And thank you."

They walked back to the car. Without another word, Hugo got into the back and slid across the seat, and Lally got in beside him, Chris following. "I'll travel with the lieutenant," Morrissey said.

The doors banged shut. Joe started the engine. Lally reached out both her hands, and held onto Hugo and Chris.

In silence, they headed for the city.

"I need your help," Joe said to Chris, while Lally was being settled into her room and Hugo was off somewhere getting coffee. "That is, I could do what I have to alone, but it would be a whole lot easier with back-up, and I can't ask another police officer."

"Anything," Chris said instantly.

"It's illegal." Joe wasn't exactly sure why he was involving Webber, except that all his instincts were still pushing him to trust the man.

"Is it for Lally?" Chris asked.

"I hope so."

"Name it."

Joe kept his voice low. "Tell Hugo you're beat and I'm taking you to my house for a rest." He saw Webber's hesitation. "Morrissey says they're going to be taking X-rays and assessing Lally for a while before they decide what to do, and I've already asked one of our bomb squad people to sit in."

"Where are we going?" Chris's blue eyes were alight with relief. There was nothing worse than waiting when you were afraid for someone you cared for. He'd done enough of that over the last few months for a lifetime.

"I'll tell you on the way."

The doorman at Fred Schwartz's apartment building, a burly man of around fifty, with beery breath and a ready smile that didn't touch his eyes, eyed Joe's badge with undisguised distrust.

"I can't let you in unless Mr Schwartz says it's okay."

"Mr Schwartz is in the hospital. We're here to get some stuff for him."

The man still looked dubious. "I should call and check with him."

"He's too sick – they won't let you talk to him," Joe said.

The man wavered. "I don't have a passkey."

"No problem, Mr Schwartz gave us his key."

"Who's your friend?" The doorman eyed Chris.

"A friend of Mr Schwartz's, here to help."

"I've never seen him here."

"I've only been here at night," Chris said.

The doorman hesitated a little more, just enough to let Joe know he was not above a little financial incentive. Two twenties changed hands.

"Don't mess anything up, will you?"

"We won't," Joe said.

"I'll need you to sign for anything you take out, okay?"

"Whatever you say," Joe told him.

"I should come up with you, but I can't leave my post."

"We wouldn't expect you to," Chris said.

They were in luck. Schwartz's corridor on the twenty-second floor was deserted. Joe, working deftly and silently, was through with the lock in less than a minute.

"A little knowledge comes with the territory," he said quietly.

"If I wasn't so scared for Lally," Chris muttered nervously, "this would almost be fun."

"Don't start enjoying it too much," Joe said, opening the door. "I won't have my sister consorting with criminals."

"Let's hope the neighbours don't call the cops then."

"Let's hope."

They stepped inside and shut the door.

It was quite dark in the hall. Joe waited several seconds until he felt certain they were alone, then switched on the light. Everything looked as it had when he'd visited just over a week earlier.

Chris wrinkled her nose. "What's the smell?"

"Some kind of menthol rub. I smelt it when I was here before."

"What do we do now?"

"We start looking." Joe looked at Chris. "You have to have steady hands if you're going to help." He took off his heavy outdoor gloves, stuck them in a pocket of his zip-up jacket, and handed Chris a pair of latex gloves, pulling on a pair of his own. "Remember this is an illegal search. The more you help, the greater your share of the guilt. The more careful we are, the better our chances of getting away with it."

Something was nagging at Chris. "What if we do find something? Wouldn't it be ruled inadmissible in court?"

"Uh-huh." Joe walked silently into the living room. The drapes were drawn, as they had probably been when Schwartz was taken to the hospital the previous night.

"So what's the point?" Chris followed three feet behind.

"The first point is maybe we get to help Lally through this thing as safely as possible." Joe was very calm. He was always calm when he was doing something, it was sitting on his ass that made him crazy. "The second is we use – *I* use – whatever we find very carefully."

"How?"

"Never mind how." Joe flicked a switch and the crystal chandelier sprang into brilliant life. "Just start looking."

"What I am looking for?" Chris stared around the room.

"You know as much as I do. Just make sure you don't smash anything, and leave everything the way you find it. If you pick up a rumpled cloth or a crooked cushion, study it before you pick it up, and get the angle exactly right when you put it back."

"This place is quite something," Chris said.

"Sure is," Joe agreed grimly, looking at the brocade-covered furniture and velvet drapes and Persian rugs. He gazed up at the woman in the ornately framed portrait that hung above the sofa. The painting Schwartz had claimed had been painted by his non-existent father. Joe ought to have known right off that she was no housewife. He wondered how much of this stuff had come from Eva Schwartz's brothel.

"How about I take the bookshelves?" Chris asked.

"Fine. Flick through every book – there could be papers, plans, whatever – and check behind them carefully. Look for a safe, panels that move, anything."

"What if we find a safe?" Chris wondered where Joe would draw the line.

"We'll worry about that when we do."

There was no safe. Their search of the sitting room and kitchen yielded nothing, the bedroom, bathroom and closets even less. The bed was unmade, so it was clear that Schwartz had been taken out of the apartment in a hurry, yet nowhere was there a single scrap of evidence to incriminate him. Joe felt sick at heart and intensely angry with himself. The search could lose him his job, but worse by far, if it came to a prosecution it could lose them Schwartz. Four people were already dead, and Christ-alone-knew how many were in danger. And Lally . . .

"You still think it's him?" Chris said.

Joe gritted his teeth. "Yes."

"Do we go on looking?"

"There's nowhere left to look, not here anyway."

"Maybe he has a garage or storeroom or something?"

Joe nodded. "Maybe."

"Think the doorman might tell us?"

"For the right price."

It cost Joe fifty bucks to ascertain that Schwartz had no more than a parking spot in the underground car park, and another twenty to persuade the doorman to tell them the number of his bay. The car was a well-polished old Studebaker.

"Let's get the trunk open," Joe said.

"Are you going to force the lock?" Chris was freezing cold. He'd gone from snowy New England to hot Florida and back to even more frigid Chicago, yet he'd hardly noticed the temperature till now.

"Why would I do that?" With a grim smile, Joe pulled out a small bunch of keys and tried just two before the lid groaned open. "Ask me no questions," he said lightly, "and I'll tell you no lies."

Both men peered into the trunk. It was tidy and clean. They saw a spare tyre, a jack and a tool kit. Aside from that, there was a tartan blanket, neatly folded, a US road atlas too large to fit into a glove box, and a big flashlight. It was the car trunk of a methodical, organized man, but it was no help at all.

Hope fading fast, they headed back to the lobby.

"Find what you were looking for?" the doorman asked.

"Not yet," Joe said. "Does Mr Schwartz have a lock-up garage anywhere, or a storeroom maybe?"

"Maybe."

The front doors opened, and an icy blast of air accompanied two young men, both bearded and wearing fur hats, into the building. The doorman greeted them obsequiously, and waited until they'd disappeared on their way upstairs before he returned his attention to Joe and Chris.

"So what now?"

"You were saying something about a storeroom." Joe was as pleasant as he could manage.

"I was?"

"You were," Chris said.

The man gave one of his smiles. "I must be losing my mind."

Joe's wallet emerged again. "Anything coming back?"

"Could be." He stared greedily at the fifty in Joe's hand. "Yeah, it seems to be getting a little less fuzzy."

"This is it," Joe said with finality.

The flicker of despair in Joe's eyes that went way beyond the professional hunger of even the keenest police officer, transmitted itself to the doorman, who would normally have snatched the fifty dollar bill and been grateful for his most profitable morning in years.

"It's not enough."

Chris made a move towards him, but Joe put out a restraining hand, and through his haze of anger, for just an instant, Chris wondered again what he was coming to. He'd never experienced so many moments of aggression in his entire life as he had over the past few days. He was an artist and the father of a ten-year-old girl. He realized he hadn't even thought about Katy for almost four hours.

"It's okay," Joe said, calmingly. "This is it, and he knows it." He held on to the last fifty. "Where is it?"

"What?"

Joe held his temper. "The storeroom."

"I didn't say anything about a storeroom."

"Listen, you bastard – " Chris's voice was almost a snarl.

"Take it easy." The doorman raised both his hands in defence. "It isn't a storeroom, is all I mean."

"So what is it?" Chris demanded.

"An apartment."

"Where?" Joe asked.

"Here."

"Schwartz has two apartments?" Joe was disbelieving.

"Sure has."

"Why didn't you mention it before?" Chris asked.

"You didn't ask."

"What number is this apartment?"

"1510."

"I don't suppose you have a passkey to that either," Joe said.

The doorman shook his head. "But I'm sure Mr Schwartz gave you his set for that one with the others." His smirk was back. "Why don't you go use it?"

Joe and Chris were already at the elevator.

"Hey, what about my fifty?"

"You'll get it when we come down."

Joe punched the fifteenth floor.

"Hey!"

The doors began to close.

"So sue me," Joe called quietly.

There were two locks on the front door of 1510, both newer and tougher than the one on Schwartz's first apartment. Twice, Joe had to stop work when neighbours and visitors passed on their way to and from the elevator.

"This is it, Joe, isn't it?" Chris felt his excitement rising.

"Maybe."

"Don't you have a feeling about it?"

"I'm way past trusting my feelings." The second lock gave.

"All *right*," Chris said.

The first thing they noticed when they entered apartment 1510 was that it was oppressively warm. The next thing they noticed was that the walls of the entrance hall were covered with artwork of varying kinds – paintings, drawings, carvings, tapestries, samplers – all of them relating to dragons. The last thing, though neither of them mentioned it, was that there was an atmosphere in the place that set their teeth on edge.

"Is this weird or what?" Chris murmured.

Silently, Joe shut the front door and drew his gun. "Stay back," he whispered, and headed for the room to the right of the hall. He opened the door and went in, fast but careful. No one home. He put the gun away.

"Shit," he said.

"What?" Tentatively, Chris came through the door. The blinds on the windows were drawn, and the light in the room was an eery kind of early twilight.

"Take a look at those guys," Joe said.

Chris stared into the glass enclosures. "Lizards?" He gave an involuntary shudder. He'd always hated reptiles, knew it was foolish, when they were harmless, but there it was.

"Lizards," Joe confirmed.

The two big green iguanas reposing on wood chips in the largest central vivarium, regarded the men unblinkingly. To their left, four tiny leopard geckos, huddling close together on a decorative branch in their smaller glass-walled home, also watched and waited. The right hand enclosure, medium-sized, its floor covered with sand and a couple of rocks, was empty.

"The big ones look like dinosaurs," Chris said, unable to tear his eyes from the iguanas.

Joe shook his head. "Dragons." The artwork was all over the walls in this room, too. "Our man has a fixation with dragons."

"Does that help us?"

"Not anyway I can think of."

"Weird," Chris said again.

"Let's get moving."

Joe put on the latex gloves again, and Chris did the same. There was just the one room, plus a kitchen, a bathroom and a large walk-in closet. Joe took the kitchen, while Chris went over the bathroom

176

– finding nothing except terry towels, soap, toilet tissue and disinfectant – and then picked his way carefully through the closet.

"Nothing."

"Same here."

They took another look over the main room. But for the lizards, it might have been an ordinary living space. The floor was parquet, without rugs, and it was far more modern in style than Schwartz's main apartment, the furniture – a black leather couch, one matching armchair with footrest, a glass and chrome table with two straight-backed chairs – minimalist, but comfortable enough.

"It's very clean," Chris said. "Almost sterile."

Joe knew. It looked like a regular living room, but every pore of his skin, every hair on his body, every nerve end told him that this was where Schwartz had carried out his work.

"Come on," he said.

"Not much to look through."

Joe nodded towards the state of the art compact disc player and the small black matt-finish cabinet beside it. "You take the discs." He pulled out his keys and selected one of the two small screwdrivers on the chain. "I'll check the speakers."

They set to work in silence, Joe intent, Chris uncomfortably aware of the six sets of reptilian eyes watching them.

"I think they're hungry," he said, trying not to look at them.

"Concentrate," Joe said.

"Right." Chris bent back to his task. "Wagner," he said.

"What?"

"The CDs are all Wagner operas."

Joe started on the bookshelves, cut from the same matt-black wood as the cabinet. Books on German mythology, and on opera, on the care and breeding of lizards, and at least a dozen books, some of them leather bound and gold tooled, on dragons. There was nothing, no neat little parcels of evidence hidden at the back of the shelves, no convenient clues concealed within the books themselves.

They both finished at the same time. Chris knew Duval was going to make them search the enclosures next. He loved Lally, but he hated the idea of getting too close to the big suckers with the pointy crests and dewlaps.

"I'll take the iguanas," Joe volunteered.

"Okay." Chris felt sweet, guilty relief.

The central vivarium was big enough for Joe to get right inside, hardly stooping at all. He took off his jacket and hung it over one of the chrome and glass chairs, then unfastened the glass doors. The bad smell hit him instantly, of the creatures' droppings and a dish of what looked like mouldy dog food in the far corner. Joe stepped through, trying not to inhale, his feet squelching on the damp, soiled wood chips. The big lizards backed away warily, and he got down on his haunches and started digging around with his hands.

Chris watched him, putting off the moment, and then he pulled himself together and got the geckos' door open, grateful that this enclosure wasn't big enough for him to get right inside. The pretty creatures scuttled to the back, and he knelt down on the parquet, took a deep breath and stuck his head and upper body through, raking his hands through the damp, smelly sand on the floor, forcing himself to comb thoroughly, the way the lieutenant was next door, glad of the thin layer of latex that made it possible to feel around effectively without physically touching the dirt.

"Nothing here," he said, after a while. "Except lizard shit."

"Same here." Joe was still feeling around, his frustration starting to mount again. He knew he was right, he just *knew* it, and yet still there was nothing to show for it, no hard evidence, no damned proof that Schwartz was their man.

Chris extracted his head and arms and straightened up, resisting the temptation to brush the dirt off his hands, knowing Duval would make them clean up when they'd finished. "I'll take the other one," he said, emboldened by its emptiness.

"Uh-huh."

This time Chris had to get right inside to make a thorough search, but there was nothing living in there, and it didn't smell too bad. He got down on the floor, and his knees sank right into the coarse sand. There was a rock over to his right. He took a breath, and began feeling around.

"I've got something."

Joe jerked up, hitting his shoulder on the glass wall to his left. "What?"

"I don't know – " Chris felt around some more with his left hand. "Could be paper – " Excited, he plunged his right hand, wrist-deep, into the moist sand, and his fingers closed on it: "It feels like papers, a whole bunch of them, I think – it's hard to tell through the gloves."

Joe was out of the iguana enclosure and right behind him.

"Take it slow and gentle," he said. "Don't rush."

"I'm getting it – "

Out of the corner of his right eye, Joe saw the sand to Chris's side shift and ripple, just a little, like a tiny quake –

"Watch out," he said, too late.

"Jesus!" Chris screamed, a strangled cry of pain.

"What?"

"My *hand!*" Chris tried to keep his voice down, but something down in the sand had his right hand, something with teeth so sharp they were like razors, and they weren't letting go. "Jesus, Duval, it's got my hand!" Desperately he struggled to pull free, but the thing was hanging on. "Help me, for Christ's sake, Duval, *help* me!"

Joe stuck his head and upper body through the opening, but there wasn't enough space for them both inside.

"Webber, there's no room – you have to get out of there!"

"I can't!" Chris tore at his right wrist with his free left hand, but the weight of the damp sand was making it harder – and then suddenly it came clear, popped right out into the air, and there was a creature hanging off his palm – just hanging by its teeth, the thin latex torn, the flesh pierced – and it was a sturdy thing about the size of a big rat, its scaly skin banded with pink and black, and Chris thought he was going to throw up or pass out, but then the pain turned to agony, and he screamed again instead.

"Pull it off!" Joe yelled. "Get out of there so I can help you."

"I *can't!*"

Joe reached in as far as he could, got his right arm around the other man's waist and dragged him out. Chris fell hard onto the wood floor, yelping with pain. Joe grabbed his outdoor gloves and took hold of the creature with both hands, pulling as hard as he could, but its teeth were deeply embedded in Chris's palm and he couldn't dislodge it.

"Do something, Duval, for Christ's sake!" Chris pleaded. "Shoot it – get it off me, just get it *off!*" His head was spinning, the agony was more acute than anything he'd ever experienced.

Joe pulled his gun. "Stay still," he ordered. "Don't move a muscle."

"I don't care if you shoot me, too – just get it *off* me!"

"I'm not going to shoot." Joe raised the weapon and brought the butt down with all his strength on the animal's head. Its grip relaxed instantly, but the teeth were still tangled in the other man's flesh, and Joe had to grasp its jaws to extricate them completely.

"Got it." He flung it away from them, towards the bookcase, and it landed with a dull thud, either dead or stunned. Chris lay very still, his hand a bloodied, torn mess, his face ashen, his eyes closed.

"Webber, you okay?" Joe knelt beside him and felt for his pulse.

"No," Chris said, still not opening his eyes. "I'm not okay."

"Let's get you to an emergency room."

"I think it poisoned me," Chris said through gritted teeth.

"I don't think lizards are venomous," Joe said.

"This one was. Take my word for it."

179

Joe got up and fetched a clean towel from the bathroom, and bound up the hand, but the blood, still flowing freely, soaked right through in seconds.

"Come on," he said, starting to help him up.

Chris opened his eyes. "The papers," he whispered.

"We have to get you fixed up first."

"No, get the *papers*." Chris was starting to sweat, and his whole body was trembling, but Lally was still in danger, and he was damned to hell if this was going to be all for nothing. "He buried them – the son of a bitch buried them – " He shut his eyes again, it was just a tad more bearable with them closed.

Joe got back into the enclosure and dug up the papers, his eyes darting everywhere as he dug, mindful that there might be another of the beasts under the sand. Webber was right, there were a whole bunch of papers, all bound together with elastic, and they were wet and filthy with dirt and blood and excrement, but he knew they were what they'd been looking for, and as he climbed back out, the desire to stop and take a good look at them was almost over-powering. But Webber's colour was getting worse by the minute, and his breathing was a little laboured, and Joe had an idea that he was right about having been poisoned, and if they didn't get him the hell out of there right away, the man might even die.

"You got them all?" Chris murmured weakly.

"Every last one." Joe put on his jacket, rolled up the stinking papers and stuck them inside, zipping himself up tightly. "Shit," he said.

"What?"

"We should take that bastard with us." He went and looked down at it. It looked dead enough. "It'll help them to treat you."

"Shoot it first," Chris said.

"No need." Joe went into the kitchen, took a stack of cloths from one of the cabinets, came back into the living room and wrapped up the lizard, careful, even with his thick gloves, to keep clear of its teeth.

"There were some plastic bags in the closet," Chris said, struggling to stay with it. "Are you sure it's dead?" He was shivering violently now.

"As a doornail." Joe stuck the lizard in a bag and started to help Webber to his feet. "Come on, let's get moving."

Chris leaned heavily against him as they went out through the front door.

"Will the papers be admissible?" he whispered, trying to keep a grip on his mind, trying to stay upright. "I mean, didn't we just burglarize that place?"

"I don't know," Joe said, though he knew damned well that there was every chance their case against Schwartz was going to go down the toilet because of his illegal search, and the thought of that was too unbearable to contemplate. "Don't worry about that now."

They were heading for the elevator.

"They can't stop you using them to help Lally, can they?" Chris's voice was becoming slurred.

"Are you going to pass out on me, Webber?"

"I'm trying not to."

"Good. No, they can't stop me using them to help Lally."

"Duval?"

"What?" The elevator was on its way up, and Joe was wondering what their friendly extortionist doorman would make of them now.

"Are you going to lose your job?"

"Maybe."

"I hope you don't. You're a good cop."

The elevator doors slid open.

"You can give me a reference," Joe said. "Unless we're both in jail."

While Webber was being attended to in the poisons unit at Chicago General, Joe called John Morrissey at the Howe Clinic to check on Lally.

"She's in X-ray as we speak," Morrissey said. "Your man Valdez is with her, supervising. And Detective Cohen's been in touch to say that Dr Ash got back this morning, and that he's getting his team together to fly over here. If he'd known Lally was here, he'd have been here by now – seems his flight from Honolulu stopped over in Chicago."

Joe cursed silently. "How long till they get here?"

"Flight's due in at six-fifteen."

Joe glanced at his watch. Three thirty-three.

"How do you feel about waiting for Ash?"

"Depends what the X-rays show," Morrissey answered. "On the one hand, I'm keen to get your sister's pacemaker out as quickly as possible – on the other hand, since Ash put it in, he may have the edge when it comes to removing it."

Joe was using one of the payphones in the hospital corridor. He faced the wall and kept his voice low. "Tell Valdez I have something," he said. "It may make a difference to whoever does take the thing out."

"How long till you know more?"

"I can't say yet. How long till you have the X-rays?"

181

"Last I heard, Detective Valdez wanted us to up the kilo voltage, use a higher penetration beam to help us see more."

"Mightn't that be harmful?"

"Not at all – in fact, with higher penetration, less X-ray is absorbed in the body."

"How's Lally coping?" Joe's insides were tight as a drum. He didn't know if he could handle hearing that she wasn't coping well. He needed all his resources now to get on with the job, to help her in the most practical way he could.

"On the surface, she's coping remarkably. She's a brave young woman."

"I know she is," Joe said.

When the initial rush to take care of Webber was past, the attending physician came out into the waiting area to tell Joe that his friend had been bitten by a *Heloderma suspectum*, more commonly known to them as the Arizona Gila monster.

"That and its Mexican cousin," the young, dark-eyed doctor said, unmistakably excited despite his work fatigue, "are the only known poisonous members of the lizard family."

"What are you doing for him?" Joe asked.

"Unfortunately, there's no antivenin for the Gila monster – "

"But he's going to make it, isn't he?"

"Fatalities are very rare, Lieutenant, but we don't have too many statistics, and I've never seen a Gila victim first-hand, so you can rest assured we'll all be watching Mr Webber very closely."

"He looked pretty sick to me." Joe was worried as hell. Webber had been vomiting and semi-conscious when he'd last seen him, and his hand, with the cloth removed, had looked a bloody mess.

"I'm told it's an agonizing bite," the doctor explained, "so part of the physical reaction is shock. Mr Webber's BP and pulse were way down when you first got him to us, but we've already seen an improvement there. He's been given a corticosteroid and tetanus toxoid, and he'll be needing some heavy-duty analgesia for pain."

"Can I see him?"

"I'd wait a while. We're going to be running a bunch of tests and, as I told you, keeping a real close eye on him. Best for him if he gets a little rest."

"How bad's the damage to his hand?" Joe thought about the way Lally had looked at Webber at O'Hare. "He's an artist."

"Too soon to tell." The doctor was already moving, on his way back to business.

"Great," Joe said, to himself. "Really great."

The clock on the wall told him it was a quarter to four. Lally had been at the Howe Clinic for almost three hours. Nine floors up in this same hospital, Jess was lying in her bed, fighting as hard as she could to hold onto their unborn child. In Memorial Hospital, about three miles away, Frederick Schwartz, mass murderer, was being cared for like the solid, deserving citizen they'd all, deep down, thought he was – for hadn't he, Cohen, Lipman and Valdez all found good old Fred the most plausible, most dependable – most *likeable*, for fuck's sake – individual at Hagen Pacing?

Every part of Joe that could churn was turning back-flips, including his brain. The proof he'd been praying for, blood- and shit-stained, but conclusive nonetheless, was still rolled up inside his zipped-up jacket. Enough evidence, Joe guessed, to put Schwartz away for the duration. Except that Lieutenant Joseph Duval had broken all the rules and screwed the whole thing up. He couldn't even hold the documents back for a few hours, in case the blueprints and figures he'd had just a brief glimpse of in apartment 1510 might be of help to Ash and Morrissey when they took out Lally's pacemaker.

That's what matters now. Saving Lally and the others.

Three forty-nine and counting.

Joe forced himself to the coffee machine, commanded himself to cut out the panic and to choose a course of action.

Under the circumstances, there was only one course left.

He dumped his polystyrene cup in the nearest trashcan, and headed, under heavily clouded skies that promised a fresh load of snow, for Chicago Memorial. He stayed at the hospital for just fifteen minutes, keeping away from Schwartz but talking to one of his physicians and one of his nurses.

By the time he got back in the Saab, Joe knew, beyond reasonable doubt, that Schwartz's sickness had nothing to do with the flu, and that it was almost certainly connected with a bite they had found on his heel – probably, Joe guessed, from the same venomous lizard that had torn Webber's hand half to shreds in apartment 1510.

By the time he'd started the motor and was pulling out into the noisy, hectic city street, the new plan was already three-quarters formulated in Joe's mind.

33

Monday, January 25th

As Monday afternoon dragged slowly by, his fever continuing to rise, the man named Frederick Schwartz lay under a single sheet in his private hospital room, and let himself drift back into the past again. He preferred it there, even the darkest memories, for remembering the wickedness reinforced his strength, steeled his will against them.

The chapel. His shiny black shoes. The long white scratch on the pew. The coffin. He was eleven years old and he understood precisely what was happening. Mother's body lay inside that box, cold and waxy and unreal. Her golden hair neatly curled, framing her face, her bright lipstick and pale powder applied by the undertaker, almost, though not quite, the way she liked it. Mother was dead. He would never see her or touch her or hear her again. And in just a few more minutes, her body and the coffin would be gone from his sight, for ever, to be consumed by the fire.

She had planned her own funeral. The doctors had said she would live to a ripe old age, but she hadn't believed them. And she was right, the doctors had lied, which was why he was sitting on the front pew next to his cousin Beatrice, who had worked in Mother's special place, listening to the music Mother had chosen. Her beloved Wagner. He felt like crying, but his eyes remained dry, for she had told him not to weep.

"Heroes don't cry," she had said, "unless they're all alone."

The music ended, and the small congregation knelt again to pray. A splinter dug into his left knee and he concentrated on the pain, pushed the knee harder into the wooden floor, and when he rose again, his eyes bright but still dry, cousin Beatrice whispered: "It's okay to cry, Freddy." And he raised his chin high, and his expression was full of contempt.

"Heroes don't cry," he said.

The moment came closer. When the doors would open and the coffin would slide away to be burned. Mother said she had always wanted to be cremated, like Brünnhilde on her husband's funeral pyre in *Götterdämmerung*.

Wagner rose again, soaring and magnificent. He watched the doors smoothly open, was intent now on Mother, hidden from view in her box, gliding on her way to the flames and to heaven. He felt suddenly happy for her, for it was as she had wanted it, beautiful and heroic and more mysterious in its dignity than being put into the earth. And he wondered if she had already found his father, or if they would not find each other till after the cremation.

The doors closed again. The congregation rose, but still he sat, until Beatrice nudged him, and he stood, and slowly, silently, they began to file out of the chapel.

The explosion was massive, deafening, cutting off the music, flinging them all to the ground. He could not speak, could scarcely breathe, but he was not hurt, his arms and legs still moved. Someone screamed, someone wept.

Slowly, painfully, he sat up. The doors to the furnace had disappeared and the cavern beyond was filled with flame and black smoke. Hot cinders floated through the air like fireflies.

The coffin was gone. Mother was gone.

He'd thought that the last crime against her, but then they wrote about it in the *Tribune*, and on the bus on the way to school, he saw two women reading that page of the newspaper, and he watched their faces, waiting for their horror.

They laughed.

They covered their open mouths with their hands and rolled their eyes and shook with mirth. He stared at their ugliness, at their wickedness, and then, slowly and clearly, he saw, for the first time, how right Mother had been to warn him about the dragons that lived in the world outside their home.

"They take on many forms," she had said.

She was right.

34

Monday, January 25th

A l Hagen professed to be well enough to go over the documents with Joe and Howard Leary. His hospital room at Memorial, eight floors above Schwartz's own room, was brightly lit and cheery with flowering plants, and Hagen himself looked a whole lot better than he had when Joe had last seen him at home just over a week before.

"I'll be out of here by tomorrow morning," he told them. "The doc only had me admitted because I passed out in the street, but it was nothing much, just the after-effects of that damned flu."

"This whole fiasco can't have helped," Leary said.

"Are you sure you're up to this?" Joe asked, pulling up one of the chairs to the bedside.

"Your sister and the others need all the help they can get," Hagen said, still heavily burdened by responsibility.

"I appreciate that, sir."

Leary sat down on the other side of Hagen's bed. He was natty in a well-cut sports jacket, his red hair crisply combed as always, his eyes avid with curiosity. "What do you have for us, Lieutenant?"

The documents were in an attaché case, leaning up against Joe's right leg.

"Before I show them to you," he began, "I need to ask if you're willing to keep this off the record." He paused. "I also have to request that you don't ask me where or how I obtained the papers you're going to see. I have no right to make these demands, but if you do

186

ask me any question on that score, I won't answer them, except to tell you that even the smallest comment from me could ultimately jeopardize this whole case."

Hagen and Leary exchanged glances.

"I have no problem with that," Leary said.

"Nor I," Hagen confirmed.

Joe opened the attaché case and laid the documents out on the bed. Each individual sheet of paper had been separated and encased in a plastic folder.

"First objective," he said, taking a smaller slip of paper from an inside pocket, "is to crosscheck this serial number with those on the documents." He paused. "There are a lot of numbers – I wish I could offer you more people to assist you, but under the circumstances that's not possible."

Hagen read the serial number. "Your sister's?"

"Yes." Joe looked right at him. "I have no right to ask this of you either. If it's too much for you, you should tell me."

"Nothing is too much."

They worked together. The serial number of Lally's pacemaker came up on two out of the six documents.

"I wish it weren't so," Hagen said, "but there isn't any doubt."

Joe felt sick to his stomach.

"We should get to work on the rest," Leary said. "Why not take a break, Lieutenant? You can't help any more."

Joe stood up. "I'll be outside." He paused. "We don't have too long."

"We know that," Leary said and, glancing up briefly, he smiled at Joe. It was the first genuine, warm smile that Joe had seen on his face, and it filled him with a new brand of despair. He had always functioned on instincts as much as hard facts, and faced with Leary, Hagen, Ashcroft and Schwartz in those early days, he had picked Leary – as had the others – for his first choice as bad guy. Over the years, Joe had gone through frequent bouts of self-doubt, had always been his own worst critic, but never in his whole career to date, had he felt as ineffectual, as guilty of poor judgment, as *impotent*, as he did right now.

He gave them twenty minutes, then went back inside.

"What do we have?"

"Everything," Hagen said, "and nothing."

Joe waited, his throat so tight and dry it was painful.

"Tell me." Joe sat down.

"They're remarkable," Leary said. "Minutely, perfectly detailed records of everything that was done. Ingredients, method, projected results."

"What's the bad news?" Joe asked.

"It's a game," Hagen answered. "He – whoever this is – "

"We all know who it is," Leary said, grimly.

"No." Joe's tone was firm, almost harsh. "We don't. You mustn't."

"Whoever this is," Leary went on, "is playing with us." He took a breath. "There are six documents, all of them variations on a theme. We know how he did it. We know how he turned our pacemakers into bombs. But the crucial details – quantities, timer settings and serial numbers – are different enough in each set to make them useless."

"But that's not the worst of it," Hagen said. "All the documents give details of homemade pacemaker batteries created on the outside to look identical to the real thing, but each containing a smaller ba.tery, some circuitry, a detonator and a timing device to count down." He swallowed. "Four of the documents detail batteries with a half-ounce of plastique explosive added, though not all."

"And the other two?" Joe wasn't breathing.

Leary took over, his voice stronger than Hagen's. "If either of these two documents is the real thing, we're looking at two alternative forms of detonation. One solely operated by timer, as in the others. One by a kind of hair trigger, using conductive glue."

"In other words – " Hagen was looking sicker again.

"They could blow any time," Leary said.

Joe felt as if everything inside him had stopped again.

"Especially during explantation," Leary added.

"And correct me if I'm wrong," Hagen said, softly, "but I believe I've read that like plastique, conductive glue doesn't show up on X-rays."

No one spoke for several seconds.

"Quite a game," Leary said.

"Unless we can establish which – if any – is the authentic document," Hagen said, "we still won't know precisely which, or how many, devices have been sabotaged – "

"Or which of the detonation methods have been used," Leary added.

Hagen's tone and face were still gentle but grim. "And since your sister's number tallies with one document detailing plastique only, and one detailing the conductive glue, we have no way of knowing just how volatile her pacemaker is."

"If either of those documents is the authentic one," Leary clarified, "it's very bad news. If it's one of the others, it's possible that the only real danger to her could be that the smaller battery would have a shorter life."

Joe was back on his feet. There was only one person who could tell them what they needed to know, and so far as Joe was concerned, it was a rock solid bet that a man capable of playing these kinds of games with people's lives would not volunteer the information unless he felt compelled to do so.

Everything they needed now was locked inside Schwartz's head.

He drove to the Howe Clinic, found Valdez and Morrissey and looked at Lally's X-rays. They looked past the stainless steel casing of the pacemaker's battery case, and there was a smaller dummy battery and the circuitry that told them, without a grain of doubt, that Lally's device was certainly one of Schwartz's, though they couldn't tell if it was benign or deadly. Joe felt like going back to Memorial Hospital and killing the son of a bitch with his bare hands, but instead he took Valdez and Morrissey into his confidence – the more people who knew about the mess, the more trouble his career was in, potentially, but that was another story for another day – and Valdez confirmed pretty much what Hagen had said about conductive glue.

"Bombers use it instead of running wires – it conducts electricity and we can't see a goddamned thing on X-rays."

"What about magnetic resonance scanning?" Joe wanted to know.

"Magnetic resonance imaging," Morrissey corrected. "Unfortunately, MRI isn't suitable for pacemaker wearers."

They all looked back at the lit X-ray pictures on the wall.

"So we could be looking at plastique and this glue stuff right now," Joe said, "and just not be able to see it."

"You got it," Valdez said, grimly.

"What now?" Morrissey asked.

"We need the right document," Valdez said.

Joe said nothing, fought to hold himself together, to use his anger and his fear, to pump it all into strength and clarity.

"What are you going to do, Lieutenant?" Morrissey asked softly.

"I'm going to get what we need," Joe said.

The Howe Clinic felt more like a large, sumptuous and tranquil private house than a hospital. There were flowers everywhere, not grand displays, but lovely, simple splashes of colour charmingly arranged to cheer and calm. The paintings were mostly landscapes, and framed photographs of grateful patients hung on almost every wall.

When Joe came in to see her, Lally, ordered by Morrissey to rest, was compromising by sitting up, still fully dressed, on top of the bed in her pretty pastel-coloured bedroom on the third floor. Hugo, gaunt from worry and lack of sleep, was sitting in an armchair on the window side of the bed.

"Hi, gorgeous," Joe said, lightheartedly, as he entered the room and bent to kiss the top of her head. "You look okay – are you okay?" He glanced at Hugo. "Barzinsky, you look like hell."

"Thank you," Hugo said.

"I am okay," Lally said, "but I think I'm going a little stir-crazy."

"You've only been here a few hours," Joe pointed out.

"I'd like to be back in Key West."

"I wish you could be."

"How long before they do something?" Hugo asked.

"A little while yet," Joe replied.

"You know we're waiting for Dr Ash," Lally said.

"I think it's nuts to wait," Hugo said for about the twelfth time.

"What's another few hours?" Lally's sense of unreality had returned with the X-ray session, though she thought that perhaps the tranquillizer Dr Morrissey had persuaded her to swallow had something to do with it.

"Can't you talk some sense into your sister?" Hugo pleaded with Joe.

"I agree with her," Joe said. "There's no imminent danger."

"How can you *say* that?"

"Easily," Joe lied. "The people who died all had their pacemakers implanted for much longer than Lally's had hers, so another few hours aren't going to make any difference."

"Why don't you trust Dr Morrissey?" Hugo wanted to know.

"It has nothing to do with not trusting him," Lally tried to explain. "But Dr Ash and Joanna King and Bobby Goldstein are all on their way, and since they put the thing into my chest – since Dr Ash was the one who threaded those wires through my veins into my heart – I figure no one else knows his handiwork as well as he does. Surely that makes sense to you, Hugo?"

Hugo looked at Joe, saw him nod, almost imperceptibly.

"I guess so," he said.

"Where's Chris?" Lally asked Joe.

"At my house, sleeping."

"Good," she said. "He must be exhausted."

"We're all exhausted," Hugo said, a little tetchily.

"Why don't you get some sleep?" Lally asked. "I keep telling you to."

"I'm not leaving you."

"I'm perfectly fine," she said.

Joe was mindful of time slipping away. "I have to go, sweetheart," he said gently. "Is there anything you need?"

Lally shook her head. "Not a thing." She smiled at him. "It's really a lovely place, don't you think? There's no hospital smell, and it's so *quiet*. When no one's talking, and the TV's off, you can hardly hear a sound."

"It's a fine place," Joe agreed. He saw no necessity to tell Lally that the reason her room was so silent was that every other patient in her wing had been moved, prior to her arrival, to a safe distance. What Morrissey had said at O'Hare about others not being at risk was true enough as far as it went, but as Tony Valdez had said hundreds of times, anyone who was complacent about any kind of bomb was either insane or very dumb. Bombs were unpredictable, and though Joe was still praying that Lally's pacemaker was one of Schwartz's benign dummies, if it wasn't, there was no way of knowing for sure that it would behave in the same way Marie Ferguson's or Alice Douglas's had.

"How's Jess doing?" Lally asked.

"She's doing great. No more pains, and they'll probably be sending her home – or at least to her mom's – tomorrow."

"That's wonderful." Lally saw the urgency in her brother's eyes, and reached for his hand. "You can go, Joe, honestly. I really am okay."

"I know you are." Joe held onto her hand for another moment. "You do what they tell you, sis, okay?"

"I promise." Lally paused. "Will you come back before they operate?"

"You bet I will."

He forced himself to walk slowly to the door. The instant it had closed behind him, he began to run.

It was twenty minutes before six.

Commander Jackson had a dinner to attend. He was sitting behind his desk, resplendent in a tuxedo, and he was impatient to get away.

"This had better be good, Duval. Mrs Jackson is waiting, not to mention the one hundred and ninety-eight other people expecting to hear my speech."

"It isn't good, sir," Joe said. "What I'm hoping it will be is off the record, at least for another twenty-four hours."

"What have you done, Duval?" The words were uttered on a sigh. "Or can I guess?" Jackson shook his head in frustration. "For the love of God, tell me you didn't search Schwartz's apartment."

"I wish I could."

Jackson stood up, walked around the desk, checked the door was properly closed and pulled down the blinds on the window through which he could see and be seen by the detectives in the open plan office outside.

"You'd better sit down," he told Joe.

They faced one another, the desk separating them.

"You need coffee?" the commander asked.

"No, thank you, sir."

"You better tell me then."

"Are we off the record?"

"Maybe."

"I need to know, Commander."

"You don't need to know anything, Duval. You just need to tell me the whole miserable fucking truth and when you've finished, you need to keep your mouth shut."

Jackson seldom swore. Joe knew it was not a good sign.

He told him everything.

"Is that it?"

"It is." Joe waited.

The commander's jaw was set tight. "So, to sum up your day's work, you not only ignored my express orders and conducted not one, but *two* illegal searches – you also broke into both apartments, you bribed one civilian and involved a second in your crimes, which have resulted in his injury and hospitalization."

Joe knew the time had come to keep his mouth shut.

"And now you're asking me to ignore all that, and to let you run with the case for another twenty-four hours."

Again, Joe said nothing.

"Do I have that right, Lieutenant?"

"Yes, sir."

"Tell me again why you think I should give you that time."

"Because I think I can finish it."

"What you mean is, you think you can help give your sister a better chance of survival." Jackson's voice was stony.

"I mean I think I can do that," Joe said as steadily as he could, "and break Schwartz at the same time."

"Using inadmissible evidence." The documents lay on the desk, plastic folders piled almost three inches high.

"Plus what we now know about his condition."

"Don't tell me any more." Jackson's dark eyes were narrow and very sharp. "Give me one good reason why I shouldn't just suspend you right now and hand the case over to someone who understands our state and federal laws."

"Whose hands would be tied because my searches were illegal."

"Your hands are tied too, Duval."

"Only as far as the evidence I found during the search."

The commander stood up, walked over to the dark wood wall on his left, and stared at the photograph that included Marie Ferguson's father. For several moments, he remained deep in thought, and then, at last, he turned around.

"Is the rest of this plan of yours legal?"

"It is."

"Is it ethical?"

Joe hesitated only briefly. "It may not be strictly orthodox, but in my opinion it is ethical."

"In your opinion." Jackson didn't trouble to hide his sarcasm.

"Yes, sir."

"Does this plan involve any other member of the police department?"

"No, sir." Joe paused. "Except for the Bomb and Arson team already on alert for Lally's surgery."

"Does anyone know where the documents were found?"

"No, sir. I believe that Hagen and Leary have a pretty shrewd idea that Schwartz is our man, but they've agreed to ask no questions."

"Do you believe" – the commander looked Joe straight and hard in the eye – "do you honestly believe that my letting you go ahead with this may save the lives of others as well as your sister?"

Joe looked back steadily. "Lally's the guinea pig for every other one of Schwartz's victims. If her pacemaker does turn out to be a bomb, we'll be able to assist other hospitals around the country."

"And do you believe you can still get me a case against Schwartz?"

"I think I can."

Jackson waited several more seconds. "You have till eight o'clock tomorrow morning."

It was more than Joe had hoped for. "Thank you, Commander."

"You'll be on your own. I won't let another officer help you on this, not Lipman, not even Cohen."

"I understand that."

"And after the deadline, you may be on suspension."

"Yes, sir."

"I want your word on something, Duval."

"Yes, Commander."

"If you realize at any point during the next" – Jackson checked

193

his watch – "fourteen hours, that you've made another mistake – that it's going wrong – you come to me right away. Other than that, I don't want to know. The only other news I want from you is a result."

"Yes, Commander."

"You realize you could lose your job, whichever way it goes."

"Yes, sir."

"Which is a goddamned waste."

"Thank you, sir."

"Don't thank me. I'm about as angry and disgusted with you right now as I've ever been with any officer under my command."

"I understand that, sir." Joe stood up. "I'd better get going."

"You had." Jackson paused. "I'll pray for your sister."

"Thank you," Joe said again.

In silence, they walked back to the front door.

"So far as I'm concerned, Duval, you have not been here."

"No, sir."

"That's as much for myself, as for the sake of the case. I'm not prepared to stand up with you on this one."

"I wouldn't expect you to," Joe said.

Jackson's hand was on the door knob.

"If you go down, you go down alone."

It was snowing when Joe walked out of the station. He unlocked his car door and got in. The clock on the dashboard read twenty-five minutes after six. If flights were running to schedule, Lucas Ash and his team would have landed by now and would shortly be on their way to the Howe Clinic, and before much longer, everyone and almost everything would be in place for Lally's surgery. The rest – the missing link – was still in Schwartz's head, and it was entirely up to Joe now to extract it.

The commander was right. He had never felt so alone in his life.

35

Monday, January 25th

H ad Sean Ferguson not been drinking whisky in John Morrissey's private sitting room at the clinic when he arrived, Joe would probably not have contemplated involving yet another civilian. But the grieving man was so avid to help, and without him, Joe knew, they might not even have gotten this far, and for better or worse, Joe was still working on instinct.

"I have a plan," he told them. "And I need your help."

"You've got it," Ferguson said.

"Don't be so hasty, Sean," Morrissey cautioned.

Ferguson ignored him. "Anything you need, Lieutenant."

Joe told them what he needed.

"I'm told that Schwartz is on the way to a full recovery," he summed up, "but at this stage, he still feels lousy. I want him to go on feeling lousy, because the worse he feels, the better chance I believe we have of making him see our point of view."

"Why can't you just confront him with the documents?" Morrissey asked.

"I've told you why," Joe said, bluntly. "Because I found them during an illegal search. Because I screwed up. Because I think Schwartz would call in his attorney and then we'd be dead in the water."

"Is he right?" Ferguson asked Morrissey, and took a sip of whisky. "Could Schwartz be made to go on feeling lousy?"

"Without endangering his life," Joe added.

"Certainly he could," Morrissey said. "If a physician was willing to do it." He paused. "There's no way Chicago Memorial would permit a patient to be duped in that way." He looked directly at Joe. "Which is why you want Schwartz transferred to the Howe."

"If you agree."

"I have no particular problem with bringing him here." Morrissey's face was grim. "It's the rest of your plan that goes against everything I believe in."

"Just a few harmless drugs," Joe said. "And a little extra heat."

"You make it sound so easy, Lieutenant."

"John isn't a natural risk-taker," Ferguson told Joe. "He's already committed the clinic to a degree of danger by agreeing to let this surgery go ahead here – which I know he's doing as much for Marie as for your sister, if you'll forgive my saying, Lieutenant."

"I know that," Joe said. "It makes me no less grateful."

"But now, if I have this right," Ferguson went on, "you're asking him to break more moral and ethical codes than I can even begin to count. I can understand why you're willing to put your career on the line, Lieutenant, but John Morrissey's a doctor, not a cop, and a damned fine one, and this city's already lost one good physician in my wife."

Joe held his breath.

"I, on the other hand," Ferguson said, a new glint in his eye, "have nothing to lose."

"What are you suggesting, Sean?" Morrissey asked.

"I think I'd make a fair physician."

"You'd make a lousy physician," Morrissey said.

"Correct me if I've misunderstood" – Ferguson looked at Joe – "but once the drugs have been administered, your plan wouldn't call for me to do any actual doctoring, would it? It's mostly talk, isn't it?"

"That's about right," Joe agreed.

"It's insanity," Morrissey said flatly. "It could get you arrested."

Ferguson was matter-of-fact. "Marie is dead, John. This man killed her. She was thirty-two years old, and she was my life."

The three men were silent.

"Okay," Morrissey said, at last.

Joe waited, every muscle taut.

"I'll allow beta blockers to be given, which will slow his heart-rate, and I'll allow the heat in his room to be turned up." Morrissey paused. "And if you two want to do a little play-acting in this clinic, I'll turn a blind eye."

Joe breathed again. "Thank you, Doctor."

"You do know how unethical this is, don't you, Lieutenant?"

"I do."

"And you understand the risks, to us all?"

"Yes, sir, I do."

"I'm far from convinced that I'll be able to persuade Memorial to let us have him."

"Just make them understand we won't be endangering him," Joe said.

"I'd say that was another debatable point, Lieutenant."

Joe said nothing more.

While Morrissey spoke, behind closed doors in his office, with the Chief of Medicine at Chicago Memorial, Joe, too hyped up either to cat nap or to visit with Lally or go anywhere near Hugo Barzinsky, paced the Persian rug with Sean Ferguson in Morrissey's sitting room.

When Morrissey came back in, Joe's pulse-rate went sky-high.

"They bought it."

"Thank God."

"What are we waiting for?" Ferguson asked.

Morrissey held up both hands, slowing them down. "I gave my word that the patient's health will not be endangered, and that their responsibility for him will terminate the instant he's off their premises."

Joe checked his watch again. It was twenty minutes after seven.

"Let's do it," he said.

"Lucas Ash should be here any minute," Morrissey reminded Joe. "How much do you want me to tell him?"

"Nothing at all about what we're doing," Joe replied. "Just tell him that we may be getting close to having vital information about the make-up of Lally's pacemaker, and that it could be deadly to start without it."

"Makes sense to me," Ferguson said.

Morrissey sighed. "The more we know, the better, no doubt about that."

"So are we agreed?" Joe asked.

No one dissented.

"All right," he said.

"Has anyone heard from Chris?" Lally asked Hugo at seven twenty-six.

"Not as far as I know."

"He must still be sleeping," Lally said.

The tranquillizer she'd been given a few hours ago was wearing off, and though she hated the muzzy feeling it had given her, the downside was that she was now a whole lot more alert than she wanted to be.

"Can I do anything for you, sweetheart?" Hugo asked.

"No." She got out of bed for the tenth time in the past hour, went over to the window on the left side of the room and stared out into the dark.

"You're supposed to stay in bed."

"Like it would make a difference."

"The doc must have his reasons."

Lally didn't turn around. "Dr Morrissey has no more idea about what is or isn't going to happen to me than you have, Hugo. The only reason they want me to stay in bed is to keep me out of everyone else's way."

"My reading," Hugo said, "is that they want you to rest as much as possible in case your pacemaker isn't up to doing its job as well as it ought."

"Thanks, Hugo." Lally turned away from the window. "Just what I needed to hear to make me feel better."

"It sounded worse than I meant it to," he said wretchedly.

"No, it didn't. Either my heart explodes or stops."

"Shut the hell up, Lally," Hugo said, with feeling.

Lally sat down moodily at the built-in dressing table, and stared into the mirror. She looked normal enough. She'd changed into her favourite Garfield nightshirt that travelled most places with her for comfort. Her hair hung in a single long loose plait over her right shoulder. Her face still glowed from the Florida sunshine. Only her eyes, unmade-up, weary and afraid, betrayed the way she really felt.

"You're just grouchy because Chris went off to sleep." Hugo tried a change of tack.

"I am not," she said tartly. "He spent days looking for us, and then that flight – of course he had to get some sleep."

"Then you're grouchy because he's slept for so long."

"If I am grouchy, it has nothing to do with Chris." Lally's voice grew tighter. "The real reason I'm grouchy" – suddenly she was on the brink of tears – "is because I feel as if I'm sitting here on some kind of glitzy Death Row, waiting for someone to come and tell me if I'm going to be reprieved or not."

Appalled, Hugo jumped up. "I'm so sorry." He bent and put his arms around her shoulders as the tears, at last, began to fall. "I didn't mean to make you feel worse – I know how scared you are – "

198

"I don't think scared quite covers it." Letting the hot tears flow, Lally couldn't figure out how she'd made it this far without weeping. "I'm sorry," she sobbed against his sleeve, "I can't help it."

"You're being so brave," Hugo said, despising himself, for now he was crying too, and that was no help to her at all. "Oh, God, look at me – I'm sorry, sweetheart – "

Lally lifted her face to look at him, and managed a smile.

"Your nose," she said, "is so red."

"You're no oil painting yourself," Hugo said.

She drew away, pulled several tissues out of the Kleenex carton on the dressing table, handed two to Hugo and blew her own nose with the others. Briefly, she glanced back at her reflection, then looked away again. She thought of Chris's portrait of her in her dance clothes. She wondered if she would ever take a class again, ever see her studio again, or the house.

She wondered, more than anything, why Chris hadn't called.

Chris had never been especially obsessed by a fear of dying. Like most people, he had occasionally wondered what his final hours would feel like, had been torn between the desire to be able to prepare, to die well, and the hope that he would go fast and easily, preferably when he was asleep.

He knew now what dying felt like. It felt like hell, but what hurt more than the agony in his hand and arm, what was squeezing the breath and strength out of him even more than the effects of the deadly venom in his blood-stream, was his inability to talk to Katy or Lally. He was glad, he supposed, that neither of them could see him this way – especially his sweet little Katy, and she'd be okay, he knew she would, once Andrea got herself back on her feet, and Andrea would, she'd have no choice, with him gone. But to leave Lally this way, when they'd hardly begun, to abandon her when she was so vulnerable and frightened and in such mortal danger, without another word, without a chance to hold her or to tell her how he felt about her, that he loved her more than he'd ever loved any woman, that he'd do anything for her, that he'd give his *life* for her. And he supposed, in a way, that he had done just that, and maybe that should have been some comfort to him, and maybe if he could know that Lally was out of danger, that finding those documents had been enough to save her, he might be able to feel a degree of solace. But as it was, here he was, all alone in this awful, painful, lonely place, tortured by tubes and needles and surrounded by well-meaning strangers, and he was dying, *dying*, for fuck's sake, because of a stupid, goddamned lizard, and he didn't know if Lally was being operated on, or if it was over, or if it had even begun . . .

At twenty after eight, Frederick Schwartz woke from a restless, dream-laden sleep to find a dark-suited man and two white-coated orderlies with a gurney at his bedside.

"What's going on?" His vision and voice were fuzzy from sleep, fever and drugs.

"You're being transferred to another hospital, Mr Schwartz." The man in the suit held his medical chart and a sheaf of papers.

"Now? Why?" Schwartz peered at the man's name tag, but couldn't quite make it out. "Why can't I stay here?"

"Because you need specialist care, which we're not equipped for here."

"What kind of care?" Schwartz felt vague, out of control.

"I'm told you're going to a clinic with a specialist poison and venom unit, where the bite on your heel can be attended to properly," the man said.

"Is that really necessary?"

"I'm sure it is." The man held out a sheet of paper on a clipboard. "I need you to check this over and sign, please, sir."

"What is it?"

"It's a document confirming your discharge from Chicago Memorial. All straightforward, but I'd like you to be sure to read it before you sign."

Schwartz took the clipboard. He was still weak, though less so than the previous day. "I feel a little better, actually."

"I'm glad to hear that."

"I don't really understand why they're moving me now. I figured the treatment was working."

"I'm just following orders, sir. All I know is they ran some tests, which showed that the poison in your system is still creating a few problems." The man smiled. "I'm sure there's no cause for concern."

Schwartz tried to focus on the man's face. "Are you a physician?"

"No, sir, I'm just an administrator." The man paused. "Would you like me to obtain a copy of the test results, sir?"

A wave of nausea gripped Schwartz's stomach. Better to get this over and done with. "No," he said, "I guess I can trust you." He held out his right hand for the pen.

"Thank you, sir."

"Better safe than sorry," Schwartz said, and signed.

"Always," the man said.

* * *

Lucas Ash came to see Lally in her room at eight thirty-five.

"Well, what in blue blazes am I doing here?" he said as soon as he walked into her room and saw her. "You're blooming, Lally."

"That's fine, doctor." Lally grinned at him from the bed. "So can't we just get on a plane together and fly straight back to Massachusetts?"

"Suits me, but I understand the nervous Nellies at the airlines won't let you do that." Ash sat on the edge of her bed and took both Lally's hands in his. "So I guess we'll just have to humour them, and get this nonsense over with as quickly as possible, okay?"

"Okay." Lally liked the feel of his strong hands on her icy ones. "You don't really believe my pacemaker could be one of those, do you, doctor?"

"Do you think, under the circumstances, you could call me Lucas?"

"You're evading my question, Lucas."

"I don't know is the honest answer, Lally." Ash paused. "I know that when I checked it over before I implanted it – when I held it in the palm of my hand and touched it with my fingers – it looked and felt exactly as it was supposed to. I've implanted dozens of that specific type, all of them made by Hagen Pacing."

Lally had forgotten the intense, violet blue of his eyes, such a very different blue from Chris's. She fixed her gaze on them. "That still doesn't mean it's impossible that it is a bomb, does it?"

"No, Lally. I'm afraid it doesn't."

She took her hands out of his. "It was very, very kind of you to make the journey, Doctor."

"Lucas," he corrected, gently. "And since I was the one who put the damned thing in, I see no special kindness in being the one to take it out again."

"Dr Morrissey said that the others were coming, too."

"Joanna and Bobby are here. They're helping to set things up now."

A new kick of nervousness hit Lally's stomach. "So it won't be long?"

"A little while yet," the doctor said. "Try to be patient, okay?"

"Do I have a choice?"

In final preparation for his confrontation with Schwartz, Joe went back to the killer's second apartment. He took a good, long look around. He studied every painting, the dust jacket of every book, the sleeve notes of every compact disc, the meticulously embroidered words of every sampler.

The surviving lizards watched him as he worked. Joe felt their eyes on him and experienced anger for their helplessness. From an early age, he had disliked zoos, had hated seeing animals in cages. These creatures would, if they were lucky, end up in Chicago Zoo, or with some other private collector. More probably, they'd end up being destroyed.

It had not been difficult concluding that the lizards represented dragons to Schwartz. It was not hard coming to the realization that there was a connection for the killer between these mythical creatures and his mother, the madam, though apart from the messages and warnings contained in those homespun samplers, those unsettling gifts to her son, there was no way of knowing just how bizarre a mother Eva Schwartz had been. *Pretty bizarre*, Joe guessed. And responsible, if not for the manner of her death or its aftermath, for the life that had come before, the life that had begun the warping of her son.

Leaving Schwartz's apartment, Joe called Chicago General, first to check on Webber's condition and then to talk to Jess.

"My bag's as good as packed," she said. "Ready to go back to Mom's." Her voice was cool, the atmosphere between them, even on the telephone line, strained and unhappy. "Unless, that is, I get to come home."

"Not quite yet, Jess," Joe said. "Soon."

"Are you coming by later?"

"I'm not sure. I hope so."

"Still on the same case?"

"Yes."

"How much longer?"

"Not long."

"I want to come home," Jess said. "Sal wants to come home."

"And I want you both there. But it's too soon."

Jess's voice was searching. Joe could imagine her eyes. "Do you still swear you're not in danger?"

"I swear it," he said.

"But you are in trouble."

"Nothing I can't resolve."

"I wish you'd tell me."

"I know."

But he told her nothing, about Lally, or about Schwartz, or about the possible imminent demise of his career. He knew it was wrong not to tell her, that it went against everything he believed in about marriage, but he could not afford to diminish his strength at this point, and so he tried to convince himself that his silence was for the sake of their unborn baby, and he said nothing.

He needed, badly, to confide in someone. More than anyone, he wanted to talk to Sol Cohen, to explain to his wise old pal why he was risking his whole career, why he was letting himself abandon the solid rock upon which the world of police work was founded, in order to be sucked down into the insane nether world of Frederick Schwartz for a battle that went against every rule and every ethic. But Joe could not and would not draw Sol into this day's madness. God knew he'd involved too many people already.

Anyway, he wasn't sure if he could explain it all, even to himself.

Sick as he felt, Schwartz knew that something was up. The first doubt had tickled him a few moments after he'd signed the discharge papers at Chicago Memorial, and then, during the ambulance ride to the clinic, he had begun to realize that something untoward was happening to him. For one thing, he knew that he was recovering. He still had a fever, was still in discomfort, but it was less severe than it had been, and he felt more lucid. For another, instinct warned him that they were on to him. There had been no visit from the lieutenant, nor from any other police officers, but nevertheless he knew that the next stage of the game, the face-to-face confrontation he had been anticipating for more than a week, was now imminent.

He found it interesting that he was not afraid.

They settled him comfortably in his new room. It was an attractive, elegant room, more suited to a hotel than to a hospital, with dark wood furniture, pale cream paintwork and beige fabrics. The nurses changed the IV in his arm, attached electrodes to his chest, wrists and ankles, switched on the EKG monitor and left him to rest. They were soothing and kind, and it was not unpleasant to be the object of so much attention and gentleness. It reminded him of his mother. But then, most things did, one way or another.

When Joe walked into Schwartz's room for the first time, just after ten o'clock, the other man was sleeping and, watching him for a few moments, Joe became conscious of a new and special stillness, a kind of perfect silence, taking control of his own mind. It was a rare form of concentration, of absolute focus. He had experienced it only once before, just before he'd begun his final interview with the arsonist. His own tenacity and the killer's ego had brought that man to his knees. Vanity, and the overpowering need to be recognized, ultimately, as a member of a select club: as one of the

203

chosen species of mass murderers. Schwartz's reign of terror might have been born out of revenge, but Joe would bet his last cent that ego had long since taken over.

Schwartz opened his eyes.

"How are you, Lieutenant?"

Joe thought he might have been awake all the time.

"I'm just fine, sir. How about you?"

"Wondering what I'm doing here."

"You know what you're doing here."

"Yes," Schwartz said. "I think I do." He paused. "Tell me, Lieutenant, how did they find out about the Gila monster? I didn't tell them."

"No, sir. I did."

"And how did you know?"

"A friend of mine got bitten by one of the same creatures. When your physicians at Memorial told me they were concerned by a bite on your foot, I recognized the signs."

"That's some coincidence," Schwartz said, pleasantly.

"Of course," Joe added, "it helped that you'd both gotten your bites at the same address."

The two men watched each other. The room was hushed. The only sounds came from the machine monitoring Schwartz's heart, and from his own breathing, slightly laboured.

"How did you get in?" Schwartz asked.

"With a search warrant," Joe lied.

"On what grounds did you get a warrant?"

"We found you might have had a motive, sir."

"Really?" Schwartz's intelligent hazel eyes seemed calm.

"We learned about your mother."

"What about my mother?"

"About her death." Joe spoke quietly. "About what happened at the crematorium."

"I see."

"We searched Mr Hagen's apartment, too."

"Because of his mother." Schwartz smiled.

"That's right." Joe paused. "We didn't find anything there."

The smile remained on Schwartz's lips, not touching his eyes.

Joe opened the attaché case he'd brought into the room with him, and took out the xeroxed copies of the six documents. "We did find these, sir, in your apartment."

"I see," Schwartz said again.

"I wonder," Joe said, with great courtesy, "if you would do me a favour, and tell me which of these records is the accurate one?"

Still Schwartz smiled. "I'm sure you do. Wonder, I mean."

"Would you do that for me?"

"I don't think so."

"That's a pity."

"Are you going to arrest me now?"

"No."

"Why not?"

"Truth?"

"I'd expect nothing less of you, Lieutenant."

"Because I need your help."

Joe glanced behind him, drew up one of the comfortable, well-padded chairs, and sat down. The stillness inside his mind persisted, and he welcomed it, for he knew that without it there was no chance of besting this man.

"There's a young woman here, in this clinic."

Schwartz said nothing, just listened.

"Fifteen days ago, she received a pacemaker implant. Until last night, she believed herself over her illness, her troubles behind her. She believed that her pacemaker had healed her, was taking care of her heart. She knows different now."

"I'm sorry for her," Schwartz said.

"Are you?"

"Why not?"

Joe held onto the stillness, gripped it tightly like a man fighting to stop himself from lashing out, or even killing.

"Then you'll help her."

The smile had gone, but the hazel eyes were affable. "How could I do that, Lieutenant?"

"In a few hours' time, a surgeon is going to cut into her again, not knowing exactly what he's going to find, and the young woman is going to have to go through all that not knowing whether she's going to live or die." Joe held out the documents. "If you can tell me if one of these records is accurate, it may mean her not having to go through all that."

The hush was back in the room.

"May I see the papers, please?"

"Of course."

Joe placed them on the bed, one set beside the other, and waited. Schwartz did not touch them.

"I'll tell you what I'll do, Lieutenant."

"Yes?"

"I'll see the young woman."

The stillness in Joe fractured a little. "That's impossible," he said.

"I thought you were trying to appeal to my better nature," Schwartz said.

"That's true."

"Then let me see her."

For a long moment, Joe looked into the hazel eyes.

"Forget it," he said.

"Then don't expect my help," Schwartz said.

Joe sank into a chair in Morrissey's office, and looked at the doctor and Ferguson. "I wasn't expecting that."

"Nor was I." Morrissey looked at Joe. "What do you think? Might it be worth putting your sister through it?"

Joe shook his head. "Even if he did cooperate after seeing her, we couldn't trust him not to play games with us. He knows he's running the show right now, and we need him vulnerable. We all know the only way of being halfway sure of Schwartz is by going ahead with the plan."

Morrissey checked his watch. It was almost ten-twenty.

"The staff are all appraised," he said.

"And you?" Joe looked at Ferguson. "Are you ready?"

"Ready as I'll ever be."

"It's a curious thing, Lieutenant," Morrissey said. "I hate this whole thing more than I can easily express to you. Simply permitting this charade to go ahead in my clinic goes against everything I believe in."

"Just remember it's for Marie," Ferguson said.

"And for Miss Duval," Morrissey said. "And for all the other victims of this man, and yet I still know how wrong it is." He paused. "So why am I allowing it to happen?"

"Because you're a human being," Ferguson said, "as well as a doctor."

"And because you've never met anyone like Schwartz before," Joe added, softly.

Morrissey stood up.

"And pray never to again," he said.

36

Monday, January 25th

Lally had a bad feeling. It had nothing to do with her pacemaker or with her heart. It had everything to do with Chris. It was almost ten-thirty, and she had not seen or heard from him since around lunchtime, just after they'd arrived at the clinic. She'd tried calling Joe's house and had left messages on the answering machine, and she had asked everyone who would listen, but no one seemed to know where Chris was. For a little while, she thought he might have gone home. It would make sense for him to go to Katy, or to Andrea. But not without telling her. Not without saying goodbye. And anyway, someone else would have told her. Hugo would certainly have told her.

"You're not leaving this room without telling me what's happened to Chris," she ordered Joe when he tried to dive in and out on one of his flying visits. "Is he sick or something?"

"Chris is fine," Joe said, lying through his teeth.

"You wouldn't lie to me, would you, Joe?"

"You know I wouldn't."

"But you do know where he is, don't you?"

"Yes, I do."

"Is he doing something for you? Is that why he hasn't called?"

"Yes."

"Can't you tell me what's going on?"

"No."

"Sometimes, Joseph Duval, I almost hate you."

"No, you don't, you adore me."

They shared a swift, strong hug.

"Joe, what's going on?" Lally, not about to let him leave, drew away. "Lucas and the others are here now – why can't we get this surgery over and done with?"

Their two matching sets of grey eyes met and held.

Joe gave in and sat on the edge of the bed.

"Because there's a slim chance – and I mean a real slim chance – that we may get some information that could help make the surgery even safer." He paused. "It could even mean that Ash might not have to operate at all, though we'd all have to be a million per cent sure."

Lally still looked deep into his eyes.

"You've got the man." She felt a charge of excitement.

"I can't talk about it, Lally."

"But you have got him, haven't you?"

Joe held both her hands. "Don't get your hopes up, sweetheart. We're all working on it, but neither Morrissey nor Ash think we should hold your surgery up any longer than is safe, and I agree with them."

"I understand that," Lally said.

"Are you okay to be alone now?" Joe asked. "I saw Hugo taking a nap in the waiting room. I could go wake him."

She shook her head. "Leave him. He's exhausted, poor man."

"He's still crazy about you, isn't he?" Joe said.

"I think so," Lally answered softly.

"All these men, Lally Duval, pining away for you."

Lally kept her hands in his. "You like Chris, don't you, Joe?"

"He's married, sweetheart."

"I know. But you do like him, don't you?"

"Yes." Gently, Joe removed his hands. "Yes, I do."

When Joe had left the room, Lally lay back and tried to rest, tried to focus on the slender hope he had brought her but, for the time being at least, her heart and the pacemaker were not quite uppermost in her thoughts. She had never been as big on intuition as her brother, but despite Joe's reassurances about Chris, Lally thought she had one of his famous warning spine-prickling hunches now.

Chris was in some kind of trouble. She was sure of it.

By eleven o'clock, Schwartz was not feeling quite as good as he had. He was uncomfortably warm again, and pretty sure that his fever had risen a degree or more in the past hour, and the EKG monitor attached to his body by all those damned electrodes was beginning to make him edgy.

"Do I have to have that thing switched on all the time?" he asked one of the nurses when she came in to check the new bag on his IV and to straighten his pillows.

"It's nothing to worry about, Mr Schwartz," she answered, soothingly.

"I'm not worried," he said, tartly. "The noise is irritating me."

"I'll have a word with Dr Kaminsky, shall I?"

"Dr Kaminsky, I gather, is my physician?"

"He is, sir, yes." She finished his pillows.

"What exactly is his specialty, nurse?"

"Poisons, sir. And envenomations."

Schwartz lay back and restlessly batted at the bedclothes with his right fist. "It would be nice if Dr Kaminsky would take the time to come and see me. I've been here for over an hour and a half."

"I'm sure he'll be in to see you very soon now, sir."

The nurse left the room quietly, and Schwartz stared up at the ceiling. Until the last half-hour or so, ever since the visit from the lieutenant, he'd been pretty certain that this transfer had been some kind of ploy to put him under the same roof as the young woman with the pacemaker – if, of course, she existed at all. *They want to play with me, I'll play with them,* he'd thought, confidently. But he was feeling sicker again, and he knew that the damned lizard, the shitty little captive dragon that he'd boiled into infinity, had done its work too well, and it was starting to mess with his mind again, and he needed to be clear, he needed to be sharp with the lieutenant, with all of them.

The monitor bleeped erratically.

He didn't like the way he felt.

As few employees of the Howe Clinic as possible had been drawn into Joe's plot. Two night nurses, two orderlies, no one else. And all they knew was that the heating in Schwartz's room was to be turned gradually higher, that ventilation was to be kept to a minimum, that they were to appear not to notice any discomfort themselves and that, for reasons they did not need to know, Marie Ferguson's husband was, so far as Schwartz was concerned, to be known as Dr Kaminsky, a specialist in the treatment of poisoning and envenomation.

Lally Duval's room was on the third floor of the clinic. Schwartz's was on the second. Every other, regular patient had been moved to the far side of the building before Lally's arrival, and John Morrissey had spent more than two hours visiting each one in turn, explaining that a localized electrical problem had necessitated the transfer from their preferred rooms, and that they would be compensated for any inconvenience caused.

Like Lally and Schwartz, Hugo was growing restless. Seeing Joe walking past the waiting room where he'd been napping, he jumped to his feet and called to him.

"What's going on, Joe?"

"Things are moving."

"What things?"

"You could use a shave, Hugo."

Irritably, Hugo rubbed his beard. "Joe, I'm not asking you to disclose police business, but Lally's going nuts in there."

"I've spoken to Lally, she's doing okay."

"She wants to know where Webber is." Hugo wasn't giving up easily. "I know he left with you at lunchtime when you said you were taking him to your place – I bought that, and so did Lally. But now she hasn't heard from him all day, and under normal circumstances I wouldn't give a damn if she never heard from him again, but circumstances aren't normal, and she's really upset."

Joe was itching to move on, but he knew that Hugo was Lally's dearest friend and distraught from waiting, and so he let him finish.

"I know she's upset, Hugo, but I think I've put her mind at rest."

"You know where Webber is?"

"I do."

"Did you tell Lally?"

"I told her there was nothing to worry about."

Hugo's soft brown eyes were suspicious. "Is that the truth?"

"Absolutely." It wasn't that Joe didn't trust Hugo, but he was a soft man, and he doubted if he was capable of successfully lying to Lally for more than five minutes.

"Lieutenant."

Joe turned around and saw Morrissey at the top of the staircase.

"Kaminsky's about ready," Morrissey said.

"Good." Joe turned back to Hugo. "I have to go."

"You've had a breakthrough, haven't you?"

"Yes."

"Who's Kaminsky?"

"No one you need to know about."

"Is this breakthrough going to help Lally?" Hugo persisted.

"Maybe," Joe said.

Joe and Morrissey walked down the staircase to the second floor.

"How ready is Ferguson?" Joe asked.

"As ready as he can be."

"Do you think he's going to be able to handle it?"

"I thought I was the one with all the doubts," Morrissey said, drily.

"Don't kid yourself," Joe said. "Schwartz killed Ferguson's wife. I'm having nightmares about Kaminsky throttling his patient."

"Sean Ferguson's smarter than that, Lieutenant," Morrissey said. "He knows what we're trying to achieve, and he knows he has to treat Schwartz with kid gloves. We've gone through the basics – he knows how to take a pulse and read a thermometer, and he can bluff his way through an EKG recording – "

"What if Schwartz suspects something?"

"Then Sean'll fly by the seat of his pants."

They reached Schwartz's floor. Ferguson, white-coated, a stethoscope around his neck, was pacing the corridor near Schwartz's room.

"He looks nervous," Joe said.

"At least he looks like a doctor."

Ferguson approached them. "Would you buy a diagnosis from this man?"

"Sure I would," Morrissey said.

"You wouldn't lie to me, John, would you?" Ferguson adjusted his Kaminsky name tag.

"I wouldn't lie," Morrissey said.

"What if he asks me something medical I can't answer?"

"Stall," Joe said. "Don't invent stuff in case Schwartz knows what you're talking about. Remember he's a brilliant man."

"I'll remember."

"Break a leg," Joe said.

"Just don't come to me to have it set," Morrissey said, grimly.

When Ferguson entered Schwartz's room at ten minutes before midnight, the patient was lying on his back staring at the ceiling. At the sound of the door, he slowly turned his head and looked at the dark-haired young doctor.

"Dr Kaminsky, I presume?"

"That's right, Mr Schwartz." Ferguson-Kaminsky smiled down at his new patient. "I'm sorry not to have been able to come sooner. How are you feeling?"

"I've been better, I've been worse."

"You look warm."

"I have a fever."

The doctor glanced at Schwartz's chart, then removed the thermometer from its antiseptic-filled container on the wall beside the bed, and stuck it in the patient's mouth. He drew up a chair, and took Schwartz's pulse.

"Okay, let's take a look." He checked the thermometer and noted down the reading on the chart. "Up a little," he said.

"It was down a few hours ago," Schwartz said.

"So I gather."

"I don't think the move did me much good."

"I hope it didn't cause you too much discomfort."

"Not too much, though I thought I was recovering well at Memorial, and now I'm not so sure."

"It happens in cases such as yours, Mr Schwartz."

"What happens?"

"Some generalized improvement, giving way to renewed deterioration."

"So I'm deteriorating, am I?" Schwartz sounded almost amiable.

"Your condition is giving us some cause for concern." Ferguson-Kaminsky patted him on the hand. "But it's nothing we can't fix."

"I'm glad to hear that, doctor."

"Provided we act promptly."

The hazel eyes watched the doctor carefully. "What do you want to do?"

"Let me start by explaining the problem, Mr Schwartz."

"That would be nice."

"You're aware, I believe, that there is no effective antivenin with which to treat the bite of the Arizona Gila monster." Ferguson-Kaminsky saw Schwartz nod. "In the majority of cases, bite victims make a complete recovery, but there are some whose hearts become affected."

Schwartz glanced over at the EKG monitor, then back at the doctor. "You're telling me my heart's been affected."

"I'm afraid so." Ferguson-Kaminsky paused. "The bad news is that once the venom has begun to act on the heart, any damage is irreversible. The good news is that in your case the damage has been to the sinoatrial node, causing it to function abnormally and creating arrhythmia, as shown in your EKG recordings. Do you understand me so far?"

Schwartz was silent for a moment.

"May I see these recordings?" he asked.

"Certainly." Ferguson-Kaminsky stood up and tore off a long strip of paper from the machine's read-out. He studied it himself for a minute, then sat down again and laid it out for Schwartz to look at. "The spiked readings are spaced out at quite regular intervals, as you see, which means the heartbeat is quite regular, but it's a little too slow."

"So why is that good news?" Schwartz said.

"Because although we can't repair the damage, we can easily correct its effects."

Schwartz lay back against his pillows.

"No," he said.

"Have I missed something?" Ferguson-Kaminsky asked.

"No, I won't have a pacemaker," Schwartz said.

"That is the treatment indicated," the doctor said. "In fact, it's the only treatment we can offer you."

A small smile played at the corners of Schwartz's lips. "If I were to believe what you tell me, Dr Kaminsky, there are antiarrhythmic drugs available."

"As an adjunct, perhaps, but quite insufficient on their own."

Schwartz shook his head.

"No pacemaker," he said.

Ferguson-Kaminsky nodded. "I can well understand your misgivings, under the circumstances."

"I'm sure you can."

"Maybe I can just offer you one more reason to change your mind."

"I doubt that."

"I believe Lieutenant Duval has told you that we have another patient suffering from a Gila monster bite."

"In this clinic?" Seeing the doctor nod, Schwartz's lips twitched in another slight smile. "The lieutenant didn't tell me that. Another coincidence."

"Hardly. This is, after all, a specialist unit."

"And now we're all happily under one roof."

"Not so happily," Ferguson-Kaminsky said. "The condition of the other patient is deteriorating rapidly."

"Surely even you must admit that is a coincidence," Schwartz said. "You just finished telling me that the majority of Gila monster bite victims recover completely, yet here we are, two out of two, going downhill fast." He paused. "I imagine you're going to give this other patient a pacemaker?"

"Unfortunately we can't."

"Why not?" The sneer behind the question was unmissable.

"Because in his case it's too late for that," Ferguson-Kaminsky replied. "And unless we act fairly swiftly, I'm afraid it may be too late for you, too, Mr Schwartz."

"I'll take my chances, doctor."

"It's your decision, of course."
"And it's made."

37

Tuesday, January 26th

While they stepped up the heat in Schwartz's room and a nurse went in to tweak his IV, increasing the flow of beta blocker drugs now being delivered into his system, the Howe Clinic's number one operating room was almost ready for service.

"Will your boss agree to wear a bomb suit?" Tony Valdez asked Bobby Goldstein.

"You have to be kidding." Goldstein, who'd been persuaded to try on an American Body Armor suit, felt like a blimp or some kind of space age monster.

"Dr Ash will not agree to wear one," Joanna King said, scathingly, "and neither will I."

"You'd be well advised to, ma'am," Valdez said.

"If I wore one of those," King answered, "I couldn't do my job effectively. And neither I nor Mr Goldstein will be anywhere near as close to the patient as Dr Ash."

Humbled and perspiring, Goldstein began to dismantle his suit.

"Are you wearing panty hose?" Valdez asked King. "I only ask because some bombs can be set off by static electricity, and just wearing nylon can do it."

"I'll remove my panty hose before we begin," King agreed calmly.

"And any other garments that might create static." Valdez looked at Goldstein. "That applies to you, too, sir."

Goldstein began a mental re-run of everything he'd put on his body since getting out of bed that morning.

"There's no carpet in here, which is a plus." Valdez wasn't letting up. "If you won't consider wearing body armour, ma'am, we'll be insisting you all wear special cotton coveralls – no metal zippers or buttons."

"As long as they're sterile," King said.

"They will be. And we have wrist straps to reduce your body's static electricity – "

"Excuse me," Goldstein broke in.

"Sure," Valdez said.

"All this talk about electricity." Goldstein, out of the bomb suit, was still perspiring but growing paler. "We'll be working with all kinds of electrical stuff during the procedure – monitors, X-ray equipment – "

"Can't be done without," King interrupted.

Valdez looked at her through clear, narrow eyes. "We don't need any heroes here today, Miss King."

She looked straight back at him. "You won't be getting any."

"Our understanding," Goldstein said, "was that we're dealing with a fairly small explosive device here – "

"If we're dealing with one at all," King added.

"In our business," Valdez said, crisply, "a bomb is a bomb until we know different. That's how we stay alive, or try to. Bomb disposal is all about unknown quantities and taking no chances. And by the way, just because this nutball's only blown away one victim at a time so far, doesn't guarantee we don't all go up today."

"A happy thought," Goldstein commented.

"Listen, people" – Valdez wasn't giving up – "I'm not going to kid you that I don't want to scare you – I do, because at the end of the operation, I want all of us, including the patient, to be able to get up and go home."

"I think we'd like that, too," King said.

"Do you know the first thing a cop does when he suspects he's found a bomb?" Valdez asked. "He clears the area. Everyone leaves – and I mean *everyone* – except the experts."

"We get your point," Goldstein said. "But Ms King's right about the armour – we couldn't do our jobs properly wearing that."

"That's okay." Valdez grinned. "If the explosion's big enough, the suits don't stop you dying, they just help hold your body parts together."

"Great." Bobby Goldstein grimaced.

"Just great," Joanna King said.

Frederick Schwartz's mind, not quite asleep, not quite awake, was wandering again. Back and forth, into the past, back into the present.

His heart-rate was too slow, he knew that, could hear it on the monitor, and it was getting harder to breathe, he was so warm, too warm. He was perspiring again, and he hated that, he was a fastidious man. He longed to be back in his own place, his special place, he needed to be in control, and he was losing it again, and he was surrounded by people he could not trust, and the dragons were out there, and they were coming closer, closer . . .

They're lying, I know they're lying. But the green lines on the monitor weren't lying, machines didn't lie, and maybe Kaminsky was speaking the truth, and maybe this was the greatest irony of his life, maybe he did need a pacemaker to keep him alive, but he could never let them do that to him.

Kaminsky and Duval were laughing because they thought he was afraid they might put one of his own pacemakers into him, but Schwartz knew no doctor would ever do such a thing, however much they might want to, and he knew that *was* what they wanted, more than anything. Especially Duval, the damnable, smiling, ever-courteous lieutenant, whose grey eyes watched him so carefully, and who hated him, despised him, wanted him dead. *They think I'm afraid to die, but there are worse things than death.* Mother understood that, she warned him. About dragons, about the ways in which they were created.

He shut his eyes and his mind spun, remembering Mother's teachings: serpents born asexually from eggs of roosters incubated in dung, animals changed into dragons. Humans too. *Man and metal*, Mother had told him. Man and metal, brought together, and the worst could happen, the most terrible thing imaginable, there could be nothing worse. Mother had been terrified of the dentist, not because of the pain, she had never feared pain, but she had never allowed him to put metal fillings into her mouth, and he remembered, too, one day, after one of the women at *Eva's* had fallen and broken her leg, and they had taken her to hospital and put a pin inside to hold the bone together, and Mother hadn't ever let her come back to work again. Man and metal. The woman was one of her best workers, but she couldn't trust her any more, she couldn't be near her any more.

And then, at the end, Mother had let them put the metal into her own body, the box into her chest, the wires into her heart, and she had died. It hadn't changed her, but it had killed her, it had destroyed her, and so he had become her Siegfried again, and he had taken his revenge, and now they wanted to stop him, and he would not let them.

*   *   *

217

At a few minutes before one in the morning, a little while after Hugo had finally been persuaded that he would be more use to Lally if he got some real sleep for an hour or two, Lally, her Garfield nightshirt hidden under a sweater, and wearing her red and white striped socks for extra warmth, emerged, after almost twelve hours of captivity, from her room.

She was hungry, she was tired and, increasingly, she was feeling more irritable than afraid. You couldn't just lie around hour after hour being terrified of sudden and violent death; your mind simply couldn't sustain that level of fear, no longer really believed it might happen. Lally didn't know any more whether she felt more like a victim or a prisoner, she only knew she wasn't prepared just to lie there in that pretty pastel bedroom any longer like some stir-crazy Sleeping Beauty, and so she was going for a walk, she was going to find Lucas Ash or John Morrissey or Joe or maybe even Chris, and she was going to start making some demands of her own.

She half expected someone to jump on her the minute she opened the door, for some armed guard or vigilant nurse or one of Joe's pals to push her gently but firmly straight back into her room again, but no one stopped her – there seemed to be no one around at all.

She walked a little way along the corridor. The quietness she'd noticed soon after her arrival, and that she'd put down to the thickness of the bedroom walls, was just as noticeable out here. The place felt deserted, almost ghostly, as if she were the only patient in the place.

Realization struck her. She was the only patient.

Softly, she tapped on a door. No one answered. Slowly, carefully, she opened it. Another pastel room, prettily furnished like her own, but empty, the bed neatly covered. She shut the door, opened another, then another.

Fear returned, then irritation again, then anger. Morrissey had told her that Marie Ferguson, his partner, had been in bed with her husband when her pacemaker had exploded, and he had been unharmed. *They were about as close to each other as they could get. And nothing happened to him. Not a scratch.* If that was true, why the hell was she being treated like Typhoid Mary, and if they were so goddamned scared of her, why hadn't anyone had the decency to tell her, or Hugo for that matter?

Lally turned on her heel and stalked back along the corridor, looking for someone, anyone, who could answer her questions. She came to the staircase she'd seen on her arrival, elegant and circular. *Up or down?* Or maybe it didn't matter, maybe there was no one else left in the whole clinic, maybe they'd all abandoned her the way Chris had, and they were waiting now to see if she would blow or not.

She went down to the next floor, turned to her right, then changed her mind and went the other way.

People. Two, no three people, standing in a huddle outside a room. She stalked toward them. One nurse, an orderly, and Joe.

He looked up and saw her. "Lally, what the – ?"

She walked right up to him, saw the orderly and nurse both throw an anxious glance at the door behind them. "I got tired of lying around like Camille. I'm not sick, Joe, and I'm not stupid, and I want to know what's going on in this place, and I want to know it now."

Joe put his arm around her. "Let's get you back upstairs."

"No." She shook him off. "Joe, I mean it. Stop treating me like some tender little coward and tell me the truth. Why am I the only patient here?"

"You're not," Joe said.

"Don't lie to me. I checked, and there's no one else in my corridor, all the rooms are empty." She hardly paused for breath. "If it's because you're all afraid I'm going to go up like the Fourth of July, then you could at least – "

"Shut up, Lally." He took her arm again and steered her firmly back towards the staircase.

"I will not shut up." She dug her feet into the carpet and refused to be moved any further. "I've been lying up in that room for a whole day, and first of all everyone claims they were going nuts trying to find me so they could take this thing out of me, and then we had to wait for Lucas Ash to arrive – "

"Lally, for Christ's sake keep your voice down," Joe hissed at her. "You wanted to wait for him – "

"But he arrived hours ago, and I'm still waiting."

"I explained that to you."

"You explained *nothing* to me, and I'm sick of it."

"You're just upset, sweetheart – "

"Of course I'm upset, Joe!"

"I told you to keep your voice down." Again, he tugged at her arm, trying to draw her away, and again she resisted. "Lally, let's go back to your room and I'll tell you everything."

"Tell me here," she said.

"I'll tell you upstairs."

Suddenly she knew.

"He's here, isn't he? The one who did this. He's here in that room."

219

Joe kept his hand on her arm, as if he feared she might break into a run and go for Schwartz's door.

"I'm right, Joe, aren't I?" Lally demanded. "He's in there, and you're trying to get him to talk." She waited. "That's it, isn't it?"

"He's here," Joe said.

"You can let go of my arm now." He released her. "Thank you."

"Will you come upstairs with me?"

For a moment, Lally stood still.

"I want to see him."

"No," Joe said.

"But it might make a difference."

"No," he said again.

"He wanted to see her."

Morrissey's voice behind her made Lally spin around.

"Did he?" she asked.

"It's not going to happen," Joe said.

"Why not?"

"Because I don't trust him."

"He's not armed, is he?" Lally asked.

"Lally, it's not a good idea." Joe paused. "Anyway, he's a lot weaker now than he was when he suggested seeing you."

"Is he sick?" Lally wanted to know. "What's wrong with him?"

"That's a long story," Joe said.

"Maybe now's the perfect time," Morrissey said.

"I don't agree," Joe argued.

"You said yourself he's weakening." Morrissey spoke reasonably. "Whatever he said to Kaminsky, he's human, and no one really wants to die, not when there's a chance."

"Who's Kaminsky?" Lally asked Morrissey.

"The doctor treating Schwartz," he replied.

Lally turned back to her brother. "Joe, let me see him." She felt stronger and more positive. "He's never met any of his victims, has he? Like the doctor said, he's human. Maybe seeing me might turn him around."

"The man's a mass murderer, Lally," Joe said. "He's no different to a serial killer. Most killers get a kick out of seeing their victims suffer."

Lally was immovable.

"What are you trying to get him to tell you?" she asked.

Joe looked at Morrissey. "What do you think?"

"I think you should tell Lally what we need. It can't do any harm."

Lally waited. "Joe?"

For several seconds, Joe said nothing. Then he shook his head. "Ah, what the hell," he said.

They insisted she sit in a wheelchair, partly, Morrissey said, because it was the policy of the clinic, but mostly, Joe said, because Lally was entering that room as a victim making a plea. Standing over him, she was a potential threat; in the chair, she was vulnerable.

Joe wheeled her in at one thirty-five. Lally had been warned about the heat and stuffiness in Schwartz's room, and that it was vital she appear unaffected by it, but still the discomfort startled her, made it all the harder to keep calm.

Schwartz was still awake.

"Lieutenant," he said.

"Sir," Joe said.

"Busy night. I thought I was the only one awake."

"We're all pretty much awake," Joe said. His hands on the back of Lally's chair were clenched too tightly, and he made himself relax them. "This is the patient I told you about earlier. You remember you expressed a wish to meet her."

"I remember." Schwartz was clearly in physical distress, but he seemed in perfect control as he looked at Lally. "How do you do?"

Lally met his eyes. "Not bad, considering."

"I thought perhaps the lieutenant had invented you."

"I'm real enough," Lally answered, steadily. "As you see."

"Do you have a name?" His voice came with an effort.

Lally hesitated.

"We won't bother with names, if you don't mind," Joe said.

"And if I do?"

Joe said nothing.

For a brief moment, Schwartz closed his eyes, as if he was in pain. Then he opened them again. "I'd like you to leave us alone."

"No," Joe said.

Lally looked at the man in the bed, and then up at her brother. "Please," she said, softly. "I'll be fine."

"It's out of the question." Joe was adamant.

Lally looked back at Schwartz. His skin was pasty white, with patches of hot colour on both cheeks. His upper lip was beaded with sweat, and his eyes, it seemed to her, were suffering. His breath sounded wheezy.

"Please," she said again.

Schwartz's eyes flickered.

"I believe you still need my help, Lieutenant Duval," he said, looking straight at Lally.

221

"We do," Joe said.

"Then please leave us alone."

Joe looked long and hard at Schwartz.

"I'll be right outside the door."

Lally took a few moments to steady herself. She looked around the room, noting the masculine touches that replaced the feminine pastels of her own bedroom on the floor above; the dark woods, softened by cream paintwork and beige curtains, the Turner print on the wall facing the bed. She let her eyes wander over the surfaces, across the fabrics, felt as if she were earthing herself before touching something that might give her an electric shock. And then she forced herself to look directly at Schwartz.

"There isn't too much time," she said.

"Maybe not."

"For either of us." She paused. "I'm not here just for myself."

"Oh, I'm sure you want to live," Schwartz said.

"Of course I do. But I want those other people to have the same chance."

"Why wouldn't you?" The words were dismissive, mocking.

The heat in the room made it hard for Lally to breathe easily, but she knew she had to conceal her discomfort from him.

"They told me what happened to your mother," she said. "I'm sorry. It must have been devastating for you."

"Devastating is a good word."

Lally swallowed. "But I find it hard to believe that your mother would have wanted innocent people to suffer."

"Do you?"

"I do."

"I assure you my mother would have expected me to avenge her death."

"And you have," Lally said. "Four people have already died. Isn't that enough?"

"It's very hot in here," Schwartz said. "You find it warm, too, don't you?"

"Not particularly," Lally said.

"You look warm."

"Maybe I'm not very comfortable being with you."

The EKG monitor beeped erratically for a moment, unnerving her. Schwartz's breathing seemed to become more of an effort, the wheeze grew louder. Dr Morrissey had told her that the overheating was not harming him, but Lally found that hard to believe. She felt perspiration starting to form on her back, and she knew that her cheeks were flushed.

"Nothing more to say?" Schwartz asked.

She shook her head. "Except to ask you to help me. And to help yourself. Tell them which document is real. And let them give you the treatment you need."

"That they say I need."

"I believe them."

"That's your prerogative."

"They wouldn't lie to you, not about something like that."

"They lied to my mother," Schwartz said.

For a moment, Lally's hands tightened on the arms of the wheelchair. "I'm a dancer, you know. I teach ballet to small children, and I bake for a café in a village in New England." She paused. "I'm not married, and I have no children of my own, but I hope to some day. And I love my life."

Schwartz's smile was cold. "What a lucky girl you've been."

"Yes," she said.

"And yet you still want more?"

"Yes," Lally said again. "And so do all those other people."

Schwartz said nothing, just kept watching her. Lally looked at his face and at his eyes, and she no longer saw suffering. On the contrary, she thought she almost detected a kind of pleasure. The eyes were very hard now, almost clinical, and she realized, with a fresh shock, that he was looking at her the way a biologist might regard a specimen prior to dissecting it.

"You're not going to help, are you?" she said, softly.

"I think not," he answered.

And Lally knew then that Joe had been right, that Frederick Schwartz didn't care about her, and that there was not one single part of him that felt guilt for the deaths that had already occurred.

She knew now that there was no escaping the fact that there might be a tiny bomb lying just under her skin. That she was going to have to endure the uncertainty of the second operation. That unless someone was able to establish precisely what this man had done, any number of people might, at any time, die.

And that Schwartz didn't give a damn.

"Ash wants to operate now," Valdez told Joe thirty minutes later, in the third-floor corridor not far from Lally's room. "He says he can't see the sense in waiting any longer. He wants Lally as calm as possible, and that's going to get tougher the longer she has to wait."

"She's resting right now," Joe said. He kept his voice low, though there was no one in earshot. "Al Hagen just called – someone else who can't sleep. He discharged himself from Memorial a couple of hours ago, and he's on his way over here now. He says he wants to talk to Schwartz, says he's known him for ten years, and he thinks there's a chance he might be able to get through to him."

"If Schwartz has been planning his revenge for the whole ten years," Valdez said, "Hagen can't have known him all that well."

"I told him he can have ten minutes," Joe said, grimly. "I need more time anyway – I'm not finished planning yet." He paused. "Tell Ash that if there's a chance – *any* chance at all – of finding out for sure what's inside my sister's pacemaker, I intend to grab it before he starts taking unnecessary risks with her life."

"He's afraid we may be running out of time," Valdez said. "I'm not sure I don't agree with him."

Joe's stomach was clenched tighter than a fighter's fist. "The shortest period so far between implantation and detonation was Marie Ferguson's at three weeks. Lally's had hers for just sixteen days."

"That guarantees nothing except hope," Valdez said, gently, "and you know it. And now that we could be talking about a different kind of detonation, it means even less."

"Which makes it all the more vital that we get the information out of Schwartz." Joe felt another of those out-of-control surges of panic and rage, and struggled to master it with a deep breath. "Aside from the fact," he went on, gritting his teeth, "that Lally's my sister, this is the first of these things we've had that's still intact. It's in everyone's interest to keep it that way."

Valdez didn't argue. "So you want me to tell Ash and his team to get some sleep?"

"Absolutely."

"Don't you want to ask Lally what she thinks about it?"

"No way," Joe said, almost violently. "It's two-fifteen, I hope to hell she's asleep, and she may know about the documents, but she doesn't know anything about the detonation, and I want to keep it that way."

"Okay." Valdez held up his hands. "You're the boss."

When Al Hagen entered the stiflingly hot room on the second floor, Schwartz was sleeping restlessly, moaning a little, very softly. His forehead, illuminated by the night light, was damp with perspiration, and there were two little oxygen tubes in his nostrils. His left arm, with its IV attached, lay still on top of the covers, while the fingers of his right hand strayed across the sheet like a blind creature seeking some lost prey.

For several moments, Hagen stared down at the man in the bed, trying to reconcile what he now knew about him with what he had believed for the past decade. His misconceptions overwhelmed him. For all the combined gifts and knowledge that Howard Leary and Olivia Ashcroft had brought to Hagen Pacing, it had, for a long time, been Fred Schwartz that Hagen had depended upon to keep things running smoothly, reliably. Safely.

Hagen thought back to the hours and days after the first deaths in Boston and Chicago, to the shattered reaction this man had presented to them all. Schwartz had seemed more stunned than any of them, more guilt-wracked, but even the guilt – more than anything, the guilt – had been a staggeringly fine acting performance.

"Man and metal," Schwartz muttered.

Startled, Hagen scrutinized him. He was still asleep, and dreaming, his eyelids moving rapidly, his mouth contorting as if in pain.

"Fred," Hagen said.

Schwartz went on sleeping.

"Fred," he said again, a little louder.

"Man and metal." Schwartz's dreaming voice was slurred, like a drunk's.

"Fred."

Schwartz opened his eyes and stared up at Hagen.

"Hello, Fred."

"You." Schwartz's pupils were dilated.

"That's right," Hagen said, warmly, gently. "I've come to see you, to talk to you. To ask you for your help."

"Help."

Hagen was uncertain if the word was mocking or wary. He moved in closer to the bed.

"Keep away," Schwartz said.

It was fear, no doubt about it.

"Come on, Fred," Hagen said, soothingly. "We all know the truth now, and I think I can maybe begin to understand why you did it, but it's over now, and this is your chance to put things right – "

"Go away." The pupils were so black now, so dilated with fear that they seemed almost to overwhelm the irises. "Get *away* from me."

"You have to think of all the good work, great work, you've done over the years," Hagen persisted. "This isn't what you want to be remembered for, Fred, for pity's sake."

"My name is not Fred."

Hagen stared at him. The man seemed almost terrified, and

maybe he was in some kind of delirium, but in spite of the fear, in spite of the still slurred voice, Schwartz was looking right into his face, and Hagen felt that the terror and hatred in that gaze was directed at him, was *for* him.

He kept his own tone gentle. "What do you mean, Fred?"

"You know."

"No, I don't know. Why don't you tell me?"

"You know who I am. I know who you are."

Hagen felt his stomach turn over.

"Who am I, Fred?"

"You're Hagen." He pronounced the name oddly, differently, the German way. Hahgen.

"And you?" Hagen's voice was very hushed. "Who are you?"

The pupils sharpened a little, the whole suffering, sagging face seemed to tauten, to grow prouder.

"I'm Siegfried," Schwartz said. "And I know why you're here."

"Why am I here, Siegfried?"

"To kill me." Schwartz seemed to summon all his strength. "But I'm going to fight you, Hagen, all the way."

For another moment, confusion swamped Al Hagen. And then, abruptly, something clicked into place in his mind, and he realized without a doubt that Frederick Schwartz was beyond reason, that whether or not he had been rational ten years ago when he had been hired to work at Hagen Pacing, he was now certifiably insane.

"He's gone mad," Hagen told Joe, in Morrissey's office.

"What happened?" Joe asked.

"He was out of it when I went in, talking in his sleep. 'Man and metal.' He kept saying that – 'Man and metal'. And then, when I woke him up, he took one look at me and his eyes almost popped out of his head, and he started telling me to get away from him – he was terrified, I mean, really terrified."

"It's probably the heat and his condition taking their toll," Morrissey said.

"No," Hagen disagreed. "Oh, I'm not saying they haven't tipped the balance, but I'm telling you it was me he was scared of." He shook his grey head. "And believe it or not, I think this all has something to do with opera."

"Opera?" Morrissey queried.

"Go on." Joe's tone was sharp.

Morrissey was sitting behind his desk, while Joe paced. Hagen sat down in one of the visitor's chairs, facing the doctor.

"Are either of you familiar with the works of Richard Wagner?"

226

"To a degree," Morrissey answered.

"Lieutenant?"

Joe recalled Cynthia Alesso, Hagen's assistant, telling him and Lipman on their first morning at Hagen Pacing that her boss was crazy about Wagner. He went on pacing. "Just go ahead, please."

Hagen shook his head. "I don't know if this is relevant, or any help to you, but for the first time ever, Schwartz used the German pronunciation of my name – Hahgen instead of Hagen." He paused. "And when I kept calling him Fred, he said – and he was way out of it, as I told you – but he said that that wasn't his name, that his name was Siegfried."

"Siegfried the dragon slayer," Morrissey said.

"Exactly."

Joe stopped pacing. "Could one of you explain that to me?"

"Richard Wagner wrote a fifteen-hour operatic cycle," Hagen told him, "that was divided up into four separate operas, and the whole thing was called *The Ring of the Nibelung*. It's wonderful stuff, pretty heavy in its way – too long for many people – and it's loaded with symbolism and mythology."

"The great hero's name," Morrissey took it up, "is Siegfried, and he's sometimes known as the dragon slayer because he kills the dragon guarding the Nibelung gold."

"And in *Götterdämmerung* – 'Twilight of the Gods'," Hagen went on, "which is the final opera in the cycle, a character with my name kills Siegfried the hero."

"Though what all that has to do with Schwartz and what he's done," Morrissey said, "beats the hell out of me."

Joe thought about the bizarre paintings and drawings and tapestries on the walls in apartment 1510 – the samplers signed with an elaborate *'E'*, his mother's signature. "It could have a lot to do with Schwartz," he said slowly. "He has an obsession with dragons."

"Really?" Hagen looked confused.

"You said he was talking about man and metal?" Joe asked.

"That was what he kept muttering in his sleep. Does it mean anything to you, Lieutenant?"

"It certainly means something to him." Briefly, Joe shut his eyes, trying to recall the words on one of the samplers. "Something to do with one of the ways dragons are born – some really off-the-wall myth about mixing metal with flesh and blood and coming up with monsters."

"Do you know," Morrissey asked Hagen, "if Schwartz is an opera fan?"

227

"He's a Wagner fan, like you, sir," Joe answered, looking at Hagen. "His place is jammed with discs and tapes – and he had a CD of *Twilight of the Gods*. I thought, for a while, that Schwartz might be trying to emulate your lifestyle, that it was a sign of admiration, a kind of hero-worship."

They all fell silent for a long moment.

"So what are we saying here?" Hagen asked, slowly. "We already know Schwartz blamed his mother's pacemaker for failing to save her life." He paused. "I bought the company in the mid-seventies, years after her death, of course, but if Schwartz was already fixated by the Siegfried and Hagen myth, I suppose pinning the blame on a company called Hagen Pacing was just a hop and a skip away." He shook his head. "But that only adds to his motivation, doesn't it? I don't see it helping to get anything more out of him."

"I do," Joe said.

"How?" Hagen asked.

Joe didn't respond, just met Morrissey's glance.

Hagen got the message. "You want me to go."

"If you don't mind," Joe said. "I want to thank you for your help."

"I've done nothing."

"You've done more than you know," Joe said.

When the door closed behind Hagen, Morrissey looked at Joe. "What are you planning now, Lieutenant?"

"Where's Mr Ferguson?"

"Somewhere in the building. Why?"

A new hit of adrenaline had sharpened Joe's flagging system again. "Schwartz is right on the brink, isn't he? He's mixing up his myths, blurring the edges of fantasy and reality – we have to use that, ethical or not. Without Schwartz's confession, those documents are useless. If I can't find a way to break him, he'll go free, and all those other patients out there will be no better off than when we started."

"I ask you again," Morrissey said, "what are you planning?"

"I'm planning," Joe said, "to try and scare him half to death." He read the disapproval on the physician's face. "Schwartz isn't going to talk any other way, we all know that." He went on slowly, still working it out. "What we can't be sure of – short of crawling inside that fucked-up mind of his – is if, ultimately, Schwartz is going to be more terrified of dying, or of this crazy man-and-metal thing."

"You want Kaminsky to try again?"

Joe shook his head. "Kaminsky alone won't change Schwartz's mind, but I do have an idea that might tip the balance. It's more than a little bizarre, and it'll take some time to set up, but it might just work."

"Maybe I'd be better off not hearing this," Morrissey said.

"Do you want to pull the plug?" Joe asked.

"How can I pull the plug on a plan I know nothing about?"

"Let's not kid ourselves." Joe owed it to Morrissey to be realistic. "If things go wrong, who's going to believe you knew nothing? We've already involved members of your staff – there are witnesses. It could mean major trouble for you and the clinic."

"I'm well aware of that, Lieutenant." Morrissey smiled wryly. "I've already done more than enough to get myself into all kinds of trouble. But I'm not a young man – I'll be retiring soon enough, anyway. And I owe Marie a great debt." He paused. "But I am still a doctor, and when all is said and done, no matter what Schwartz is guilty of, he's still a patient in my clinic. I can't become personally involved in any form of mistreatment."

"You won't be."

"Do you give me your word he won't be harmed?"

"I do."

Morrissey nodded. "Then as I said, I can't pull the plug on something I know nothing about."

Joe checked his watch. Ten past three in the morning, and the whole investigation was still as big a mess as it had been. There was just this one remaining chance, this one more insane shot at trying to break Schwartz, and if he failed, Joe knew that he'd have no more reason not to give Ash the go-ahead to take Lally into surgery.

Less than five hours remained until the commander's deadline expired, and his career went down in flames. Right now, that was the least of his worries.

229

38

Tuesday, January 26th

A t four-fifteen a.m., Frederick Schwartz was dreaming again, wild, dark nightmares in which his mother was punishing him, burning his skin with her cigarette, in which a great scaly dragon bore down on him, its breath so hot that he felt stifled, suffocated, in which he screamed and wept and no one came to save him. In which Hagen stood, silent and shadowy, in the background, his sword drawn and all hope gone.

For several moments, Sean Ferguson watched the man who had killed his wife, and suddenly, for the very first time in all his years, adult and childhood, he experienced the urge to end another human being's life. He wanted to pick up one of those pillows and place it over this madman's face, to push and push until the laboured breathing stopped and the insane, poisonous, evil blood ceased flowing through his veins –

And then Schwartz gave a wheezing, choking breath, and his right hand clutched spasmodically at the damp sheet covering him, and the brief, murderous impulse left Ferguson. Killing him now would help no one. Duval's way was better.

Ferguson-Kaminsky took a deep breath of stifling air, and bent over the bed. "Mr Schwartz, wake up."

Schwartz moaned.

"Come on, Mr Schwartz, you're okay."

Schwartz woke with a jolt, sweat streaming off him, eyes dark with terror.

"You're okay now," Ferguson-Kaminsky said. "It was just a dream."

"Where is he?" Schwartz's voice was a hiss.

"Where is who?"

"Where's Hagen? I saw him – he was here."

"Mr Hagen was here earlier, but he's gone home." Ferguson-Kaminsky's bedside manner was so gentle and calming he marvelled at it himself. "But I've come to talk to you again about letting us treat your condition."

Schwartz shook his head weakly from side to side.

"Where's Hagen?" he asked again.

"I told you, sir, he left."

"I don't believe you."

Ferguson-Kaminsky sat on a chair beside the bed. "Listen to me, please, Mr Schwartz, because I have something important to tell you."

The wild eyes narrowed. "You want to put metal into me."

"I want to put a pacemaker into you, yes." The doctor paused. "You remember I told you about the other patient bitten by the Gila monster? Do you remember I told you that he was very sick, that it was too late for him?"

"I remember. I remember all your lies."

"Not lies," Ferguson-Kaminsky said. "He died, Mr Schwartz. The other man died because it was too late to help him. And you're going to die too, unless you let us help you now."

"I don't believe you."

"What will it take for you to believe me, Mr Schwartz? Do you want to see the other man? Will you believe me then?"

The eyes grew even narrower, filled with contempt and suspicion. "You're all such liars," he said.

Ferguson-Kaminsky stood up. "I'm not lying to you, Mr Schwartz. I wish I were." He walked over to the door connecting that room to the next and turned the lock in the door. "Come in, orderly," he called.

The door opened.

Schwartz stared.

A green-coated orderly stood in the doorway, and there was something behind him. A gurney covered with a white sheet.

"Doctor?" The orderly waited.

"Please bring it in."

The gurney slid through the door.

"Thank you, orderly." The door closed behind the other man.

"What is this?" Schwartz sounded contemptuous, but Ferguson-Kaminsky could almost taste his fear.

"I'd rather not put you through this," he said, still gentle.

231

"Through what?" Schwartz's breath wheezed. "This charade?"

Ferguson-Kaminsky moved closer to the gurney and lifted the sheet away from Chris Webber's chalky, peaceful, dead face.

Schwartz shrank back in his bed. "It could be anyone." His mouth opened, like a fish gulping air. "People in hospitals die all the time."

"Take a look at his right hand," the doctor said. He came back towards Schwartz's bed, bent and pressed a button, raising the head end.

"What are you doing?" Schwartz gasped, panicking.

"Just making it easier for you to see," Ferguson-Kaminsky said. "You know what the lizard's bite looks like – those grooved teeth make a mess, don't they?"

"No." Schwartz turned his head away.

"I want to prove to you I'm not lying."

"Take him away."

"Just take a quick look." Ferguson-Kaminsky went back to the gurney, lifted the sheet on Webber's right side, raised his hand. Bloodless now, the wounds stitched up. Lifeless. "Shall I wheel him closer?"

"No!"

Schwartz clamped his eyes shut. Cold, clammy dread clutched at him. He couldn't breathe, his heart fluttered wildly in his chest. He had only ever seen one human corpse and he had never forgotten. *Mother, grown waxen and cold. Mother, with her hair sweetly curled and her eyes closed for ever.*

"Take a look," Ferguson-Kaminsky said again. "Open your eyes and take a look – feel him, if you like – and then you'll know I'm not lying to you about the pacemaker."

"*No!*"

Frederick Schwartz fainted.

In Morrissey's sitting room Joe, alone, was pacing again. From time to time his steps brought him face to face with his reflection in the big mirror on the wall over the unlit fireplace. He looked haggard, older than he had just a week ago; the thin face with its pointed nose looked thinner, the dark hair had maybe a little more grey in it, but mostly it was his mouth, so grim, so set, that showed what he'd been going through. No wonder Jess had looked so disbelieving whenever he'd told her his troubles were nothing he couldn't handle.

The door opened and he spun around.

"No go," Ferguson said, quickly, seeing his face.

Chris Webber entered the room behind him. The grey-white

make-up they'd applied to his face and upper body was partly wiped away, and he was warming up again after they'd plunged his right hand in ice in case Schwartz wanted to touch it, but he still looked like a zombie in a third-rate horror movie, his true pallor showing through, contrasting with the still feverish glitter of his eyes.

"He didn't buy you as a corpse." Joe's voice was flat, defeated.

"Oh, he bought me only too well." Chris's injured hand had been swiftly rebandaged by Morrissey, and he wore a white sling around his neck. "He freaked out."

"And then he passed out," Ferguson added.

"So what's next?" Chris asked.

The door opened again, and Morrissey came in with Lucas Ash and Tony Valdez.

"We need a moment with Lieutenant Duval," Morrissey said to Chris and Ferguson. "If you'll excuse us."

Silently, the two men left the room.

"I want to operate now," Ash said to Joe. His face was set. "I understand how you feel, and believe me, I'd rather be going in there knowing exactly what we're up against, but under the circumstances, I think we have to get this thing out of Lally as fast as we can."

"For what it's worth," Valdez said, "I agree."

"I'm not through with Schwartz yet," Joe said. The panic was back, deep inside. He felt like a child, helpless and frustrated, wanting to cry, to kick and scream until he got what he needed.

"The OR's ready," Ash went on, steadily. "My team is ready, the bomb people and half the Chicago Fire Department all seem to be well and truly primed. And to be candid, Lieutenant, I think you're letting your personal fears get in the way of your professional judgment."

"How do you figure that, Doctor?" Joe was icy.

"Because on Sunday morning," Ash said, crisply, "when you and I spoke for the first time – that's approximately forty-four hours or so ago – I got the distinct impression that you considered my being in Hawaii and cut off because of a storm, almost as great a crime as if I'd tampered with the pacemakers myself." Ash softened his tone. "Now I know it was because you believed that every second counted, that your sister's life was in imminent danger, but that danger hasn't passed. And I know that part of the reason you're stalling now is because you're terrified of what may happen in surgery – "

"Aren't you?" Joe challenged. "You ought to be."

"Of course I am – I'm not a fool, Lieutenant." Ash paused. "And I don't know what your plans are for this man, and I don't want to know, but surely you must realize that even if you do pull off a miracle and get him to talk, we can't take anything he says now at face value. Your sister's pacemaker will still have to be explanted, and we'll still be going into the unknown."

"He's right, Lieutenant," Morrissey said. It was the first time he'd spoken since they'd entered the room.

Joe said nothing. He knew, without being reminded, that Schwartz's word wouldn't count for spit without corroboration, and he knew that Ash was right, too, that he was stalling now mostly because of his fears for Lally. And that if he didn't make a decision now – *right* now – his own fears might be what killed her.

Ash looked at his watch. "I have four forty-two, gentlemen. With your permission, I'd like to go and wake Miss Duval to let her know that we're down to our final preparations, and that we'll be ready for her in the OR at five-fifteen sharp."

Neither Morrissey nor Valdez spoke.

Joe stared into Ash's handsome face. As Lally had when she'd first set eyes on him almost sixteen days before, he felt almost troubled by that face, was aware, ludicrously, that he might feel more confident if it were marred by some small imperfection.

"Four forty-three," Valdez said quietly.

In the seven or so seconds that followed, Joe thought about Jack Long and Marie Ferguson, and Sam McKinley and Alice Douglas, and all the other as yet nameless victims out there, going about their business in blissful ignorance. But the only face Joe saw in his mind was Lally's. For one more frantic instant, he sought some kind of divine inspiration, but none came.

"Go for it," he said.

Chris and Ferguson watched silently as the cardiologist and Valdez left the room, saw the determination of the way they walked away down the corridor, and they both knew, without being told, that a decision had been made.

Without a word, Ferguson knocked on Morrissey's door and they both went right in. The two men were sitting in armchairs, Joe slumped sideways, his body language telling them all they needed to know.

"They're going to operate?" Ferguson asked.

"At a quarter past five," Morrissey said, softly.

Chris looked at his watch. Everything inside him froze.

"What now?" he asked.

"We wait," Morrissey answered.

Chris ignored him. "Duval?"

Joe said nothing.

"So what now?" Chris's voice hardened. "Is that it? You're giving up?"

"No, I'm not giving up," Joe said, wearily. "Just taking a break."

"I had a feeling," Ferguson said, "before we were asked to leave, that you had more plans for Schwartz."

"I did," Joe said.

"So what are they?"

"Maybe we should let the lieutenant have a few minutes," Morrissey intervened. "He'll want to visit with his sister, and then I think he should try to rest a while."

"He can rest later, when it's over, when there's nothing left to try."

Chris knew how harsh he sounded, how unlike himself. He saw that Duval was almost at the end of his rope, and he knew how that felt – and maybe his own sudden rush of strength was only temporary and born out of the knowledge that he was not, after all, going to die. But he had this conviction that his body had beaten the Gila monster's venom so that he could join in the fight to at least *try* to help Lally, though it did look now as if only Ash could do that for her. But he could see Duval was fading fast, and Chris, maybe more than anyone here, knew how much trouble the lieutenant was in, and that *bastard* was still hanging in, and he was damned if he was going to let them all just give up when there might still be a chance of nailing him.

"Duval, what's the plan?" he asked, still tough.

Joe came out of his slump. "Okay," he said, slowly, taking a moment to regroup, to refocus on what he'd been brewing up in his mind before Ash had come in.

"Good." Chris relaxed a little.

"Is Schwartz still out?" Joe asked Morrissey. "I'd like him out a while longer. I *need* him out."

For an instant, Morrissey paused. Then, tiredly, he got to his feet.

"I'll give him a sedative. He'll sleep for an hour or so."

Joe felt a new pang of guilt. "Thank you, Doctor."

Morrissey nodded and left the room.

"What do you have in mind?" Ferguson asked Joe.

"One last shot," Joe said. "If this doesn't work, we're dead." He managed a smile at Webber. "No part for you in this, except waiting."

"That's okay," Chris said. "So long as you're not giving up."

"What is it?" Ferguson asked.

"It's really off the wall."

"So's Schwartz," Ferguson said.
"I just think it might be the last push he needs."
"Then go for it," Chris said.
"Dr Morrissey'll hate it."
"Then we won't tell him," Sean Ferguson said.

39

Tuesday, January 26th

"Talk about *déjà vu*," Lally said when they wheeled her into the OR. It was fifteen minutes after five on the nose, and the winter world outside the clinic was still dark and sleepy, but in this room, there was no time, no season.

"Hi, Lally," Joanna King, sleek in cotton coveralls, greeted her warmly.

"Good to see you again." Bobby Goldstein, not so sleek, came to give her a kiss on the cheek. "Though I never guessed back in Holyoke you had such a taste for the dramatic."

Lally looked around the room, taking in the preparations that had been made for her surgery. The glass walls had been partly boarded up, partly diagonally taped, the way some people prepared windows in storm risk areas of New England to stop them blasting lethal shards of glass if they broke. There were no oxygen or other gas cylinders, and Lally guessed they had been removed in case the worst happened. But what really made her stomach quake and raised the tiny hairs on her arms were the two astronauts talking so earnestly to Lucas Ash over at the far end of the room.

"Bomb technicians," Joanna King said.

"Known as bomb techs or bombers to the initiated," Bobby Goldstein embroidered.

"Goldstein's an expert now," King mocked.

Lally looked away from the men in their protective clothing and the cardiologist still listening to them so carefully. She tried to focus on Joanna King, just as elegant and statuesque as she remembered, and on dear, kind-faced, humorous Bobby Goldstein.

"You can't begin to imagine how grateful I am that you've come here for me," she told them. "But are you sure it's safe for you to be doing this?"

"We wouldn't miss it for the world," King said.

"Personally, I came for the pizza," Goldstein grinned. "Chicago's where it all began, you know."

"I think you'll find that was Italy," King said, drily.

"Not the real thing," Goldstein argued. "The real thing started in a place called *Pizzeria Uno* right here in Chicago, which is where I vote we all adjourn to when this nonsense is over."

"I'm with you," Lally said.

Joe had brought Chris to her room, fleetingly, just before she'd come down to the OR, and the evidence that he was all right had been a joyous relief, yet the bandages on his hand and his stricken face were proof enough that her fears for him had been justified. And then Hugo had been there too, and there had been no time for explanations, and she'd said her farewells to them all at the elevator up on the third floor, had embraced them and refused to let any of them come any further with her, and frankly it had been almost a relief to have the elevator doors slide shut, blocking off their three anxious, stressed-out faces.

"How was Florida?" Joanna King asked.

"Beautiful."

"We heard your boyfriend went chasing down there after you, and brought you back in a private jet." Goldstein's eyes twinkled behind their spectacles. "Is it true?"

"Pretty much," Lally said, "except he isn't my boyfriend."

"Sounds like he ought to be," King commented.

"Lally, my dear, I'm sorry to have kept you waiting." Lucas Ash, handsome as ever, came striding towards her with one of the astronauts. Lally's stomach, steadied slightly for a moment by the banter, took a new dive. "Ready when you are."

"Ready as I'll ever be," she answered.

The man beside Ash removed the head part of his bomb suit, and Lally saw that it was Tony Valdez.

"Hi, Tony," Lally said.

Valdez's grin was bordering on lazy, his whole demeanour deceptively calm and laid-back. "I just want to tell you that none of us believes we're going to be needed here today," Valdez said. "The stuff on the windows, our suits, the firemen outside the door – it's all purely precautionary."

Lally didn't know what to say. Her mouth was very dry.

"Okay," Ash said, gently. "Want to get up on the table, Lally, so we can make a start?"

"Not really," she said, hoarsely.

"I'd sooner have done this in a catheter lab, the way we did it the first time around," Ash said. "But apparently this suits the rest of the team rather better, so I thought I'd better fit in. It looks more forbidding, but it makes no real difference."

Lally got up on the table.

"Since you're an old hand at this," Ash said, "I don't need to waste time explaining everything to you, except just to say that what we're going to do first is exactly the same as we did before, only in reverse order."

"And then?"

"And then we all take a deep breath, and I put in a new pacemaker." Ash smiled at her. "Not one, I hasten to add, made by Hagen Pacing."

"Poor Mr Hagen," Lally said. "He called me. He was so upset."

"I know," Ash agreed. "I met him, too."

Sitting upright on the flat, terrifying operating table, Lally had never felt more vulnerable. She remembered the first time, remembered how afraid she had been, afraid of the procedure, afraid of pain, afraid of it not working. Afraid of dying. She remembered Charlie Sheldon telling her that the pacemaker implant would be nowhere near as nice as a day on the beach, but nowhere near as nasty as having a tooth pulled. She knew now that, compared to this, the first operation *had* been a day on the beach.

"Music," she said, suddenly.

Everyone looked at her as if they feared she'd flipped out.

"Last time we had music," she said. "Mozart."

"Did we bring our tapes?" Lucas Ash asked Joanna King.

"Of course."

"You want Mozart, Lally?" the doctor asked.

"I'd prefer Prokofiev, but I don't mind."

Joanna King was already checking through the cassette tapes in a cardboard box. "No Prokofiev. Will Tchaikovsky do?"

"Maybe Mozart might be better." Lally managed a grin. "Less exciting."

"She means she wants the doc calm, not dancing," Goldstein said.

"Mozart it is," King agreed.

Valdez approached the table, a pair of protective goggles in his gloved hand.

"Take them away," Ash said, irritably. "I told you I won't have anything impairing my vision."

"They're not for you, Doctor, they're for Miss Duval."

"What for?" Lally asked.

"Just in case," Valdez said.

"Forgive me," Lally said, startled by the calm of her own voice, "but if the worst does happen, I don't think I'll be worrying about my eyes."

"Fair enough." Valdez smiled at her and moved away.

"Anyone have any more interruptions?" the doctor asked.

No one said a word. Mozart flowed softly into the room.

"All set, Ms King?"

"Yes, Doctor."

"All right, Lally?"

"Yes, thank you." Her voice was down to a whisper.

"Then we'll begin."

Chris and Hugo sat in the waiting room on the third floor in silence, both men surrounded by plastic coffee cups and encased in their own private thoughts and fears, self-recriminations and rage and impotence. The clock on the mantelpiece ticked on. Outside, down on the streets, the gentle whir of early morning traffic grew gradually louder.

From time to time, Hugo looked across at Webber, saw the sling and the bandaged hand, and the evidence that the man had been sick was etched all across his face, and though no one had told him what had gone on, Hugo knew it had something to do with Lally, and the guy looked like a goddamned hero. And Hugo hadn't liked him before, but now he hated him for that, hated that he, who had loved Lally for so long, had been unable to do a *thing* to help her.

Chris felt Barzinsky's dislike, and in other circumstances he might have pitied the man, but right now his own mind was jammed with other emotions, none of them too pretty. Guilt upon guilt upon guilt, weighing him down, guilt about abandoning Andrea and Katy, guilt about failing Lally; for neither his escapade with her brother, nor his brush with death, nor his performance as a corpse had achieved a fucking *thing* so far as she was concerned – she was still down there in the OR facing the nightmare on her own, and Duval and Morrissey hadn't even wanted to let him see her before they took her down, had told him he looked too lousy, that Lally would go into surgery worrying about him, that she had enough problems without adding to them. But Chris had insisted, and so they'd given him just one minute, and she'd taken one look at his hand and arm and though he'd told her that it was nothing, that he'd taken a bit of a fall, he could tell she didn't believe him, and so after all that he probably *had* added to her burden, and oh shit, he didn't like himself too much . . .

The door opened and Morrissey looked in. Hugo jumped up, but Chris found his legs would hardly move.

"News?" Hugo asked.

Morrissey shook his head. "Too soon."

Hugo sat down again.

"You should be resting," Morrissey said to Chris.

"No chance."

"You should at least put your feet up."

"I will," Chris said, not moving.

"How're you feeling?" the doctor asked.

"About a thousand per cent better than I was."

"But still pretty lousy?"

"I'm okay," Chris said. "Thank you."

Hugo's irritation level rose again. "Why can't we wait down there, closer to the OR?"

"It's off-limits." Morrissey was looking haggard. "Even to me."

All three men thought about the reason why. All three shuddered.

In spite of Mozart, the atmosphere in the operating room was thick enough to slice as Lucas Ash injected local anaesthetic close to the area where he would cut the recently healed skin above Lally's left breast.

"All right?" he asked gently.

"Fine," she lied.

"You will be," he said.

She looked through his little fold-up glasses into the keen blue eyes.

"Thank you," she said, softly.

"Haven't done anything yet."

"Thank you, anyway."

She closed her eyes, and tried to project herself out of the OR. She thought about Chris and how awful he'd looked when he'd come in, finally, to see her, and she knew that all her bad feelings about him had been justified, and even in that brief moment they'd shared she'd realized for sure – if there had been any real doubt – that she was in love with him. Now, keeping her eyes shut, she built up a mental picture of him, remembered the way he'd looked in the harbour at Key West, the relief on his face when he'd found her. She remembered the flight to Chicago, the bad weather and the shock and fear all mixed up together, only the knowledge that Chris was beside her keeping her going. She remembered their one evening together at her house in Stockbridge, with Katy asleep upstairs in her bedroom. She remembered what a loving father he was, and what a concerned husband, and she remembered that he'd left his daughter, at a time when she needed him so badly, because Lally was in danger, and she hadn't really had a chance to tell him how she felt about that, and maybe it was as well, because there was still Andrea at home, and whatever happened here today, Chris would have to go back to face his wife and their problems. But still for now, it was so good to think about him, to think about his face, his strength, and she fastened onto that, held it tight in her mind.

"Ready to start now, Lally," Dr Ash said.

Lally opened her eyes.

"You're clear on what I'm going to do, aren't you?"

She nodded, unable to speak.

"You understand that when we've disconnected the first pacemaker, an external device will take over temporarily, until the new one's in place. Just to avoid any unlikely hiccups." Ash smiled. "Okay?"

"Okay."

She felt, rather than saw, the bomb techs in their astronaut suits move closer to the table; felt the tension rise, like mercury in a thermometer, as King focused on her X-ray pictures, Valdez hovering beside her, scanning the images of the pacemaker generator box and its wires. And again, she looked into Lucas Ash's face, into those clear, intent eyes. And she trusted those eyes, trusted his fingers, and when he told her to lie absolutely still now, she obeyed him without a word.

When Schwartz came to, he was in another place. Not in his room, but in an unfamiliar, cold place, with white walls and steel trolleys and a curious odour. He was lying on a hard, unyielding bed, and his vision was blurred, and his arms and legs were so heavy he could hardly move them.

There was a shape beside him, looming over him.

"Who's there?" His voice came out slurred and thick.

"Almost ready," a man said.

He blinked his eyes hard, and his vision cleared a little. Dr Kaminsky was standing to his left, wearing a green gown, a mask over his nose and mouth, a hypodermic in his hand.

"What's going on?" Schwartz tried to sit up, but it was impossible, and he realized there was another man behind him, holding him down by the shoulders. "What have you done to me?"

"Just relax, Mr Schwartz," Kaminsky said.

"I want to get *up* – " Schwartz struggled for a second, but he was too weak, and he felt so heavy. "My legs," he moaned. "My eyes – I can't see – "

"That's just the sedative we gave you – you were a little distressed, remember?" Kaminsky's voice was soothing. "Now try to be calm."

"What are you *doing* to me?" Schwartz's voice was so slurred, his mouth was so dry, he was having trouble swallowing.

"We're preparing you for your pacemaker," Kaminsky said, pleasantly.

Schwartz shook his head violently. "No – I told you no pacemaker."

"You signed a consent, Mr Schwartz."

"I signed nothing!"

"Sure you did. When you were transferred from Chicago Memorial. You signed it then, remember?" Kaminsky squirted fluid from the end of the syringe the way he'd seen countless actor-doctors do it in movies. "We have to save your life, Mr Schwartz, we're bound by medical ethics to save your life."

"More lies." Schwartz moaned. "You can't do this."

"We have to," Kaminsky said.

"You can save lives, too," another voice said, softly.

Schwartz turned his head towards the voice, tried to focus but failed.

"Who is it?" Another man, gowned and masked. He couldn't see his face. The terror grew. "Hagen – is it Hagen?"

"One last chance, Siegfried," the voice said.

"Oh, dear God, help me." Schwartz moaned again.

"You help us, we'll help you," the man told him.

He came closer, and Schwartz saw that it was not Hagen, but the lieutenant, and he was holding some papers. And his mind cleared a little then, and he remembered the documents, the records of his work – his brilliant, heroic work – and for a moment he was utterly, perfectly lucid again.

"You're bluffing, Lieutenant."

"No." Joe moved right in to the table. "I give you my word."

"I don't believe you."

"One last chance," Joe said. "To be Siegfried, the true hero, instead of one of them."

"Man and metal," another voice whispered.

Schwartz turned his head, and Kaminsky was holding up the oh-so-familiar generator box of a pacemaker in his gloved hand.

"Man and metal," Kaminsky said. "That's what you fear most, isn't it, Siegfried? More than death, more than Hagen?"

"Are you going to tell us what we need to know?"

Schwartz turned his head again, and the lieutenant was there, with the papers in his hand, and his face was so calm, so set, so *evil*.

"Last chance," Kaminsky said.

And every terror that had ever haunted Frederick Schwartz, from his earliest nightmares all the way to this final horror, seemed to swirl around in his brain, blanketing him, swamping everything, confusing it all, all the long-held motivations and desires for justice and vengeance, turning his blood to ice and his bowels to water.

He believed them now.

"I'll tell you," he whispered.

"Do you swear it?" the lieutenant asked, his face taut as a mask.

Kaminsky held the pacemaker box over his face, so close to his lips that he could almost taste the metal on his tongue. "Sure you won't change your mind?"

"I'll tell you," Schwartz whispered again. "I swear it, on my mother's memory. I'll tell you everything."

Ferguson-Kaminsky turned away. Joe came closer.

Lally's eyes were tightly closed, and she could feel Lucas Ash's breath on her neck, steady and light and calm, like his hands.

"I have it," he said, very quietly.

She heard a soft flutter of activity around the operating table.

"Lally, the external pacemaker's taken over for now. You feel okay?"

"I think so," she whispered, her eyes still shut.

Another long minute passed.

"It's out," he said.

Lally half opened her eyes. She saw it, in the palm of his latex-covered hand. She kept very still, hardly daring to breathe, heard movement to her right, saw another hand, more thickly gloved, outstretched to take it.

"Careful," Lucas Ash said, gently, as it left his palm. "It's slippery."

The other man dropped it.

"Jesus!"

It was like watching a slow-motion horror sequence in a movie. The little bloodied metal box sliding off the gloved hand, starting

244

to tumble through the air, free-falling, spinning as it descended through space –

"No *way!*"

Joanna King's tackle was the most graceful, the most sublime, anyone in the room had ever seen. Her two hands outstretched and cupped, catching the box as her body hit the linoleum floor, knocking the breath out of her.

No one said a word.

A second gloved pair of hands took it from King's, the movements steady now, confident, perfect.

Lally raised her head a little way, saw the box put inside a small containment vessel that, in turn, slid smoothly into a larger one. She saw the two astronauts pick up the container, saw them start walking, calmly, slowly towards the exit, and the swing doors opened, and she heard voices outside, hushed, almost reverential, and she heard the slow squelching tread of rubber soles on linoleum, and they were walking away.

The doors swung closed. The Hagen pacemaker was gone.

Goldstein walked over to King, still on the floor, and gave her his hand to help her up.

"Lawrence Taylor," he said, "eat your heart out."

"That was some tackle," Ash agreed.

"Not bad," King said, dusting herself off, "if I say so myself."

Lally lay back on the table. A wave of emotion welled up in her, a mixture of laughter and tears, of delayed panic and inexpressible relief.

"If my heart survives that," she said, shakily, "it'll survive anything."

For a moment, Lucas Ash reached for her right hand and held it.

"Ready for the new one?" he asked her.

Her eyes were wet.

"Ready," she said.

40

Tuesday, January 26th

"**D**o you understand that you have the right to remain silent?"
Joe asked Schwartz, with no one else except Ferguson to
hear. "Do you understand that anything you say can and may be
used against you in court or other proceedings? Do you understand
that . . .?"

Joe knew that in the past eighteen hours he had done much
more than break rules. He had violated a man's rights, he had
exhorted others to break the law, he had put one civilian in physical
danger, had placed the future of a fine physician and a first-rate
clinic at serious risk, and he had told more lies than he had in his
entire life. He had done it for his sister and the others like her. He
had done it because he could not endure the spectre of Schwartz
walking free. He had done it because – once the whole roller-coaster
ride had begun gathering momentum – he had seen no viable
alternative. He had done it, some might say, for the greater good.
None of that made it right.

Yet he continued a while longer. He read Schwartz his rights
right there and then in the whitewashed laboratory at the Howe
Clinic, while he knew – while he damn well *knew* – that the man
was too demented, too sedated, to comprehend what he was being
told. And all the time Sean Ferguson, brimful with vengeance for
his beloved Marie, went on playing Kaminsky, holding the little
pacemaker like some miniaturized Damoclean A-bomb; and Joe
knew that Ferguson would do anything he had to, lie through his
teeth, even perjure himself in court – not to help a cop with his job

on the line, but because Schwartz or Siegfried or whoever the hell good-old-Fred had turned out to be, had murdered his wife, which was why Lieutenant Joe Duval knew he could go on violating this man's rights all the way to Jackson's 8 a.m. deadline if necessary, and at least no one would ever get to hear about it from the lips of this particular witness.

The sedation and the lingering effects of the beta-blockers and temperature extremes meant that Schwartz was slow getting started, but he had already identified one of the documents he'd buried with the Gila monsters as the true record of his labours, and Joe already knew that the whole idea of the conductive glue hair-trigger detonation had been an elaborate fiction, and he had a pretty shrewd idea that though the confession had begun slowly, once Schwartz got going, nothing much would stop him. Many murderers talked when they thought it was all over – some just gave up the game and went to sleep, but many talked, often so goddamned relieved that they forgot all about attorneys and their rights. Some killers, though, simply relished the spilling of their guts as the continuing fulfilment of their great, dark, ongoing ego trip, and Joe was as confident as he could be that Schwartz would be one of these, spurred on by the terrors of Kaminsky and his little metal box.

At five minutes before eight, with Lally safely tucked up in bed and Al Hagen and Howard Leary already helping the police and FBI in the final tracking down of Schwartz's victims, Joe interrupted the session to call Jackson. Within a half hour, Cohen was sitting in on the confession, back in Schwartz's second-floor room, and they were rolling tape, and everything was starting to spruce up nicely and Joe dared to believe that – even if Lieutenant Joseph Duval was down for the count – at least there was reason to hope that the case against Frederick Schwartz was back on track.

"I began," Schwartz told his two-man audience, "last August. One weekend, that was all it took for me to work it out, though I guess, one way or another, I'd been working it out most of my life."

There was still a tremor in his hands, but his voice was less slurred now, and though he paused for a moment, neither Joe nor Cohen said a word. They both knew it was coming, all coming now, they could feel it, they could always feel it in the air when a confession was working its way up and out of the dark and messy recesses of a long-term killer.

"The real work was child's play for me," Schwartz went on. "I started in the last week of September. Six pacemakers, twice a week, for eight weeks, four of them dummies, two of them the real thing. I could easily have done more – I could have killed hundreds, more if I'd chosen to. But I didn't need more. I'm not a violent man by nature. That was enough to punish them all."

"Who were you punishing?" Joe asked.

"You know who."

"Tell me anyway."

"The doctors. The ones who lied. The ones who laughed." The hazel eyes were so hard to read now, blank, almost blind with memory. "And him most of all. That was what I wanted most, to finish him."

"Who, most of all?" Joe asked, softly.

"Hagen, of course." He said the name the German way, Hahgen, the way he'd said it hours back when Al Hagen had come to see him, and Cohen looked up, surprised.

"Can you tell us his full name?" Joe said, for the sake of the tape.

"Albrecht Hagen." Schwartz's lips turned up a little at the corners. "He wanted to kill me, you know."

"What makes you think that?"

"It was written. Mother told me." Schwartz gave a tiny shrug. "Hagen kills Siegfried, everyone knows that."

"Who's Siegfried?" Cohen asked, still confused.

Schwartz turned to face the older detective, and the disdain was clear in his expression and in his voice.

"I am Siegfried," he said.

Joe closed his eyes for an instant, letting relief wash over him. *The crazier the better,* he thought. On the tape, another cop listening. Which ever way he tried to squirm later, whatever he told his attorney, Frederick Schwartz would not now walk, would not go free.

Lally was safe, and the others out there had a chance. For Joe, right now, that was more than enough.

Twelve hours later, Chris Webber felt torn apart all over again, between relief, anger and frustration. He was gladder than he'd ever imagined it was possible to be that Lally had been safely brought through her nightmare, and that her brother had nailed Schwartz. But if he had allowed himself to fantasize at all about what might happen next between himself and the woman with whom he knew, without a shadow of doubt, he was deeply in love, he certainly had not envisaged that almost the first thing he would have to do was to leave her side and go back home to Stockbridge.

"What's happened?" Lally asked, when he came to tell her. It was nine-thirty in the evening, and she'd been sleeping for most of the day. After her surgery, John Morrissey had admitted Chris to the clinic as a patient so that he could fully recover from his own ordeal and be monitored for any after-effects, and he had been resting too, until a while ago.

"I called Katy," he said. "Seems Andrea checked herself out of her clinic."

"Oh," Lally said, softly. "I see."

"No, you don't." Chris shook his head. "She's wrecked our house, Lally. She's out of control, and that's why I have to go back."

"Of course you do," she said.

The room was very quiet. Hugo, on the verge of collapse when the crisis had passed, had gone back to Joe's house, and Joe, this evening, was still heavily embroiled in police business. Schwartz was still in the clinic, under guard, where he would remain until morning. Lucas Ash had said he wanted Lally to have as few visitors as possible until next day; but knowing now that he would have to check out early in the morning to catch the first flight back to Albany, Chris had crept out of his own room, across the corridor from Lally's, and come to see her.

She looked so lovely, those soft grey eyes so tired and still vulnerable, yet so luminous with relief and the joy of being alive. She wore a white man's shirt instead of a nightdress, and her hair, freshly washed by one of the nurses, hung loose over her shoulders. No make-up, not even a hint of lipstick, but Chris knew he'd never seen a lovelier woman.

"When are you going to tell me?" she asked him.

"Tell you what?"

"Where you were, all that time. What you were doing. What really happened to your hand."

"I can't tell you," Chris said. "Because of Joe."

"I know. Joe told me not to ask you."

"There's not much to tell, anyway."

"I know that you were helping Joe. Helping me."

"I didn't do much."

"I don't believe that." Lally paused. "I was scared."

"I know you were."

"Not just for myself – " She smiled ruefully. "I was *terrified* for myself. But I was scared for you, too. When you didn't come back after I checked in here – "

"I wanted to be here," Chris said.

"That wasn't a reproach," Lally said swiftly. "It's just that I had this awful feeling something had happened to you." Tentatively, gently, she reached out and touched his bandaged hand. "I guess it was just this."

"I guess."

They fell silent. With the corridor still devoid of other patients, and in the late evening stillness, the hush in the room was almost too complete. If she was home at the end of a day, Lally thought, if she sat in her sitting room all alone – no Hugo, no TV, no music, with even Nijinsky prowling outside – it was still never totally silent. There was the ticking of the French carriage clock she'd inherited from her parents, there was the occasional creak, the comfortable voice of a good old house, and there were the night birds and the wind in the trees and the cars on Lenox Road, and the reminders of neighbours and friends, doors banging, dogs barking, voices, laughing or arguing or just living.

"It's too quiet here," she said to Chris.

"I know."

"I can't wait to get home."

Chris said nothing.

"Oh, Chris, I'm sorry." Lally touched his hand again, careful not to grasp it properly in case she hurt his wound or overstepped some unspoken boundary. "I didn't think."

"It doesn't matter."

"Of course it does. You must be so worried about Andrea and Katy." She winced a little.

"Are you in pain?" Chris asked, quickly, anxiously.

"No, not at all – Lucas gave me something." She paused. "I was just thinking that this is really my fault."

"How do you figure that?"

"If you'd stayed home, if you hadn't come chasing after me and saving my life, you'd have been there for Andrea when she needed you."

"That makes it my fault, not yours."

"You thought she was safe," Lally said. "You thought she was being looked after."

"There you are then," Chris said. "No one's fault."

Lally thought about Andrea Webber, about her violence and vulnerability and misery, and guilt flooded through her. "I should have insisted you went back as soon as you got me here," she said. "It was selfish of me to want you with me."

"Did you want me with you?"

"Oh, yes." Lally hesitated. "More than anything."

"Thank God for that," Chris said, softly.

They were silent again.

"You know it's over," he said, after a while. "My marriage is over."

"You can't be sure of that," Lally said. "Not now."

"I've been sure of it for a long time. I told you that the night Katy stayed with you, when you made me supper and let me talk. I needed that more than anything, and you just sat there and let me."

"Anyone would have done the same."

"No, they wouldn't," Chris said. "And no one else would have come to check up on Katy the way you did."

"Sticking my nose in."

"You did it because you cared."

"I'm Katy's teacher. How could I not care?"

"Another teacher would have handled it differently, probably filed an official report." Chris paused. "You thought I was abusing Katy, didn't you?"

"No. Not really." Lally tried to remember exactly what she had thought. She was so tired still, it was hard work just thinking. "I knew it had to be a possibility, but I couldn't believe it. I didn't believe it was Andrea, either. You both seemed such – " She broke off.

"Such good parents," Chris said wryly.

"You are," Lally said quickly. "And you said yourself that Andrea loves Katy more than anything – she's sick, she can't help herself. Which is why you have to fly home in the morning, and you don't have to worry about me any more. I'm okay now." She smiled into his eyes. "Thanks to you."

"Thanks to a lot of people." Very gently, Chris took her right hand with his good left one. "They all seem to love you so much."

"I know. I'm very lucky."

"Hugo, especially."

"Yes."

"Is there – ?" Chris's face coloured a fraction. "Is there something special between you and Hugo?"

"Yes," Lally answered, and watched his eyes darken. "We're best friends."

"That's all?"

"It is for me."

"Poor Hugo," Chris said.

Lally smiled again. "He was very suspicious of you, you know."

"Was?"

"He can't hate you now, after what you did. I think that irks him a little."

251

"I think your brother feels the same way."

"I expect so."

"All these people, wanting to protect you, loving you." Chris still held onto her hand. "It's because you're so special."

"I'm nothing special," Lally said.

"Oh, yes. You are."

"Thank you."

She closed her eyes for a minute, and when she opened them again, Chris was looking at her so intently and with such naked love that she had the greatest urge to move into his arms, to hold him and let him hold her. But Andrea was still there between them, as forcefully as if she were physically there, in the room, and so Lally just lay still and said nothing and did nothing.

"I have to let you sleep now," Chris said, gently. "Dr Ash would shoot me if he knew I were keeping you up."

"You should rest, too," she said, looking at his injured hand.

"I'm fine."

"If you were fine, Dr Morrissey wouldn't have kept you here."

"That was just because he knew I wanted to be near you."

They were still again for a moment.

"Did you see him?" she asked, quietly.

"Schwartz, you mean?"

Lally nodded.

"Kind of," Chris said.

"I met with him, you know."

"Joe told me."

"He was so cold," Lally said. "I suppose I thought it would make a difference to him, seeing me – I don't know why I thought that – I guess it was very naive of me." She paused, thinking, remembering. "I thought, he's still just a man, a human being – he's only done this because of what happened to his mother, whom he loved." She shook her head. "I thought that if he was capable of that kind of love, I might be able to touch him."

"Maybe you did."

"No." She was clear on that. "Not a bit."

"Your brother says he's insane."

"But so clever, too. Able to do all that, and to fool everyone – people who worked with him every day, who'd known him for years."

"You always hear that, don't you?" Chris said. "When they arrest serial killers, the neighbours always say he seemed so normal, so ordinary, a bit of a loner, but nothing special."

Lally took a deep breath and let it out slowly, gently. Her heart beat easily, healthily, powered by its new, safe, regular pacemaker. She knew the routine now. Another couple of days here in the clinic, then a check-up, back in Massachusetts, with Bobby Goldstein taking care of the fine tuning. And then back to normal, the way Lucas Ash had told her the first time.

"I'm going to be okay now," she said to Chris.

"I know," he said, quietly. "It's all over."

"For me, anyway."

"You mustn't think about the others."

"I can't help it."

"Not now, anyway. Now you have to concentrate on getting strong, on getting over it."

"I feel pretty good, considering," Lally said.

"You look wonderful," he told her.

"Do I?"

He nodded slowly. "You're very beautiful."

"No, I'm not. I'm tall and skinny and my nose is too long."

"Your nose is perfect," Chris said. "Trust me, I'm an artist."

She smiled again.

"Will you say goodbye before you go in the morning?"

"It'll be very early."

"I don't mind."

"And it won't be goodbye," Chris said.

"Of course it won't," Lally said, lightly. "We'll see each other, whatever happens. I'll be teaching again in a few weeks and – "

"That's not what I meant."

"I know."

An image of Andrea Webber floated, unbidden, into Lally's mind.

"I'd better get some sleep now," she said and, very gently, she took her hand out of his. "You, too."

Reluctantly, Chris stood up. His head still swam with fatigue and his hand still throbbed.

"I'll be just across the corridor if you need me," he told her.

"I won't need anything," she said.

"All the same, I'll be there."

"Stop worrying about me, Chris."

"Easier said than done."

41

Wednesday, January 27th

At a quarter past three in the morning, Schwartz was awake. They had allowed him to rest for quite a long while, and now he was feeling better. He was able to breathe more easily, was perspiring less. He was growing stronger.

The night staff checked on him hourly. The last nurse had come in at a quarter to three. Pulse, temperature, blood pressure. A tweak to the drip feed still attached to his left arm. The EKG monitor had been removed during the afternoon. He did not miss it.

The room was cool and comfortable, the bed linen smooth and dry and soothing. He had slept a little, and now he was alert. Unlike the young police officer in a chair near the door. His guard. Sleeping peacefully, his fair head slumped down over his chest, snoring gently, his throat constricted by the tightness of his uniform collar.

Schwartz knew that there was not much time left. He was not going to die from the Gila's bite. By morning he would be strong enough for them to transfer him to a prison hospital, perhaps even to a regular jail cell. And then it would be too late.

Mother had come to him in a dream while he had slept.

There is a dragon here, in this house, she had told him.

He was awake now, very clear in his mind, very lucid. No fever to delude him, no doctor or policeman to terrorize him. He knew that Mother was watching over him, and that she was right. There was a dragon, on the next floor, almost directly above his head, and Schwartz knew that it was his destiny to kill it.

You must be silent and swift, Siegfried, Mother had whispered in his ear. *You must make yourself invisible. And you'll need your sword.* They had all relaxed their vigil now. In their presence, he had been quiet and unresponsive and obedient ever since the tape recorder had been switched off and the lieutenant and the pudgy-faced older detective had left. They thought he was still sick and exhausted, and they had what they wanted from him for the moment, and he knew they had all been working, all through the day, probably all through this night, piecing together information he had given them, contacting the patients in need of explantation. They were finished with him, for now.

And his guard was sleeping soundly.

Lally, too, was asleep. Dr Ash had offered her a sleeping pill, but she had told him she didn't need it, though the truth was that she didn't want that kind of drugged oblivion. She had escaped death, and now, more than anything, she wanted to re-establish control over her life. She wanted to allow time to idle by, to feel everything, be it pleasure or pain or sheer normality. But her talk with Chris had drained her, and in the end, fatigue had overtaken all other thoughts, all other emotions, and sleep had won.

He stood at the foot of the bed, gazing down at her. There was a night light fitted behind the top of the curtains, just enough to illuminate the patient for the staff, but not bright enough to disturb her.

She looked more peaceful in sleep than she had during their meeting the previous night, but otherwise much the same. Female, with a sweetly shaped face and softly rounded arms, long brown hair spread out fanlike over the white pillow. She looked human. But he knew better.

A dragon takes on many forms. Mother had told him. *Man and metal.* She had the metal inside her, in her heart.

He had his sword. He had found it in the deserted galley kitchen on his floor, together with an orderly's green coat. His magic cloak. Invisible and armed. Siegfried, the dragon slayer.

She stirred a little, and he stood motionless, hardly breathing, but then she grew still again, lips slightly parted. She looked so innocent, almost child-like. A lesser man might be fooled.

He moved silently around the bed until he stood directly over her. He felt a new, great strength flow through him.

And he raised his sword.

Lally opened her eyes, saw the knife, saw his face, and screamed, but it came too late, and the long blade flashed down and sliced into her arm as she tried to thrust herself away.

"Help me!" She screamed again, shrilly, piercingly.

The door crashed open, flooding the room with light.

"Lally, get *clear*!"

Schwartz raised the blood-soaked knife a second time, and Lally rolled away off the bed and crashed down onto the floor, searing the wound in her chest, knocking the air out of her lungs.

"Son of a *bitch*!"

Chris hurled himself at Schwartz, eyes wild, bellowing with rage, grasping at the madman's arm, grabbing for the knife. The blade cut through the bandages on his bitten hand, drew fresh blood as they grappled for control, and Chris almost fell, but still they wrestled, and Chris was hitting Schwartz, great, maddened punches into his belly, and Lally, trying to crawl away, could hear the killer's groans, could almost hear the breath being squeezed out of him, yet still the knife was in his right hand, and she saw the light from the corridor flashing on the bloody blade as Schwartz thrust up again towards Chris's stomach –

She heard the shot before she saw Joe in the doorway. The sound was deafening, final.

Schwartz stumbled back, stretched out both his hands. The knife tumbled, soundlessly, to the carpet and bounced, twice, sprinkling blood into the air, and Schwartz, too, fell, heavily onto his back against the wall. And Lally heard the sound in his throat, half gasp, half cry, saw the shock on his face and the bloodied mess on his side where the bullet had exploded into him.

Joe reached him first, his gun still raised, and kicked the knife away, and Lally, on the floor a few feet away, knew there were other people in the room, running, calling out directions, but she hardly noticed them, hardly felt the pain in her own arm where he had stabbed her, or in her chest where she had struck herself when she'd fallen. She was watching Schwartz, seeing the staring of his eyes and the trickle of blood at the side of his mouth.

The last two things Siegfried saw were the dragon's blood on his sword hand, and Joe Duval's face, peering down into his own.

Slowly, painfully, he lifted his hand to his lips and licked it, tasting salt, tasting triumph, and for a moment he closed his eyes. And then, opening them again, he stared up at Joe, and his expression grew perplexed.

"But you're not Hagen," he murmured, dying. "I thought it would be Hagen."

Lally tried to stand but, dizzy and trembling, she sank back down onto her knees, and Chris, tearing his eyes from Schwartz, rushed to help her, put his arms around her and held her tight.

And Morrissey bent and checked the dead man's pulse.

Epilogue

Life went on with the strange, flat normality of anticlimax.
Chris returned to Stockbridge a day late, while Lally stayed
on at the clinic for another few days. With Schwartz dead and the
case against him proven beyond doubt, Joe's career seemed
salvageable, after all. Isaiah Jackson's anger hung between the two
men like a constant, silent reproach, but Jess and Sal were back
home with Joe again, and Lally was safe, and if Joe had claimed to
have any real regrets about his handling of the case, he knew he'd
have been a damned liar.

Of the thirty-two lethal pacemakers, Schwartz's Midnight
Specials, seventeen had been implanted in patients. For Jack Long,
Marie Ferguson, Sam McKinley and Alice Douglas, help had come
too late. And for one more victim, a fifty-five-year-old bus driver in
Philadelphia, dead at the wheel of his vehicle just a few hours after
the killer's confession, taking with him one young passenger and
injuring three more. The remaining twelve devices had been
explanted without incident.

Lally's pacemaker, when taken apart by the bomb techs, proved
to have been one of Schwartz's dummies, its battery small and
inadequate, but minus plastique. Deadly enough, potentially, in its
way.

It would be a while before Lally felt truly normal again. Lucas Ash
and John Morrissey had both suggested a short course of
counselling to prevent her from bottling up her fears and memories

of the nightmare, and Joe, from long experience of dealing with victims, agreed with them. But Lally knew that just going home, getting back to teaching ballet and baking cakes and croissants for *Hugo's* would be the best therapy for her. And spending time with Chris and Katy.

Especially Chris.

Lally knew now, without question, how she felt about him, but she knew, too, that their closeness had been brought about by their respective traumas, and that as long as he remained married, there could be no certainty about a future with him. Andrea Webber was a very sick woman, and they were all going to have to be very careful and gentle with Katy if she was not to be torn apart.

In Stockbridge, waiting for Lally to come home, Chris Webber couldn't see too far into the future either, but he knew that he loved Lally Duval more than he'd ever loved any woman, and that Katy cared for her, too. He knew, also, that it was only a matter of time before he and Andrea divorced, and he was a little consoled by the knowledge that this had been an inevitability long before he got to know Lally.

He was painting another picture of her. His hand was still bandaged and painful, but he had the mobility he required in his fingers, and he wanted – he needed – to get the image onto canvas while it was still so vivid, so *entrancing*, in his mind. Lally, with her hair blowing in the breeze, her shoulders and arms bare, her long slender legs showing through the thin fabric of her skirt. Lally, with the joy of seeing him so transparent in her face. The way she'd looked in the moonlight in the harbour at Key West.

He was working more slowly than he liked, but it was coming, it was taking shape. If it was ready in time, he would take it to Logan Airport when Joe brought her home from Chicago.

>>> If you've enjoyed this book and would like to discover more great vintage crime and thriller titles, as well as the most exciting crime and thriller authors writing today, visit: >>>

The Murder Room
Where Criminal Minds Meet

themurderroom.com